Kenneth's Queen

Anna Chant

Anna Chant asserts the moral right to be identified as the author of this work. No part of this publication may be reproduced, distributed, or transmitted in any form or by any means, including photocopying, recording, or other electronic or mechanical methods, without the prior written permission of the author, except in the case of brief quotations embodied in critical reviews and certain other non-commercial uses permitted by copyright law.

Standard Copyright Notice
All rights reserved
Copyright © Anna Chant
2016

Cover design by Jonathan Chant-Stevens
Technical support from Alexander Chant-Stevens

For my three lads,

Alexander, Jonathan & Benjamin

The name of Kenneth Mac Alpin's queen is unknown to history. The name she bears in this book has been created from the Gaelic word for woman – Bean and the Welsh (possibly a similar language to the Pictish language) name Banon, meaning queen.

Part One: Year of our Lord 833

Chapter One

"Ouch!" cried Baena, not for the first time.

The others gathered in front of the circular assembly hall of Abernethy ignored her while the old man working on her wrist continued what he was doing. Baena considered whether to protest again. She had more sense than to actually flinch as the man inserted the needle and rubbed in the soot and copper. She'd seen enough marks ruined by careless movement to want to risk the intricate blue and black knot the old man was marking on her.

Baena opened her mouth, but before she could make a sound her mother looked up from her stitching.

"Do not be a child, Baena. Remember who you are."

Baena glared resentfully at her mother, who serenely added another stitch to the tunic she was making. Her mother was still a beauty with her flaming red hair and her tall, willowy body, barely thickened by the six children she had borne. Baena always felt insignificant in her presence. Her own hair was also red, but not so bright and although she had seen over fifteen years she didn't even come up to her mother's shoulder. The storytellers still sang songs of the great beauty of Sabina. Baena doubted that any would ever sing of her.

"The delegation from Dal Riata will be with us soon," continued Sabina. "Perhaps even this day. There must be none of this child's nonsense once they arrive."

"I care nothing of what they think of me," Baena glanced at her wrist, reluctantly admiring the marking.

"Be silent, child," Sabina scolded. "Your father has arranged this match with the Gael lord and that is the end of the matter. You will obey him."

Baena lowered her eyes which had filled with tears. As a Daughter of the Third Royal House, she could never admit that she was afraid. "I do not wish to marry a foreigner."

Causantin, her father strode up to the hall in time to hear these words. He felt a pang at seeing his daughter so despondent and tried to reassure her.

"He is not really a foreigner, my child," he said gently.

"No, he is not," Sabina added. "Through his mother he is a Son of the Sixth Royal House. He is our kinsman."

"That is true, "agreed Causantin. "But it is not what I meant. You will have heard many times of the battle against the forces of the Angles, just a year ago now."

Baena nodded.

"There seemed no hope for us. They had pursued us across the land until we were trapped. All of us, Pict and Gael alike were surrounded by those savage Angles. All seemed lost. Cinaed, your betrothed, was there with his father, Alpin and his grandfather King Eochaidh of Dal Riata and many another Gael chief and Pict lord. That night our noble King Oengus had a curious dream. I know not how he slept for I slept not a wink."

Baena, Sabina and the others around the hall listened intently. Although they had all heard of this battle many times, they had never heard it from the lips of Causantin himself.

"In the morn he told us of his dream. He said that the blessed Saint Andrew himself had come to him and promised to send us victory," Causantin shrugged. "To tell the truth I did not believe it. I thought Oengus was telling a pretty tale to put heart into the men. That is good for the young lads like your brothers and of course, young Cinaed, but worthless for old soldiers like myself and Alpin. I simply prepared myself to die bravely."

"Go on, Father," Baena said breathlessly, forgetting her imminent handfasting for a moment.

"The lines formed and we were waiting for the attack when Eochaidh looked up. The sky was of the clearest blue, cloudless except for one. And that cloud marked the sky with the holy cross of the blessed Saint Andrew, its arms reaching over us all. He was an old man, but Eochaidh strode forward and stood beside Oengus. No words passed between them, yet they gave the order to charge as one and they led the charge as one. We all of us fell in behind them – Alpin, Cinaed, myself, everyone. We cared not who were Picts or Gaels. We were one people and together we were a victorious force. Eochaidh died not long after the battle, but the Gaels accepted our King Oengus as their own battle lord."

Baena was silent. Her father's words were compelling. She could almost see that white cross uniting the two armies and the awe on the faces of those battle-weary men. But try as she might she could not visualise the face of her betrothed. Her opposition to the match had been so great that she had refused to ask her father a single question about him.

"He appeared a good man, Baena," her father seemed to know what she was thinking. "Tall and brave."

"And an excellent match," added Sabina. "With the royal bloodlines of both the Picts and the Gaels."

"But I am promised to Drust," Baena made one last protest, although if the Gaels were almost here she knew it was hopeless. "Of the First Royal House," she added for good measure.

"Not promised, my child, although we did once speak of a match. He too is a fine young man, but he is not for you. I pledged you to Lord Cinaed as the battle ended as a symbol of our victory."

"Why would he want to wed me? He's never even seen me."

Causantin smiled fondly. "I told him of your virtuous nature and your great beauty. How could he refuse?"

"He'll be very disappointed then," Baena muttered under her breath.

"No doubt he wishes to strengthen the Pict royal bloodline," Sabina put in. "With his mother's blood and you at his side he could be chosen as Rex Pictorum one day."

"Or if not, perhaps the throne of Dal Riata will be his. My child, you could be a queen!" Causantin said with satisfaction. "In any case, you will meet him soon. A messenger has arrived. The Gaels will be with us by nightfall."

"Nightfall?" Sabina exclaimed. "Why did you not say sooner? We must ensure that everything is ready to greet them."

Sabina flung aside her stitching and swept into the smoky hall, followed by Causantin. Baena believed that Drust stood a much better chance at being crowned Rex Pictorum than this Cinaed. But with only the old man and a couple of serving women left around her it seemed pointless to say it.

As nightfall approached with still no sign of the Gaels, Baena began to hope for a brief respite. But her hopes were dashed when the cry of the watchman floated down from the tower.

"The banner of Dal Riata! Gaels approaching!"

Baena was quickly dressed in a white woollen tunic. With shaking fingers she fastened a pale, grey cloak with an enamel brooch. Some of the children had woven a wreath of flowers for her head and her hair was vigorously combed until her scalp ached and left to flow down over her shoulders.

"You look beautiful, my child," Causantin commented fondly when he saw her.

Baena gave a nervous smile, but she noted the slightly indulgent look on her mother's face and knew that her father's affection was blinding him. She cheered herself with the thought that once Cinaed had seen her and realised he had been lied to about her beauty, he would probably ride away again.

Many from the households of Abernethy began to gather with them, drawn by curiosity about the expected guests as well as the mouth-watering smells of the preparing feast. Deer, pigs and a side of beef were roasting on the fire and flagons of heather ale had been set out to revive the travellers.

As the last rays of the sun were falling on the low hills that surrounded the fort a group of riders came over the final earth bank. As they dismounted and handed their horses to the willing hands waiting to assist them Baena fixed her eyes on the men of the group and tried to work out which one was her betrothed. There were about fifteen in the group including one woman. An older man took the hand of the woman and walked towards them. The rest were all young men who followed in a loose band. With their travel-stained clothing, it was impossible to tell their rank apart. They accepted with smiles and waves the many greetings called to them and. as they came closer to the hall where Baena and her parents stood, formed a more orderly procession.

"Welcome, my Lord Alpin!" cried Causantin, moving forward and clasping the hands of the older man.

Baena kept her eyes lowered, but peeping upwards she studied the faces of the two younger men who stood a step behind him.

Alpin was a tall man whose tawny hair was streaked with grey. He bowed before Sabina. "The songs do not do your beauty justice, my lady! May I present my Lady Unuis? And of course, Lord Causantin you will remember my sons Cinaed and Domnall."

Baena's heart beat faster, as she tried to work out which was which. Both men were tall. One had a head of unusually blonde hair and he stood carelessly behind his father, looking around him. The other was slightly darker. He kept his gaze focused courteously on Causantin, a smile of greeting on his lips and this was the one who stepped forward and bowed.

"Indeed, I remember our campaigns against the Angles well, Lord Causantin. It was an honour to fight alongside you. I am most happy that our blood is soon to be joined in peace."

Baena scarcely heard her father's reply as she stared at the man. And he was truly a man. When she had been told of him she had expected a boy, like Drust who was just over a year older than herself. This man towered over her. A faint scar on his cheek did little to mar his appearance and hinted at the battles he had endured.

Causantin pulled her forward. "Lord Cinaed, may I present my most treasured jewel, my daughter the Lady Baena? My child, this is Lord Cinaed Mac Alpin"

The man's intense grey eyes were fixed on her for a second, but as he took her hand his smile was kind. "My lady, it is an honour to meet you at last."

Baena stammered a greeting, as he bowed over her hand. She was still shocked by how old he was. He had definitely seen at least twenty years. She had imagined that the battle the previous year had been his first fight, but as he raised her hand to his lips, his sleeve fell back and looking at the scars on his arms she realised that he must have fought many times.

He continued to talk kindly to her as others were presented to her parents and she thought in sudden resentment "he thinks I am but a child."

Chapter two

After the first awkward greeting, Baena spent no more time with Cinaed that evening. As the night drew in torches were lit and the travellers settled down for the feasting. Baena got glimpses of him talking and laughing in a rowdy group. The heather ale flowed freely as platters of meat, fish and barley bread were passed around accompanied by dishes of last autumn's hazelnuts and skewered mushrooms.

Baena was relieved to sit quietly with the women while secretly scrutinising her future husband whenever she got the chance. He was very much the centre of attention and watching her brother Hago filling his cup at every opportunity, Baena felt irritated at the way they were all favouring him.

"May I sit with you, my lady?" a short, grey haired woman sat next to her as chunks of apple cake and raspberries preserved in honey were dispensed. "We were not presented earlier. I am Unuis of the Sixth Royal House, wife of Alpin."

Glad of the opportunity to speak to Cinaed's mother, Baena greeted her warmly, feeling ashamed of herself for not seeking her out sooner. They sat in silence as they watched Cinaed laughing at a comment Domnall had made and Unuis seemed overshadowed by the vitality of her sons. But Baena felt instantly comfortable with her and began to talk with her in a way she even found hard with her own mother

The next morning Baena was up early. Having barely slept, she was glad to get out of the stuffy chamber she shared with the other unwed women and into the bright morning. The settlement was quiet, which was not surprising. The feasting and drinking had gone on well into the night and as she headed towards the church she suspected that there would be few at Morning Prayers that day.

Baena herself scarcely listened to the priest as he intoned the words to the small group who had made it. Her thoughts were overwhelmingly of her impending marriage. Queen of the Picts or Queen of Dal Riata! It sounded very fine. But it was likely that neither title would be hers as she felt fairly certain that Cinaed's claim to either crown was weak. She didn't even know when the marriage would take place although it was unlikely to be in the next day. Cinaed still had to receive the matching mark on his arm and it would surely be too soon to put on another feast.

In any case, she knew that she would not be going away yet. Cinaed and his father would be busy during summer securing their shores against the raids of the Norsemen and Cinaed had agreed that Baena could remain with her parents for the time being. She felt a grudging flicker of gratitude towards him that he was at least allowing this.

The prayers finished and, as she rose from her knees, Baena looked around, smiling at the people she had known all her life. There was only one stranger present – a strong looking, dark haired young man, who she realised must be one of the Gaels.

"Baena!" came a call, as she left the church.

Baena turned and her face lit up. "Drust!"

Drust was a handsome seventeen-year-old, with his dark hair falling onto his shoulders and sparkling vivid blue eyes. He took hold of Baena's outstretched hands and kissed them both. The Gael man she had seen in the church looked at them curiously as he strode past. Baena quickly pulled her hands away, aware that the man had cast many a backwards glance at them.

"Oh Drust, I am not supposed to talk to you while they are here." She gestured to the Gael. "I'm sorry."

Drust bowed, but whispered, "Meet me in the old place. Please."

The old place was a little hollow just beyond the final earth bank of the fort. The gorse bushes and brambles surrounding it made it almost impossible for anyone to see in until they were already inside. As children Baena, Drust and their kin had often played there. She knew she should not meet Drust, but the longing to talk was so strong that she wandered casually towards it. Pulling a hood over her head, she hoped that no one would recognise her.

Drust was already waiting in the hollow. He smiled when he saw her and held out his arms. Baena flung herself into them and for a few minutes they just clung together.

"You must escape this marriage. You must," he whispered

"But how? I have begged and pleaded. No one will listen. They just keep telling me what a good match it is."

Drust snorted. "I think I would be a better one. No Gael blood in my veins."

"I know," Baena whispered, resting her head against his shoulder.

"I thought your father would relent. He dotes on you even more than your brothers."

"It's all because of the battle last year. He has some idea of sealing the truce with my marriage. Suddenly all he wants for me is this Cinaed!" she spat the final word out.

"But you are meant to be mine." Drust's face darkened with anger. "Perhaps we should run away, leave Pictavia behind. Maybe to the south there is some settlement that would welcome us."

"How can we do that?" Baena asked more practically. "Every place we stopped for food or shelter we might be held and returned in disgrace."

"Do you want to escape this marriage or are you already Cinaed's creature?" Drust demanded.

"No! I will never be Cinaed's creature! But I do not think running away is the answer," Baena protested, shocked at Drust's outburst.

"There is something we could do," Drust said slowly. "He would walk away from the marriage for sure."

"What?"

Drust's hands went to the leather ties at the neck of her tunic. Baena stepped back. "What are you doing?

"He would not marry you if you had lain with another," Drust said, a smile curving his lips.

Baena crossed herself. "I know he would not, but I cannot. My name would be ruined."

"Your father would have no choice but to let you marry me."

"But your father could refuse," Baena pointed out miserably. "In fact, he probably would. He would think very poorly of me. I must go to my handfasting a maid."

Drust scowled at her. "I am starting to think you want to wed him. If you truly wish to marry me you must delay the ceremony while I think of something."

"I'll try," said Baena looking pleadingly into his eyes. "But I don't know how easy it will be. I am not leaving after the handfasting."

"We can't do anything once you are his wife. You will belong to him then." Drust looked even angrier. "We must take action before the ceremony."

"I just meant that I will still be here while Lord Cinaed is fighting on the coast."

Drust smirked slightly. "Perhaps some obliging Norseman will see to it that he never returns."

Baena nodded, although she felt very uncomfortable. However much she wanted to escape this marriage, it seemed wrong to wish for a brave, young man to be slaughtered by the Norse scum.

Drust pulled Baena back to him and they clung together once more before Baena whispered, "I must go."

"Well, this is a pretty picture!" A voice made Baena and Drust spring apart. Cinaed, Domnall and the Gael she had seen outside the church were stood in the hollow. All three wore the same look of contempt on their faces.

"You were right to warn me of this, Graunt," Cinaed said to the Gael.

"I don't care what you've seen!" Baena announced defiantly. "I was promised to Drust before my father met you."

"Well, now you are promised to me," Cinaed said mildly while the other two men bit their lips and looked at the ground. Baena glared at them, but Cinaed continued "You must return now. I will have no scandal attached to my name."

"I will not go with you!"

"You will or I will carry you back to your mother."

"I will not let you lay a finger on her!" Drust stepped forward.

Baena's heart swelled with pride at his defence, but it was quickly dashed as Domnall and Graunt failed to hold in their laughter and even Cinaed smiled.

"Lord Drust, your courage impresses me. I hope you will join our campaigns against the Norsemen soon. We have need of brave young men like you. But this is not the place for your heroics. The Lady Baena is for me, by the word of her father. Now please go, unless you wish Graunt to remove you by force."

Baena felt like crying with frustration. For a moment she had hoped that he would walk away from the match in anger, but instead they had been treated like a couple of naughty children. "Go!" she whispered to Drust.

"But..." he looked at her incredulously. "What about them?"

"They'll not harm me. Just go."

Drust pushed past the Gaels with as much bluster as he could manage, much to the men's amusement.

Cinaed held out his hand. "Come, my lady. You must return."

Baena tried to ignore him, but he caught hold of her arm as she swept past. "I hope you will behave with more propriety once we are married. Now, accept my escort with good grace. If you do not you will leave me with no choice but to throw you over my shoulder and return you by force. Then everyone will know of your character."

Baena shrank back at the anger in his voice. She did not trust herself to speak but bowed her head in agreement. She was miserably aware of Domnall's look of amusement as he and Graunt left the hollow.

A glimmer of sympathy appeared in Cinaed's eyes as he relaxed his grip on her arm. "Try to accept this, my lady. It will not be so bad."

The next few days passed in a blur. Baena knew that Cinaed had been marked with the same intricate knots as herself and the next day many of the men went hunting, returning hours later flushed and triumphant with the makings of a magnificent wedding feast. Storytellers and pipers arrived at Abernethy from all over Pictavia and many a person stopped their work to join in the festivities.

Baena loved music and would have joined them, but as was the custom she was kept secluded for the two days before the handfasting. In the chamber she worked on stitching tunics and lining cloaks while outside the merriments continued. She had spoken no further words to Cinaed as he had escorted her from the hollow in silence. Only the firm grip on her arm had shown that he was even aware of her presence. When they had arrived back at the hall, all three men had bowed politely to her, but Baena could see the disgust in their faces. Now she would not meet Cinaed again until they were to be man and wife. Every time Baena thought on this she felt like weeping. This would be a poor way to start a union.

On the evening of the second day her mother swept into the chamber carrying the wedding raiment. In spite of her dread, Baena could not help but be pleased. The woven cloth of the tunic had been dyed with woad to create a blue that would match the summer sky and embellished with white stitches.

"So, my daughter, tomorrow you are to be wed." Sabina settled herself down beside Baena. "Is there anything of marriage that you wish to know? I do not know if he will have any expectations of you before he leaves, but you understand about the wedding night, I trust."

Baena's heart quaked at the thought of sharing her bed and probably also her body with the angry stranger. Her mother made no mention of her transgressions and Baena realised that Cinaed and his companions had not reported them. For a second she felt grateful to him. Her mother's wrath was legendary and Baena had no wish to face it tonight.

"No, Mother. I understand my duties," Baena said quietly.

"Good," Sabina said as she stood. "We expect you to do us credit at the ceremony. Get some sleep now. Tomorrow will be a long day."

Chapter three

Baena felt the nerves gathering before dawn. She lay on her pallet for what seemed like hours, staring at the gradual lightening of the sky through the smoke hole in the ceiling. Eventually, a serving girl brought her a cup of water from the holy well and told her that it was time to get ready.

More water was brought so that Baena could be cleansed for her wedding, but no food. Even past the hour of Morning Prayer when Baena would usually break her fast there was nothing. She longed for some food to settle the fluttering in her stomach. Even a dry oatcake would do, but as a bride, she was expected to maintain her fast. She would next eat at the feast that came after the handfasting

They draped the blue tunic over her head. In the morning light it was even more beautiful than it had been the previous evening. But as a girdle was tied round her waist Baena looked down disdainfully at her slender body. She imagined that she looked like a child who had stolen her mother's clothes.

"Sit down my lady, we must comb your hair." The woman was gentle enough, but Baena's nerves were so strained that she felt every knot that was tugged.

Sabina arrived, dressed in a tunic lavishly embroidered with silk thread. Bangles of silver jangled on her arm and gold glinted round her throat. She looked magnificent and Baena felt more dissatisfied than ever with her own appearance. Sabina placed a circlet of harebells on Baena's loose hair and looked critically at her.

The women all gazed at her. "You look so beautiful, my lady," one gasped and the others all nodded.

"As beautiful as this morning," said another.

"You look well enough, my child," Sabina said at last, but she sounded pleased. "This is a gift from your father." She clasped a heavy gold chain around her neck. "And this is from the Lord Cinaed."

A further gasp of admiration came from the women at the bangle of gold and amber that Sabina was fastening around Baena's wrist. The bangle was beautiful, but Baena looked at it resentfully. It was his obligation to provide her with a bridal gift so hardly worthy of the approval it was getting. One of the women held out a silver mirror and

Baena looked at her reflection without vanity. Her mother was right. She looked well enough, but no more than that.

One person who did not share this opinion was her father. When he arrived to escort her to the handfasting Causantin looked on in amazement.

"You are the most beautiful daughter. Why, you look just like your mother on our wedding day, does she not, my love?"

Sabina smiled but did not contradict him.

"Young Cinaed will not believe his luck when he sees you. Come, my daughter. It is time."

Baena tried to smile as she took her father's arm. Her mother took her place on Baena's other side and they led her out to the cross on the hill. Baena couldn't help but wonder if Christ himself had approached a cross with more dread.

The old stone cross was elaborately carved with knots and other even more ancient symbols. A crowd was gathered around, which parted as Baena drew closer. The three made a striking sight. Causantin's face may have been scarred from battles, but his figure was as tall and upright as any man's. Sabina, elegant and beautiful drew many eyes. Between them, Baena felt insignificant, but she looked fresh and young to the admiring eyes that watched.

Cinaed was waiting at the cross. Dressed also in blue with a light cloak clasped to his shoulders his tall figure had attracted considerable admiration. A ready smile was on his lips as he accepted the good wishes of the watchers. He turned to them as they drew near. As his grey eyes rested on Baena he smiled slightly and he looked approvingly on her. His hand reached out to briefly clasp hers and as he bowed over it, she noted the mark on his wrist, identical to hers.

Father Fergus stepped forward and began to intone the sacred words of Saint Columba that would bind them together.

"Bring forth the threads," he said at last. Baena kept her eyes downcast to hide her dismay at this final step.

Causantin and Alpin came proudly forward each bearing a cord. One blue, one white. The priest twisted them together.

"Cinaed, son of Lord Alpin, Clan Chieftain of Dal Riata and Lady Unuis of the Sixth Royal House lay forth your arm to be bound to this woman."

Cinaed extended a muscled arm and smiled encouragingly at Baena.

"Baena, daughter of Lord Causantin of the Third Royal House and Lady Sabina of the Fourth Royal House lay forth your arm to be bound to this man."

Baena froze. Until that moment she had been certain that Drust would have a plan and something would happen to stop the marriage, but there would be no going back from this. Cinaed frowned, anger marking his face. She looked anxiously at her parents. Causantin smiled and gestured at her, but Sabrina's eyes glared at her. As if she had spoken Baena could hear her hiss in her head "Do not disgrace us."

Baena looked back at Cinaed. Fury had narrowed his eyes, but his arm was still outstretched. Shakily she stretched out her own. Behind her, the watchers let out an audible sigh of relief.

Cinaed grasped her hand once more, much tighter this time but Baena refused to show any sign of pain. The priest took the twisted threads and wound them round and round their wrists.

"Once that you be forever true, twice to bless you with babes and thrice for the blessing of the Lord God, our heavenly father."

With the last word, he tied the cord in a knot. Baena longed to shrink away from the feel of that hairy, muscled arm now bound to hers. His fingers were still entwined with hers in a way that must have looked loving to the watchers. Only Baena could feel the strength in those fingers that pressed into her hand. She kept her own hand as relaxed as possible in the hope of releasing some of the pressure, but her bones still felt crushed. Baena stole an upward glance at her new husband. He was looking down at her, but there was no softness in his eyes. His prize was now secure, but Baena wondered if he would ever forgive the humiliation of her hesitation.

Chapter Four

The people cast sprigs of heather over them as they processed to the wedding feast. Cinaed said nothing to her but smiled cheerfully at the crowd of well-wishers. The day was fine so tables had been set up around the roasting pits and Cinaed led Baena to a bench draped in blue cloth. Awkwardly with their hands still tied together, they sat down.

And so began a steady procession of people each presenting their dishes to the couple - slices of fat pork and venison, honeyed oats, preserved cherries and jugs of mead and heather ale. Baena, who had been so hungry earlier, now found it hard to even nibble at anything. Cinaed, on the other hand, seemed in great spirits, laughing and joking with the people, and complimenting them on the foods they presented. Everyone went away commenting on his good humour, but Baena knew that her own downhearted look had been noted and the look in his eyes when he glanced at her became increasingly icy.

"I am so proud to call you Son!" exclaimed Causantin, embracing them both.

"And I to call you Father!" Cinaed smiled back.

"So what do you think of my little flower? Is she not every bit as beautiful as I said?"

"Indeed, you are rightly proud. She is much admired."

Baena cringed at the veiled insult, but her father failed to notice the slightly sour tone in Cinaed's voice.

"I know you will take care of her."

"You may rest easy. I shall endeavour to be everything she deserves in a husband." He glanced at Baena as he spoke and she struggled to keep her face expressionless at the coldness in his gaze.

Baena noticed a similarly cold look in the eyes of Sabina who was the next to greet them and knew that she had disappointed her mother. Inwardly she cursed herself for her hesitation at the cross. She had delayed the marriage by mere seconds and probably won her husband's undying resentment.

Alpin, jubilant on the heather ale planted a loud kiss on Baena's cheek

"My lad, you've a bonny bride there!" he cried as Unuis gave Baena a quick embrace.

She looked worried and whispered in Cinaed's ear. Cinaed frowned at his mother and shrugged slightly. Unuis gave a smile, taking him into her arms. As she moved on Cinaed's eyes followed his mother.

At the end of the well-wishers came Father Fergus who had returned to remove the bindings from their wrists. The length of cord was divided between them and knotted into individual wristbands. Baena tried to hide the relief she felt as her slender arm was free once more, although she reflected bitterly that now she would never be free of the man who sat next to her. Smoothing down her sleeves she placed her hands in her lap and gave a swift glance at Cinaed. He had placed his arm on the back of the bench as he looked attentively at the priest and Baena shivered inwardly at the thought of that strong arm still so close to her.

"The blessings of Christ and Saint Columba be upon you, my children," Father Fergus announced and around them people cheered.

The afternoon continued with dancing. As the pipers and drummers whirled around them, Cinaed rose to his feet and pulled Baena into the traditional dance. Baena concentrated on her steps, trying to ignore the feel of his grip around her waist. It was a relief when the dance ended and he bowed solemnly to her. The people watching clapped and smiled on them as Cinaed led her back to the bench. Once there he put his hands in his lap, leaning forward to watch the rest of the dancing. Sadly, Baena remembered weddings where the couple had danced every dance together and felt like weeping. She knew this was often the lot of women of the Royal Houses, but raised on the stories of the love between her parents she had hoped for better. As the evening drew on she scanned the groups of Pict men, but there was no sign of Drust. Perhaps it was just as well.

At that time of year night barely touched this settlement of the Picts, so although the shadows were lengthening it was still light when the ladies took her away to prepare her for bed.

Blankets were piled in the bridal chamber, but still Baena shivered as the women fussed around her. Some of the older ones pushed sprigs of white heather beneath the straw mattress, said to bring fertility.

"Leave!" gestured Sabina. "My daughter does not need all of this!"

The women scuttled from the chamber, leaving Baena alone with her mother. For once Sabina seemed lost for words. Sensing her daughter's fear she gathered her in her arms. Baena buried her head in her shoulder and tried very hard not to cry.

When Sabina let go her own eyes seemed luminous with tears.

"My child, I feel you have already displeased him."

Baena bowed her head as Sabina sought for the words to best advise her daughter.

"I do not know what he will expect of you this night, but try to please him. If you can then everything will be well between you. Bless you, my child."

One last embrace that Baena wished would never end before Sabina left without a backwards glance, leaving Baena with absolutely no idea as to how she was to please Cinaed.

As she lay on the bed, dreading the moment when she would be alone with her husband, a sound of raucous merriment approached, singing and laughing. Baena recognised the voices of Domnall and Graunt and even her own brothers. Soon it was directly outside the doorway to her chamber.

"My friends, my kin. I thank you all. But I will continue alone!" Cinaed's voice sounded cheerful.

"Are you sure, Brother?" came Domnall's voice. "You know what to do?"

Much laughter greeted this.

"Oh, he knows!" Graunt's voice was blurred by the quantities of heather ale he'd drunk. "I could tell you of some nights!"

"But you won't," laughed Cinaed. "At least not here! I'll bid you all good night!"

"Will be a good night for you, Brother, with that pretty young bride!"

Baena cringed at his words, but outside she heard Cinaed laugh and shoo his companions away until the laughter moved off. Baena bit her lip and lay tensely as Cinaed pushed aside the door hangings.

In the dim light Baena could see that he had cast off his wedding finery and was dressed only in a simple robe. He kept it on as he lay next to her on the mattress, propped up on his elbow and looked intently at her. She clenched her fists together as she waited for his next move.

"You're just a child," he said at last and turning his back on her he lay down and said no more.

Baena was stunned and more than a little outraged at the nerve of this barbarian Gael rejecting a Daughter of the Royal House. Firmly quashing the relief that was coursing through her she dwelled angrily on the rejection until sleep came at last.

Chapter five

The light woke Baena early. Turning, she looked at her husband. He still had his back to her and his hair fell over his shoulders. No doubt sensing he was being watched, he rolled over and looked at her.

"I am glad you are awake. There is much to do. We ride this morning."

"You... you're leaving this day?" Baena exclaimed in considerable surprise.

Cinaed frowned slightly. "We are leaving, as soon as you can be ready."

"No! I am staying," she cried in panic, unable to believe he would so quickly forget the agreement.

Cinaed reached out and took her hand. "No. You are my wife now and your place is with me. Do not disgrace us both by arguing."

Baena snatched her hand away. "I'll not leave. You promised I could stay here!"

Cinaed's eyes narrowed. "I have changed my mind."

Unsurprisingly there was a huge row. Causantin was bewildered at the turn of events.

"But why? What of our agreement?"

Cinaed looked at the crowd that had gathered around them. Domnall was grinning and the other Gaels also looked amused, but the Picts were angry. Baena looked down. For the first time she wore the caul of a married woman and hoped it would conceal her embarrassment. Cinaed had hold of her arm, keeping her firmly at his side, as he shook his head. "I would prefer not to say."

Causantin flushed angrily. "That is not good enough. I ask as father to son, why are you going back on our agreement?"

Alpin stepped forward and placed a hand on Baena's shoulder. "Now then Causantin, you'd not hold the boy to an agreement he made before setting eyes on his bonny bride would you? Naturally he's changed his mind now he's seen her."

"You are headed for the campaigns against the Norsemen. He'll not spend much time with her. Baena is safer here with us."

"Cinaed wants his wife," Alpin said firmly. "You can trust him with her safety."

"She is too young," Causantin protested. "That was our deal."

Alpin folded his arms. "She is Cinaed's now. The decision lies with him."

All eyes turned to Cinaed. "Causantin, I would speak with you and your lady alone," Cinaed said after a long silence.

Still frowning Causantin took Sabina's arm and headed to a deserted chamber, smoky from the morning fires. Cinaed pressed one hand against Baena's back to usher her along as well.

"Explain yourself, Cinaed," Causantin said, folding his arms.

"If I leave her here I shall no doubt return to find her belly swelling and not by me," Cinaed said brutally.

The colour drained from Baena's face and she avoided looking at either of her parents.

"Nonsense," Causantin maintained firmly. "Baena is a virtuous woman. She would never dishonour the marriage."

"And yet just days ago I found her in the arms of that puppy from the First Royal House," Cinaed bit back. "Is that your idea of virtue?"

"Drust!" Sabina spat. "Baena, you were forbidden to have anything to do with him."

For a long time Causantin just stared at Baena, before turning back to Cinaed. "We will guard her. I swear she will not see him again," Causantin pleaded.

"No. She comes with me."

"And if I refuse?"

Cinaed shrugged. "She is as yet untouched. The marriage can be dissolved if you wish."

Baena's heart leapt. Then she saw her mother's angry face and wondered if staying was really preferable.

Causantin shook his head. "There must be something we can do to persuade you. Some deal could be struck."

Cinaed took a long look at Causantin. "My lord, I am sure you are sincere in your intentions to guard her virtue, but it is clear to me that this will not be enough. Either I leave today with my wife or I leave an unwed man. The choice is yours."

"Promise me she will be safe with you," Causantin sighed.

Cinaed nodded. "She will be well cared for. I give you my word on that."

"But you are headed for the coast, perhaps even a battle with the Norsemen. You'll not take her with you?"

"No. She will stay at Dunadd with my mother. There is no safer place."

"Very well then, my son," Causantin said sadly. "Take her with my blessing."

"Thank you." Cinaed turned to Baena who was feeling close to tears. His eyes softened slightly. "I shall give you some time to make your farewells." And with a small bow to Sabina he left them.

Sabina narrowed her eyes. "I told you not to disgrace us. And what do you do?"

Baena shrank away from her mother. "I... I'm sorry."

Causantin held up a hand. "No. There will be no reproaches. Our daughter is leaving. I do not know when, if ever, we will see her again. Our last moments together must not be spent in anger."

"Oh, Father!" Baena flung herself into his arms, tears streaking her face. "I am sorry. I will make you proud."

"I already am, my child."

They clung together until Causantin released her. "Dry your eyes, my child. We must not keep him waiting. He has reason to be angry with you now, but he is a good man. I would not have given you to him if he were not."

"I know, Father." Baena blinked back further tears and straightened herself. "I shall be a good wife and I shall never forget the dignity of a Daughter of the Third Royal House. Farewell Father."

"Farewell, my dear child. Send word to me when you can so I know you are well."

"Farewell Mother."

"Farewell Daughter." Sabina tried to remain formal, but a corner of her mouth trembled as she placed her hands on Baena's shoulders. "Remember your heritage. You are of the true royal house of this land, from before these Gaels ever crossed the sea. Never forget this." The formality collapsed as she looked at her anxious daughter. "But all the same, be dutiful and obedient to your husband. It is a poor start you have made with him, but in time if you please him he will look on you with more kindness."

Baena wiped the last traces of tears from her cheeks and exited the chamber with her head held high. Gesturing to one of the women she called "Pack up my apparel and fetch me a riding tunic."

Ignoring the smirking Gaels she swept majestically into her chamber. She kept her composure as members of her kin gathered to pass little gifts, thanking them graciously for beaded necklaces, an iron cross, earthenware bowls and pots of honey. She knew these must have been hastily gathered, as no one had expected to leave today.

"Enough!" she exclaimed trying to laugh, as one more little nephew moved in to embrace her. "I thank you all. I shall miss you all. Farewell."

Outside her horse was waiting. At the sight of this one friend who was to go with her, her composure nearly broke. She stroked its nose until she could look up again.

"Are you ready?" Cinaed had approached her. There was no anger in him now, only an indifferent respect.

Baena took one last look at her parents, who were looking on with both sadness and amazement at her transformation from careless girl to Lady of the Royal House. She looked gravely back at Cinaed and nodded.

Cupping his hand he helped her to mount the horse before mounting his own.

"May the blessings of Christ and Saint Columba be upon you and guard you on your travels. God speed your journey." Father Fergus moved among the party making the sign of the cross as he went.

With the cries of farewell echoing around them they trotted away from the settlement. Baena kept her eyes fixed firmly ahead, but out of the corner of her eyes she could see the tears on the faces of the Picts who lined the way to wave and it took considerable effort not to allow her own eyes to fill.

As they left the populated area the horses picked up speed and cantered over the grassland. The scent of heather and gorse filled the air and the sun shone down on them. Baena had no idea how long this journey would take. She only hoped that the weather would hold for it. If there was one thing she hated it was riding in the rain. The weight in her heart eased once there were no more kin to wave at her and she could concentrate on guiding her horse through the bushes, all thoughts of home pushed resolutely from her mind.

However if she thought she had seen the last of her friends she was wrong. At the very edges of their land stood a boy, bareheaded on a rock. It was Drust. Cinaed frowned and looked warningly at Baena. "Ride on!" he snapped.

But Baena dared to reign in her horse for an instant. She looked steadily at Drust, a slight smile on her face. She wondered if he was having the same memories as her – the splashing as mere children in the loch, the gathering of firewood for the roasting pits, the dances together on feast days and, yes those stolen kisses when their parents had discussed the possibility of their marriage.

The Gaels were all silent as they waited curiously for Cinaed's reaction. But none came. Drust dropped to one knee and Baena gently inclined her head. One tear escaped her eyes as she urged her horse on, but she did not look back.

Chapter six

The journey took several days, across sweeping moorlands and through dense forests. At nights they begged shelter at farms and settlements and slept on the floors of smoke filled dwellings. If no residence was in sight in the high hills they crossed, the men rigged up shelters from stout sticks and skins and lit great fires to keep the wolves away.

On such nights Baena, exhausted from the days riding crept into her tent as soon as she could, but lay there unable to sleep listening to Cinaed laughing and joking with his father and other men by the fires. Only after she heard him call a cheerful goodnight to Domnall and Graunt and felt him creep in next to her to fall almost instantly to sleep did she relax enough to rest herself. Often she dreamt of her family and the busy scene back at Abernethy. When she woke she wept at the bitter realisation that she was still with these strangers as they made their way across the land.

One day, as the sun glistened on a sea loch Alpin reigned in his horse and breathed in deeply. "Aah, I smell the furnaces of Dunadd!"

Baena could smell nothing out of the ordinary and suspected this was fancy on his part. She looked at the loch and realised in awe that she must have crossed the land. Feeling more distant from her family than ever she looked at her companions. Cinaed had reigned in his horse next to his parents and the three of them smiled at each other. Domnall was joking with the other young men, all eager to be home. Only Baena stood alone.

"It will be good to return," said Unuis

"Has this journey tired you, my dear lady?" Alpin asked his wife.

"A little," she admitted.

"I did say that you did not need to come, Mother," Cinaed added.

Unuis smiled on him. "Nonsense, my son. Of course I would see you wed, but it will be good to return."

Alpin seemed to suddenly remember Baena and called over his shoulder to her, "And does the journey tire you too, my daughter? Well, then let us hurry on. Come Cinaed, bring your bride home."

Cinaed gave Baena the briefest glance. He'd spoken to her only when necessary the entire journey and he didn't speak to her now.

"Of course Father, by all means let us hurry." And he urged his horse on, racing ahead with Domnall.

At length they came down from the hills onto a flat plain.

"That is Dunadd," Unuis said to Baena, gesturing across the plain.

Ahead a stone fort rose out of clouds of smoke. It was the largest stone building Baena had ever seen. For a while she could only gaze in wonder at the castle terraces and the crags of rocks above. So this was the journeys end.

"It was not so big the first time I saw it," Unuis said, smiling at Baena's astonishment. "The lower enclosure was added by Alpin's father, King Eochaidh."

The younger men, Domnall and Graunt included urged their horses to greater speeds and galloped across the plain, vying with each other to be the first back. For a moment it looked that Cinaed might join them, but then he seemed to think better of it and rode much more properly beside Baena. She looked at him anxiously, hoping for some sign of welcome on his face, but he was looking directly ahead. He seemed unaware she was even there.

As they got closer she could hear the noise of clashing metal and could now most definitely smell the furnaces. They rode among small dwellings and many people stopped what they were doing to call a greeting or to stare curiously at Baena. Before the great wooden gates of the fort, boys waited to take their horses and the travellers climbed the steep path to enter the hall.

Baena was glad to be handed a welcome cup of hot heather ale. She sipped it while taking a look around her new home. The hall was dominated by a huge table, on which great jugs of ale rested. It seemed to be full of men, who clustered around Alpin, Cinaed and Domnall, giving them news and firing questions. There was no sign of Unuis and Baena wondered if she had been claimed by some domestic matter or simply slipped away to recover from the journey.

When she next looked up she met Domnall's piercing blue eyes. He grinned, then dug his elbow into Cinaed.

"Brother, should you not be taking your bride to her chamber. Show her how you conduct matters at Dunadd!" he jested.

Alpin roared with laughter. "Indeed my boy, what are we doing keeping you here? Go!"

There was good-humoured laughter and more sly jokes as with a rather forced smile Cinaed ushered Baena from the hall. In silence, she followed her husband out to a round dwelling.

It was pleasant enough. The circular walls were hung with cloths that no doubt kept it warm in winter. She noticed her packs already lying on to of coffers, as she tried not to look at the bed that dominated the room.

Baena stood with her head bowed while Cinaed just looked impatiently at her. Sighing, he reached out and took her hand. Baena was unable to help her reaction at his touch. She flinched and Cinaed dropped her hand, a look of rage spreading across his face.

"Ah, yes. I know your tastes run to a very different man," he started in a low, angry voice. "But there shall be nothing of that nature here. I will not have my name disgraced. If you do not behave with honour and propriety at all times you will be punished in full accordance with our laws. I trust you understand this."

Baena nodded fearfully, although she had no idea how their laws stood on such matters.

"It is clear to me that you were allowed to run wild back in your land. That is now at an end. Here we work hard and you will be expected to bear your share. I will have no man say that the Lord Cinaed has a lazy, slattern for a wife."

Baena's resentment built up at the injustice of his words. She had never shirked her duties and was no stranger to the hard work needed to keep these great forts running.

Cinaed folded his arms and looked at her with narrowed eyes. "I have indeed made a very poor bargain. From this day you will strive harder to please me."

Baena burst into tears, hating herself for her weakness. Cinaed made a disgusted sound and swinging round he stalked from the chamber. Baena sank to the ground and sobbed her homesick heart out. She tried desperately to understand why she had been sent here. Even if her father had not wished her to marry Drust there were surely plenty of other Pict men he could have chosen.

She stiffened as soft footsteps entered the chamber and she wondered what Cinaed wanted with her now. But it was not him. Gentle arms were wrapped around her. Baena raised her face to see Unuis' worried eyes looking at her.

Fresh sobs burst out of her as Unuis pulled Baena's face against her shoulder and gently stroked her hair.

"Hush child. This day is hard, but do not weep. All will be well."

Unuis was right. Life did improve as she settled down to her new life. She saw very little of Cinaed. At meal times she took her place next to him and he greeted her with the deference due to her rank but spent the occasion talking to Alpin and Domnall or any visitors that had come to Dunadd. At night he came late to their chamber and slept on a pallet away from her.

Baena couldn't help but be impressed with how many visitors there were as men visited from all over Dal Riata and beyond, even on one occasion as far as the court of the Emperor Louis. But it was not long before they heard of a very different kind of visitor. The fleet of the Norsemen had been sighted in the seas off Dal Riata. Alpin summoned his men to head to their boats, moored in the sea loch.

In her life Baena was to witness many times the troops assembling in the great plain beneath Dunadd, but she never forgot her amazement at the sight this first time. The noise alone was beyond anything she had experienced as horses neighed, men shouted orders and women and children wept to see them leave. Drinks were handed out to the men to refresh them before they set off.

Alpin was already standing by his horse talking to Unuis. He accepted a cup of ale from Baena with a brief thanks. She turned away to see Cinaed, Graunt and Domnall, dressed in short riding tunics and breeches, coming from the fort. They seemed to be teasing their kinsman Gregor, a young man not much older than herself. Cinaed was laughing, his arm draped around Domnall's shoulders. Graunt laughed too, clapping Gregor across the back. As they came upon Baena their laughter disappeared. The four of them paused a moment to accept the cups that Baena was offering. Cinaed quickly downed his drink and turned away before she could speak the traditional words of blessing. Graunt looked at her with a touch of disgust in his eyes as he went after Cinaed, but Domnall gave her a cheerful wink before leading Gregor to his horse.

As the men rode away Baena got one last glimpse of Cinaed talking to Gregor. She gave a sigh of relief at their departure as Unuis stood with her and took her arm. Baena glanced at her and the smile on her face faded. The older woman had clearly been weeping as her husband and sons rode into danger. Suddenly Baena felt ashamed of her relief and every day the men were away Baena went to the church and for Unuis' sake prayed for Cinaed's safe return.

The prayers were answered as the men returned jubilantly two moons later. The raids had been far fewer than they had feared and the coast had for the most part been successfully defended.

While Cinaed had been away Baena had slept in Unuis' chambers, but with his return, she moved back with resignation to her own.

However that night Cinaed did not appear, not even to lie across the room. When this was repeated over the next few nights Baena breathed a sigh of relief and returned to Unuis.

Baena discovered quite by accident exactly where Cinaed was spending his nights. One autumn day as the light began to fade she took some cloths down to the church. As ever when she visited here she lingered a little to pray for her family. The church was always peaceful with a faint smell of incense clinging to it. She lay the freshly woven cloths on the stone altar, wondering, as she did every time she came, at the stone of pure white among those grey blocks. Other than that white stone the only other decoration was an elaborate golden cross. Baena knelt there in a quick prayer before making her way back to the higher levels of the fort.

As she headed back she saw Cinaed come through the gates into the courtyard. The men had been hunting that day and Cinaed appeared to be among the first to return. He did not spot her lingering in the shadow of the church and she slowed her pace a little so as not to have to engage him in a conversation that always seemed so hard.

Across the courtyard, a blonde woman had just come out of one of the storerooms and to Baena's astonishment Cinaed grinned, whistling at her. Baena frowned, trying to place the woman. Then it came to her. Her name was Annis and she had recently come to the fort to serve Unuis.

Annis whirled round, her face lighting up with a welcoming smile. Cinaed strode quickly across the courtyard to pull her into his arms, kissing her passionately. Baena shrank back in horrified amazement, although there seemed little chance of either Cinaed or Annis noticing her. Annis laughingly pushed Cinaed away, gesturing up to the fort. Cinaed laughed too, whispering something in her ear and to Baena's total disgust the pair slipped into the storeroom.

That evening Cinaed greeted her at the meal as politely as always, but as the evening drew on Baena caught the knowing glances and sly grins that Domnall and Graunt both gave him and she reflected bitterly that for a man who wanted no disgrace on his name he was doing very well.

Chapter seven

An excited stir went through Unuis' chambers a few days later when Cinaed entered. Unuis looked up in surprise as it was unusual to see any of the men during the day other than at prayers

"What brings you here, my son?" she asked.

Baena, who was watching him from lowered eyes thought she saw a fleeting glance between him and Annis.

Cinaed bowed over his mother's hand. "I came to tell you we will have guests this evening. The Pict men who fought with us on the coast are returning home. They are making camp in the plain this night and some of their leaders will dine with us."

"What House are they from?" Unuis asked.

"The Third for the most part."

Baena's heart leapt. "Is my father with them?" she burst out without thinking.

Cinaed glanced at her, looking irritated at the interruption. "I believe so," he replied.

Baena forced down the anger that no one had thought to tell her that her father and possibly other kin had been fighting that summer. "I must go to him."

She stepped forward, but Cinaed blocked her path. "I do not think so. I do not want my wife visiting army camps."

"But-" Baena began.

"You will do as I say and remain with my mother."

An icy silence descended on the room and Baena's eyes filled with tears. Before her vision blurred she could see that Annis was smirking.

"Cinaed, it is natural for the child to be eager to see her father," Unuis said, gesturing to the other women to leave.

"I am sure it is," Cinaed replied. "And she will be pleased to welcome him this night."

As the women filed out Annis gave Cinaed a sidelong glance, but Cinaed was stood with his arms folded, his eyes fixed in irritation on Baena. He took no notice of her.

Once the women had left Cinaed lowered his voice, but he sounded no less severe. "That young lord from the First House that you are so attached to may be there," he said and Unuis gave Baena a sharp glance. "I trust I do not need to remind you to avoid any conversation with him. If you make any attempt to be alone with him you will be severely punished."

Baena bit her lip and nodded.

"Good." Some of the anger died away. "I will take my leave now, Mother." He bowed and left the room with no further word.

Baena felt wretched. It was torture to know that her father was so close, but she was unable to go to him. Feeling Unuis stare at her Baena kept her eyes downcast. Unuis had been her one friend since arriving here, but now perhaps even she would turn against her.

"Well, we must make the necessary preparations for our guests," Unuis said as the silence became uncomfortable. She did not ask about Cinaed's comments but treated Baena with her usual affection for the rest of the day.

The evening seemed to take a long time to arrive, but at last, Baena was able to head to the hall to prepare the welcome cups. She could hardly contain herself as she served both Gaels and Picts alike until eventually Alpin escorted her father into the hall. Baena longed to run across the room and throw herself into his arms. But she had to remain patient still further while Causantin cheerfully greeted both Cinaed and Domnall. Fortunately, she did not have to wait any longer. Keeping his hand on her father's arm Cinaed ushered him past the other men and brought him towards her.

"Your daughter has been most eager to greet you," he said with a charming smile at Causantin.

"Baena, my dear child!" Causantin held out his arms and Baena flung her own arms around him, unable to speak.

"I will leave you to your reunion," she heard Cinaed say.

Causantin pushed Baena away slightly so he could look at her properly. He seemed pleased with what he saw.

"You have grown these last months," he said. "I can see that this marriage agrees with you well. Did I not tell you what a fine young man I had chosen?"

"Yes, Father," Baena said quietly, wondering how her father could be so deluded. She wondered what her father would say if she had replied, "Yes, a fine young man who has rejected me every night of our marriage to lie with others."

But, of course, she said nothing of this as she handed her father a cup of ale. It might cause a terrible row or perhaps her father would simply chide her for her failure to please her husband. Given how he seemed so determined to fawn over Cinaed, Baena suspected that the second possibility was much more likely.

At that moment, she caught sight of Drust entering the hall. He saw Baena immediately and gave her a long look. Baena allowed herself to briefly meet his eyes. She couldn't help thinking how different everything would be if her father had permitted her to marry Drust. She would probably be with child by now and her life would be among friends.

Her father seemed to read her mind as he commented, "Not with child yet?"

"No, Father."

"Well, these things take time, but I hope you do not keep him waiting too long. A young warrior like himself will want sons and lots of them. Your mother presented me with our first son less than ten moons from our handfasting."

"I know," Baena said despondently.

"Just keep praying to be blessed."

"I will, Father," Baena replied, thinking grimly that prayer was indeed her only hope. It would take God himself to arrange a virgin birth.

The hall had filled up now and already people were taking their seats at the great table. Cinaed came over to them and invited her father to be seated.

"May I sit with my father?" Baena asked.

Cinaed raised his eyebrows and Causantin quickly said, "A wife's place is with her husband, my child."

"It is." Cinaed agreed, stretching out his arm.

Reluctantly Baena laid her hand on it, feeling like weeping. She could hardly believe that this brief conversation was the only contact she was to be allowed with her father.

Cinaed's eyes fixed for a moment on where Drust was sitting with a group of other young Pict men. He glanced at Baena. Her hand was resting obediently on his arm, but her dejection was clearly to be seen in the droop of her head. He ushered Causantin to a space further up the table and placed Baena's hand back on her father's arm. She looked up at him in surprise.

"I think at such a happy reunion the normal customs should not apply," he said jovially to Causantin. "I will entrust my lady to your care this night."

Any gratitude Baena felt at this vanished as Causantin replied "My daughter is most fortunate to receive such kindness. I thank you, my son."

Wondering again how her father could be so taken in she sat next to him on the bench and to forestall any further questions on her marriage she asked after her mother and brothers. As he talked she felt such a longing for her home even though she knew it was likely she would never see it again.

As everyone ate their fill talk among the men got louder with jokes and songs a plenty. The women began to retire and reluctantly Baena rose from the table.

"When do you ride on, Father?" she asked, as Cinaed joined them once more.

"At first light, my child. And as you know well it will take several days to return."

"Then say your farewells now," Cinaed instructed.

"But might I not say them in the morn?" Baena asked, hardly able to bear the thought of saying goodbye again so soon.

"I have already told you that the army camp is no place for my wife," Cinaed replied a hard edge creeping into his voice, although his face remained courteous.

Causantin nodded. "I am happy to see you with so protective a husband. My dear child, it will be good to bring such pleasing news of you to your mother. Fare you well."

Causantin kissed Baena's cheek as Baena stammered some words in return that she knew did not come close to what she wanted to say. Cinaed bowed to her, as the singing grew louder.

"I'll bid you good night, my lady," Cinaed said. He put a hand on Causantin's arm and led him back to the festivities.

Baena hurried across the hall, hoping to leave before the tears started to fall. She kept her head bowed and did not notice the man standing before the doorway until she collided with him. She looked up and started to apologise. But her apologies stuttered to a halt as she realised it was Drust's eyes that were looking down on her.

She sprang back, but he caught her hand. "I thought you were never going to talk to me," he said.

"Drust! I... I must not. I have been forbidden. Please let me pass."

Drust leant back against the wooden beams that formed the doorway. "Once you did not care for what others said. Are you now so completely the great Cinaed's property?"

"No!" Baena cried instinctively before reflecting on her grim reality. "Oh, I don't know. I must not speak to you. He will beat me for sure. Please, Drust!" Baena cast a quick look back into the hall. Cinaed and her father had their backs to her and even if they turned it was possible that they would not see what was happening in this dark, smoky corner of the hall.

"You were meant to be mine, Baena," he hissed.

"I know, but my father had other plans. Please do not cause trouble for me. Let me pass!"

"Are you troubling my lady?" a voice asked and whirling round she saw Graunt standing behind her. Her heart sank. After Cinaed, this was the last man she wished to see. She knew he would report these events to Cinaed and then she would be punished. Cinaed had never specified what punishment she would receive. She guessed it would be a beating, but perhaps it would be even worse.

"You go join the men if you are one, my lad!" Graunt gave Drust a shove and Baena could no longer hold back the tears. Graunt looked at her through narrowed eyes. "Do at least try not to disgrace the honour of Lord Cinaed."

Baena wiped her eyes. Several of Unuis' women spoke highly of Graunt and she wondered whether to appeal to him not to betray her to Cinaed. But seeing the contempt in his eyes made her hesitate.

"I'll bid you goodnight, my lord," she said in as calm a voice as she could manage.

She walked steadily until she was out of the hall and then she fled across the courtyard. She had already intended to sleep in her own chamber that night so that she might weep in peace. But now she had a more pressing reason. If Cinaed wished to vent his anger on her, at least no one would witness the punishments she must endure.

Chapter eight

Baena passed a sleepless night expecting Cinaed to burst into the chamber in a rage at any moment, but he did not come. As the sky began to lighten Baena's fear gave way to anger. Even with her father nearby Cinaed had still chosen to lie elsewhere. Thoughts of her father gave Baena an idea. Since Cinaed was likely to punish her anyway, she decided there was nothing to lose from trying to see her father one last time. She dressed quickly, putting on a hood and left the chamber.

Outside she was shocked by how light it had become, but by the noises she could hear drifting up from the plain she knew the Picts had not yet left. Praying that no one would spot her she hurried down the steep path that led to the main gates. If these gates were bolted as they often were overnight her plan would come to nothing, but with the visitors camped in the plain there was a good chance they would be open. Pulling the hood firmly over her head to obscure her face from the watchmen she headed on.

She was in luck. The great wooden gates stood partially open. Almost running she slipped through and ran straight into a man coming the other way. It was Domnall. Judging by the sack over his shoulder and the dog at his heel he had been out after rabbits. Baena's hood fell back in the collision and Domnall's mouth dropped open when he saw her.

"Are you running away from my brother? You know I can't allow it, but I can't say I blame you!" he said.

"I am not running away. I just want to see my father one last time before he rides on," Baena said sullenly, certain that she was about to be escorted back in disgrace.

"Do you know how many men are down there?" Domnall asked. "You'd never find him."

Baena turned away. She had always known that it would be hopeless, but Domnall caught her arm.

"I assume Cinaed does not know you are out?"

Baena shook her head, making no attempt to deceive him. She expected Domnall to be angry, but instead he gave a broad grin.

"Come on then. I'll take you down there!"

"Really?" Baena asked, not sure she could have heard him correctly.

"Yes, but hurry. They'll be gone soon. And if Cinaed finds out I shall deny all knowledge of helping you."

Baena nodded and linking arms they hurried down together, Domnall's dog trotting behind them.

Down on the plain Baena understood what Domnall meant about not being able to find Causantin. Men were running everywhere, some loaded with bundles. Horses paced impatiently and dogs sniffed among the debris. Men were shouting and some of the comments were decidedly coarse. And as she spotted half naked serving lads loading up the horses she also reluctantly conceded that perhaps Cinaed was right not to want her there.

"The Lord Causantin of the Third House?" Domnall asked one of the Picts.

"Over there," the man pointed.

Domnall kept his hand under Baena's arm. "If we see that fool, Drust, you keep well away from him. I do not know what happened last night, but Cinaed was not happy with him."

"Of course I will," Baena snapped back, angered by the way all the men seemed so keen to believe the worst of her.

They had to ask several more men before Baena spotted her father through the crowd. They were just in time. He seemed to be about to mount his horse and was shouting some last orders at his men.

"Father!" she called, running to him.

Causantin caught her in an embrace. He looked startled. "My child, what are you doing here?"

"I had to say a proper farewell," she said.

"But the Lord Cinaed-" Causantin started

"The Lord Cinaed has an important matter to attend to," Domnall stepped forward. "He apologises for not being here to bid you farewell himself. He trusts me to keep his lady safe."

"My Lord Domnall, that is most kind of you," Causantin said still looking uncertain, as well he might at seeing Cinaed's wild younger brother in a position of trust.

"Father, you will send my love to Mother and all my brothers and the children won't you? Tell them I think of them often."

"Of course, my child. They all think often on you. Now one last kiss, my daughter. We must ride."

Baena flung her arms around him wanting to never let him go. Causantin had to prise her away and passed her back to Domnall.

"Farewell, my child," he cried, mounting his horse.

"Farewell Father," Baena cried through her tears. "May God speed your journey!"

Causantin's horse moved away and others soon followed. Domnall pulled Baena away from the thudding hoofs and gave her an awkward hug.

"Come, Sister. You must get back," he said, his blue eyes, free for once of mischief, were sympathetic.

"No, I would watch them go," Baena said quietly, her eyes straining for one last glimpse of a friendly face.

"Don't be a fool. They will all be awaking up there," Domnall gestured at the fort. "You will be missed."

Baena still did not move, no longer even caring about punishment. There was nothing Cinaed could inflict on her that would be worse than the pain in her heart at that moment.

The sympathy in Domnall's eyes faded. "Baena, come now or I will return alone and tell Cinaed exactly where you are."

Her father was already out of sight among the other riders so Baena wiped her eyes and allowed Domnall to pull her along. He moved swiftly until they reached the path back to the fort.

"Pull your hood up," he told her. "And pray you can get in without being seen."

Baena did as she was instructed, but just as they got to the wooden gates they could hear whistles coming from the courtyard and a dog barking excitedly.

"That's Augus," Domnall whispered. "Cinaed will be with him."

Baena shrank back against the rocks. "What shall I do?"

Domnall thought for a moment then grinned. He was clearly treating this as a great jest. Baena was grateful to him for taking her to see her father, but she couldn't help resenting his attitude. It was easy for him. Even if Cinaed was angry with Domnall, he would not care. Scuffles between the brothers were not uncommon and Domnall had proved that he was more than capable of holding his own against Cinaed. It would be a very different matter for her.

"I'll go ahead. Perhaps I can distract him. You'll never make it into the fort. What about the church? Go in there. It will be of no matter if you are seen coming out later."

Baena nodded, her heart thumping. They crept up the path until they could just see into the courtyard. Cinaed was throwing scraps of meat to a huge dog who jumped up eagerly to grab them from the air. As Cinaed ruffled the dog's head Domnall winked at Baena and strode boldly in.

"Cinaed!" he called cheerfully. "A good morning to you!"

"And to you, Brother. Where have you been so early?" Baena shrank back as Cinaed turned to greet Domnall.

"Rabbits!" Domnall tossed the sack at Cinaed.

Cinaed peered in. "Not bad, Brother," he grinned. "But I think Augus would have got more!"

"Nonsense," Domnall scoffed. "That mutt could never beat Oden."

"Are you sure?"

"Shall we test it?" Domnall asked, whistling to his own dog.

Cinaed grabbed Augus by the neck and Domnall tossed the rabbits one by one to the other side of the courtyard.

"Ready?" Domnall asked.

As soon as the brothers let go of their dogs, Baena darted into the courtyard. She did not look to see which dog was winning and only hoped that Cinaed's attention on the dogs would not waver. It was with relief that she made it inside the church and slumped down trembling against the wall.

From the noise outside she guessed that it was Cinaed's dog that had won the competition. She reflected that at least that would put him in a good mood although this seemed rather harsh on Domnall. She was just wondering how long to linger in the church when she heard another voice.

"Cinaed!" It was Unuis and she sounded worried. "I can't find Baena. She didn't sleep in my chambers last night and she's not in hers either."

Cinaed's good humour vanished. "If she is down there…" he said ominously.

"She won't be," Unuis insisted. "She is a good girl."

"I know you have a kindness for her, Mother, but I think it is blinding you to her faults," Cinaed sighed. "I need to speak to her myself as I have heard that puppy from the First House was sniffing around her again last night."

"She may not have done anything to encourage it," Unuis pleaded.

"Then where is she?" Cinaed demanded. "I shall have to go down there to ask if any have seen her and she will have made me a laughing stock."

Baena felt worried. She wondered if any of the Picts still there would remember seeing her.

Perhaps the same thought had occurred to Domnall for he spoke up. "Before I went out I saw a woman go into the church."

"That would make sense, Cinaed," Unuis spoke eagerly. "She would want to pray for her father's journey."

"Would you not recognise her, Brother?" Cinaed asked.

"It was scarcely light and the woman wore a hood. It may not have been her." Domnall said casually.

"Mother, would you check for me?"

Baena quickly ran to the altar and knelt before the white stone, trying to look as if she had been there for a while. Unuis entered softly, but nonetheless, Baena jumped as if startled out of her devotions.

"There you are, child," Unuis commented with relief. "My son is looking for you."

Baena did her best to look puzzled and a bit stiff as she rose from her kneeling position, although she hated deceiving Unuis. Cinaed too looked relieved when he saw her.

"I believe you spoke to Lord Drust last night against my expressed instructions?" he said.

Baena nodded, silently cursing Graunt.

"May I ask why?" Cinaed asked with icy politeness.

Baena felt angry at the injustice of this questioning. "He blocked my path, my lord. Perhaps if you had escorted me safely from the hall instead of hobnobbing with my father it would not have happened."

Domnall who was watching from a hay bale laughed delightedly at this, something that did not help Cinaed's mood.

"Child, you must not speak so." Unuis moaned.

Cinaed looked unimpressed at her outburst. "I see, so just one day in the company of your Pict family and you return to wildness. I had hoped that the guidance of my mother would cure that. I am glad that we will not be seeing your father or any other member of your family for a long time. You are trying my patience, considerably. If my mother's gentle guidance does not teach you how to behave I shall have to use more forceful methods."

Cinaed did not wait for an answer before stalking away, his face like thunder.

"Baena, why speak like that to him?" Unuis asked.

The fight was gone from Baena now and she was sorry to have upset Unuis. "I did not invite Drust's attentions. I swear it."

"I know, child," Unuis frowned at Domnall. "Why did you laugh? You made everything worse," she snapped.

Domnall got to his feet. "Did I?" he said insolently. "You have no idea how much worse I could have made things, Mother." Domnall spat the last word with contempt. He winked at Baena and sauntered away after Cinaed.

Baena looked at Unuis, wondering at the different relationship Unuis had with her sons. She felt that it was Unuis' one fault to favour Cinaed so much. Domnall was certainly rash and a little wild, but he was also cheerful and friendly. Baena couldn't help but think everything would be much better for her if Cinaed was a little more like his brother.

Part Two: Year of our Lord 834

Chapter 1

Soon after her first Yule at Dunadd news came that shattered the truce with the Picts. In spite of the extravagant festivities, Yule had been a lonely time for Baena. Since her father's visit Cinaed had spoken to her even less than before and she missed the fun and jests she would have enjoyed if only she had still been with her family.

But the loneliness was only to get worse. It was uncertain who had started it but reports came that members of the Seventh Royal House had encroached on the Gael territories. Cursing all Picts Alpin rode off to defend them. Skirmish after skirmish followed.

"So much for the great Pict alliance," Annis said tossing her head.

The other women clustered around her. Her affair with Cinaed was an open secret among the women and she had begun to dress well above her station, often far finer than Baena herself. Following her lead, the other women began to treat Baena with contempt. The language of the Picts and the Gaels was not so very different and Baena had never had any trouble with it, but now some women pretended not to understand her or to mock her accent. Others took to whispering behind their hands and laughing when she passed.

Unuis was unwell and Baena had no wish to make her feel worse by complaining of how the women were treating her. Whenever Unuis had no need of her Baena took refuge in the church where she prayed for Unuis to recover and for the truce to be reinstated. Sometimes she prayed for Cinaed's safe return, but nowhere near as often as she knew she should. They had been wed for well over half a year now, yet still Cinaed took no interest in her. She began to despair of ever bearing a child while he lived.

For a while it seemed as if neither prayer was to be answered. Unuis deteriorated further until Baena feared for her life. But to everyone's relief, the day came when the crisis passed. Slowly Unuis was able to sit up again and even rise from her bed. But she remained very weak.

Just as Unuis seemed to be recovering there was more bad news. At least, Baena considered it bad news, but the other women rejoiced.

"I bring news from the Lord Alpin!" the messenger announced when he had been ushered into Unuis' chambers. "They have won a great victory. Oengus, King of the Picts and pretender to the crown of Dal Riata is no more. Lord Alpin slew him with his own hands!"

The women laughed and cheered. Unuis smiled weakly. "And Alpin's sons. Do they still stand?"

"They do. The Lords Cinaed and Domnall both fought most bravely. Many a Pict fell at the end of their swords."

Annis smiled proudly at this, but Baena turned away. Oengus was Drust's uncle and well known to her. On many an occasion as a child, he had picked her up to show her musicians or storytellers. In recent years he had even honoured her with a dance on festive occasions. When a marriage to Drust had been discussed Baena had begun to consider him close kin.

"Tears, my lady?" Annis smirked when Unuis was resting. "Your lord husband is part of a glorious victory and you shed tears?"

"What else can we expect, Annis?" another woman chortled. "She's a Pict!"

"Oh yes, I forgot," sneered Annis. "You were meant to bring us eternal peace or something."

The other women laughed.

"The Lord Cinaed must be well pleased with his deal," Annis jeered. "Peace and an heir. That was all he wanted. But you have delivered neither."

"Barren and a Pict!" laughed another of the women. "What a fine bride for the son of our Lord Alpin."

"I'm surprised he keeps you with him," Annis shrugged. "He cares nothing for you, you know."

Baena ignored her and fled to her chamber as soon as possible to pray for Oengus without disturbance.

Whether Annis had any real knowledge of Cinaed's opinions Baena never knew, but a conversation she overheard a few weeks later made her wonder. Alpin, Cinaed and the other men had returned as heroes and feast after feast was ordered. Unuis was still not well, but she always made the effort to be present and appear to celebrate the Pict defeats. To help her Baena took on as many of her duties as she could and so it was that one day she was in the shadowy hall alone preparing for the latest festivity. On such occasions the costliest silver platters and hanging bowls were brought out from the treasury and Baena was engaged in wiping them clean of the dust and spiders that had crept under their wrappings. Alpin was just outside the open door talking to his sons and Graunt as they polished their armour and sharpened their swords.

"The Picts are in disarray," Alpin said cheerfully. "We must press our advantage before the summer is over."

"Where next?" Domnall asked.

"One of the higher houses I think. The First or the Third are both high ranking. One of them."

In the hall, Baena felt her heart sink at the thought of the confident Gaels attacking her father's territories. She knew that Oengus' death would have hit them hard.

"Can we attack the Third?" Graunt asked. "What of Cinaed's alliance?"

"It is unfortunate," Alpin replied. "I fear I made a mistake there. A match to secure the peace seemed a good idea, but I am starting to think the Picts can never be trusted."

Cinaed had remained silent through all this and did not say anything now.

"Could the marriage not be dissolved?" Graunt asked.

Baena dropped her cloth at this suggestion and reflected on how much she had always disliked Graunt.

"I don't see how," Alpin replied. "I should think all the Pict royal houses would join together to avenge such an insult to one of their own. We have no reason for dissolving the union, do we?"

"The marriage hasn't been consummated," Domnall piped up. "Has it Cinaed?"

"Be quiet you fool," Cinaed hissed.

For a moment the only sound was the clanking of armour then Alpin spoke once more. "Is this true?" he demanded.

There was silence again, but either Cinaed had nodded or Alpin took the silence for assent for his next question was "Why ever not? She's pretty enough. How can she be still untouched?"

"Such matters are my own concern, Father," Cinaed said stiffly.

"I thought it was strange that she was not with child yet," said Alpin. "Is she refusing you?"

"Father-"

"If she is refusing her duties she must be taught otherwise," Alpin said. "Cinaed, you are one of the strongest men alive on the battlefield. Why are you so lenient with women?"

"She is not refusing me," Cinaed said slowly. "I would thank you, Father, to let me conduct my marriage in my own way."

"But if you do not care for the girl then the marriage could be dissolved. She can be returned a maid to her father. The Third House will not like it, but under these circumstances, their complaints will not move the rest of the Pict Royal Houses."

Inside Baena felt humiliated at being discussed in this way. She tried to imagine returning home as an unwanted bride. Her parents would probably blame her for her failure to please Cinaed. The assumption for everyone would be that there was something wrong with her and it was unlikely that any other man of rank would want her. With Oengus' death, Drust would now be one of the highest ranking members of the First House. Even as an unwed woman she would be a little lowly for him. As a rejected wife there would be no chance.

"I hear your little blonde companion is with child," Domnall added helpfully.

Baena's mouth dropped open. No wonder Annis had been so smug lately.

"I know nothing of such matters," Cinaed replied.

"Cinaed, could you not put your efforts into getting your wife with child?" Alpin sounded puzzled. "Other women can wait until later."

There was a crashing sound of armour being cast aside. "I have said, Father, that I will manage this myself. I neither need nor want any advice."

"Why did you bring the girl here?" Alpin asked. "I thought after the handfasting night you were so taken with her that you wanted her with you. But now you're saying you hadn't even touched her! If you had left her over there dissolving the marriage would be even easier."

"I had my reasons." Cinaed's voice sounded a little fainter and Baena guessed he was walking away. "This matter is not for discussion. The decision on whether or not to dissolve the union is mine and mine alone."

There was silence for a moment. Baena stared at the shiny silver platter in front of her in despair as it dawned on her how precarious her future was, resting as it did in the hands of the man she always managed to annoy.

"What is the matter with the boy?" Alpin demanded. "She's pretty. Even prettier now than at the handfasting. It should be no hardship to sire a child on her."

"I think he finds her over feisty," Graunt said slowly.

"Feisty?" Alpin exclaimed. "I've never heard her say more than a few words at a time. More likely it's the Pict blood that puts him off. He won't want any more Pict blood in his children. But then why won't he agree to send her back? Do you two know why he even brought her here?"

"We do," Domnall replied.

"And?"

"Cinaed swore us to secrecy," Graunt said. "My lord, I would ask you not to press us on the matter."

"I suppose it has something to do with that dark haired Pict lad that Cinaed threw his drink at last year," Alpin said shrewdly. "I thought that was unlike him."

Domnall and Graunt remained silent. "What of this blonde girl? Who is she? Would she make Cinaed a suitable wife?"

"No," Domnall and Graunt said together.

"Unless you want your eldest son to be wed to the daughter of a cow herder," Graunt added.

"No, I do not," Alpin said wryly and Baena couldn't help feeling relieved. Bad as it would be to be rejected at least she would never hear of Annis in her place. "Oh well, I expect Cinaed will tire of her once she gets great with child. Perhaps then his pretty, young wife will be more appealing."

"Maybe we do not want her too appealing, my lord," Graunt said slowly. "These Pict women are often overindulged in their own land and even control their lords."

"That is a myth," Alpin snorted. "I do have some experience of Pict wives you know!"

"It is true that no woman could be more dutiful than the Lady Unuis," Graunt said. "But what of the Third House? Did you see the Lady Sabina? I felt she had a firm grip on the matters of the Third House."

"Cinaed's wife is her daughter," Domnall put in. "And in spite of what you have heard, she can be both feisty and disobedient."

"Is she? Then Cinaed needs to discipline her. The boy is too soft with women. He always has been. Perhaps I should push harder to dissolve the union. There will be no rule of women here."

"My Lord, I think we should attack the Third Royal House next," Graunt suggested. "If the girl is still untouched it will make dissolving the union even easier. Or if she is a true wife by then it will ensure she understands that she cannot influence Cinaed. I think it would be wise to keep some distance between them."

Baena twisted the cloth tightly in her hand and wished with all her heart that she could twist it round Graunt's neck. If Graunt was continually dripping this poison into Cinaed's ear it was no wonder he had rejected her.

"I can't make my battle decisions based on Cinaed and his troublesome wife," Alpin said. "We attack the First Royal House. They have the Kingship. But once we are victorious over them we will move on to the Third and to hell with the alliance!"

Baena had heard enough. She fled back to Unuis' chambers feeling her future was bleak. Either she would be sent away in disgrace or she would be forced to share her body with the enemy of her Father and live out her life as a stranger in this land. She did her best to compose her face as she entered but was not helped at the sight of Annis. Despite her loose tunic, Baena could see that her stomach was swelling. Domnall was right. Annis was bearing Cinaed's child. The child that Baena so wanted to bear.

"Is all prepared for tonight, my child?" Unuis asked.

Baena tried to smile at the pale woman. "Yes. Everything is ready."

"Wonderful. So many victories over the Pict scum to celebrate!" Annis commented with a smile.

Baena narrowed her eyes as she fantasised about grabbing hold of her blonde hair and shaking her hard. If it caused the loss of her child so much the better. She clenched her fists to restrain herself from running her nails down Annis' face and ruining it forever. With an effort, she swallowed her anger and took Unuis' hand.

"Is there anything else you need me to do?"

"No, child."

"Then I will leave you to your rest," Baena kissed Unuis' cold face, feeling again the twinge of fear that she was not recovering as she should.

Baena headed to her own chamber suddenly wishing for her own mother. Sabina had always been so strict and her temper was fierce, but her advice would be welcome now. She remembered on her handfasting night Sabina had advised her to try to please Cinaed and that if she could all would be well. The trouble was that she had no idea how to please him and this was no matter she could discuss with Unuis. Baena took out a mirror and studied her face. Alpin and the others had called her pretty, but if she was she could see no sign of it in her anxious eyes. She looked at the bed and shuddered at the thought of what she would have to do to conceive the child she so desperately needed. Everyone called Cinaed handsome, but Baena had never admired the looks of that cold-eyed man. However, she knew she had no choice.

That evening she dressed carefully, choosing a tunic that Unuis had once said suited her well. She pulled her girdle a little tighter than usual and over her head she wore her prettiest caul in a shade of blue that matched her eyes.

When she entered the hall she could see Cinaed talking to his father. They were laughing together and so Baena assumed their quarrel had been made up. Perhaps it even meant that Cinaed had agreed to Alpin's suggestion to dissolve the marriage. Cinaed bowed to her as she approached in his usual manner, but looking pleadingly into his face she could see no interest and he quickly continued talking to others.

Alpin kept his gaze on her a little longer and although Baena tried to smile at him there was no answering smile back. Instead, his face was stern and his eyes as cold as his son's. That night Baena lay alone in her chamber, weeping at the knowledge that yet again she had failed to please her husband.

Chapter two

That summer Alpin had summoned men from clans all over the land to attack the Pict territories and there were rumours that he would claim the crown of Dal Riata in the autumn once they were victorious. As the preparations for war had proceeded there seemed to have been no time for the men to consider Baena's own future. Neither Alpin nor Cinaed mentioned the possibility of the marriage being dissolved, but when Unuis was not watching the other women treated Baena with even more contempt and Cinaed did not give her even the most cursory of farewells before he rode away.

Dunadd seemed a different place with so many men away and more of the women needed on the farms. As the weeks went by they received reports of many a skirmish and it seemed that there was no stopping Alpin, as he fought his way across the territory of the First Royal House. When Baena went to the church these days she just knelt with no idea of what prayer to make when she knew that every victory for Alpin brought an attack on the Third House a little closer.

Often she wondered what prayers Unuis made. She never mentioned her own Pict blood, but Baena was sure that it was this that had made them so close.

With even more work to do for those that remained at the fort, her days were busy. One grey afternoon they were weaving blankets which could be sent out to the troops. Unuis began to load up the shuttles with thick black wool and Baena looked anxiously at her thin arms. She had hoped that with the warmer weather Unuis' condition would improve, but she still looked very frail.

"My lady! My lady!" the watchman burst in on them. "Lord Alpin's banner has been sighted. The clan will be here before nightfall!"

Unuis looked up from her loom in surprise "The men are returning? There was nothing in Alpin's last message to suggest they would be returning so soon."

"They were still in the territory of The First Royal House," Baena tried to keep her voice neutral, but she couldn't help but think of Drust. She expected that he would be fighting to defend his family's land. She wondered if Alpin's return meant that the First House had been defeated. If so the attack on her own family would be even closer.

"You'll be glad to welcome Lord Alpin back, my lady," Annis said to Unuis. "And perhaps your sons will be with him."

Unuis barely repressed a smile and looked pointedly at the baby in Annis' arms. To Baena's dismay, the child was a boy, named Grimmach and just over two moons later Annis was looking as pretty as ever. She wasn't sure if anyone had sent word to Cinaed that the child had arrived, but with such a sight waiting for him on his return, Baena doubted whether Cinaed would tire easily of his mistress.

Baena ground her teeth. She reminded herself that if Cinaed wished to beget bastards across Dal Riata then that was no concern of hers.

"Enough time in speculation," Unuis said. "The men will be hungry when they return. We must make ready. Baena, take these cloths to the store. Prepare a welcome feast."

As Baena gathered up the cloths she noticed Unuis take Annis' baby in her arms and again she was struck by how fragile the older woman seemed. Baena hurried from the room, her arms laden with material and tears in her eyes. She resolved not to resent Unuis from taking pleasure in what was surely her grandchild.

By the time the army arrived the hall was bustling with activity. Huge pots of soup thick with barley were simmering on the fire, the aroma mingling with the smell of the peat smoke. Platters of smoked meats were set out. Baena and Unuis were arranging the welcome cups when Cinaed burst into the room. Baena stopped what she was doing and stared at him.

His tunic was torn and dusty and Baena could see new cuts on his arms. He stood in the doorway his eyes darting around the hall then he slumped against the doorpost as he caught his gasping breath. Everyone froze and waited for him to say something, although it was obviously going to be nothing good.

Unuis went white as she too stared at her son. Baena put an arm around her and could feel her body trembling.

"Mother," he said struggling to find the words, as he came closer to them. "My father... Alpin... He is dead."

A cry went up from around the hall. Unuis shut her eyes and fell against Baena. She gestured for a stool and eased Unuis down onto it. Cinaed wiped his forehead, the pain etched into it. Annis hurried forward with the welcome cup of hot ale, but Cinaed took it without looking at her. His attention was fixed on his mother and he went to kneel at her side. Baena kept her arms around Unuis, her mind hardly able to comprehend what Cinaed had just said. It seemed impossible that the great chief had been defeated.

"He fought bravely, mother. He led us as he always did."

Unuis opened her eyes and clasped Cinaed's hands. "Tell me everything, my son. Spare me no details."

"Everything was going well. We encountered little opposition and were deep in Pict territory. Father thought we should attack one of the main settlements."

"Why, oh why did he do that?" Unuis moaned.

Cinaed took a long draught of his hot ale. "He was right. The last thing they were expecting was so bold an attack."

Domnall and Graunt came quietly into the hall, carrying a stretcher between them with a shape covered in cloth lying on it. Like Cinaed, they looked exhausted and uncharacteristically subdued. A strong smell like rotten meat came from the stretcher, overpowering the aromas of the cooking. The girl who took them their cups retreated gagging at the stench.

"The battle was going our way," Cinaed continued. "Victory should have been ours. Father was fighting one of the highest born Pict lords. He... He was beaten."

"You are a liar, Brother. That is not how it ended," Domnall interrupted.

Unuis stroked Cinaed's cheek. "Please, my son. Tell me exactly what happened."

Cinaed swallowed and shut his eyes as if trying to blot out some memory. "The young Pict Father was fighting knocked the sword from his hand. He could have finished Father with one blow there and then, but he didn't."

"I wish he had," muttered Domnall. "Father should have died in the glory of battle."

"I tried to fight my way to him, but by the time I got there several Picts had hold of him." Cinaed rose to his feet and shook his fist. "That damned Pict held a sword to his throat. He told me to call back the men or Father would die."

"You should have ignored him," Domnall cried. "We should have charged. I know Father would die and perhaps some of us would too, but it would be a glorious ending."

Cinaed looked wearier than ever and ran a hand over his eyes. "You may be right, Domnall, but I hoped to save Father. I thought they would grant Father his freedom if we fell back. I expected a ransom demand but we would have gladly paid that. I gave the order to retreat."

There was silence. Baena tightened her arm around Unuis' shoulders. As Cinaed's face set into sharp lines of rage she felt certain that they were about to hear something truly terrible.

"As we fell back that Pict boy watched us. Even as we retreated I thought there was a smirk on his face. Once we were a distance away he raised his sword," Cinaed's voice broke. "I ordered the archers to fire, but it was no use. Mother... they hacked off his head."

Unuis' mouth opened, but no scream came out. Her hand flew to cover it as Cinaed fell back to his knees and took his mother's hand again. Baena stared at him, her horror at this account of the battle mingling with her shock at seeing Cinaed so grief stricken.

"They slaughtered him like an animal!" raged Domnall. "We should have attacked again. We need revenge."

Cinaed looked up at his mother. "I failed. I am sorry," he shook his head sadly before turning to look at Domnall. "But we shall have our revenge." He stood up straight and tall. "By my father's soul I will have revenge, but it will be at a time when our revenge will be victorious."

Unuis looked pleadingly up at her sons. "Alpin's body. Do you have it all?"

"They threw his body after us, Mother. But..." Cinaed hesitated "they took his head. It was placed on a spike in front of their gateway."

Tears rolled down Unuis's cheeks. "Is his head still with the Picts?"

"Certainly not!" roared Domnall. "I would not allow them to treat Father's body with such dishonour. I and some of the men went back under the cover of darkness. We stole it from them."

"Let me see," Unuis said, staggering to her feet.

"My lady, I think he should be prepared for burial first," Graunt said, hesitantly.

"Let me see," Unuis repeated, leaning heavily on Baena.

Domnall pulled back the cloth. The body lay, as they had seen many bodies, except this one ended in a jagged red cut. The head that lay next to it was unmistakably Alpin's. The thinning hair was matted and blood stained while the sightless eyes seemed to stare at them fixed in permanent horror. The cheeks were mottled and decaying. Screams from the women pierced the air and Baena heard the retching sound of someone being sick.

If there was any colour left in Unuis' face it drained out now and she slumped against Baena. "Bring blankets and some of that hot ale," Baena called struggling to support Unuis.

Cinaed crouched down next to her to help ease Unuis onto a thick rug and for the first time seemed to notice who Baena was. His eyes narrowed.

"Get out, you little Pict. This is not your place. Get out!"

Baena gaped at him, one arm still around Unuis. "But..."

Cinaed stood up and grabbed hold of her arm. He pulled her roughly to her feet. "I said get out!" he pushed her away. "Do you know who did that to Father?"

Baena shook her head fearfully, as she backed away.

"Your lover, that's who!" Cinaed spat the words out and a gasp went up from the hall.

"Drust!" Baena managed to exclaim.

"Yes. Drust." Cinaed advanced on her. "I suppose you think he is a great hero now, don't you?"

"No... No! I don't," she cried.

Cinaed's strong hands gripped her shoulders tightly and he shook her. "Perhaps I should send him your head," he snarled. "Would that be the sort of revenge you barbarians understand?"

"Please, my lord ... stop. You're hurting me," Baena begged. Cinaed looked angry enough to indeed hack off her head.

Cinaed gave her one last shove. "Get out!"

Baena turned and stumbled to the exit, as she did she heard Unuis murmur "Cinaed, Cinaed. Stop, my son. It's not the child's fault."

But she didn't hear his reply as she choked back her sobs. Ignoring the dejected-looking men entering the courtyard she streaked out into stormy twilight.

Chapter three

Baena spent a cold, uncomfortable night, huddled in a blanket in the corner of a store room. Occasionally she dozed, but mostly she sobbed, unsure if her tears were for Alpin, herself or poor bereft Unuis. As dawn touched the sky she stretched her cramped limbs and headed out into the fresh air. She looked at the brightening sky and wondered if this would be the last time she would see the sun rise over Dunadd. The look in Cinaed's eyes the previous night told her clearly that he would soon send her away. She shivered wretchedly as she reflected that it would have been better if she had died instead of Alpin. Her life might as well be over. Once back in her own land, she would be regarded by all with pity and contempt.

A few people were around, but there was none of the cheerful bustle that usually permeated the air at this time. Baena looked at the stone fort and the round houses that surrounded it. Smoke emerged from some holes, but she could almost feel the grief hanging over the settlement despite these small signs of normality.

Baena shivered and pulled the blanket around her before trudging to the upper terrace. She half expected to be challenged and sent on her way, but the hall was empty apart from the huge fighting dogs who had no doubt cleared the remains of the welcome feast. She guessed that many of the men were already at the church.

Baena headed directly for Unuis' chamber, even if it was just to say farewell. She doubted whether Unuis would be asleep, but she pushed aside the door hangings gently.

"You can't come in here," a voice hissed. "The Lord Cinaed does not want you near his mother."

Annis was sat on a low stool holding her baby. Several of the other women moved to block her way, the animosity in their eyes obvious even in the dim light of the single candle that was burning.

"I just want to see Lady Unuis. I want to care for her," Baena pleaded, humiliated at having to beg for entrance from her husband's mistress.

"She won't want a Pict here. No one wants you here," Annis whispered viciously. "Especially not the Lord Cinaed. They say you're still a maid so I don't suppose you'll even be here much longer. We'll be glad to see the back of all Picts."

Baena was considering whether to point out that Unuis was also a Pict when a weak voice called out "Is that Baena?"

"Do not concern yourself, my lady. We will keep her away," Annis' voice changed miraculously to gentle and soothing.

"Don't talk nonsense, Girl. Let her in."

"But my lady, the Lord Cinaed-"

"Does not rule my bedchamber. Let the child in."

Reluctantly the women moved aside and Baena ran to Unuis, falling on her knees by her side.

"Leave us. I would talk with Baena alone."

The women muttered among themselves as they left and Annis' eyes shot daggers at her as she hoisted her baby onto her shoulders. Hearing Cinaed's name mentioned, Baena hoped Annis would not go straight to him. The last thing she wanted was another bitter scene in front of Unuis.

"Oh Unuis, I am so sorry. I am so sorry about Alpin. I never ever wished for this."

"I know you didn't, my child. Light some more candles. Let me see you properly."

Baena did as she was bidden. Turning back to Unuis she was shocked. The woman had aged overnight and looked even thinner than she had the previous day.

"Unuis, is there anything I can do? Let me help you."

Unuis stroked Baena's hair with a shaky hand. "Perhaps, my child. Perhaps."

There was a short silence as Baena waited for Unuis to continue. Unuis smiled a sad smile. "I do not mind so much for myself. It is Cinaed that concerns me. He loved his father so much. They were inseparable. I shall be with Alpin soon enough and then Cinaed will have no one."

"No, no Unuis. I know you have been ill this winter and now you have suffered a grievous blow, but you will be well again."

"I do not think so, child. Even before the news of Alpin, I suspected I was not destined to be long in this world. The winter was hard, but the spring has come and gone and there is not even much left of the summer. Yet I am no better."

"Oh Unuis, please do not talk so."

"Hush child. No tears for me. I do not wish to speak of myself. Cinaed."

"He will be fine," Baena faltered, wondering what Unuis expected her to do. "He has many friends and his brother."

"True. Graunt is a good lad. Did you know he was Alpin's nephew? He has been with us since Alpin's sister died when he was not much more than a babe. But it will be different for Cinaed with the men now that he is their leader."

"What of Domnall?" Baena asked, puzzled that Unuis did not appear to have the same concern for her younger son.

"I do not trust Domnall," Unuis said matter of factly.

Baena gaped at her. "What?"

Unuis seemed almost amused. "Oh, Domnall is not my son. Has no one told you this? I have raised him as my own, but he is not. I do not think he truly loves Cinaed. Since the moment he could walk, Domnall has been jealous of him."

"How did this come about?" Baena was amazed. "I'm sorry, I shouldn't be asking you this."

"Yes, you should, my child. It is right that you should know. I was ill for a long time after Cinaed was born and was unable to fulfil my duties. We were living on the sacred Isle of Iona at the time. There are many Norsemen in those parts. Alpin took a Norse girl as his mistress. She was Domnall's mother. Perhaps if I had died, Alpin would have married her. I know not. In the end, I survived and she did not. She died giving birth to Domnall."

"And Domnall stayed with you?"

"Cinaed was always a strong, healthy little lad, but he was the only one. I had not quite seen fourteen years when I married Alpin. The birth, not even a year later, was too much. I was damaged beyond full recovery." Unuis smiled gently at Baena. "I feared for you when I first saw you at the handfasting, not much more than a child and advised Cinaed not to put you through childbearing too soon. I believe he listened to me."

Baena was too surprised to nod as she was suddenly presented with a very different reason for Cinaed's rejection of her.

Unuis smiled again. "It is good to know that a boy will still listen to his mother. I'd not worry about you so much now. You have grown into a woman this last year. It was a kindness of Alpin not to expect me to bear another, but for him, one son was not enough. He decreed that Domnall should be raised with Cinaed. I know he loved both his sons, but I have never been sure of Domnall. That is why when I am gone I wish you to be there for Cinaed."

"I am not sure how much use I can be to him. He hates me now. I do not even know if he will keep me with him."

"Do not hold last night against him, my child," Unuis pleaded. "He was angry and his grief is intense. He should not have taken that out on you. His anger is against all Picts, but you were the one in front of him." Unuis made a wry face. "Apart from me, of course."

"And he is half Pict himself. Indeed, he is all Pict, according to our laws."

"True. And maybe one day you will remind him of that although you will need to pick your day wisely. He does not like to be reminded of it. But that day is not today," Unuis gave a brisk shake of her head. "And I am not gone yet. But remember my words. Promise me, Baena."

"I promise. I will try to do as you want."

"You're a good girl. Alpin will be laid to rest today. Go ready yourself and I shall do the same."

Baena dressed in a plain grey tunic and covered her hair with a black caul. The bell had not yet tolled, but she left her chamber anyway, glad to be out in the air. She made her way down the terraces towards the church, where, as she expected, people had begun to gather. On a rocky outcrop beyond the church, she spotted a man standing alone. Despite the hood over his head, she knew it was Cinaed by the sight of the great dog Augus lying at his feet. She hesitated, unsure of what action to take, but then wondered how she would feel if it was her father lying dead. She missed him intensely and she knew that only if Cinaed did send her away would she be likely to see him again. But at least he was still living. Remembering Unuis' request she took a deep breath and headed towards Cinaed, even though she knew she was leaving herself open to further attack.

"I am sorry about your father," she said quietly, as she came up behind him.

"Thank you." Cinaed did not turn round.

"He was a most courageous man." Baena continued, not really sure what to say. Alpin had always been casually affectionate to her whenever they met until the truce had broken down, but she could not feel that she had known him well.

Edging closer to him Baena could see the far way look in Cinaed's eye. "Yes, he was. But he was more than that. I remember him teaching me to swim in the seas off Iona and being at my side in my first battle. I was most afeared as all boys are, but his guidance gave me courage."

His body drooped with exhaustion, which was hardly surprising. He had undoubtedly spent the night by his father's side. Probably he had spent the last few nights there. She blinked back tears at the thought

He turned and stared at Baena for a moment. He looked bewildered and for the first time Baena truly wished she could comfort him. She suddenly understood what Unuis had been saying. It would be hard to show this face to the men he was supposed to lead. Still unsure what she would do, she took another step towards him, but at that, a strange look came over his face as his eyes bored into her.

"I was always prepared to see my father die in battle. I suspected it would happen one day. But to see him hacked to death by that... that..." his eyes narrowed angrily and for a tense moment Baena wondered if he would strike her. She braced herself for the blow, but with a futile, angry shake of his fist, he turned away from her. "Leave me."

Chapter four

Alpin's funeral rites passed with a dignity that was a fitting tribute to the man. Baena had wondered where she should stand in the church. She had no wish to further antagonise Cinaed by standing too close, but on the other hand, she could not disrespect Alpin by keeping her distance. She hesitated at the door as others entered, but when Unuis arrived surrounded by grey clad women she extended her hand to Baena and the two entered together.

The stone building was cold. Heavy incense masked the stench from the coffin that lay before the altar. Cinaed and Domnall, dressed in plain tunics, stood before it, their heads bowed. As custom dictated everyone filed past to murmur their own prayers. Unuis took her time, standing by the coffin with silent tears flowing down her cheeks. Baena wondered what she was thinking. Clearly she had felt more than just a dutiful affection for Alpin, but it was impossible for Baena to guess how deep her feelings had run. Unable to bear the grief on the widow's face Baena looked ahead of her directly at the altar. A black cloth had been laid over it, flowing down towards the white rock at its base.

Unuis wiped her eyes and laid her hand on the coffin, but as she did so she swayed, as if about to faint. Cinaed quickly put an arm around her waist and supported his mother to a bench. Baena felt almost relieved that he was distracted, as she laid her own hand on the coffin. Trying not to think of the grisly remains inside she lowered her head.

"Farewell my Lord Alpin. Rest in peace. God have mercy on your soul," she prayed, before moving to the bench next to Unuis.

It took a long time for the clan to shuffle past the coffin to take their places at either side, cramming into all corners of the church. Eventually the priest stepped forward to begin the funeral rites. Their faces pale, but composed, Cinaed knelt at Alpin's head and Domnall at his feet. There was a rustling as everyone in the clan who was able followed the action. Baena wished she could dissuade Unuis from kneeling on that cold stone floor, but knew it would be pointless to even try. She knelt next to her as close as she could, hoping the feeling of her presence would offer some comfort.

"May God have mercy upon us. Go in peace my children," the priest intoned at the end.

Everyone rose from their knees and stood with their heads bowed low. As the gentle sound of strings floated around the church, Baena's eyes filled with tears at so much sorrow. Gently she put an arm around Unuis. Cinaed and Domnall took up places on either side of the coffin. The brothers looked at each other with grief apparent in their eyes as they prepared to do the last service they would ever perform for the father who had loved them both. They were joined by their kinsmen Graunt and Gregor and two old companions of Alpin named Mathan and Guire.

Bowing low before their dead leader, they raised the coffin onto their shoulders and carried it slowly from the church. As they passed by every clansman and woman bowed down before following the sombre procession.

On the plain below them was the burial ground, where a hole had already been dug next to the grave of Alpin's father, the old warrior king, Eochaidh who had helped to briefly unite the Gaels and Picts under the cross of the blessed Saint Andrew. Her marriage to Cinaed had been supposed to strengthen the union, but Alpin's death had surely torn it forever apart. Alpin had never been acknowledged as a King of Dal Riata, but nonetheless, he would lie among kings. Baena felt that this was no less than he had deserved.

Chapter five

A period of intense mourning followed the funeral. Men and women went about their daily tasks as normal but dressed in plain, usually dark clothing. At the end of the day, only fish was served with their meals and there was none of the music and laughter that usually characterised the evenings.

The day after the burial Unuis became ill again and took to her bed. Baena felt frightened, wondering how much more the widow would be able to take. She nursed her devotedly, barely leaving her side. Slowly Unuis began to recover.

Cinaed visited his mother daily, but while these visits always gave Unuis great joy, Baena spent them tensely, wondering if this would be the day that Cinaed would tell her to leave Dunadd. However, Cinaed made no comment on Baena's presence. Other than the odd glance in her direction he paid her no attention at all

On one occasion about ten days after the funeral Baena, needle in hand, was adjusting some of Unuis's tunics, which now hung too loosely on her slight frame when Cinaed entered the chamber.

"The clan chieftains will be arriving in a moons time. We must make a decision on the kingship of Dal Riata," Cinaed told his mother, after his usual enquiry to her health.

"Will you put your name forward?" Unuis asked, raising her eyes to study her son's face. He looked calm, but all merriment had gone. His eyes were weary and he appeared many years older.

Cinaed shook his head. "No, Mother. I have too little experience in battle leadership. The chiefs would never accept me. All I would achieve is to anger the man that does get selected."

"So many leaders have died in the last years. Who could be selected? Would you not take the crown if you were asked?"

"Of course, Mother." There was a short silence and it was clear to Baena they were both thinking that if Alpin had lived he would probably have been an undisputed choice. "But I won't be asked. There are some good warriors among the chiefs. Father's cousin Aed, perhaps. Or there's Lord Fie. I have never fought alongside him, but I hear he is skilled. I would pledge our clan to either of them."

"Will we remain here in the King's house?"

"I expect I will be away. Perhaps defending the coast against the Norsemen, although I still plan to get my revenge on the Picts of the

First House." Cinaed clenched his fists and his eyes darted a sharp glare at Baena. She felt suddenly nervous as she wondered if he would order her away, but he continued more calmly, "No king would expect you to leave. Especially not while you are ill. Perhaps one day we will return to our own territories. Iona even. But we will speak of this when you are well again."

"Oh, Cinaed…" Unuis began to protest.

"No Mother, you will be well again. Soon we shall have good food and your ladies will take care of you." Cinaed threw another glance in Baena's direction and frowned. "I hope they are, in any case."

"Of course they are, my son, the very best care, but… it is in God's hands."

"Prayers shall be said every day for your recovery." Cinaed kissed his mother's hands. "Say nothing more, Mother. I know you will recover."

But when the day of the gathering of the chiefs arrived, Unuis still had not risen from her bed. As usual, Cinaed visited her immediately after morning prayers. The official mourning for Alpin was now over, but Cinaed was still dressed in a tunic of a grey so dark it was almost black.

"Mother, would you not be well enough to rise from your bed this day? Just to greet the chiefs as they arrive."

"I am sorry, my son. I can scarce walk across my chamber."

"There should be a lady present to provide the welcome cups. It would not be for long."

"You have a wife, Cinaed," Unuis said gently.

Cinaed's grey eyes fixed on Baena. She saw him frown and braced herself for a humiliating rejection. But he nodded curtly. "Very well. Make yourself ready, my lady. The first arrival may be soon."

Unuis gave a satisfied smile. "Baena, my child, pass me that little coffer. There is something you should have."

She rummaged in the little box, before pulling out a silver and enamel brooch. "This traditionally belongs to the wife of the chief," she said pressing it into Baena's hand.

"I should not take this from you," Baena said, tears in her eyes as she feared again that Unuis was leaving them.

"Nonsense, child. It is rightfully yours now. Wear it this day with my blessing."

Cinaed continued to frown, but he made no objection. His face was expressionless as he and Baena left his mother's chamber. She glanced at him, wishing that she did not find it so hard to talk to him. He seemed lost in his own thoughts and whatever they were, it was clear they were not pleasant ones. He said nothing until they reached their own chamber.

"Do not delay," he said, as he left her there.

Feeling obliged to match Cinaed's sombre attire, Baena changed into a grey tunic, made from the finest wool and edged in black thread. She fastened the brooch to her cloak, before hurrying nervously to the hall to carry out her first duties as Lady of the Clan.

"Are you really going to let a Pict greet the chiefs?" Graunt was saying to Cinaed as she entered.

"My mother is ill. There is no one else."

"There must be someone. What about Mathan's lady? Her rank is high," Graunt suggested.

"It would be a huge insult to Cinaed's wife to put someone else in this position today," Domnall commented.

"I find I do not care if I insult a Pict," Graunt replied, with contempt. "And given your father's death, I am surprised that it bothers you so much."

Cinaed scowled at him, but Domnall had noticed Baena hesitating in the doorway. He gave her a sideways look. "If I had ridden a long way to be here, I think I would rather be greeted by Cinaed's pretty wife than Mathan's lady."

"Be quiet, Brother." Cinaed snapped.

Domnall jeered. "Just because you do not like to look at your wife, Cinaed, does not mean that others do not.

Cinaed darted a quick look at Baena and shrugged. "I have made my decision. My wife will welcome the chiefs."

"What of the matter your father spoke to you of?" Graunt said. "You will find it harder to do that if you have had her beside you on this day."

Baena hated standing there, as they discussed her as if she were not there. She guessed that the matter Graunt was speaking of was the end of her marriage.

"I will not discuss that with you," Cinaed said, sounding angry, as a shout from the watchman proclaimed that the first banner had been sighted. Cinaed glanced again at Baena. He looked irritated that she had barely moved from the doorway. "Start preparing the cups," he commanded.

"I still think you should put your name forward to be King," Domnall said, as Baena tried to steady her shaking hands enough to pour the drinks without spilling them. She had no wish to anger Cinaed any more that he already was. "As Eochaidh's grandson, you have a true claim."

"I keep telling you I will not," Cinaed replied, in a somewhat weary tone. "Our clan will have power by supporting the new king."

"Perhaps I should put my name forward," Domnall said.

To Baena's relief, Cinaed's face lit up in a gleam of amusement. "Dal Riata needs a strong king. Not a fool of a boy!"

Domnall laughed, but any retaliation he might have made was lost as the watchman called again. The first chief was now arriving. The three men strode over to Baena. Swallowing her nerves, she handed them each a drink, looking in vain for some sign of approval from Cinaed. It felt ridiculous to be so worried. She had served drinks on numerous occasions, but this one was different and the presence of Cinaed and Domnall on either side of her, only made her feel worse. Cinaed took a mouthful of his drink.

"Domnall, Graunt, speak with as many as you can before the debate starts. I would know where the support lies. Baena, do not speak unless you are spoken to." He looked at her, clearly irritated again. "And try to smile. You are supposed to be welcoming."

Baena looked at him out of frightened eyes, knowing that she must appear more worried than ever. She half expected him to order her away, but instead the annoyance faded from his face. He put his hand on her shoulder and half smiled. "You will be fine."

As the first arrivals came through the door, Cinaed stepped forward to take the hands of an older man, who bore a faint resemblance to Alpin.

"Welcome to Dunadd, my Lord Aed."

Baena stared after him, still feeling the touch of his hand on her. "The drinks, my lady," Graunt said sharply.

Recovering herself, she hurried forward with cups of foaming heather ale, an anxious smile of welcome on her face.

"Many thanks to you, my lady," Aed said, bowing to her, his kind smile offering her the first hint of reassurance. "It is good to be welcomed here by so fair a face. I had no idea your wife was so beautiful, my boy," he called to Cinaed.

Baena blushed and saw Domnall shoot Graunt a triumphant grin. Cinaed simply nodded to Aed, as he greeted the next arrival.

Chief after chief arrived and Baena quickly forgot most of the names. She did take a good look at Lord Fie, as someone that Cinaed had suggested as a possible King. He was a tall, dark-haired man with a quiet charm. His gentle air contrasted greatly with the accounts of his military prowess.

Eventually the last chief arrived and, for Baena, the true work began. The next few days were an endless round of preparing and serving food and drinks. Talks went on late into the night, often only breaking off for prayers. Baena, rushing into the hall with yet another jug of ale or platter of food, found it impossible to tell how the gathering was going or if they were any closer to selecting their king. It sounded raucous with much fist thumping and shouting.

"What is happening?" she whispered to Domnall at one point.

"Hard to say," he told her. "The chiefs are evenly split. Cinaed has put the support of our clan behind Aed. He thinks Aed will be the better king and as he is our kinsman, it would be advantageous to us. But Fie has many supporters. Lord Coulym has also put his name forward."

"Lord Coulym," Baena stared. "Isn't he-"

"Just three moons older than me," Domnall finished with a grin. "But it would appease the supporters of both Aed and Fie, who would be angered if the other was chosen. It would serve Cinaed right if we ended up with a fool of a boy on the throne after all."

Baena hid her smile at this comment, as she continued with her work.

In the end, the process took nearly four full days and a large part of the nights. Baena became aware in a change in the mood of the men as the evening of the fourth day arrived. Cinaed rose from the table as Baena came to remove the latest platter. She grimaced at the state of the hall. The dogs would be delighted once they were allowed in.

Looking jubilant, Cinaed came towards her. "Prepare a celebration, my lady. Lord Aed is to be proclaimed king."

Chapter six

It was with relief that Baena saw the feast on the great table before leaving the men to their rowdy merriment. It was too late to see Unuis this night and Baena felt a twinge of guilt that she had neglected her over the past few days. Making her way wearily to her chamber she quickly undressed. Shivering, she got into bed with a shawl wrapped around her shoulders and began to unbind her hair.

It was a surprise when Cinaed too came into the chamber shortly after her. Baena knew that the celebrations would go on long into the night, but the jubilant expression on his face had gone. It was replaced by the look of strain he had worn since his father had died. She felt a sudden wave of sympathy, as she realised that he had not truly been able to back the king he wanted. The king he had expected to support that autumn was his father. It was no wonder he had little heart for the celebrations.

Despite her feelings, Baena looked nervously at the dismal expression on his face. Whenever before they had shared a chamber, he had always come much later. It had been easy to feign sleep. This night there would be no avoiding what he had to say.

He sat down on his pallet, shaking loose his own hair. "You have done well these past days," he said suddenly. "The King was most appreciative."

"I was honoured to be the one to welcome him, my lord," Baena replied.

As Cinaed removed his shoes, Baena returned to combing her hair, trying to complete the task quickly. Glancing up as she finished she was startled to find Cinaed's eyes still fixed on her. She tensed, wondering if he was about to tell her that their union was over. Such an announcement would be doubly humiliating with Dunadd so full of people. He crossed the chamber and sat down on the bed, his eyes not wavering from her face. Baena cast her eyes down and waited for what he was about to say.

At first, Cinaed did not say anything. Instead, to her amazement, he reached out to caress her face, running some strands of hair between his fingers and stroking them with a gentleness that she found hard to believe possible from such a strong hand. Smiling he took one of her hands in his. "You have grown so beautiful, Baena."

Shocked by the compliment, Baena could only stammer, "Thank you, my lord."

Cinaed frowned, making Baena's heart sink. She should have known that she would do something to annoy him. Frantically she tried to work out what it was.

"I have a name," Cinaed said to her.

Baena felt confused. "Yes, my lord," she replied.

"Use it."

"Yes, my lor-," Baena stopped short, unable to help laughing at her mistake. As the smile lit up her face it brought an answering one to Cinaed's. Baena found herself looking into grey eyes that were sparkling with laughter, while his hand continued to stroke her cheek. "Yes, Cinaed," she said breathlessly.

Cinaed's smile faded and he took his hands away from her. There was a strange expression in his eyes. "The day I returned to Dunadd," Cinaed said awkwardly. "I was angry, but it was wrong to have taken my anger out on you."

Baena stared at him, shocked that he was apologising. The grief was etched into his face even deeper than ever and her shock only increased as she realised how much she longed to comfort him. She put her hand over his. "It was a difficult day for you."

Cinaed clasped her hand, his face relaxing as if he had gained some comfort from her touch. He looked at her, a slight smile returning to his lips. "I want an heir."

Baena's heart began to thump. Despite her own longing for a child, she had always dreaded lying with this man. But this night there seemed nothing threatening about him. She swallowed hard. "If it is within my power to provide you with one, I will," she said quietly.

Cinaed moved closer to her. "Do not be frightened of me," he murmured, slipping an arm around her waist and leaning forward to brush his lips softly against hers. She was totally unprepared for how that kiss would feel. It was nothing like those long ago kisses with Drust. Her hand tightened around his.

Cinaed pulled his head back, with a slightly rueful expression. "I am a brute springing this on you now," he said. "I know you must be tired. You need not receive me this night, but I hope soon."

As he made to stand up, Baena clung onto his hand. Her lips were still tingling from his kiss. To her surprise she realised she wanted him to kiss her again. "I am not tired," she whispered.

Cinaed's smile widened. Putting both his arms around her he pulled her against him. She felt his lips in her hair and on her neck. Tentatively she put her own arms around his waist, still not certain if this was the right things to do. As he released her she wondered for a moment if she had offended him by her action, but he was still smiling. She blushed at the look in his eyes as he began to unfasten his belt.

Baena watched him as he cast off his tunic. For the first time the strong muscles in his arms and chest did not seem to threaten her. She noticed too the scars that marked his body, hating that anything had hurt him. He grinned as he saw her watching him. Slipping under the covers with her, he took her back into his arms.

"I fear I am not as beautiful as you," he said. "But I hope you do not find me too displeasing."

Baena had gasped at the feel of his body against hers. "No, no. Not at all," she stammered before the gleam in his eyes told her how he was teasing her. She smiled shyly at him, thinking that when he looked at her like that he was the most handsome man she had ever seen.

Her breath quickened as he unfastened the pin that was clasping the shawl around her shoulders. He smiled reassuringly at her, as he removed it. His arms felt warm against her bare skin as he pulled her down against the pillows, his lips finding hers once again. Eagerly she responded to his kisses, welcoming the touch of his hands on her. She was unable to believe how this day was ending, yet overwhelmed with happiness that this first night together would not be the ordeal she had always feared.

The next morning Baena awoke when Cinaed removed his arm from around her and got up from the bed. Watching him from under lowered eyelids as he dressed she tried to make some sense of what she was feeling now that she was truly his wife. It had been bewildering how his mood had changed so quickly from irritation to tenderness, but remembering the feel of his hands and lips so gently on her, it seemed strange that she had ever dreaded a night with him. She could only hope that she had managed now to please him. After the kindness he had shown her in the night it would be hard to experience his anger again.

Baena propped herself up on her elbow, smiling to herself as she looked at his tousled hair, thinking it made him look younger than usual. His face seemed to have lost the careworn look that had been there since Alpin's death. When he turned away from her to tie back his hair, she pulled on her own tunic.

She smiled as she realised Cinaed was watching her, but before either of them could say anything the sound of a bell made them both start. It was already the hour for prayers.

"Hurry," Cinaed said, pulling on his shoes.

He waited for her, while she quickly bound up her hair. As she adjusted the folds of the caul over her head, he looked at her critically.

"I must look a fright," Baena said, reflecting on the speed at which she'd dressed.

Cinaed laughed. "You look beautiful," he said, putting his arms around her and kissing her passionately.

It was Baena that eventually pushed him away with considerable reluctance, murmuring, "We will be late and then what will everyone think?"

"That you are an obedient wife and that I am a very lucky man," he said with a teasing grin.

Baena went scarlet, as still smirking, Cinaed escorted her from the chamber. Outside in the grey autumn light, she looked around her, feeling that everything seemed different. She realised that her place here was now secure. Dunadd was her home.

"What are the King's plans for the Pict border?" she asked Cinaed fearfully, her thoughts going to her other home.

Cinaed looked at her with some sympathy. "The Picts are our enemies, Baena. You know that."

"They are my people, not my enemy," Baena protested.

The frown, she had been dreading, marked Cinaed's face, but as he looked into her pleading eyes, he sighed. "I need you to be with me. It will reflect badly on me if you are not."

"I am with you," Baena said, her happy mood dampening. "Does that mean I must forget my family?"

Straight away she regretted her words, frightened that she would undo all the good the night had done. To her relief, Cinaed shook his head with a smile. "No, I do not forget your family and the alliance with them still stands. I swear to you that I will not attack your father's territories, but I can make no promises on what the other clans do."

Baena nodded. With the prayers just starting there was no time to say anything else. As they came to an end, Domnall winked at Cinaed.

"You left the feast early, Brother," Domnall looked from Cinaed to Baena. "Were your celebrations of a more private nature?"

Cinaed grinned and cuffed Domnall about the head. Baena shook her head in embarrassment, frowning slightly at Domnall. She remembered how Unuis had told her that Domnall was not to be trusted. The affection between the brothers seemed genuine, but Baena suddenly felt a shudder, as she watched the playful exchange.

"Baena!" a voice called.

Looking around she was delighted to see Unuis up from her bed, talking to Graunt and the new king. Leaving Cinaed and Domnall to their scuffle, Baena made her way towards them, dropping to her knees before the King.

"My eternal obedience, my Lord King."

Aed pulled her back to her feet. "No kneeling necessary, my dear lady. Your hospitality the last few days has been very much appreciated. I fear we have kept you extremely busy."

"I am honoured to have been of service, my lord," she said.

Aed smiled benevolently. "I would bestow a small gift on you, my lady, as a token of my thanks."

To Baena's surprise, Aed removed a silver chain with an amber pendant from his pouch and draped the costly gift round her neck. Unuis gave her a proud smile as she stammered her thanks.

"And I shall not forget what I owe to you, Cinaed," he said as Cinaed and Domnall came up behind them. "I shall always remember how you were the first to pledge your clan to my service." His face grew grave. "My boys, I have not yet offered you my condolences for Alpin. That was a terrible affair. You will avenge yourselves?"

"With your permission, my Lord King," Cinaed replied.

"Of course we will, my lord," Domnall put in. "The Pict scum will regret the day they killed my father. We will slaughter the lot of them."

Baena kept her face expressionless. She would not disgrace Cinaed, but inside she flinched at his words.

Aed laughed. "That would be a huge task."

"Not all," Cinaed said. "As you know, my lord, I have an alliance with the Picts of the Third Royal House and I would ask you not to order me to break the terms."

Baena looked gratefully at him, but Cinaed's expression was bleak as he added, "I reserve my revenge for one man in particular."

In the awkward silence that followed, Cinaed moved away from Baena, a fierce look in his eyes.

"Well, nothing can be done on that until the spring at least," Aed said slowly. "But on to happier matters, I believe young Gregor is of your clan? He seems a goodly lad."

"Gregor is of my clan and my kin," Cinaed replied.

"He has an attachment for my niece and has asked my brother for her hand. Would such a match meet your agreement?"

"If it does yours, my Lord King," Cinaed said. "Clan Mac Alpin would be honoured by such an alliance."

"Excellent. I know it is too soon for such celebrations in your clan, but we will speak of this again," he said, as he left them to greet more of his new subjects.

Cinaed gave Domnall a satisfied look. "You see, Brother, how advantageous it is to support the King. He seeks to ally himself even more closely with us."

"Cinaed," Unuis interrupted, looking worried. "Graunt said that you left the celebrations early last night. I am concerned for you."

Cinaed raised his eyebrows, smiling mischievously at his mother. Her eyes widened in astonishment, as he put both his arms around Baena. "When Graunt has a wife of his own, perhaps he will understand why I might choose not to feast with men all night."

Graunt's eyes narrowed, while Unuis stared at her son, tears coming to her as she realised how genuine his smile was. She looked from him to Baena, nestled in his arms, her eyes bright and confident in a way that Unuis had never seen before. She breathed a sigh of relief. It looked like her beloved son and the Pict girl she had grown to love would be happy.

Chapter seven

Over the next few weeks, the women of Dal Riata worked tirelessly to prepare for the crowning. It soon became clear that Cinaed's status had soared as a result of his support for King Aed and the chiefs who had shown him affection as Alpin's son now accorded him a new respect. The death of Alpin could have seen their clan dwindle into insignificance, but Cinaed had ensured that Clan Mac Alpin would remain a force to be reckoned with. Cinaed played a prominent part in the coronation ceremony and among the wives of the chiefs, Baena too was treated with deference. Those weeks had been happy ones for her, as Cinaed remained most attentive. At night she would often gaze at him in the dim light as he slept next to her, wondering how she could ever have not wanted this marriage.

The crowning was the last time the gentle Unuis was seen in public. The next day, complaining of pains in her stomach, she took to her bed. Baena neglected all other work to nurse her and Cinaed was often in attendance, but Unuis grew steadily weaker.

"You must care for her better," Cinaed told the women as he and Baena arrived one morning.

"But, my lord-" one of the older women started.

"Do not excuse your failures," Cinaed snapped at her before she could finish. "Care for her better."

The women all looked helplessly at each other as Cinaed left. Unuis moaned slightly in her sleep. Baena went to her and took her hand. It was icy cold.

"We need a priest," the older woman muttered. "But I can't see the Lord Cinaed agreeing to that."

Baena blinked back the tears to see all the women looking at her.

"My lady, can you not persuade him?" the woman said.

Baena pushed back her stool. "I'll try," she sighed and went after Cinaed.

She found the men gathering outside the hall, preparing for a hunt. Dogs bounded excitedly to their masters and the shrieks of birds pierced the air. Blinking in the autumn sunlight she looked around, wondering how she would find him in this crowd.

"Sister, what brings you out here?" Domnall swept up to her, a falcon on his arm.

"I must find Cinaed. Unuis..." Baena hesitated, wondering whether the permission of a foster son would do if Cinaed could not be found. "She is failing fast," she finished soberly.

Domnall looked solemn. He passed the falcon to a serving lad and took Baena's arm. He led her through the men to where Cinaed was talking to the King.

"Should you not be with my mother?" Cinaed asked, looking annoyed as she hesitantly approached.

"I will return, but Cinaed, we need a priest," Baena said as gently as she could. "Grant us permission to summon one when she next wakes."

Cinaed frowned at her for the first time in weeks. "She does not need a priest," he hissed at her. "She needs all of you to take better care of her."

Baena blinked back the tears that had come to her eyes at the viciousness of his tone. She was exhausted from caring for Unuis and bitterly hurt that Cinaed seemed to think she was not doing enough.

"A priest can do no harm and may do much good," Aed said. "Let your lady call a priest if she thinks it best."

Cinaed stared at the King in surprise, before looking back impatiently at Baena. "Very well. Now go back to her immediately. We are leaving for the hunt shortly, but I will see her this night. I expect to see her much improved."

Baena reached out to place her hand on his arm. It was stiff and he did not respond to her touch. "Cinaed, I do not think you should be away from Dunadd this day."

Cinaed snatched his arm back and anger flashed from his eyes. "I thought you had done with your disobedient ways," he growled, loud enough for some of the nearby men to turn curiously. "Now do as I have instructed. I do not take orders from you."

Baena flushed with mortification, but before she could respond the King spoke again. He had been watching them with sympathy. "But you do take orders from me, my boy," he said quietly. "And I am forbidding you from joining the hunt this day and command you to remain at the fort."

Cinaed took his angry eyes off Baena to stare in shock at the King. "Very well, my Lord King. As you command." He gave Aed a curt bow and ignored Baena completely as he headed away.

Aed looked on Baena in a kindly fashion. "This is a sad matter, especially coming so soon after Alpin."

Baena nodded gratefully at him, unable to speak.

"Father!" Aed called to a nearby priest. "Accompany this lady. There is someone who has need of you."

There was relief in Unuis' chamber when Baena returned with the priest and they quickly lit more candles so he could read the sacred words. Unuis lay very still under the covers and only the slight rise and fall of her chest showed that she still lived. Baena stared at her pale, dry lips and reached for a chalice of wine. Dipping a cloth in the wine she wiped it gently across her mouth. Unuis stirred slightly and as the priest knelt at her side to recite the prayers of the dying, her eyes flickered open.

"Cinaed," she gasped, her head moving from side to side. "Cinaed."

Baena realised that all the women were looking at her again.

"I do not know where he is," she whispered. "And I do not think he will come."

"But she wants him, my lady. If you cannot persuade him then no one can."

After all the kindness Unuis had shown her since her arrival in Dunadd, Baena knew that she had to try to do this for her, however angry Cinaed might be. She left the chamber, but she did not have to look hard. He was stood just outside, his face pale. They looked at each other for a moment.

"Cinaed, we have done everything we can. Please come in," Baena begged.

The pain that filled his eyes was excruciating to watch. Not knowing what his reaction would be, Baena put her arms around him. Briefly, he returned the embrace. "I know," he said, pushing aside the hangings and entering his mother's chamber.

"Leave us," he said to the women.

Before she let the hangings fall back Baena saw Cinaed take his mother's hand. Unuis opened her eyes again and they filled with joy as she looked on her beloved son.

Unable to watch any more Baena backed away and joined the huddle of women in the hall. The day's tasks lay neglected as they sat in silence. As the afternoon wore on Baena could bear it no longer. She took a jug of ale and returned to Unuis. Her eyes were shut once more and Baena suspected that she would never open them again, but her hand still lay in Cinaed's.

"Thank you," Cinaed took the cup of ale Baena had poured without taking his eyes off his mother.

"Shall I stay?" she asked, gently laying her hand on his shoulder. "Or do you wish to be alone?"

Cinaed's eyes flicked briefly up to her. "Stay," he said quietly.

Baena pulled over a stool and sat next to him. The chamber was still, apart from the calm voice of the priest. Over the next hours, Unuis' breathing grew shallower and her already pale face got whiter still.

Baena slipped to her knees and closed her eyes in prayer, although that did nothing to stop the tears that slowly fell. It was not much later that a slight movement made her look up. She saw Cinaed hold a silver goblet above his mother's lips. Taking it away he studied it in the candle light, but Baena already knew that he would see no misting of her breath on that goblet. Through her tears, she looked one last time on the face of the woman who had helped her through this last difficult year. Cinaed looked down as well, his face expressionless. Sighing, he pulled the blanket over her face as the priest intoned the final words.

Chapter eight

Baena woke late the next morning. Quickly she pulled on a tunic, shocked by how advanced the day already was. Cinaed had said nothing to her after Unuis had died and it was the priest who ensured that she reached the safety of her chambers, leaving Cinaed to sit beside his mother's body.

Habit more than anything else took her back to Unuis' chambers, where she found that the body had already been removed. Cinaed was instructing the women to pack up her possessions. Even in the dim light of the chamber Baena could see how exhausted he looked and she felt guiltier than ever for sleeping so long herself.

"Forgive me," she said quickly. "I do not know how I came to sleep so long."

Cinaed ignored her apology. "See to this," he gestured at the packing. "Keep what you will for yourself and distribute to the others as you see fit. My mother will be laid to rest this afternoon. I must prepare."

There was a stillness in the room as the women packed away the possessions Unuis had accumulated in her life. Baena kept for herself some jewellery and costly cloths, while granting the other women their own items. A silver mirror to one and a fine chalice to another. At the bottom of a coffer they found two shawls of the softest wool, lined with a thick white fur.

"She made these when she was carrying the Lord Cinaed and wrapped him in them when he was a babe," one of the older women told her. "You should keep them for your own babies when they come."

Baena nodded, as she took the shawls, trying to imagine a young Unuis, younger even than herself and very frail, wrapping her new baby son in these shawls. She wondered what Cinaed had looked like then. Her thoughts then drifted to the son she hoped to conceive, the grandson that Unuis would never see. Smiling sadly she placed them on her pile.

A slight squall from the other side of the chamber startled her. Little Grimmach had woken and she watched Annis bending over his crib. Baena had as little as possible to do with Annis these days, hating the thought of her and Cinaed together. But the memory struck her of Unuis smiling at the baby, the only grandchild she would see. Slowly

Baena picked up one of the shawls and held the soft wool against her face. Suddenly feeling glad that Unuis had at least held one grandchild she crossed the chamber. Wordlessly she held the shawl out to Annis.

Annis stared at her in shock and everyone in the room went silent. Baena and Annis just looked at each other, before Annis took the shawl, a tear glistening in her eye.

"Thank you, my lady," she murmured, wrapping it around her son.

Baena still said nothing, but looking down at the baby she smiled. She didn't have to imagine how Cinaed would have looked all those years ago. He would have looked just like that.

As she returned to her tasks the women looked at her with new respect and Baena's heart felt lighter. She was certain that Unuis would have approved.

When Cinaed returned dressed in a dark tunic everything was done. He took a moment to thank the women and present them with a small token of his own. Baena held her breath as he reached Annis, but Cinaed spoke to her with no more favour than any other. She noticed that his glance lingered on the baby, but if he realised the lad was wrapped in his own shawl he made no comment.

Only when the last woman had been dismissed did he turn to Baena and motioned to her to leave the room with him.

"The funeral rites start within the hour," he told her. "You must make ready."

Baena nodded, following him towards their chamber. Cinaed did not touch her and he appeared barely aware of her presence. As they neared it they could hear Domnall and Graunt arguing.

"I'll not do it," Domnall was saying.

"You must. You can't let Cinaed stand alone," Graunt replied

"No. She made it plain I was no son to her."

"What is going on? Must you two argue on today of all days?" Cinaed demanded as they rounded a building. Graunt and Domnall, both dressed in grey tunics, were glaring at each other. They fell silent on seeing Cinaed. Domnall looked uncomfortably at the ground.

"Domnall will not stand at the coffin with you," Graunt said.

Cinaed raised his eyebrows and looked steadily at Domnall. Domnall glanced up, flushing at the look on Cinaed's face.

"It would not be right. She did not regard me as her son," Domnall muttered.

"And it seems you did not regard her as your mother," Cinaed stated, his eyes still fixed on Domnall.

There was silence as Domnall refused to meet Cinaed's eyes. Baena looked unhappily at Cinaed. She couldn't help feeling angry with Domnall for deserting Cinaed at this time and yet she knew his words were true. Unuis had not loved Domnall as a son.

"I'll stand with you if you would like," Graunt offered. "She was not my mother, but she was my aunt and I well remember her kindness to me as a boy."

Cinaed took his eyes off Domnall. "I thank you, my friend, but no. My mother had just one son. I shall stand alone." He looked back at Domnall. "Do you plan on attending the rites, Brother?"

Domnall raised his head and nodded.

"Then perhaps you will oblige me by escorting Baena to the church."

"Of course." Domnall took a step towards Cinaed as if to clasp his hand, but Cinaed turned away and headed for the lower terraces.

Graunt cast a contemptuous look at Domnall which then swept to the bundle of possessions in Baena's arms.

"Looks like you have done well for yourself, my lady," he commented.

Baena flushed in rage, but Graunt had already strode away. She turned her own steady gaze onto Domnall.

"Do not start," Domnall said angrily. "I'll not take censure from you."

Domnall returned to her chamber a little later accompanied by Gregor. The two normally high-spirited young men were both subdued and the three of them walked to the church in silence.

Inside a small crowd had gathered, but her eyes went straight to Cinaed. He cut a lonely figure standing with his head bowed in much the same place as he had stood for his father just a few moons before. When Baena reached the coffin her mind went blank. She had so much to say to Unuis that she could have stood there for hours.

"Thank you for your kindness. I was honoured to have known you," she thought inadequately before she realised the one thing Unuis would want to hear. "Let your soul be not concerned for Cinaed. I will care for him as long as there is breath in my body. I'll not forget my promise. Rest in peace."

Moving to one side she watched Domnall from under her lowered eyes as he stood a moment by the coffin. She wondered what, if anything, he was thinking.

There was no official mourning at Dunadd for Unuis, but as a mark of his respect and esteem for Cinaed, Aed ordered a fast day meal to be served that evening. Cinaed was composed throughout the meal, talking normally with Graunt and any other that spoke to him, gravely accepting their condolences. Baena ate little, just longing for the evening to be over so she could retreat to the chamber and weep in peace.

It was late when Cinaed joined her. Exhausted from grief, she sleepily watched him come in. He was forbidden from lying with her during the mourning period and so prepared himself for rest on a pallet across the chamber. After unbinding and running a comb through his hair he sat down on the pallet to remove his shoes.

All of a sudden he sank his head into his hands and Baena saw that his shoulders were shaking. In an instant, Baena forgot both her own tiredness and the rules as she shot across the chamber. Kneeling next to him, she put her arms around him. Despite his strength, he put up no resistance as she pulled his head against her shoulder. For a long time, she simply held him tightly as he sobbed, stroking his hair and laying her cheek against the top of his head. At length he calmed and lifted his head to look wonderingly at her. With his blotchy face and swollen eyes, he was unrecognisable from the handsome young chief who was always so in command of every situation and Baena's heart went out to him. She pulled him down to the pallet and then lying next to him she held him in her arms until at last he slept.

Part Three: Year of our Lord 835 – 6

Chapter one

Cinaed cursed as the fish he was trying to haul in escaped and flopped back into the water. On the bank, her bare feet dangling in the water, Baena giggled.

"That's enough of your cheek!" Cinaed grinned, splashing icy water at her.

Baena shrieked and scrambled backwards. Cinaed stood up to his thighs in the loch, the bottom of his tunic trailing in the water. Settling herself back down on the bank she wondered how he could bear it. Cinaed cast the line out once more, then waded back to the bank and sat beside Baena.

It was a day of doing nothing, which was unusual for them both. During the dark, cold days of winter Aed and the chiefs had planned their military campaigns for the next season. Winter clung on longer than usual, but at last, the snows melted and the sun shone more often than not. Cinaed announced that the King wanted them to set out for the border with Pictavia. Rumours of raids had reached them and it was clear that some territories were still disputed. This announcement triggered a new flurry of activity. Tents had to be mended and blankets woven. The tanners at Dunadd made stout leather shoes and strong packs for all the gear the clan would need for the days on the move. With her own hands, Baena stitched the banner that Cinaed's men would carry into battle. There were always some women who accompanied the clan army to prepare the meals and care for the wounded, and this year Cinaed decreed that Baena should be among them.

The first few months saw many skirmishes, but to Baena's unspoken relief no full scale battles. She was enjoying being away from the formality of Dunadd. Evenings were so relaxed, spent snuggled at Cinaed's side by a blazing fire, listening to the stories of the men and looking up at a black sky scattered with stars. His arm was always tightly around her as they both anticipated the moment when Cinaed would call out a goodnight to the men and they could wander hand in hand to the seclusion of their tent.

As mid-summer approached, Cinaed commanded that they set up camp on the banks of a huge loch, surrounded by craggy hills to take some time to replenish supplies and plan their next move.

On this day many of the men had gone hunting in the wooded slopes. Scouts had been sent out to spy on the Pict settlements and report back on weaknesses they could exploit. Until they returned discussions were futile, leaving Cinaed with a rare free day. Early that morning nets had been weighted down in the loch, but that didn't stop Cinaed wanting to catch some himself.

For a while they sat companionably together on the bank, their fingers entwined and the sun warming their faces. Suddenly Cinaed felt a tug on the line. Leaping up he began to pull it in. Soon a good sized trout flopped helplessly on the bank. Cinaed grinned triumphantly, looking less like a clan chief and more like a boy than Baena had ever seen.

"I thought you would want to join the hunt," she commented.

Cinaed shrugged. "I suppose I did, but I want to be here when the scouts return. I must hear what they have to say before discussing it with the rest of the men." He flicked water at her again. "Not so bad having me here with you is it?" he asked playfully.

Baena smiled and rested her head against his shoulder. "No, not too bad!"

Cinaed arched an eyebrow. "Do you want me to throw you in that loch?" he demanded.

"You wouldn't," Baena said, tossing her plaits over her shoulder and looking him in the eye.

Cinaed looked at her and then at the smooth waters of the loch and grinned. Putting his arms around her, he kissed her. "You sound very sure, my lady."

"Oh I am," Baena teased. "But you shouldn't be so sure I won't throw you in the loch!"

Cinaed shook his head. "No wonder I am having trouble with the men. I can't even manage my own wife!"

Baena immediately looked more serious. "I didn't know there was any trouble. How bad is it?"

"They're resisting my orders," Cinaed sighed. "Even Graunt is not supporting me. The men want to go after the Seventh Royal House or perhaps the Second. Their settlements are said to be less well protected. I want to attack the territories of the First. It will be a harder fight, but the First Royal House currently have the kingship. If we can strike at them we will send a strong message to all Picts. Besides I will still have my revenge on-" he paused abruptly and a pained look came over his face.

Drust. Baena finished the sentence in her mind as Cinaed's arm slipped from her shoulders and he moved fractionally away from her. It was ever this way. Every time Drust was mentioned a distance seemed to come between them. She tried to think of something else to say.

A cloud had passed over the sun and as the rays peeped out they shone on the dead fish that lay next to them, lighting up the iridescent scales into a sparkle of rainbows.

"Look, it's so pretty!" she exclaimed. "I always think it is a pity that we cannot make clothing out of fish skins. When the hunters return we may have deer hide and rabbit skins. They will be soft and warm, but not nearly so pretty. Just imagine a gown of fish skin."

Cinaed looked amused at her prattle or perhaps it was just relief at the change of subject. He put his arm back around her. "You would look like an angel," he said. "But you would not smell like one!"

Baena laughed. "Some angel! Can you even get red headed angels? The angels in the parchment the old abbot showed me once were all golden with golden hair."

Her voice trailed off as she hit another awkward subject. She wasn't sure how much Cinaed had to do with the beautiful, blonde Annis anymore. There were some things that were best not to ask. But on those nights back at Dunadd when he had come so late to their chamber she had lain there wondering if the war council had gone on into the night or if he was with her. Baena had been relieved that because of her child, Annis had not joined them on the campaign. Cinaed had never formerly acknowledged little Grimmach as his son, but the lad wanted for nothing and the clan made much of him.

"What's wrong?" Cinaed asked, seeing her face fall.

She smiled sadly, still thinking of the boy. "Nothing. It's just that I had hoped that I would be with child by now."

Cinaed nodded. "I had hoped it too, but we must give it time. It is in God's hands."

"But it has been nearly a year. Sometimes I have hopes for a few days, but it always comes to nothing. What if there is something wrong with me?"

Cinaed half smiled and kissed the top of her head. "You're a bit young to decide you must be barren."

Baena leant gratefully against him. He was so kind not to reproach her. She wished more than anything that she could repay him with a son.

"We must pray that God blesses us," Cinaed continued. "But in some ways, I am glad you are not with child yet. It is good to have you with me. There are times when I cannot speak to the men."

Baena nodded in understanding. After every skirmish and fight in the privacy of their tent or chamber, she had seen the confident, optimistic leader mourn for any men who had fallen. In this first campaign without his father perhaps it was as well that she was able to be with him.

"Now if want to really help, think of how to convince the men to obey me."

"What would convince them?"

"God's own messenger might." Cinaed sounded gloomy.

Baena giggled. "Perhaps it is you who needs a fish skin robe. What a fine angel you would make!"

"I think you are being cheeky again, my lady." Cinaed put his head on one side and regarded her with an amused glint in his eyes.

"Not at all," Baena made her features serious. "You would be dazzling. But I would throw you in the loch before permitting you my bed!" she dissolved back into giggles.

Cinaed laughed out loud and leapt up. Pulling Baena, he tried to drag her off her feet. Baena shrieked and dug her feet into the ground.

"Stop it!" she cried through her laughter.

Cinaed pulled her perilously close to the loch, casting an arm around her waist. For an instant she teetered on the edge before he pulled her back and looked at her smugly.

Baena looked meekly down, noting how close Cinaed stood to the edge. Then she flung herself at him, knocking him off his balance. But unfortunately for her, he kept hold of her and they both splashed into the icy water.

"You brute!" she gasped struggling to her feet, splashing water at him.

Cinaed laughed again and pulled himself easily out of the loch. He regarded her teasingly before pulling her up and into his arms. She looked at him in mock anger for a second, before the smile returned to her lips. He smiled back at her, the teasing look fading from his eyes as he brought his lips to hers. Their arms tightened around each other, as they sank down on the banks of the loch. Cinaed began to push her tunic from her shoulders.

"What are you doing?" she said, colour staining her cheeks, but her arms still wrapped around him.

"You'll catch a chill. Let it dry in the sun." Cinaed replied, throwing it to one side.

"But someone might see us!" she smiled in spite of herself as he pulled off his own tunic.

Cinaed took her back in his arms and kissed her again. "There's no one around," he murmured as he pulled her to the ground.

Afterwards they both lay on the grass letting the sun warm them. Feeling self-conscious Baena pulled her still damp tunic over her head. Cinaed smiled lazily and rolled onto his front. He was looking at the fish. It was a good catch. Five huge trout and three pike. It was likely there would be more in the nets and if the hunt was successful they would eat well that night as well as have plenty to smoke or salt for the next stage of the campaign.

"So if I did want to dress as an angel would it be possible to sew fish skin into a robe?" he asked.

Baena stared, as she began to plait her damp hair. "I… I don't know. Are you teasing me again?" she asked doubtfully for he looked totally serious.

"No. I want to know."

Baena wondered if she had a touch of the sun as she could not believe she was having this conversation. "It would be hard. Such a robe would be very flimsy. Sewing it onto existing clothing would work better. But Cinaed, you cannot really be thinking of this."

"I need to do something to make them listen. The more I think of it the better the idea seems."

"They would never believe it. They'd know it was you."

"Not necessarily. Suppose it was night time and they had plenty of ale in them and perhaps some of that Water of Life the abbot gave me. If they do realise it is me then it will be a jest they will never forget!"

Baena remembered the one small sip of the Water of Life that she'd had and thought that maybe Cinaed had a point. The men would believe anything if they'd had enough of that.

"So, can you do it?" Cinaed begged. "I'll even jump in that loch to cleanse myself for you afterwards!"

Baena burst out laughing and flung herself into his arms. "You're mad Cinaed! But yes, I will do it. Give me an old tunic, preferably a pale coloured one. I will see what I can do."

Chapter two

In secret Cinaed and Baena skinned the fish he had caught and after the meal that night Baena excused herself early to work on the robe. It was messy work and the stench of raw fish soon consumed the tent. But Baena's mind was elsewhere. She smiled to herself as she stitched, her thoughts drifting back to the idyllic day she had just had.

With the final piece of skin attached to Cinaed's old tunic she held it up, watching the scales shimmering in the candle light. Wanting to escape the smell, Baena left the tent to wash. The sky still had a hint of light and raucous noises drifted from the central fire. Two of the scouts had returned that day. Only the scout who had been sent to the territory of the First Royal House was still away.

After washing Baena went to the fire to check the women had cleared away the remains of the food. The last thing they needed was foxes or even wolves sniffing around. The men were sitting on the ground with cups still in their hands and their talk had turned to the attacks.

"Why won't you listen, Cinaed?" Graunt was saying. "We'd have an easy victory over the Second Royal House."

"It would be a worthless victory," Cinaed replied. "The other royal houses will just keep up their attacks."

"The First will be hard," Mathan put in. "Even your father could not prevail."

In the light of the fire, Baena could see Cinaed's jaw tighten at the mention of his father and she longed to go over to him.

"We have learnt from that defeat," Cinaed said at last. "A blow to the First House will be a lesson to all Picts. I am the chief. The decision lies with me."

"I agree with you," Domnall called out. "Since when has our clan been so afraid of a hard fight?"

"We are not afraid of a hard fight," Mathan said coldly. "But we would prefer an easy victory to a hard defeat."

"And what of your loyalty to my father?" Domnall sat up. "You should all be eager for revenge."

Cinaed put a hand on Domnall's shoulder. "Exactly. I am glad there is someone in this clan of cowards who has not forgotten this."

"We are not cowards, Cinaed," Graunt called. "We all want revenge, but this is not the time. The Second Royal House and the Seventh are enough of a target for now."

The men nodded and muttered their agreement.

Cinaed stood and glared at Graunt. "Are you going against me? Have you forgotten your oath of loyalty already?"

Baena held her breath as Graunt rose to his feet. Graunt was one of the highest ranking members of the clan. It was no minor matter for him to challenge Cinaed.

"I am not going against you." Graunt faced Cinaed. "But I will not let your need for revenge blind you to the best decision."

"So we get our token victory over the Second and return to feast at Dunadd, leaving the borders in the hands of the First Royal House? Is that the best decision?" Cinaed demanded.

"Feasting at Dunadd sounds good to me!" Gregor shouted out to much laughter.

Gregor's light-hearted comments were cut short as another man rose up and stood beside Graunt. "You should take the clan leadership, my lord," he said and a gasp rose up from the men. "We cannot trust the Lord Cinaed's judgement."

Baena stopped her tasks and stared at the man. Domnall had scrambled to his feet to stand with Cinaed and an icy silence descended.

"Don't be a fool," Graunt said to the man. "It has not come to that."

"I think it has," said the man. "Everyone knows that Cinaed is in alliance with the Picts. How can we be sure he will not betray us to them?"

Baena longed to go and stand next to Cinaed. It was so hard seeing him with only Domnall for support, but she knew that such an act would make matters even worse.

"Because he is Lord Alpin's son," Graunt said firmly and to Baena's relief he moved away from the man to stand next to Domnall.

"The alliance is not with the First House," Cinaed said coldly. "And it has no bearing on this campaign."

The man looked around at the rest of the clan. "I am not the only one to think this, am I?"

But if he had hoped for support he was disappointed. The men ignored him and downed their drinks. Domnall shook his head in disgust and sat back down, filling up his own cup again.

Cinaed folded his arms and looked steadily at the man. "Clan Mac Alpin, no decisions can be made until we hear from the last scout. Now retire all of you."

Baena continued to clear away the debris as the men headed quickly to their tents, shaken by everything she had witnessed. Graunt kept his eyes on Cinaed.

"I am loyal to you, but if I think you are making a mistake I will tell you. You need your first campaign as clan chief to be a success. Go for an easier target."

Cinaed looked seriously at Graunt. "Even against an easier target men will fall. Should their lives be sacrificed for my personal glory? If we go against the First House our losses will not be in vain."

"The men will not forgive a defeat. You are making a mistake and it's not the only one."

Frowning, Cinaed glanced at Baena. "I will not discuss that matter with you."

Graunt shrugged. "Very well, I'll go to my rest. I hope the scout comes back soon. The men need a decision. Good night, my friend."

Cinaed's face relaxed into a smile and the men embraced.

"I have finished the robe, my lord," Baena said in a low voice once Graunt had gone. Only Domnall was left staring into the fire.

"Have you? That was quick!" he smiled, noting the trouble in her face. "As you can see things are not good."

Back at the tent Cinaed looked pleased with the robe and immediately tried it on. The panels of fish scales had been left loosely attached so they floated around him as he moved. She had even sewed strips of skin to the hem so the shimmer floated below his knees. Baena brought out one of her own cauls, similarly adorned with fish scales.

"Are you dressing me as a woman?" Cinaed demanded, his face looking both outraged and amused.

"You must conceal your face," Baena said. "Just try it." She pushed his hair over his shoulders and standing on tiptoes she draped the caul around his head. Standing back she caught her breath at how otherworldly he looked. It would be even more effective in the blaze of firelight.

"Call Domnall!" Cinaed said admiring the way the oil lamp reflected off the scales. "I doubt I can fool him, but we can test it."

Baena shivered as she headed out again into the night. Domnall was still lounging by the dying embers of the fire.

"Brother! Come, Cinaed would speak with you."

"Has he turned you into a messenger boy, Baena? I always considered my brother a fool. I could think of many a better use for you!"

Baena repressed a shudder. She had begun to feel uncomfortable with the way he looked at her. "I serve Cinaed the best I can. Please come, Brother." She spoke as lightly as she could.

With no sense of hurry, Domnall rose from his place and put his hand beneath Baena's arm. "Lead on, my lady."

Baena fought the urge to pull her arm away and led him back to the tent.

"I almost wish Cinaed would not be there, my lady," Domnall said in a low voice, as they reached the tent.

At this Baena did pull her arm sharply away and she threw open the hangings.

"The Lord Domnall," she announced formally.

Domnall entered the tent. "Jesu!" he cried falling to his knees.

Even Baena was taken aback. Cinaed had lit more lamps while she was gone and he stood among them with his arms outstretched. Iridescent colours swirled around his person. Domnall crossed himself as Cinaed burst out laughing.

"You were the one person I thought I could not fool, Brother."

Domnall stuttered something, uncharacteristically short of words.

"It is a ruse. If I command the men to obey their clan chief dressed like this, do you think they will listen?"

Domnall looked uncertainly at his brother. "If they see you like this they would follow you off the end of the Earth. They will serve you forever."

"Good. Play your part and our father may yet be avenged."

Chapter three

Baena had completed the fish skin robe just in time. The next day the last scout returned to camp and Cinaed announced there would be a feast that night before the war council the next day.

The women of the camp spent the afternoon preparing food and Baena declared she would make her special family version of hot heather ale.

As the soft afternoon light began to thin fires were lit. Baena had arranged everything carefully so that Cinaed could make his way from their tent without being seen.

"Everything is ready," Cinaed told Baena, stealing a sip of the ale. He blinked. "By God, Baena that is a powerful brew!"

"You must not drink any. Dressing as an angel is blasphemy enough. You had better not be a drunk one!"

Cinaed laughed as he joined his men. "Save me a cup for after," he whispered.

The western sky still had a touch of light as Cinaed slipped away from the feast. Only Baena and Domnall saw him go. The hot heather ale was going down so well, musicians were playing and Domnall was entertaining them with story after story each one more improbable than the last.

Cinaed timed his return perfectly. He moved into position quietly between the two fires and stood with his arms outstretched. The robe reflected the reds and golds of the fire, so he appeared almost as if made of flame. Baena hid a smile and continued serving the men, waiting for someone to notice the glowing figure.

It didn't take long. There was a scream and a crash as one of the women dropped a platter. The men looked up startled out of their merriment. The woman was too shocked to speak and could only point at the sinister shape between the fires. All the men jumped up and Domnall rose magnificently to the occasion.

"My God, what have we done that has brought this apparition upon us?" he cried falling to his knees.

The other men followed suit, some even prostrating themselves on the grass. Shaking with silent laughter Baena knelt with them. Mistaking her trembles for fear the woman next to her clung to her hand.

"Save us!" cried Gregor

"Tell us your will," Graunt cried. "We will obey."

"You are sinners. Sinners one and all," the apparition cried in a voice most unlike Cinaed's. "You will face the vengeance of the Lord."

There were further screams. "Christ have mercy. Saint Columba save us!" terrified voices called.

"You have a Lord," the eerie voice continued. "A chief, god fearing and fair. He was appointed to lead you, as Christ led his followers. But do you welcome his guidance? Do you obey his wisdom? Do you go where he commands? You have displeased the Lord God. You will feel his vengeance! Prepare to feel his wrath!"

"Forgive us!" called Gregor. "Spare us. We will obey your bidding. We will do whatever our chief commands."

The men of the clan hurried to agree.

The figure folded his winged arms. "Do you all swear?"

"We swear. By the sacred relics of Saint Columba we swear. We will obey our chief, the Lord Cinaed," Graunt cried.

The arms outstretched. "Clan Mac Alpin, be sure you do. The Lord will be noting everything you do."

Baena edged closer to the fire. The men were so fixated on the figure that no one took any notice of her. She pushed a tub of water over the glowing embers. Clouds of steam surrounded Cinaed. By the time they had cleared Cinaed had vanished.

The people of the clan were rubbing their eyes. Some crossed themselves, others seemed close to tears. The remains of the feast were forgotten and one by one the men slunk away to their tents. The night watchmen lit extra torches and huddled fearfully together by the embers of the fire.

As the moon rose over the loch Cinaed, Baena and Domnall toasted their success with the last of the ale. No longer hot it was still very potent.

"How many of these did the men drink?" Cinaed asked.

"Enough," Baena smiled. "I don't think they'll be in the mood for a long council tomorrow."

Domnall slumped on the ground. "He's had plenty, anyway." Cinaed prodded him with his foot, before taking off his tunic. Grimacing he dipped his foot in the loch.

"You don't have to do that, Cinaed. Really. Our tent reeks of fish in any case."

"I can't attend the council smelling like this. There must be no suspicion."

It was a very brief dip before he gratefully swathed himself in the cloak Baena offered.

"Help me get him to his rest," Cinaed indicated the snoring Domnall.

Domnall roused a little as Cinaed and Baena walked him to his tent.

"Are you taking me to bed, Baena?" he cried.

"Shut up, you fool!" Cinaed shook him, pushing him onto his sleeping rug.

"Aah, join me my lovely!"

Baena turned away in disgust, as Cinaed flung a blanket on top of him.

Outside the tent, he pulled Baena into his arms and kissed the top of her head.

"Do not mind him. Men say all sorts when they are drunk."

Baena clung to him. "It is not the first time he has spoken to me in that fashion."

"If any other man spoke to you in that way, I would kill him," Cinaed said, glancing back at Domnall's tent.

"I would not want you to do that to Domnall," Baena protested.

Cinaed laughed. "Good. I will speak to him. He does not mean to offend you. He does it to annoy me."

Baena felt even more distressed at that, as she remembered Unuis' warning. "Why does he want to do that?"

Cinaed looked surprised at her intensity. "You have brothers. Did they never argue?"

"I suppose so, but this seems different."

"Perhaps. Domnall was not always favoured as a child as I was. I am not sure my father did the right thing raising him with us," he shrugged. "But I am glad he did. As young lads on Iona, we had many an adventure together. Besides, Domnall is the fiercest of warriors. It is good he is with us and not the Norsemen."

"Could he challenge you for the clan?"

"I suppose he could. He is Alpin's son just as I am. If I were to be challenged, it would come from him or Graunt." He smiled at Baena. "Do not look concerned. I do not think it will happen. We do not always agree, but as both boys and men, we have always stood by each other. Graunt and I saw our first battle together and Domnall fought alongside us not much more than a year later. I trust them both with my life."

Chapter four

It was a highly chastened and probably slightly unwell group of men that gathered for the war council the next day. After a short meeting, Cinaed announced that they would march on the territory of the First Royal House. Baena tried to hide her concern at this news. She knew very well that it would be a hard fight. As she helped the men prepare, she couldn't help but wonder which ones would not be returning.

They rode hard for several days, eventually setting up camp close to the edge of the First House's territory. It was impossible to launch any sort of surprise attack on this well-protected location so they were not surprised when a Pict messenger arrived in the camp.

"Lord Cinaed, Eogan, the High King of Picts and Dal Riata would know your intentions in this land."

Loud shouts of derision greeted this proclamation as the Gaels wondered at the nerve of the Pict king, claiming the overlordship of Dal Riata.

Cinaed clapped the messenger on the shoulder so hard he fell over. Smiling down on the man sprawling in the mud he replied "We do not recognise Eogan as the Lord of Dal Riata. All hail King Aed of Dal Riata!"

The Gaels cheered this and there was more laughter as the messenger climbed awkwardly to his feet.

"As to what we want, firstly we demand that all Picts remove themselves from Gael territory and never return."

More jeers burst from the clan and the messenger shuffled uncomfortably.

"And secondly, we demand that the murderer of our Chief, the Lord Alpin Mac Eochaidh is delivered to us for justice."

"The Lord Alpin fell in battle," the messenger protested.

Cinaed smiled a chilling smile. "Perhaps I should slaughter you now and claim you fell in battle. If I just sent your head back would your king understand my message?"

The cheers of the clan were deafening and the messenger stepped back uneasily.

Still smiling, Cinaed took the messenger by the throat. "Take this message back to your so called King, my friend. If we do not hear that our demands are to be met within three days we shall use force."

The messenger retreated as the Gaels hurled insults and even a few stones after him.

Two days passed. The men recovered from their travels and began to get restless. Cinaed had no expectation that his demands would be met peacefully and sent out scouts to spy on the Pict settlements.

"Baena, have you seen Augus?" Cinaed asked her shortly after returning from a hunt.

Baena, her mind full of the deer and hare that would need skinning, barely gave his question a response.

"He came back to the camp. I last saw him sniffing around the bones at the rubbish heap," Cinaed frowned.

"I don't know why that animal has to dig up bones. You feed him more than enough. Tell him not to bring the bones back to the tent. I'm fed up of sleeping on them!"

But by the time night came the dog had still not turned up.

"He'll come back," Baena soothed as Cinaed stood outside the tent whistling into the night.

"I hope so. I've had that dog since he was a pup and we're moving on tomorrow. The scouts have found the place for our war camp."

Next day Baena was busy tying clothes into bundles and supervising the packing of foods when the call rang out.

"Pict delegation approaching!"

Baena straightened up. This time, it was no single messenger but a group of riders who swept in so fast that there was scarcely time for anyone else to assemble. She stared at them.

"Drust!" she gasped.

Cinaed stood next to her, his face frozen into a terrifying mask of rage.

"Have you come to atone for your crimes?" he demanded.

"Not at all," Drust replied. "I have come to tell you to advance no further. You cannot beat us Lord Cinaed, any more than your father could."

Behind the horsemen a dog barked and tugged excitedly at the cord which restrained him. Only the slightest flinch gave away Cinaed's reaction at the sight of his dog in the hands of the enemy.

Drust followed Cinaed's gaze and sneered. "You should protect your property better my Lord Cinaed. It was so easy to steal him." His gaze wandered innocently to Baena. "I wonder what I should steal next."

Cinaed's eyes narrowed, as the dog continued to bark.

"It is a strange thing, is it not? I fed the dog well last night and this morning, but still he is loyal to you. You stole a bitch pup from me once. I wonder if she is still loyal to me."

Baena flushed scarlet with rage and mortification. She could feel the eyes of the clan upon her. Drust laughed, his eyes caressing her.

Cinaed picked up his sword causing Drust and his men to back away, still laughing.

"Oh Cinaed, I understand your anger! I have felt her sweetness too. I am not surprised that you wish to keep hold of such a possession. But she should have been mine. She dreams of being mine."

Cinaed strode towards the horses, raising his sword, his face like ice.

"Go home, Cinaed," Drust laughed. "The lands we have taken remain with us. But as a token of my goodwill, here, take your hound." Drust cut the cord of the excited dog who bounded happily back to Cinaed. "Fare you well, I hope for your sake that our paths do not cross again. She was promised to me, Cinaed. If we meet again I will take back my property," Drust cried out, as the horses swept out again in a cloud of dust.

Cinaed's face was white with fury. "Keep packing," he snapped at the clan. "We march on by midday."

"Cinaed-," Baena started.

"How close were you to that man?" Cinaed glared at her.

"You know a marriage was spoken of," Baena stammered. The rest of the clan had not yet moved very far and many were watching curiously.

"Did you lie with him?" he asked angrily. Baena could see the shock on the faces of the watchers. She stared at him in horror at the question.

"Answer me," Cinaed hissed. "Did you lie with him?"

Baena went red with mortification. "No! You know I did not. I was a maid the first time I lay with you. You must know that," she said trying to keep her voice low, although she knew everyone had heard.

"Then what did he mean? Do not lie to me. I was not the only one to see you in his arms."

"I know," Baena whispered, close to tears.

Cinaed produced a cross from under his tunic. "Swear by this that an embrace such as I witnessed was all that past between you. Promise me that you did not lie with him. That you did not even kiss him and that you have not lusted after him since our marriage!"

"I can't," Baena's face crumpled. "I did not lie with him, Cinaed. I swear it, but-"

"Faithless slut!" Cinaed turned away from her and stalked towards Graunt. Graunt put an arm across his back as the two men walked off.

The rest of the clan stared at Baena for a few seconds before hurrying to carry out their own work. With an effort, Baena held back the tears as she returned wearily to the task that she had started before Drust arrived. She became aware of a man standing in front of her. Looking up she saw it was Domnall.

"I really don't admire your taste," he grinned. "But if Cinaed has no further use for you, I hope you know where to come. I could show you a better time than Drust, you know!"

Baena narrowed her eyes. "Go away, Domnall. I don't know why Cinaed calls me faithless when you would cuckold your own brother at a word from me."

Domnall laughed out loud at this.

"Don't be a fool, Domnall," Graunt said coming up to them. "Cinaed is really not in the mood. Come, he would discuss the strategy with us."

Cheerfully Domnall blew a kiss at Baena, but Graunt shook his head and looked icily at her.

"Cinaed made a huge mistake bringing the Pict out here. If the battle does not go well for us Cinaed will likely lose the support of the clan."

Domnall made his eyes very wide and innocent. "Have you forgotten the vision of the other night? The men would not dare disobey."

Graunt crossed himself. "I hope not. But this enemy among us does not help matters. She reminds the men of Cinaed's own Pict blood."

Domnall smirked and pretended to inspect Graunt's face. "Your nose appears to be intact so I assume you have not mentioned this to Cinaed."

"I am not that much of a fool," Graunt laughed harshly and he shot a look of hatred at Baena. "Why did he not rid himself of her when he had the chance?"

Chapter five

A wretched day followed. Cinaed spoke to her not at all, although somewhat to Baena's surprise the women continued to obey her. When it was time to leave Cinaed helped her on her horse with a formality that made her wish he hadn't bothered and he rode beside her in icy silence.

After a few hours ride, Cinaed decreed that they were as close to the Pict settlements as they could get and the clan set up a basic camp. Only the absolute necessities were unpacked in case they needed to move on in a hurry. In the night, Cinaed lay as far away from her as was possible in their confined tent. Baena was not sure if he slept, but she did not and wept silently.

The next morning Cinaed ordered the men to prepare their weapons and armour, as they would be marching on their enemies the next day. Baena could see no sign of rebellion among the clan, but perhaps it was because Cinaed's mood was so black that none dared cross him.

"Is the attack still to be launched in the morn?" she asked, when in the afternoon she found Cinaed alone, sharpening his sword.

Cinaed did not even look up but nodded curtly.

Baena knelt down next to him and picking up a soft cloth began to polish his helmet.

"Leave it," Cinaed snapped, snatching the cloth from her hand.

"Please Cinaed, let us not be parted in anger," she begged.

Cinaed looked her firmly in the eye. "Whose victory are you praying for tomorrow?" he asked.

Baena stared at him. "Yours, Cinaed. How can you even think otherwise?"

He ignored her and returned to inspecting his sword. The blade gleamed in the sunlight, reminding Baena of the injuries that could be suffered. She knew that if Cinaed did not return from the battle she would always regret not resolving this.

"Tell me what I have done to make you doubt me."

"Done? Days before our handfasting you were in his arms."

"I know," whispered Baena.

Cinaed looked anguished. "And at the wedding, when my hand was outstretched to you, you held back. Your feelings were plain to everybody."

"I was a child, a foolish child. What of everything that has happened since? Does that count for nothing? Night after night I have lain willingly in your arms. I cared for your mother in her final days and was honoured to do it." Desperate to lighten the mood she added, "And just in these last days I sent myself half blind spending a night sewing together fish skins for you."

"Wifely devotion indeed," Cinaed replied in such a dry tone that she was unsure if she had succeeded. "And yet you will not tell me what has taken place between you and my father's murderer."

"He was my childhood friend and I thought we were to be wed. We played together. We danced together. I know it was wrong that we kissed, but it was only when a union was spoken of. Nothing more, Cinaed. I swear it."

Cinaed looked more relaxed. "And since our marriage have you been ever faithful in thought as well as deed? Can you swear to me that you have not lusted for that man?"

Baena's face burned in shame. "No," she whispered. "The summer after we were wed I wished it was him I had married. I longed so much for my home-"

"You had everything you needed at Dunadd, but nothing was good enough for you, was it?" Cinaed looked angry again. "My poor mother thought so highly of you."

Baena felt stung by this. "Your mother understood what it was to be a young girl in a strange land. Do you think your mother did not weep for her own land when she first came to Dal Riata?"

"My mother was no slut. Do not dare to compare yourself!" Cinaed raised his voice.

Baena bowed her head in despair. She had so wanted to make up this quarrel but so far she had only made it worse.

"I know she was not," Baena cried. "She was the best of women and I shall never forget her kindness to me. You must know how much I loved her."

Cinaed shrugged and he continued sharpening his sword.

Baena tried again. "You provided well for me at Dunadd, but I missed my father and mother. Surely you, who now miss both of your parents, can understand that? I do not think I really lusted after Drust, but at the time, I longed for the life in my own land that marriage to Drust would have given me."

Cinaed looked at her in silence. Baena felt encouraged by this and continued, "I do not think I ever truly lusted after Drust. I was a child.

I knew nothing of such desires. But he was my childhood friend, one I was very fond of."

"Did you see him when he came to Dunadd?"

"Only in the hall, I swear it. I was a child then. I am a woman now and as a woman, I have felt nothing for him. As a woman I have given my heart to no man but you." Baena had bowed her head so she did not see Cinaed's face brighten. "Please forgive me, my lord, for my child's foolishness at our wedding and my ungrateful thoughts since."

"Oh, my love," Cinaed took her in his arms and buried his face in her hair. Baena slumped against him in relief, all thoughts of the battle forgotten. "I forgave you for that a long time ago. I intended never to mention it. It was only because I thought-"

"As a woman I feel nothing for him," Baena repeated. "And I will swear it by whatever sacred oath you wish."

Cinaed smiled and shook his head. "No oath means more to me than your word."

Baena reached up and pushed the hair from his eyes. Looking up into them she smiled back. "You have my word. But was it wrong for me to feel affection for my old childhood friend?"

"No, it was not wrong, but I am not sure there is much of your friend left. He was just a boy then."

"He has changed so much. I suppose I have too, but there is a vicious streak in him that I never thought to see."

"He's been to war, Baena. It changes a man. Before a man goes to war he is sheltered. Oh, I know life can be hard in the settlements. We see old and young alike waste away to disease. We hear the screams of the women in childbed. Sometimes the harvest fails and we know we will go without that winter. But all this is nothing compared to the realities of war."

Cinaed raised his sword, watching the light shine from the sharp edge, before continuing, "I do not know if you can understand. Before I went into battle I did not know if I could kill a man. Like all boys, I had bragged about such ambitions, but in my heart I did not know if I could. I wonder if anyone can. But once you are in battle it all changes. The noise, the flashing weapons, the terrible cries of the wounded and dying. Your kin and your friends may be falling around you. Suddenly you must injure or be injured, kill or be killed. The urge to survive takes over and you fight. But you are forever changed in some way."

"How?" Baena asked breathlessly, half horrified half fascinated by the picture Cinaed portrayed.

Cinaed shrugged. "It varies. Some, Domnall for example, fall in love with the excitement. They live for the next fight. He grew up on stories from his Norse kin on the glories of battle. Perhaps that is why he loves it so." Cinaed gave a wry smile. "I sometimes think he believes he is doing his enemies a favour by killing them in battle and dispatching them to the feast halls of the heathen gods."

Baena shivered and crossed herself.

"Others and I believe your old friend Drust is one of these, love the cruelty they can display so freely on the battlefield. Once they have fought they may be unable to leave that cruelty behind them. I would not wish to be the son of such a man. All fathers will chastise their sons when necessary, but I have seen men inflict the most brutal punishments on their sons for the most minor of misdemeanours." Cinaed shrugged. "I think you would be foolish to wish to be the wife of such a man."

Baena clung on to his arm. "I do not wish to be the wife of such a man and I know I am not. So how did war change you?"

Cinaed was silent for a moment. "From my first fight, I have always regretted the waste of men. I am no coward and I know it is often necessary to fight. Our lands must be defended and increasing them is glorious indeed. But these fights over an established border are a waste. I saw the strength we could amass when Gaels and Picts fought together against the Angles. That was a fight to be proud of. That is why I agreed to our marriage. If Gaels and Picts would stand together we would both be great. But divided as we are, both are weaker."

"Do you feel our marriage has failed?" Baena asked nervously, hearing the regret in his voice.

Cinaed clasped her hand tightly. "Between us two? No. I could never think that. But our marriage was supposed to be more than just you and me. Now my father is dead and our borders are in disarray. So yes, our union has failed. I can never regret our marriage and can only hope that you will not either. I know you have said you will pray for my victory tomorrow-"

"Of course I will," Baena interrupted, almost in tears. "Stop thinking otherwise. Tomorrow will be the most wretched day for me. I shall spend it frightened for the outcome and praying that you will come safely back to me."

"But what if I was fighting your father? It could happen one day. I have sworn I will not attack his territory, but what if he attacked ours? Or joined one of the other royal houses to defend their territory? I cannot be certain that he will not support the First House. It is possible even that I face him tomorrow. Would you still pray for me then?"

Baena closed her eyes in pain. "Forgive me, Father," she thought as she opened them to look Cinaed in the eye. "Yes I would," and the tears spilt out of her eyes. "But will you hate me if I say I would pray even harder that such an event should never occur?"

Cinaed half smiled. "No, of course I would not hate you. I think you are wise to make such a prayer."

"Your father intended to attack the Third Royal House," a voice said. Baena looked up to see Graunt standing there. He did not look impressed at their entwined hands.

"I am not my father," Cinaed said lightly.

"No, you are not. He would never take battle advice from a woman," Graunt commented. "Or a Pict."

Cinaed stood up and looked at Graunt out of unblinking, grey eyes. Graunt looked somewhat uncomfortable. "The men will not like it either," he added.

"The men will do as they are ordered," Cinaed said. "And I trust you will as well. We have surely been friends for too long for you to keep standing against me."

"I am not standing against you," Graunt said, emphasising the last word. "I am advising you to be careful where you seek counsel. That is all."

Cinaed smiled chillingly. "I am always careful," he replied.

Chapter six

Baena slept little again that night. Feeling Cinaed's warm presence next to her, she longed to hold him close to her and never let him go. Of course, she did no such thing but lay as still as possible so as not to disturb him and dreaded the morning.

All too soon the early light filtered through their shelter and the birds started up their joyful chorus. Baena was sure that if she had been a man she would have snatched up a bow and shot the lot of them. How could the birds sing so merrily over these men who were about to risk their lives?

Swallowing her fears Baena dressed and maintained a cheerful smile as she supervised the breakfast preparations. She knew it was important to feed the men well, as who knew when they would next eat a good meal. As she spooned the nourishing oat porridge into bowls and filled platters with salted meats she looked at the men with pain, as she realised that for some, maybe many of the men, this would be the last meal they would eat. She served Cinaed herself, still maintaining her bright expression. There would be far too much time to weep once the men had left.

The men came together for Morning Prayers and afterwards Baena could see Cinaed talking to Domnall and Graunt. In spite of their serious mood, there was no sign of tension between them. As Domnall and Graunt both nodded Cinaed smiled and embraced them both. He held up a hand to silence the chatter of the clan. He was dressed plainly in a short brown tunic over breeches, but Baena swallowed over the lump in her throat as she looked at him. Even on the most magnificent of occasions he had never looked as handsome to her as he did now. The clan were quiet as flanked by Graunt and Domnall, Cinaed addressed them all.

"My friends, my kin today we march to battle. Today we engage with those wicked Picts and shall take back what is ours. We shall make sure they do not lay claim to even the tiniest piece of Dal Riata ever again!"

Loud cheers greeted this. In spite of her fears Baena felt herself smile at the adoration the clan so clearly still felt for Cinaed.

"God willing, we will, at last, have our revenge on the man who killed my father, your great Chief, the Lord Alpin, may God have mercy on his soul."

The men crossed themselves. Some hurled a few curses of their own onto Drust's head.

"Look at the man on either side of you. Your life lays in their hands and theirs in yours." He clapped Domnall and Graunt on their shoulders as he spoke. "Be willing to lay down your life for that man and accept his sacrifice to save yours. Fight for the clan, my friends! Fight for me! Fight for the glory of Dal Riata! Victory will be ours!"

Baena could hardly hear Cinaed's last words the cheers were so deafening. Baena felt her mood lifting. They would be victorious and she hardened her heart against the Picts that must fall.

"Make ready, my friends! We advance now!"

In the chaos that followed, Baena found Cinaed fastening his sword belt. She watched him unseen for a second, taking in his tall figure and the muscles that bulged through his clothes. His sun-streaked hair moved slightly in the morning breeze and he appeared calm enough. His face lit up when he saw Baena and she flung herself into his arms.

"There you are! I thought I was going to have to leave without a farewell kiss!" Cinaed said cheerfully.

Baena looked up at him, her hands winding around his neck and pulled his face down for a long kiss. His arms felt so tight around her that it almost hurt as they clung together.

"Baena," he released her and lowered his voice. "If the battle is not successful I will send a message and you must flee. Do not worry about packing up the camp. Just get away."

"But-" Baena began to protest.

"No, do not wait for me, my love. The men who will guard the camp know of a safe refuge for you. If I am able I will join you there. As the wife of the chief, you must be as a mother to the clan. Your duty is to lead the other women and the wounded to safety. Give me your word, Baena, that you will do this."

Baena nodded. "I will do whatever you command, my lord. You have my word."

Cinaed nodded and tried to smile. "Apart from anything else it would be dangerous for you to remain here. I am sure that Pict scouts would quickly locate this camp and I do not think you can presume too much on your old friendship with Drust to keep you safe. You would be a valuable prisoner to them and I think he would not hesitate to hurt or defile you to get at me."

Baena could not help the pain in her eyes, but she nodded and Cinaed gave her one last embrace. "I am a brute for saying this to you. Just be safe, my love."

"I will," she whispered. "But you will be victorious. I know it."

Cinaed kept his arm around her as he walked to his horse at the head of the mass of men, where Domnall and Graunt both bowed to her. Although Graunt still seemed disapproving of her, it was clear that this opinion was not shared by the rest of the men who cheered loudly as Cinaed gave her a long, last kiss.

Baena's face began to ache from maintaining the smile as Cinaed urged his horse on, his arm waving a farewell. She kept her smile as Domnall, Graunt and man after man rode past. Only when the last foot soldier was out of sight did she collapse to the ground and let her tears flow.

The first day an army is away is always the worst for the people waiting behind. Remembering Cinaed's instructions to lead the remainder of the camp, Baena set the women to work to keep their minds off the fighting.

"Fetch water from the river," she commanded. "We shall wash the bedding so the men may have a place of comfort when they return."

The priest approached her. "With your permission, my lady, could the watchmen help construct a shelter so I may care for the wounded."

Baena nodded and by the end of the first day, they were ready when some wounded men were brought back to camp.

"What news?" she cried, scanning the group anxiously for Cinaed.

The man at the head of the group bowed low. "The Lord Cinaed sends his greetings, my lady." Baena felt faint with relief that Cinaed was still alive. "We have made good advances on the Pict territories and our losses are far fewer than theirs. He commands you to be of good cheer and charges these men to your care."

Pleased that they had washed all the bedding Baena ordered the women to make the men comfortable. As each was laid down the priest moved among them, assessing the treatment they needed. Baena followed him, helping as much as she could. It was a messy business, cleaning off mud, excrement, sweat and blood. So much blood.

Baena sat by one man, his face battered and bruised. Some cuts were so deep and as Baena watched fresh blood spurted from them. She had wiped his face clean before she realised to her horror that it was

Gregor. He had a deep wound to his thigh and another in his side. The priest shook his head as he tended to the wounds.

Gregor screamed in pain as the priest worked and Baena took hold of his hand, her eyes widening as she saw the extent of the injury. She wondered whether it was even worth bandaging them, as the bindings were quickly spotted in crimson stains. The agitation of the young man increased and Baena helplessly tried to soothe him by stroking his hair. She was relieved when the priest moved on and Gregor could lie still. She returned later to Gregor with food once all the wounded had been treated as best they could to see if there was anything further she could do.

"You must eat," she begged, trying to spoon porridge into his mouth. "It will make you strong again."

But Gregor moaned and turned his head away. Baena wiped the porridge from his chin and considered trying again. His skin felt burning hot. Dipping a rag in some cool water Baena gently sponged his face and hands. Eventually she fell into an exhausted sleep beside him.

She woke with a start in the blackness of the night. Instinctively she reached out a hand to see if Gregor's fever had broken. He felt cool to the touch and she felt an overwhelming feeling of relief, which was instantly dashed. He felt too cool.

Baena let out a cry.

"What grieves you, my lady?" the priest called. He entered the shelter accompanied by a watchman with a flaming torch in his hand.

The light confirmed what Baena already knew. Gregor was dead. She looked sorrowfully at the still face.

"He was wed to the King's kinswoman just a few moons back," the watchman said quietly.

Baena nodded sadly. "I believe his wife is with child. I pray that will be a comfort to her. Rest in peace Gregor," Baena whispered, as the priest pulled the blanket over his face.

"Leave him, my lady. There is nothing more you can do tonight. We shall lay him to rest in the morn," the priest told her.

Tears of sorrow and exhaustion flowed down Baena's cheeks.

"You did all you could, my lady," the watchman tried to comfort her. "Everyone is saying how much you did."

"It wasn't enough," she sighed as she reached her own tent.

"Some wounds are beyond help."

Baena's last thought, as exhaustion took over once more, was that this was of little comfort.

Chapter seven

Two further men died during the night and it was a sombre group that gathered by the hastily dug graves.

"Keep Cinaed safe," Baena prayed, after the funeral rites had finished, before hurrying back to nurse those still living. She was pleased to find there were definite signs of improvement with many of them. One even declared that if the battle continued another day he would march back to join it.

That evening more casualties were brought back, including Graunt and Domnall. Baena's heart contracted at the sight of them. She couldn't imagine that those two had strayed far from Cinaed's side.

Kneeling next to Graunt she carefully cut away his tunic, horrified by the drying blood that was underneath. She held his hand as the priest checked the slash he had received across his belly. It was long, but fortunately not too deep. In spite of the animosity between them, she hoped he would recover. She would hate to have to break the news of his death to Cinaed.

"Cinaed still stands," Graunt half gasped, seeming to read the question in her face, as she wiped the blood from his stomach and legs. "The fighting was fierce this day, but our advances against the Pict scum were great."

Baena ignored the insult to her people and asked, "Is he uninjured?"

Graunt hesitated. "No serious injury, my lady."

Baena's frightened eyes flew to Graunt's face, forgetting her dislike for this man. "What do you mean?"

"He is able to fight on, my lady. He would not leave the fight and you should not wish him to." Graunt shut his eyes against the pain and said no more.

But Baena felt the reproof in Graunt's words and flushed.

Dealing with Domnall was harder. He had taken the news of Gregor's death badly and was desperate to return to the fight. No sooner had the priest bandaged the wound to his leg, he was struggling back to his feet. Crimson flooded through the woollen bindings.

"What are you doing?" Baena cried, rushing to put an arm around him. "Lie back down."

Domnall could barely stand without Baena's support. "Have a horse ready. I am returning."

"You are not," Baena replied, trying to pull him down. Even injured he was stronger than her. "Domnall, lie down or I will summon the watchmen to tie you down."

Domnall wavered on his feet and sank back down onto the furs. "I'll not stay here. If I am to die, I will die in conflict, not lying here on a rug."

"Fine!" snapped Baena. "If I think you're dying I will instruct the watchmen to give you a kicking. Now lie still, you fool."

Domnall scowled while next to him Graunt winced as he fought the urge to laugh. Baena sank to her knees next to Domnall. She took his hand. "I am so sorry about Gregor," she whispered.

Domnall turned his face away and closed his eyes. Baena looked back at Graunt. His eyes too were closed, screwed up against the pain. She felt so helpless, knowing that she could do nothing more for them than she had for Gregor. All she could do was pray that they would be luckier.

She was feeding Graunt the next day when a watchman burst in, excitement on his face.

"My lady, the banner has been sighted. The clan is returning!"

Baena looked at him, hope struggling in her eyes. "Is it victory do you think?"

"The banner was held high, my lady. It must be."

"Quick! We must prepare food and ale. Take word to the others."

It was hard to continue calmly feeding Graunt. Her mind was racing as endless possibilities ran through her head. A victory did not necessarily mean that Cinaed was alive.

"You should go and prepare for Cinaed's return, my lady," Graunt told her.

Baena wanted nothing more than to do that. She had imagined herself welcoming Cinaed back looking her best, not in the old, stained tunic that she was wearing. But she shook her head.

"Presently, my lord. Now, try to eat a little more."

Graunt was being kept as still as possible to allow the injuries to heal, so was only slightly propped up to allow him to be fed. It was a messy, slow process, as Baena had to stop between every mouthful of food or ale, to wipe his face. However she was pleased that he was able to eat. So far he appeared to be recovering.

Once Graunt had eaten as much as he could, she looked at Domnall who was lying with his eyes closed. She had decreed that she alone would care for these two, so that the responsibility if they died would lie only with her. Earlier she had changed Domnall's bandages. The injury seemed to be healing, but the process had clearly exhausted him. Gently she pushed back some blonde strands to lay her hand on his forehead. He stirred slightly and she couldn't help but smile at how innocent he looked. To her relief there was no sign of a fever, he was simply sleeping. With nothing more to be done there, she rushed outside to join the welcome preparations. Outwardly she was calm, but inside her heart was thumping. Suddenly Augus was bounding towards her. The huge dog jumped excitedly at her in greeting. Baena tried to calm him as the first horses rode towards them.

It was a dusty, weary group of riders who emerged from the trees. Baena scanned them, but to her horror could not locate Cinaed among them. Her heart beat even louder as she looked at the men. It was with relief that she saw them accepting the refreshments with a good cheer that would surely have been impossible if their leader had fallen. And then she saw another group of horsemen. Straggling behind the first group this group were riding pillion and Baena's face broke out in the first real smile since the men had set off. Looking dishevelled, with his arm bandaged up explaining why he was not able to ride his own horse, was Cinaed.

Baena ran to the horse as Cinaed painfully dismounted. His pale, exhausted face lit up as he saw her.

"Victory! They have agreed to our demands. The settlements of Dal Riata are safe once more."

Baena, her face beaming, handed him a cup. "But you are hurt!"

"Just a scratch." His smile slipped. "Others were not so lucky. Mathan was slain and others."

"Some men died here as well," Baena said quietly. "We lost Gregor. I am so sorry, Cinaed."

"I heard. I know you did your best, my love, but I am not surprised." Cinaed shook his head sadly. "His injuries were terrible."

Baena put her arms around him and pleased to be able to give some good news she quickly said "Domnall is recovering well. And I am hopeful of Graunt too."

"Thank God!" he replied.

"What of Drust?" she asked hesitantly.

"He still lives," Cinaed said, shortly. "My revenge must wait. I could not risk any more men, once they agreed to withdraw from our territories."

The late afternoon was busy, as the few women of the camp served food and drink to the weary men. And there were more injured to tend to. The shelter where the wounded lay was crowded now and so when Cinaed entered he did not notice Baena soothing a man in the corner as he weaved his way through the prostrate men to see Domnall and Graunt.

"So victory was ours in the end," Graunt said to him.

"Yes, we prevailed," Cinaed replied, looking cheered at the good spirits Graunt was in.

Domnall scowled. "I should have been part of it."

"You were, Brother. That last charge you led was decisive. The Picts never recovered from it and today was mostly negotiations. Your sacrifice was not in vain."

Domnall's face relaxed and he appeared more cheerful.

"Cinaed," Graunt said, sounding serious. "I must say something to you about your lady."

Baena froze in her work, wondering what she had done wrong now. Cinaed frowned at his friend. "I know you consider her a Pict viper waiting to strike us and have often counselled me not to trust her, but even injured as you are I will not allow you to say a word more. I believe her to be true."

Baena's heart lifted at Cinaed's defence, but she was even more surprised when she saw Graunt nod. "That is what I wanted to say. I withdraw my reservations about her completely. She has shown such care and tenderness towards the men, their own mothers could not have cared for them more devotedly. She has been an angel in our midst, even with the most awkward of men," he finished with a black look at Domnall.

Cinaed laughed, as he also looked at Domnall. "Such skill indeed! Graunt, your words are much appreciated. She is in truth an angel."

Baena came towards them, smiling. "Do not be foolish! I have given the men such care as I could. Nothing special."

Graunt struggled into a sitting position. "My lady, if my manner has ever offended you, please accept my apologies. I am eternally grateful for the care you have given to me. I do not think I deserved it."

Baena felt tears prickling her eyes. "My lord, it is all forgotten. I am just happy you are recovering so well. Now, Cinaed, I must check your injury."

"No need, my love. I told you, it is but a scratch."

Baena folded her arms and looked sternly at him.

Domnall laughed. "You should do as you are told, Brother. Otherwise she will have you tied up and kicked. A hundred Picts are not more terrible than her!"

Cinaed grinned and put his good arm around her shoulders. "Very well, but not here. You can care for me in our own tent."

"You didn't really tie him up, did you?" Cinaed asked incredulously, as they left the shelter.

"I threatened to. He was hell bent on returning to the battle even though he could barely walk! Was I wrong to show him so little respect?" she asked suddenly anxious.

"You did well, my love. I am so proud of you. You have undoubtedly won many hearts this day." And as they reached their tent he kissed her deeply.

For a second Baena rejoiced at the kiss. Until that moment, she had not realised how scared she had been that she would never again feel his arms around her, but she pushed him away. "There will be none of that, my lord. Not until I have seen to your injuries."

Cinaed smiled, pulling her back to him. "I begin to see why Domnall was so afraid! But I, my love, am made of sterner stuff!"

Chapter eight

When she was finally allowed to look at Cinaed's injuries Baena was relieved to find that the gashes across his arms had already scabbed over. They did not seem to be overly troubling him, as he presided over the victory celebrations.

After several days, the clan started a leisurely pace back to the lands of Dal Riata. First they visited the disputed territories to ensure the agreement with the Picts was being met. Cinaed was pleased to find that Gael farmers were already moving back and King Aed sent fresh men to ensure that all would continue to go smoothly. Eventually Cinaed decided they had done enough and announced that he would head to his own lands in the far west rather than return to Dunadd.

But even with the slower pace, Baena felt exhausted. At night she crawled into her tent and was asleep before Cinaed joined her.

One night he came earlier. Smiling when he saw she was awake, he took her into his arms, but Baena froze at his touch. Instinctively she pushed him away. In the dim light, she could see that he looked surprised and immediately she felt ashamed.

"I'm sorry," she whispered. "Of course I am happy to fulfil my duties."

"You don't look happy," Cinaed said, sounding hurt. "Is it still just a duty for you?" he asked softly.

"No, oh no. Do not think that. It has not been that for a long time," Baena protested with tears in her eyes. "When you were away I longed for you every night. But please not tonight."

"Or the past few nights I think," Cinaed commented, but seeing the misery in her eyes his face softened and he gently stroked her hair. "I am not reproaching you, my love. I am concerned. Are you ill?"

Baena burst into tears at his kindness. "I don't know," she sobbed into his shoulder. "I am just so tired."

Cinaed looked even more worried and put his arms back around her. "Don't cry, please Baena. I know these last weeks have been a strain on you. Soon we will be home and all will be well. Get some sleep. You will feel better in the morn."

But she felt no better the next day. In fact, she felt worse. Dragging herself up to help with the morning preparations, she was violently sick.

Cinaed took one look at her and ordered her back to rest.

"We'll camp here a few days. You're not fit for travelling."

"But the men want to get home. We can't delay."

"There's not a man in the camp who would want to make you ride while you are ill. Get some more rest. I'll send someone to bring you some food later."

Baena sank back onto the furs with relief and slept some more. Later when one of the women brought her food she ate the porridge hungrily but sent away the greasy meats.

Feeling better, a thought struck her. Her monthly bleeding that had occurred with irritating regularity hadn't happened for a while. She tried to count back to work out when it had last come and realised it was well over two moons ago.

A sudden surge of excitement went through her. Quickly she fastened on a tunic. She pulled it tightly against her and looked down. Her stomach was still flat, but she was sure her breasts were more rounded. For a while she just sat among the bedding hardly able to take it in. Running her hand over her stomach it seemed impossible to imagine that there might be a child in it, but the signs were all there. Her face lit up and she muttered a quick prayer of thanks that she could finally say the words to Cinaed that she had been so longing to utter. Pulling on shoes she hurried from the tent in search of him.

She found him sitting around a fire talking with several of the other men. They all stood up as she approached.

"You're looking better," Cinaed commented with obvious relief.

"We are all praying for your health, my lady," Graunt told her.

"Thank you." She bowed her head in acknowledgement of the good wishes and tried to keep her expression calm until she could speak with Cinaed alone. "Cinaed, may I speak with you when you have time?"

"I always have time for you," he said, taking her arm and leading her away.

Once they were alone he looked quizzically at her. "You do look so much better. Quite radiant in fact."

Baena beamed up at him. "Yes, oh yes I am! Cinaed, I believe I am with child!"

Cinaed's mouth dropped open, his face lighting up into a huge grin. Gathering her in his arms he spun her around.

"Are you sure?"

"I think so. My monthly bleeding has stopped. The exhaustion and the sickness are all signs."

"We must take good care of you." Cinaed shook his head. "As well as we can out here in any case. This is the best news. When will the babe come do you think?"

"I think in the spring if all is well."

"Are you able to travel?" he asked anxiously. "I'd like to get you to my home, but not if it will harm the child."

All feelings of sickness had totally gone out of Baena's head. "Oh yes. I feel quite well now. I think it would be better to travel now than when I am bigger."

Cinaed thought for a moment. "We could ride less each day. Leave later, stop earlier if that will be easier? Or you could ride pillion with me? Or-"

Laughing, Baena stopped any further suggestions with a kiss. "Try not to worry about me, my love. I am sure I can manage."

It was some weeks later that they came down from rocky cliffs and saw the sea before them. Cinaed had decided that he wanted their child born on the sacred Isle of Iona, his own birthplace.

"Is it not overrun by Norsemen?" Baena commented, looking out at the choppy waters beating against little islands. Cinaed had told her that Iona itself was out of sight so she knew that it must be a long way over that grey sea.

"There are some settlers there, but Iona hasn't been attacked for a long time," Cinaed grimaced. "Probably because there is little left to steal. It's as safe as anywhere on this coast."

Baena looked again at the sea. She still felt sick each morning and the movement of the sea did nothing to help.

Cinaed guessed what she was thinking. "Don't worry. We won't attempt the crossing until the weather is calm."

It was a much smaller group that had travelled this far. Now they were deep in Cinaed's lands many had drifted away to their own farms and settlements and a few days previously Graunt had led some of them back to Dunadd, where their families still resided. Baena was only sorry that it was Graunt that had gone and not Domnall. Since the battle Graunt had gone out of his way to be friendly and respectful towards her and Baena forgot that she had ever disliked him.

The clan had erupted into cheers when, at a feast one night, Cinaed had announced to them all that Baena was with child. She soon found that the care she had given Graunt and the other men after the battle was repaid many times over on the journey as they competed to bring her the finest foods and warmest blankets.

Only Domnall still made her feel uncomfortable as she was unable to forget his lechery towards her. She was certain that Cinaed had chastised him for it, as his words were always respectful, affectionate even as from a brother to a sister. But his eyes seemed to be often on her with an expression that she found impossible to understand. Sometimes she thought back to the words of Unuis and reflected that if his own foster-mother could not trust him, it was surely impossible for her to regard him with any affection.

They were lucky that the next day was fair. It was the first time Baena had been to sea, so it was with some trepidation that she allowed Cinaed to help her on board. They brought thick woollen blankets and furs to wrap her against the breeze.

"Don't worry. It's an easy passage," Cinaed told her. "I was fishing off boats all the time as a boy here."

Once they set off Baena did not attempt to move around. As they passed the little islands close to the mainland the swell picked up and much to Cinaed's amusement, Baena clutched fearfully onto his hand. It seemed to take an age to cross the stretch of open water, before moving along the coast of Mull. Cinaed pointed out the seals basking on the rocks.

"Fine food and even finer furs," he commented.

Once they had rounded Mull the waters grew calmer. Cinaed looked ahead, a peaceful smile on his face. Ahead of them a grassy island, dominated by a hill was separated from Mull by a narrow channel.

"There's Iona, my love. My home."

Baena disembarked with relief, glad to feel the ground beneath her feet again. A group of monks led by the Abbot of Iona himself had come down to greet them. Cinaed bowed with respect but then grinned at the holy man.

"So you rose to be abbot! I am not surprised, Father."

The Abbot smiled. "I have, my son. I am happy to welcome you back here. And is this young Domnall? I do not think I would have known you."

"May I present my lady to you, Father? Baena, Father Indrechtus, the Abbot of Iona. He was still a brother when I was last here and was charged with the teaching of Domnall and myself."

Domnall and Cinaed exchanged mischievous looks which raised a laugh from the holy man and made Baena suspect that they had not been the most diligent of students.

"I bid you most welcome, my lady," the Abbot said and led them up the hill to where three stone crosses stood before the abbey. Looking at the stone refectory and church nestled so peacefully under the hill it seemed hard to imagine that this had been the scene of vicious Norse raids in the years before Cinaed was born. Now only goats wandered and chickens pecked in the places the Norsemen had plundered.

They spent their first few nights in the abbey guest chamber while Cinaed and the men made the necessary repairs to their own dwelling. During the day, the Abbot showed Baena the abbey with pride, despite their few treasures. In a building of oak and wattle, she was amazed to see the library of books and manuscripts and watched in awe as by just the light of a candle one of the monks dipped a quill in ink to inscribe sacred words on a piece of vellum. But most moving of all was when she was shown the sacred shrine of Saint Columba himself and she spent a long time there in prayer, thanking him for bringing her safely to her new home.

It was a happy day when Cinaed took her hand and led her to their dwelling. It was not to the same standard as Dunadd, consisting merely of a small hall with a few chambers and storage rooms surrounding it, but after the months on the move it felt luxurious to them. Baena looked forward to settling in and preparing for the arrival of her child.

One autumn evening, shortly after the equinox Cinaed made an announcement as they dined. Meals here were simple and so only a few, including Domnall and the Abbott were eating with them. The past few weeks had been among the happiest Baena had spent since their marriage. In their first days there a number of the islanders had presented themselves and offered their services. Baena had taken a particular liking to a dark haired girl, named Kieta who quickly became Baena's chief serving woman and companion. The simpler life felt almost lazy and Baena had regained her energies. She was noticeably bigger now, but not yet so big as to feel uncomfortable.

Cinaed too seemed happier. Showing Baena the haunts of his childhood or heading off to fish with Domnall he seemed in many ways to become a boy again. Baena had worried that her swelling body would be unattractive to him, but she needn't have worried. He made it clear he found her more beautiful than ever.

It was therefore even more of a shock when Cinaed announced that he would make a lengthy trip to the King at Dunadd.

"But why?" was all Baena could say.

"The chiefs are meeting. We need to plan for next summer."

"What about me?"

Cinaed seemed surprised. "You'll stay here, of course. You can't travel in your condition. Domnall, you're in charge. I know you'll look after Baena."

"It will be an honour," Domnall said, sitting up straighter.

"Cinaed, you can't go. You can't leave me!" Baena cried suddenly.

Cinaed looked shocked at her outburst. "Control yourself, Baena. You know I have responsibilities."

Baena looked miserably around the table. Every man was staring at her. Pushing back her chair she ran awkwardly from the room.

The meal must have ended early as Baena was still crying when Cinaed entered the chamber. At the sight of her, the irritation on his face faded and he took her in his arms.

"Baena, what is this? You know I can't always be with you. I shall miss you, but the time will pass and we shall be together again."

"How long will you be?" Baena asked, trying to control her sobs.

"I don't know, but I shall try to be back before our child is born."

Baena's tears flowed again. "Not until then?" she asked desolately.

Cinaed realised he'd said the wrong thing. "Maybe much sooner. As well as consult with the other chiefs I must check on my lands on the mainland and with the clansmen who are still in Dunadd."

Baena suddenly felt an icy chill. The clans people in Dunadd. No doubt that included Annis, the beautiful woman who had already borne Cinaed a son.

"How angry will you be with me if our child is a girl?" she asked.

"I won't be at all angry, my love. It is in God's hands. Any child is a blessing and you are young yet."

Of course it didn't matter. He already had a son. "So you don't care if I bear you a son?"

Cinaed's face took on the slightly wary expression that men have always worn when trying to say the right thing to their pregnant wives, knowing that they will fail miserably.

"My love, I am praying for a son and, of course, I am praying that you come safely through the birth. Whatever the outcome I will not be angry at you."

Baena refused to be comforted. If she didn't survive he already had his next wife lined up. She began to cry again.

"Can't Domnall go in your place?"

"Domnall? That young hot head negotiating with the chiefs? No, I must go. Besides Domnall may be needed here. If there is trouble from the Norsemen he will know how to handle them."

"I don't want to stay with Domnall."

Cinaed shook his head wearily. "I know he offended you over the summer, but you need have no concerns. He will not speak to you in that way again."

Baena bowed her head, knowing it was useless to protest.

"Now dry your tears. Let us not part in anger."

Chapter nine

Winter came early to Iona that year. As the ground turned icy the women all encouraged Baena to stay inside rather than risk a fall. There was plenty do with the never ending repairs of clothes, smoking and salting the fish and meats and preserving of fruits, but the days still dragged. Baena missed Cinaed intensely. The baby was moving now which led to Baena often waking in the night and although Kieta slept in the room with her, the chamber felt cold and lonely without him. It was in those times that she particularly wondered if he too lay alone thinking of her or whether he was in the arms of Annis.

She was barely aware of Yule Tide approaching and as she felt more and more uncomfortable was in even less of a mood for celebrating. She had seen little of Domnall since Cinaed had gone away, but was surprised to learn from Kieta how busy he was overseeing the repairs of buildings and increasing the food stocks for the winter. She had expected him to spend his time drinking and wenching the moment Cinaed was no longer there to keep an eye on him.

One morning he came to her chamber to discuss the Yule Tide festivities.

"It is customary for the lord and lady of the clan to host a feast for the islanders," he told her.

"In our own hall?" she asked wondering how they would all fit in.

"Of course not," Domnall replied rather impatiently. "The abbey allows us to use their hall. So, shall I tell the Abbot that we will be maintaining the tradition this year?"

"But Cinaed's not here. How can he host it?"

Domnall's impatience only increased. "I am in his place, so naturally I will host it."

Baena lowered her eyes to her stitching to hide her dismay at this comment. She remembered Unuis saying how jealous Domnall was of Cinaed. No doubt he would enjoy playing the chief in Cinaed's absence.

"I trust you will also be present, Sister," Domnall continued.

"Oh no. I can't." Baena stammered, hating the thought of seeing him in Cinaed's place.

Domnall frowned and for once, Baena could see a resemblance to Cinaed although he rarely looked like that at her anymore. "Why not?

Are you ill?" he demanded. "It is the tradition for the lady to be there and I think Cinaed would expect it."

Petulantly Baena flung aside her sewing. It was becoming too hard to do with her swollen fingers in any case. "Oh, very well. If I must."

On the Yule Night Domnall returned to her chambers to escort her to the feast. He was finely dressed in a blue tunic and russet cloak and Baena reluctantly had to admit that he looked very handsome. She was dressed in the finest tunic that could be adjusted to fit her, but it was not particularly festive and she felt very dowdy next to him.

Baena did her best not to shrink away as he wrapped a thick cloak around her. But as he took her arm, his manner remained respectful. They made their way through the wind and the sleet to the abbey in silence.

The hall of the abbey was ablaze with torches and candles and the islanders gave them a rousing cheer as they entered. Delicious smells wafted from the fire where pork, fish and seal were roasting. After the Abbot had said prayers, Domnall stood to propose the toast to the island and the abbey as was the custom.

"And lastly, my friends, let us drink to our Chief, the Lord Cinaed. I hope he too is enjoying a festive Yule Tide and will return to us soon," Domnall added at the end "And drink also to his lady for her good health as her confinement draws near."

As the islanders cheered, Baena couldn't help but feel touched by Domnall's words and to her surprise she enjoyed the feast. The islanders were all most solicitous of her and as the ale and mead flowed Domnall became an amusing dinner companion, full of stories to keep them all entertained.

When she wearied he insisted on escorting her safely back to her chambers.

"There is no need," Baena protested.

Domnall looked at her with that inscrutable expression that always made her feel so uneasy. "Cinaed would not be pleased with me if you slipped," he replied, his voice suddenly quiet. "I will return to the feast once I know you are safe. This is a dangerous time for you."

Baena stared at Domnall in sudden understanding. When Unuis had told her of Domnall's birth, she had been so indignant for Unuis at having to raise her husband's bastard son that she had spared no thought for the other woman in that tale. The one who had not lived to see her son grow into a brave warrior. Feeling an unexpected burst of affection for her brother-in-law, she laid her hand on his arm. "Thank you, Brother," she said gently. "I shall be glad of your escort."

A few nights after the feast the stormy weather calmed down and a small boat was spotted making the crossing from Mull. There was much excitement on the island as they speculated who it would be and whether he would be dark or fair.

"It's an old belief we have on the island," Kieta explained. "If our first visitor after Yule is dark it is said we will have a year of prosperity while a fair-haired one heralds a year of Norse raids."

The islanders were to be happy. It was a dark haired man and one that Baena was pleased to see.

"Welcome, Graunt!" she exclaimed trying to get to her feet when he was ushered into her chamber.

"Do not get up, my lady. A merry Yule Tide to you! I bring Cinaed's greetings."

"Where is he? Will he return soon?"

"He hopes to, my lady. He is overseeing his lands, but he is not far away. In the meantime, he asked me to give you this."

He handed Baena a small package. She removed the leather wrappings to find a brooch of finely wrought silver set with coloured glass.

"He exchanged many fine seal furs for the smiths to make you that."

Baena smiled, as much delighted by the fact that Cinaed was still thinking of her as she was with the beautiful brooch.

As Kieta served them cups of hot ale, Graunt gave Baena the news from Dunadd.

"And what of the ladies?" Baena tried to ask casually. "Did you see any of them? Annis perhaps?"

There was some understanding in Graunt's face. "Yes, I saw her. In fact, I attended her handfasting to Caulum."

"She's married?" Baena was astonished.

Graunt nodded. "Her little lad is walking and talking now. Ci... It was felt he should have the guidance of a man."

Baena tried to work out what all this meant. She looked up to see Graunt's eyes on her.

"Cinaed bestowed some lands on Caulum as a bridal gift. They departed for them soon after the handfasting. I don't suppose you will see her again."

"Graunt!" Domnall burst into the chamber. "Is Cinaed not with you?"

Graunt rose to greet Domnall. "No, and just as well. He'd have something to say about you entering his lady's chamber in this fashion."

Domnall cast an irritated glance at Baena. "Forgive me, Sister. What news?"

"Later my friend. The Lady Baena does not need to hear it all again. Tell me of your Yule celebrations."

Domnall shrugged. "We have had the feast and the monks have held their services."

"Is that all? What poor entertainment for my lady."

Domnall started to scowl again and Baena couldn't help feeling sorry for him, after his efforts to amuse her at the feast.

"Don't blame Domnall," she said quickly. "The truth is I have been poor company. He had to cajole me into that one feast."

"The islanders will light the fireballs this night. I hoped to persuade you out to see it," Domnall said stiffly.

"I'm not sure. It is still icy and I don't want to risk a fall."

"This won't do, my lady," Graunt said. "You must see the fireballs. Domnall and I will look after you."

Domnall gave her a friendlier smile as he nodded. "Of course we will. The fireballs are a sight not to be missed."

That night dressed in her thickest woollen tunic and cloak Baena headed out across the frosty island. Men with flaming torches lit her path and Domnall and Graunt each held an arm. Overhead the moon was crystal clear and the stars shone like a thousand jewels on a black cloth. Baena looked at the moon. That same moon was shining on Cinaed somewhere and she wondered if he was looking at it now. Inside her the baby stirred, pushing against her. It was feeling big now and she felt a rush of fear at the thought of getting it out.

"Is all well, my lady?" Graunt asked, noticing her expression.

Baena smiled. "Yes. Cinaed's son is lively tonight."

The ground was slippery making her glad of the presence of the two men and even gladder when they reached a point where a stool had been set out for her. She sank down gratefully, her hands moving to her stomach to try to calm the child within. Kieta brought thick furs to swathe around her and they waited for the spectacle to begin.

On the beach below them, the holy beach where it was said that Saint Columba had first arrived on these shores, a fire shone out through the night. Suddenly the low sound of a pipe floated towards them.

"It's about to start," Domnall told her.

Shadowy shapes could be seen moving around the fire, their figures suddenly illuminated in a blaze of scarlet as torches were lit. Slowly the torch bearers processed around the fire before moving away to form a ring. In the torchlight Baena could see that in the ring were more figures, holding something aloft.

The tune of the pipe changed rising higher and all of a sudden globes of fire seemed to burst from the circle into the blackness of the sky.

"They make the balls from sticks, dried grasses and animal fat," Graunt explained to Baena who had exclaimed over how well they were burning. The fireballs were moving off now to be carried up the hill. It was an eerie sight, as it was impossible to see the bearers, who were all dressed in dark clothing. It appeared almost as if the burning spheres were floating upwards on their own.

"They believe that carrying the fireballs up the hill will entice the sun to shine on us for longer," Domnall said.

"They will leave them as an offering to the fairy folk who live there," Kieta put in and then blushed as the Abbot frowned at her. Graunt gave her a sympathetic grin.

"It is a foolish superstition," the Abbot sniffed. "Only our Lord can ensure that the sun will rise. My lady, that hill is where the blessed Saint Columba would converse with angels sent by the Lord God."

Graunt crossed himself. "Meeting with an angel is a most wondrous and terrifying event," he said quietly.

Baena shot a horrified look at Domnall, but in the moonlight, she could see the mischievous glint in his eyes as he looked down at her. She pulled her hood further over her head to conceal her own amusement as they watched the fireballs moving higher.

"Domnall, do you remember when we made our own fireball and tried to join in?" Graunt asked with a grin.

Domnall snorted with laughter. "I still remember the beating my father gave us the next day as well!"

"Why?" Baena asked. "What happened?"

"We were forbidden from taking part, but we planned that no one would know," said Graunt.

"How were you caught?"

Graunt was doubled up with laughter and all she could hear was "Cinaed" and "such a fool," so it was Domnall who eventually explained between gasps. "Cinaed set his hair on fire!"

Baena smiled as the fireballs started arriving at the top of the hill. They were placed down to burn themselves out, as the bearers set off for revelry in the settlement. Under the furs, she stroked her swelling stomach again. "I can see I will have my hands full with this one."

Chapter ten

The Yule Tide festivities drew to a close and the first moon of the Year of our Lord 836 slipped by. The women who attended Baena suspected that she had just a few weeks left. Four perhaps, certainly no more than six. That first moon had brought terrible weather to the isles on the western coast and Baena began to fear that Cinaed would not return in time for the birth.

In the bad weather Baena had been glad to remain inside once again, but the Abbot persuaded her to attend the abbey for the festival of Saint Brigid.

"She once visited this holy isle and blessed the waters of our well. She has a special kindness for women in childbirth. You should come to our service so we can pray for your safe delivery my lady."

The day was cold, but clear and after the service Baena walked slowly back to her chamber. Her back ached but she was glad to feel the air on her face. There was a good view of the harbour and she could see that a boat had come into dock while she had been at the abbey. She hoped it had brought some fresh supplies. The meat that had been smoked and salted for the winter was nearly gone and she was getting tired of smoked fish.

She was about to return to her chamber when she noticed the large dog sitting outside the doorway of the hall. Upon seeing her it lumbered to its feet and bound excitedly towards her. Baena stepped back as it leapt around, worried it would knock her flying.

"Augus!" a man's voice yelled. "Get down!"

Baena's face lit up as the dog ran back to his master. "Cinaed! You're back!"

"Stupid mutt," Cinaed said to the dog, before coming towards her his arms outstretched and a smile on his face. Baena could only image the sight she must look now that she was so great with child. She could feel how puffy her face and fingers had got and was only glad her long robe meant that her swollen ankles would not add to his revulsion.

But Cinaed did not look at all revolted. For a minute he held her at arm's length and looked her up and down.

"My love, let me look at you! Why our babe grows so big." Pulling her closer his hand pressed gently on her stomach and he smiled as the baby moved against it. "And strong too! Are you well?"

"Oh yes, now you are here quite well! The ladies think it will not be much longer before, God willing, I shall present you with your son," Baena smiled, overjoyed that he was here with her again.

"Come, you're chilled. Sit by the fire and warm yourself. I have a message from your father."

"My father? Have you seen him?"

"Yes, we were both in the disputed lands. No, don't look so worried my love. There was no enmity. He expressed his great joy at your condition. He seems to imagine that this child could be Rex Pictorum one day."

"I suppose it could happen," Baena replied noncommittally, but she thought privately that between herself, Unuis and Sabina this child would belong to three of the Royal Houses and would indeed have a better claim than many who had held the title.

Baena was so happy at Cinaed's return that despite her discomfort and aching muscles the last few weeks of her pregnancy went by well enough. Cinaed was often busy training the young boys of the settlement or in council with Domnall, but at least he was with her every evening and she no longer spent the nights in cold loneliness. Her ladies told her that her child would arrive before the days and nights stood equal, so each day she rejoiced as the sun rose earlier and set later and prepared herself with a mixture of hope and fear.

The first pains struck around a moon after Cinaed had returned. She had passed a restless night, feeling her belly tighten up and then relax.

"I am meant to be meeting some leaders with Domnall today," Cinaed told her as the first glimpse of the sun was seen over the isle of Mull. "We were planning to take a boat over there." He gestured to the island. "I would be back this night, but perhaps I should not be away today."

Baena looked at him in some impatience. "No, go. The day is so fine that I want to get our chamber aired and the bedding washed. It will be easier without you around."

Cinaed laughed and kissed her. "Very well. But do not do too much. You must save your strength."

For around an hour the women worked when Baena suddenly felt a sharp pain build up across her stomach.

"Are you in pain, my lady?" Kieta asked.

Baena straightened up. The pain had gone. "No. Hurry with the work." She felt a strong sense of urgency and the sight of the women staring at her was irritating.

The women gave each other meaningful looks but did as they were commanded. The pain returned several times during the morning. At midday the women urged her to drink some gruel.

"And maybe one of these oat cakes," Kieta suggested.

Baena sipped at the gruel but grimaced at the sight of the dry oat cake. Then came a stronger pain. Kieta took the bowl from her and held her hand until it ebbed away. Baena looked at her, fear in her eyes.

"All will be well, my lady," Kieta soothed. "Your babe is ready to come. Perhaps when the Lord Cinaed returns this night he will have a fine son waiting to greet him."

Baena nodded. She sipped a little more gruel but then retched. "I cannot eat," she whispered.

Kieta signalled to the other women and they helped Baena to the chamber that had been prepared for the birth. A fire had already been lit and fresh straw was lain out. The women hung a thick blanket over the tiny window, plunging the room into shadows. The Abbot was quickly summoned for prayers.

For a long time he prayed for a safe delivery for both mother and child. Then sending the women from the room he spoke privately to Baena.

"My daughter, you bear these pains as Eve's penance for her wickedness in the Garden of Eden. You must bear them bravely and without complaint as it is God's will. There are times when God requires a woman to make the final sacrifice. If he calls you from the world this day you must pass without sin. My daughter, is there anything you wish to confess?"

With a fresh pain building, Baena's mind scrambled. But as it released some thoughts occurred to her. "Jealousy," she whispered. "I am jealous and have believed my lord husband of wrongdoing. I am short tempered and have displayed anger too freely. And I am afraid, Father. I know I must bear this, but may God forgive me I am so afraid."

"The Lord God has seen into your heart and will know that you have truly repented. The Holy Mother of God may too have known fear that night in the stable, but she bore it bravely and so will you."

The Abbot rose to go, but Baena held out a hand. "Wait. I have never confessed this before, and it is so great a sin I do not know if I can ever be forgiven. In the early days of my marriage, I had lustful thoughts for a man not my husband. Cinaed has forgiven me, but can I ever truly be forgiven?" Baena felt fresh fear bursting from her. This pain would be nothing compared to the fire pits of hell that were sure to be her doom.

"Is your heart now true to your husband? Are you faithful to him in both thought and deed?"

"Yes, Father."

"Then be at peace, my daughter. Your sins are absolved. The blessings of Christ and Saint Columba be upon you." He gave Baena a kindly smile and marked a cross on her forehead with the waters of Saint Brigid's well. "You will be in my prayers this day, my child."

After the Abbot left the women returned. They brought her hot ale infused with herbs.

"Drink this, my lady it will ease the passage of your babe," Kieta told her.

During that long day, Baena paced around the room. Time started to have no meaning. With the window covered and the door bolted she had no idea if it was night or day. At some point, she felt a gush of liquid and knew that the birth waters had gone. After this, the pains began to last longer and come quicker. She barely had time to recover from one before the next built up. It was impossible to stifle her cries.

Then she heard voices at the door.

"Come away, my lord."

"No, I must know what is happening." It was Cinaed. In the fog of pain, Baena realised it must be nightfall if Cinaed had returned.

Around her the women looked at each other. Kieta went to the door.

"We cannot open the door, my lord. My lady's time is close. It will not be long now."

More muffled voices were heard and then there was silence apart from Baena's increasingly desperate cries.

Soon after that the pains changed and she felt the urge to push.

"It won't be too much longer, my lady," Kieta said, helping her onto the straw. Some of the other women pushed amulets under the straw with whispered prayers for her protection. Baena felt more frightened than ever and clung frantically to Kieta's hand. She knew she was at that point when the evil spirits would gather to attack her and her babe and could only hope that the prayers of protection would be enough.

"I can't do this. I can't go on!" she cried at the end of her strength.

"You must," Kieta wiped her brow with cool water. "We can see the head. The babe is coming."

Baena shook her head. She could feel the babe slipping back up between each push. She had heard of too many women where the child got stuck and died. She began to cry. "I can't go on. I have failed."

"No, my lady. You have not. Keep pushing."

Given a choice Baena would have ignored her. She felt at the end of her strength. Her arms and legs were shaking from sheer exhaustion, but her body seemed to have a will of its own and somehow kept going.

It seemed an age before the pain changed again to an intense burning. The women were all suddenly very excited.

"Try not to push, my lady."

Baena held off as long as she could, but eventually, the push came. There were cries of delight from the women.

"The head is out, my lady. One more push."

Baena's spirits suddenly rallied. One more push. She could do this. There was a strange slithery sensation and she collapsed back onto the straw. Around her the women all smiled happily as they placed the wet, squirmy bundle in her arms. Baena felt tears of joy streaming down her cheeks. It was over and the pain was gone. She looked down into the big shiny eyes staring up at her, hardly able to believe that her babe was here.

"Is it a boy?" she asked.

Gently Kieta turned the baby over and everyone's faces beamed. The baby began to cry, that first croaky little cry.

"A boy. My prayers have been answered. Cinaed has a son!" Baena said as she brought her squalling son to her breast.

In the hall, Cinaed knew nothing of the jubilation that was taking place in the birthing room. For hours he had sat staring at the fire flinching at every cry he heard. He had prayed in the beginning, but now even that seemed useless.

He was so intent on his own fears that he did not even notice that Baena's cries had stopped. When Kieta burst into the hall he started violently.

"My lord, you must come. The Lady Baena has been delivered of a fair son!"

Some cheers burst from Domnall, Graunt and the other men who had waited with him. Cinaed stood up, unable to take in the words he had just heard. Nervously he followed Kieta to the birthing chamber. Pushing open the door, his eyes went straight to where Baena was lying, lit up by the torchlight. Nothing had prepared him for the sight of her. He had never seen her look so white and exhausted. Concerned he knelt down next to her and looked into her eyes. They were filled with a happiness that took his breath away.

"We have a son, Cinaed. I would like to call him Causantin, for my father if that has your agreement?"

For once Cinaed was lost for words. He could only nod as he looked down at the baby suckling at her breast. Putting his arms around them he silently vowed to protect them both as long as there was life in his body.

Part Four: Year of our Lord 838 – 839

Chapter one

It was one of the last days of summer and Baena sat on the grass, enjoying the warmth of the sun on her face. Her second son, three-month-old Aed lay on her lap while Causantin toddled around happily. Baena felt a surge of gratitude every time she looked on his little face. He was a son to proud of, so strong and sturdy. Glancing down at Aed she prayed it would be the same for him. So far he seemed as hearty as his brother, but it was early days yet.

The two and a half years since Causantin's birth had been happy ones and often Baena wished that life would always be like this. Apart from when he was needed for defence on the eastern front, Cinaed was mostly at home. Support among the clan chiefs for King Aed remained strong, but the king never forgot that Cinaed had been his first supporter and rewarded him richly. Cinaed had decided to display both his gratitude and his continued loyalty by naming his second son for the king.

Aed's birth had been far easier than Causantin's and Baena had recovered quickly. She felt proud that she had given Cinaed two such fine boys.

The peace of the afternoon came to an abrupt end when Causantin stopped his game and stared transfixed out to sea.

"Boat. Boat. Mama, boat."

Causantin was jumping up and down in excitement and Baena smiled. Causantin loved boats and that summer every time the weather had been fine he had pestered his father or uncle until they had taken him out in a little coracle.

Kieta came out of one the round houses, her own baby daughter in her arms. Two years previously, soon after Causantin's birth, Baena had become aware that even when he was talking to her Graunt's eyes had often wandered to Kieta. Her suspicions were further aroused when she noticed them in deep conversation at the midsummer feasts. She was, therefore, unsurprised but still delighted when Graunt asked Cinaed for permission to wed Kieta. Their handfasting later that summer had seen the whole island come alive with singing and dancing.

Now as Kieta started to come towards Baena she looked out to where the excited child was pointing and froze.

"My lady, they look like Norse boats!"

Baena glanced up. The boats of the Norsemen were nothing unusual in these parts, but this was not just one or two boats. This was a fleet, their carved prows sweeping relentlessly forwards. Baena leapt up, ignoring the sleepy protest of Aed.

"What are they doing here?" she gasped. "Are they raiding us?"

The two women looked at each other helplessly. Despite the rigours of childbirth, both were still young and very pretty. And everyone knew what the Norsemen did to pretty young women who fell into their clutches.

At that moment, the abbey bell began to toll.

"Quick," Baena gathered her wits. "The abbey is the best-protected place. Causantin, come with Mother."

"Boat! Boat!" the child was still beaming.

Baena had no wish to frighten him. "Causantin we must go to the abbey. The bell is calling us."

Causantin did not need telling twice. Those strict men of God had taken the little boy to their hearts and the Abbot himself was the very worst at feeding the child forbidden treats. Baena grabbed his hand and they hurried towards the abbey. They were not the only ones. Brothers and islanders alike were taking refuge. Many of the older brothers, including the Abbot, remembered previous raids by the Norsemen on Iona.

"You are welcome here, my lady," said the Abbot, outwardly calm. "I do not understand why the Norsemen are coming. Our treasure is long gone, save the bones of Saint Columba himself."

"Would they want that?" Kieta asked, wide-eyed with fear.

Baena shook her head. "They are only of value to the God fearing Norseman and I do not think they would attack the abbey. The heathen scum would, but old bones hold no value to them."

"You are very wise, my lady. We shall pray that you are right," the Abbot said solemnly

"But what of your jewels, my lady?" Kieta asked.

"I have a few," Baena admitted, "But surely not enough for a raid of this size." She looked frantic. "They can have them if only they will leave our babes alone."

"My lady, every man here will protect you to the death. Now make yourselves as comfortable as you can. I think we might have some honey cake for this young man," and he tousled Causantin's head.

They were interrupted by a loud banging on the door that made everyone jump. A few people cried out and Baena bit her lip as she wondered if the Norsemen could have arrived so quickly.

But a familiar voice made her relax. "Open in the name of the Chief!"

The heavy bolts were pulled back and Cinaed entered. He looked relieved to see Baena and the children there.

"What is happening?" Baena hurried to him. "Are they raiding us?"

"I'm not sure. They may be passing us to head down the coast. I hope so," he added grimly.

Baena's face crumpled as she looked at her sleeping baby. She felt wretched that to wish the raid away from them simply meant that others would not be so fortunate.

Cinaed understood her thoughts. "I have sent Graunt to light the beacon. We must pray that the people of Dal Riata heed our warning."

"Father!" Causantin had heard his father's voice and hurled himself at Cinaed's legs.

Despite the danger they were in Cinaed could not help but smile. He made no attempt to disguise his pride in his handsome little son as he picked Causantin up and held him high in the air. The boy shrieked with glee. Cinaed kissed him and lowered him gently back down. He kissed Baena as well and stroked the cheek of the baby.

"I must go, my love. I stopped here for just a moment to ensure that you were safe. Domnall is marshalling the men on the shore. If the Norsemen are planning on stopping here we can show them we are no easy target." Cinaed raised his voice so everyone could hear. "If there is any man or boy here who can bear sword, club or bow come with me now. Brothers who have sworn not to bear arms come also. If you can bash a drum or shriek down a pipe you can strike fear into the hearts of the Norsemen!"

There was a burst of activity in the room as men hurried to do Cinaed's bidding.

"Father, I place the life of my lady and my sons in your hands," Cinaed bowed to the Abbot.

The great door was opened once more to allow the men out and Baena had to restrain Causantin who was determined to follow his father.

"For Clan Mac Alpin and Saint Columba!" they heard Cinaed roar. The answering shout from the men was deafening, almost as deafening as Causantin's howls at the outrage of being left behind.

Baena sank down, cradling both her children close to her. She looked helplessly at Kieta and the Abbot. All they could do now was wait. It wasn't long before they heard a great noise from the beach and Baena wished she could see what was going on. The noise sounded terrifying, but there was none of the cries or howls of agony that would be expected from a battle, so she assumed that it was just a show of strength from the men.

It seemed a long time later that a thump on the door came again. This time it was Graunt.

"It is safe to come out, my lady," he said before greeting his wife. "The Norsemen have sailed past. They are headed down the coast."

Baena left Causantin in the charge of the Abbot and handed the baby over to one of the women before heading out. Cinaed was stood on the hill looking over the mainland. Joining him she could see smoke rising from a place further down the coast.

"Jesu!" she said in quiet shock and crossed herself. She had grown up with the tales of the savage Norse attacks but had never witnessed one. Watching the billows of smoke she could only imagine the terror of the residents. Men would be slaughtered outside their homes while the women would be beaten and defiled. She wondered what would become of the little children, like her own Causantin. Were they slaughtered as well or were they left to toddle through the smoking wreckage, stumbling over their father's bodies?

"We have been free of raids these last few years," Cinaed said, his helpless anger betrayed by the clenching fists.

"Is there nothing we can do?" Baena asked, although in her heart she already knew the answer.

"For them?" Cinaed gestured towards the smoke. "Pray for them. That is all. But in the morn I will send a messenger to the King. He must know that our settlements are under attack once more." He turned away, unable to watch the smoke any longer. "If only those damned Picts would stop harassing us. If they joined us we would have a chance at beating back the Norsemen." A thoughtful look came over Cinaed's face, but he said no more.

"Will we have to leave here?" Baena asked, looking across the island in regret. She had come to love it there.

"It may be," Cinaed said slowly. "Unless I can find some way to keep you all safe here."

Chapter two

Life almost got back to normal on the holy Isle of Iona, as no more Norse dragon boats were seen swooping over the waves towards them. The day after the raid Cinaed took boats to the destroyed settlement and brought some survivors back with him. His face looked bleak when he returned. He refused to describe to Baena what he'd seen, but that night she was woken by him crying out and thrashing around on his pallet. Holding him close after that nightmare painted a far more frightening picture to Baena than any he could have described.

The survivors were mainly women who had fled with nothing but their torn clothes. All were grieving the loss of husbands, brothers, fathers and even children. All were silent on what had occurred, but, with a breaking heart, Baena suspected that several would bear children with Norse features next year.

"They are demons!" Baena raged to Cinaed, after trying to comfort yet another bruised, sobbing woman.

Cinaed held her in his arms. "I have sent a messenger to the King. We need more protection on this coast."

"How can you protect an entire coast?" Baena cried and turning to Domnall she added, "I suppose you think this is all glorious battle, don't you?"

Domnall shrugged. "The King could send many more men to protect this coast, Sister, if only we didn't need so many on our eastern borders to protect them against the Picts!"

"You are blaming my people for this atrocity?" Baena shrieked, barely able to believe her ears.

"Oh be quiet, both of you," Cinaed said, mildly.

"But-" Baena started.

"No Baena, I will not make Domnall apologise for his words. The truth is I have tried many times to forge an alliance with the Picts against the Norsemen, but instead they take advantage of our weakened state to attack our borders."

Domnall was smirking at this, but Cinaed fixed him with a stern gaze. "Baena is right too. There is no glory in this warfare and you are a fool if you think otherwise. Attacking helpless women and babes is cowardly and breaks one of our most ancient laws. If any member of my clan behaved in this fashion my wrath would be terrible. They may be sailing away with coffers of treasure, but their souls will be damned for all time."

Reproved both Baena and Domnall cast their eyes down and in the silence they missed the way Cinaed was looking thoughtfully at them both. Eventually Cinaed broke the tension.

"Baena, my love, please return to the women. They have need of your care. I would speak with Domnall alone."

Cinaed did not inform Baena of what he'd said to Domnall, but a few days later Domnall took a boat to Mull. Baena was still angry with him and so did not inquire as to where he was going or when he might return. With some hesitation, Cinaed decided that they would remain on Iona for the winter at least, as poor weather meant that further raids would be unlikely.

"But I think you should return to the mainland in the spring with the babes," Cinaed told her. "I saw those women too. I could not bear for such a thing to happen to you."

Baena had never been so glad to see the onset of the stormy winter weather. A wet tunic on the way to the church was a small price to pay for the rough seas that would keep them safe.

The news when the messengers returned from the King was bad. The Norsemen had conquered much of Ireland and there could be little doubt that their own coast would be likely to face serious attack in the next years. Night after night Baena stared at her sleeping children and wondered what would become of them all.

Around a moon before Yule Tide Cinaed received another message. He listened privately to the messenger, his face tightening. Afterwards he spoke to Baena.

"If the weather remains calm we will have some guests arriving soon. Be prepared to host."

"Guests? At this time of year? Who are they?"

Cinaed hesitated and Baena was sure she saw a flicker of misery cross his face. "Some chiefs," he said at last.

Cinaed said no more, but Baena was happy to have something positive to do and gladly made the preparations. Two days later she was outside when she looked towards the mainland. To her horror, the unmistakable shapes of three dragon ships were headed straight for their island.

For a moment she froze, her gaze fixed on the boats in terror. Then screaming for Cinaed she ran back into their dwelling. She collided with him in the doorway.

"What is wrong?" he asked.

Terrified she pointed at the boats. "They are coming for us," was all she could say. Her mind raced to her innocent children as horrifying visions of their little bodies being thrown to the rocks consumed her.

Cinaed looked miserable but remained calm. "So our guests have arrived."

Baena stared at him, convinced she hadn't heard him properly. "What?"

"Make ready. Let the ale flow freely. I have much to discuss with these men."

Baena finally found her voice. "The Norsemen are our guests? Are you mad?"

Cinaed's face hardened and he suddenly looked older. "No, my love. Desperate. I would make a deal with the Devil himself to keep you and the clan safe."

"You are making a deal with the devil," Baena said flatly.

Cinaed sighed and shrugged. "I will do what I must and so must you. Support me in this Baena. Prepare the feast. I must go and greet our... guests."

Baena gritted her teeth and prepared to entertain the enemy. As she poured out the welcome cups she wished more than anything that she had some poison to drop in them. Soon she saw a group of around ten men approaching the dwelling, led by Cinaed and Domnall. So that was where he had been, Baena thought bitterly, hobnobbing with his Norse kin. She should have guessed.

"Welcome to Iona!" Cinaed announced genially as they reached the dwelling. "The holy Isle," he added. "And here is my lady! My love, may I present My Lords Gunn, Camrodd and Geirr."

Plastering on a smile as false as Cinaed's, Baena served the men.

"You have a most beautiful wife, my Lord Cinaed," Gunn said in a strongly accented voice and it took every bit of self-control that she possessed to stop herself shrinking away from the admiration in his cold blue eyes.

Domnall's face was triumphant as she served him his cup. He grinned at her in a way that showed he knew exactly what she was feeling and Baena itched to throw the hot drink over him. Seeing him here with the other Norsemen, his own Norse heritage was obvious and Baena shivered as she wondered how close he had become to them.

"You need not stay," Cinaed told her jovially. "We shall serve ourselves, shall we not?" he added to Camrodd.

"We shall miss her beauty." Camrodd took her hand and to her disgust, he kissed it. "But you are right, Lord Cinaed. This council is not for women."

"Then I shall leave you to your deliberations, my lords," Baena said as brightly as she could and left them in the hall.

The Norsemen stayed for three nights. Baena kept her distance from them and at night she and Kieta took all the children to Baena's chamber and bolted the door. At the end they took their leave with the same respect they had shown when they arrived and Geirr made a speech thanking her for her hospitality with a pleasure that seemed genuine. All the same, she felt a huge sense of relief when the dragon boats glided out to sea.

Chapter three

Once she'd watched them sail out of sight she returned to the hall. It was a mess, with platters of half eaten food and bones on the floor. Some of the tapestries hanging on the wall were stained with ale. Baena looked around in disgust, hoping that rats had not already been attracted by the debris.

"You will not regret this Cinaed," Domnall was saying.

"I trust not."

"What have you agreed?" Baena asked them.

"They have agreed to leave this stretch of the coast alone," Cinaed said slowly.

"But that's wonderful!" Baena cried in admiration. "How did you do that?"

Cinaed looked tortured. "I think you should not ask me that."

"Why?"

"Just tell her, Brother. She will find out," Domnall said, putting his feet up on the table.

"Tell me what?" She looked from one man to the other, realising that Domnall looked far happier than Cinaed.

"They have agreed to leave our coast in peace in return for information we have on the Pict defences," Cinaed said, his eyes pleading for Baena's understanding.

Baena froze in horror. "You have sent those demons to attack my people?" she said desperately, hoping that she had misunderstood him.

"It makes sense," Domnall said buoyantly. "The Norsemen stop attacking our coast and the Picts are distracted from our Eastern borders."

Baena ignored him. She stared pleadingly at Cinaed. "You cannot do this."

"I have," Cinaed replied gravely.

"They may attack my father's territories! You promised me you would not attack my father."

"I am not attacking your father. My promise stands."

"But you will set those monsters onto him. How can you do this?"

Cinaed's look of anguish deepened. "After the raid, I sent word to your father. I asked him to bring Pict men to support us, as was in the terms of the alliance. He refused. He would not even pledge his own men. He knows that you and our sons are in danger, but he has said it is our problem."

"I don't believe you! My father would never desert me." Baena felt like weeping as she wondered how she could ever forgive Cinaed for this.

"Your brothers have played a fine part in attacking our settlements," Domnall put in. "I fought against them myself last year. So much for the great union, you were supposed to bring us."

"Be quiet, Domnall!" Cinaed thundered. "I did not wish Baena to know all this."

Domnall refused to look ashamed. "I am just saying that our alliance with the Norse is better. You have made a good choice today, Cinaed. The Picts have proved they cannot be trusted."

Cinaed gave a joyless laugh. "I do not trust the Norse either. My alliance with them lasts as long as it suits me."

Domnall frowned. "And how long will that be?"

Cinaed shrugged. "Until the Picts are tired of the attacks and are willing to listen to our terms for alliance."

Domnall flushed with anger. "I worked hard to make this alliance, Brother. And you will throw it away to ally yourself with the faithless Picts?"

"Your efforts are much appreciated. But you are naïve if you thought it would be a lasting alliance. The Norsemen will leave us alone for a little while, but they would be back one day and you know it. I would prefer the alliance to be broken on my terms."

"The Picts will never ally themselves with you," Baena hissed. "Not when they hear of this."

"The Norsemen will not forgive this," added Domnall angrily. "When they find out your treachery…"

"Who will tell them? You, Brother? And Baena, will you betray me to your father?"

"You are asking me to betray my people?" Baena asked.

"And me to betray mine," Domnall added flatly.

Cinaed's grey eyes turned cold. "I see. I thought you two were the ones closest to me. But it seems I was wrong." His eyes narrowed. "Get out! Get out both of you! Pack your belongings and say farewell to your sons, Baena. Go back to your people."

"But, Cinaed-" Baena cried.

"What? Did you think I would let you take my sons? Get out! And you Domnall. Go to your kin! You are no brother of mine." Cinaed's rage rose and he stalked towards them.

Domnall fell back uncertainly, but Baena stood her ground. She had never seen him so angry and half expected him to strike her. But even so she detected the pain in his voice and suddenly she realised how hard it had been for him to take this step. He glared down at her, standing so close she was forced to step back.

"Get out of my home."

"No," Baena tossed back her hair and glared back at him.

This gesture only enraged Cinaed further. He seized hold of her arm and dragged her towards the door.

Baena pulled back, although her strength was nothing compared to his. "Stop it, Cinaed," she cried breathlessly. "You can beat me. You can even kill me. But I will not leave you. I would never leave you."

Cinaed dropped her arm and Baena stumbled back.

"You are Pict," he said.

Baena nodded.

"Then you will have to leave. I want no Picts in my clan." Cinaed no longer sounded angry, just very sad.

"Oh, Cinaed..." Baena reached out to comfort him, but he held up his hands.

"No, Baena. I told you long ago that there may come a day when you would have to decide whose victory you would pray for. That day has come. Decide. Are you Pict or are you of Clan Mac Alpin?"

The pain Baena felt at this was so severe it took her breath away, but she did not hesitate. Falling to her knees she recited the traditional oath of fidelity that a clansman must swear to the chief, amending only a part to reflect her femininity.

"And I swear by almighty God and in the name of Saint Columba to be a true clanswoman. If danger commands it I will lay down my life for the good of Clan Mac Alpin and I will serve you, Lord Cinaed for as long as there is breath in my body."

Baena bowed her head and remained kneeling before him.

"And you, Domnall? You swore that oath to me once over our father's body. Does it still have meaning to you now? I will accept no Norsemen in the clan. I will release you from your oath if you wish."

But Domnall shook his head and went down on one knee next to Baena. "I am of Clan Mac Alpin. I swear by almighty God and the bones of Saint Columba that I remain true to the oath I swore by our Father's soul."

Cinaed's face cleared. He knelt down with them and took a hand of each.

"These are dangerous times. Many will not survive, but I am determined that we will. Baena, I know how hard the bargain I have driven must seem, but I would willingly strike a worse one to keep you and our sons safe. I too swore an oath when I accepted the clan leadership to protect my people. I cannot like my course of action, but my preferences must not come before protecting the clan."

Tears poured down Baena's cheeks. "I release you Cinaed from the oath you swore not to attack my father. If you must do so for the good of our clan, you have my blessing."

Cinaed brought his head down to rest against Baena's. "Oh my love, I know how hard it is for you to say this. I thank you."

Not to be outdone Domnall said, "I should not speak for the Norse chiefs, but I release you from the blood oath you swore with those three today."

Cinaed smiled. "I thank you Brother, but it was not my blood. It was the blood of a pig."

Domnall gaped. "What? You mean the Norse chiefs swore an oath with a pig?"

Cinaed grinned rather shakily and nodded. Pulling both Baena and Domnall into his arms all three burst into slightly hysterical laughter.

When Cinaed climbed into bed next to Baena that night she looked at him in some surprise. He had lain away from her since Aed's birth as the baby still fed during the night.

"I know it is a little soon," Cinaed said reading her thoughts. "And I do not wish to get you with child again just yet. But on this night, I do not want to lie alone."

Baena moved the sleeping baby to lie on the other side of her and snuggled up to Cinaed. "Nor do I," she whispered. "Cinaed, did my father really refuse to aid us?" In her heart, she knew that Cinaed would not lie to her about such a matter.

"I am sorry, my love. I wish I had not had to tell you that."

Baena rolled onto her back and stared up at the dancing shadows, feeling bereft. Cinaed pulled her back into his arms.

"You must not blame him. He is a leader and he has to do what is right for his people, just as I have to do what is right for mine."

Baena leant her head against Cinaed's shoulder. "And I am one of your people now, not one of his."

The baby stirred and let out a whimper. Baena picked him up and brought him to her breast. Cinaed looked at his wife, her hair falling around her shoulders, as she nursed his son and smiled. "As one of my people you can be assured that wherever you or your children are I will always come to your aid."

Baena lay back down, her baby still in her arms. She smiled back. "He is cutting teeth, I think. You will not get much sleep if you lie here."

"I would still prefer not to be alone tonight," he said placing an arm around them both.

"You are never alone, my love. Wherever you are my heart is with you."

Chapter four

The Year of our Lord 839 was to be a momentous one, but at the years beginning they were merely fearful. The spring came early that year and they worried that the fair weather would bring the dragon boats over from Ireland or down from the Norse lands. Messengers began to bring reports of attacks on the Pict coasts, but their own remained at peace. It seemed Cinaed's plan was working.

However despite the peace, Cinaed decided it would be best to move his family to Dunadd and place them under the direct protection of the King. When he informed Baena of this she worried about the rigours of the journey on her little ones, especially Aed who had spent the winter going from one minor ailment to the next.

"I'd rather he took his chances on the path to Dunadd than risk a Norse raid," Cinaed commented looking at his son, who responded with a toothless grin. This little lad had soft wispy hair and Baena's clear eyes. Cinaed stroked his head. "He is well enough at the moment."

"I will be glad to be at Dunadd again," Baena said. "It is just the journey that worries me." Baena was longing to feel safe again. Every time she left her dwelling she could not help scanning the seas for fleets of dragon boats and she flinched every time the abbey bell rang, in case it was alerting them to danger.

"We will take it slowly, going over land as much as we can, since the seas are so unpredictable at this time of year. If either lad seems unwell or the weather turns against us we will stop awhile. I'm sure there's not a dwelling between here and Dunadd that would not be pleased to offer us refuge."

Baena agreed and began the long task of packing their belongings and preparing foods for the journey. There was also the sad business of saying farewell to the Abbot and the others on the island who seemed almost like kin. She couldn't escape the feeling that they were deserting these people at a time they might need them the most.

Almost too soon the day came to leave. The boat was loaded and the Abbot and all the brethren came to pray for their journey.

"Fare you well, Father," Cinaed said bowing before the Abbot. "It is woeful to go. I had thought my lads would study at the abbey as I did."

The Abbot blessed him. "I know, my son, but that would still be a few years off. Perhaps times will change again and they will yet."

Cinaed helped Baena on to the boat and settled her with Aed. Kieta soon joined her with her own baby, as Graunt too was making the move to Dunadd. Baena tried to keep Causantin with her as the boat headed over the swell of the waves, but, of course, the boy would have none of it and soon escaped to where his father and uncle were standing in the prow. Domnall laughed and lifted him up so he could see more. Baena shook her head, but in spite of the faint feelings of mistrust that she found hard to shake off, she knew that Domnall would not allow Causantin to come to any harm.

It was a short journey to Mull, where horses were loaded and saddled. Aed was strapped onto Baena's back so they could ride with Cinaed while Causantin rode with Domnall.

"It will be time to start teaching Causantin to ride once we get to Dunadd," Cinaed commented.

Then he turned his horse around and took a long last look at Iona. The abbey looked as peaceful as ever, nestled in the grasslands with the great rocky hill looming over it. Baena shared his sadness. They had been so happy there.

"I have a feeling I will never see my home again," Cinaed commented quietly.

"If the Norsemen do not attack could we not come back?" Baena asked.

"I don't know. I just have a feeling I will not." Slowly he turned his horse away.

Baena tightened her arms around his waist and leant her face against his back. "Does it matter, my love? As long as we are together."

"True." Cinaed urged the horse into a canter to catch up with Domnall, Graunt and the rest of their little band. They did not look back again.

Several days of sleet and rain delayed their journey, but as Cinaed had predicted there was no trouble finding a settlement that would grant them refuge. However, warm as their welcome was it was nothing compared to the welcome they received when they finally arrived at Dunadd. Baena had not seen King Aed since she and Cinaed had set off on campaign all those years before and so she was taken by surprise by how highly Cinaed was regarded among the Chiefs. The lavishness of the banquet laid on to welcome them took her breath away.

All too soon Cinaed had to leave. The borders still needed protecting, but he said he could leave a lot easier knowing that they were safe at Dunadd.

Baena felt the old familiar fear watching them set off, but in the frequent messages that he sent to the King, he reported that the skirmishes were much lighter than usual and that their casualties were few.

Cinaed returned unscathed before midsummer. His return took Baena by surprise, as she had expected him to be away for longer.

"The Picts have left the border. Our settlements there are safe!" he announced jubilantly on his return.

"That's wonderful!" Baena replied.

Cinaed smiled grimly. "I think they are busy elsewhere."

Baena maintained her smile. "So your plan is working."

"It would seem so. It is good news. The men can put their energies into hunting, raising crops, building new fortifications. Dal Riata can recover."

"And you? What will you do?" Baena asked.

"Teach this young man to ride, to start with," Cinaed announced swinging an excited Causantin round. Then he slipped an arm round Baena's waist and whispered, "Perhaps try to get you with child again."

Baena blushed and laughed. Aed was toddling around now and desperately trying to do everything his brother could do. A new baby would be good.

The summer was a beautiful one and the harvest flourished. Cinaed persuaded Baena to leave the children in Kieta's care and accompany him on a tour of his lands. Despite missing the children Baena loved every moment of the trip. She knew that those golden afternoons when it was just her and Cinaed cantering over the hills would be memories that she would treasure forever.

But the happy times could not last. One evening as they were celebrating the barley harvest a Pict messenger arrived.

"My Lord King of Dal Riata, I bring a message from the Lord Causantin of the Third Royal House."

Chapter five

Baena stared at the man in shock. She felt several sets of eyes on her.

"And what can we do for the Lord Causantin?" Aed asked, casually chewing his food.

"Our stockades are under siege. The Norsemen have laid waste to our coast. The Lord Causantin begs for your help under the terms of the alliance he made with the Clan of Alpin these six years past."

Howls of derision greeted this.

"The Clan of Alpin did you say? Alpin? Would that be the same Alpin that you murdered the following summer?" the King asked.

The Gaels laughed while the exhausted messenger looked uncomfortable.

"Still, that is of no matter. But I am interested to hear that the alliance still stands. I had heard from the Lord Cinaed that the alliance was no more - something he only found out when he asked for your aid in defending our coast."

The jeers raged louder than ever, but Cinaed held up a hand for silence.

"My Lord King, may I suggest that this man is taken to refresh himself and rest a while. We can decide how to best respond to this request."

The King nodded his assent and the Gaels began to talk excitedly among themselves. Cinaed frowned, deep in thought.

"Have you nothing to say, Sister?" Domnall asked. "You usually have much to say on this subject."

Cinaed's sharp eyes shot up to Domnall, but Baena replied, "I will support whatever our chief decides is best for the clan."

Cinaed looked at her in concern. "Do you wish to return to our chambers? The discussion this night will not be an easy one for you."

"No. I must hear what is said. I shall go mad with worry if I cannot."

Cinaed nodded and pushed back his stool to join the group of chiefs around the King.

Domnall sniffed. "I'd fight. It's been a tame summer."

Baena ignored him and instead kept her gaze fixed on the group around the King. The conversation was lively, to say the least, but in the uproar of the hall, it was impossible to hear what was being said.

As the discussion raged around her Baena began to pick out words, most of them insults to the Picts. More flagons of ale were brought and the conversation got even louder. One man got into a heated argument with Domnall, as Domnall pushed the suggestion to join the fight.

"Sacrifice yourself for them? Pah!" the man cried. "But what else can we expect from a clan riddled with Pict scum" and he spat at Baena.

Baena shrank back in shock as the gob hit her on the cheek and Graunt quickly stood in front of her, glaring at the man. Domnall rose up and grabbed the man by the neck.

"You will not insult the Lady Baena. Apologise!"

"It's not just her," the man jeered. "Isn't the great Lord Cinaed half a Pict himself?"

Graunt laughed viciously. "Perhaps you should say that to the Lord Cinaed's face and see how long you live."

"But I would advise you not to be such a fool," Domnall added, shaking the man until his teeth rattled.

Cinaed re-joined them at that moment only to hear the last few words that Domnall had uttered. He looked at Domnall with irritation. "No brawling here, Brother."

Domnall did not let the man go. "You may not care that this man spat on your lady, but I will not stand for it."

An icy stillness came over Cinaed as he looked at the man in Domnall's clutches. Drawing a dagger he held it to the man's throat. "If you insult my lady again you will be very, very sorry. Am I clear about this?"

The man whimpered pitifully.

"Throw him out, Domnall. We have more important matters to deal with than this fool."

Domnall was very happy to oblige, dragging him away, still protesting. Cinaed sat back down next to Baena and reached for her hand. Baena clasped it gratefully. "I am unharmed," she smiled shakily as Domnall returned. "Thank you, Brother, for your defence."

Domnall shrugged. "I'll dash his brains out on the floor if he insults us again. What decision, Cinaed?"

"No decision yet. Wait a moment. The King is about to throw the discussion open to us all."

It took some time for King Aed to get silence in the hall. But, at last, the discussion could begin.

Cinaed was the first to rise to his feet.

"My kinsmen, I cannot forgive that the alliance I made with the Third Royal House has not been honoured and so, unless the King orders it, I will not commit Clan Mac Alpin to this cause." Many chiefs muttered in surprise as this, but Cinaed had not finished. "Despite this betrayal of our alliance, I do not forget that the Lord Causantin of the Third Royal House is my father by marriage. So although I will not commit my clan, I would ask the Lord King's permission to support this cause myself as is right that a son supports his father. I free Clan Mac Alpin of any obligation to me in this matter."

There was a stunned silence as Cinaed sat. Baena stared at him, speechless, a mixture of love and fear in her heart as she wondered how Cinaed would fare in what was sure to be the most terrible of battles without his clan to protect him. A sudden vision of Alpin's bloody head floated into her mind. Caring not at all about the men who were watching Baena flung her arms around him.

"Thank you," she whispered. "It is better than my father deserves."

"You'll not go alone!" Domnall shouted. "You can free me from the obligation of the Clan, but never from that of a brother."

"I'll be with you too!" Graunt spoke up and Baena's heart swelled in gratitude. She felt better knowing that those two most devoted of companions would accompany Cinaed.

"You have my permission, Lord Cinaed. I wish you victory," the King spoke. "But what of the clans? How do we answer the Pict plea?"

A familiar looking man stood up. "Coulym," Cinaed whispered to Baena. "The puppy who would be king."

Baena bit back a smile and prepared to listen.

"We owe the Picts nothing!" he yelled and the hall erupted in cheers. "Let the Norsemen finish them off. Once they depart we can sweep in and take the Pict lands for Dal Riata!"

Domnall got back to his feet, but it was a long time before anyone would listen. Coulym's suggestion was very popular.

"I am all in favour of taking Pict lands for Dal Riata," Domnall announced once the King had managed silence again. "But it would not be so easy once the Norsemen are there. I spent much time in negotiation with the Norsemen last winter."

A ripple of interest went round the room. Most of the chiefs saw Domnall merely as Cinaed's headstrong younger brother. Suddenly they looked at him with new eyes. Cinaed watched Domnall curiously and Baena realised that even he did not know what Domnall was about to say.

"My Lords, when the Norsemen first raided our shores they wanted our treasure. But while they were here they saw our lands, so much better than their own for growing crops and raising livestock. It is this they want now rather than our treasures. If we allow them into Pictavia we cannot be certain they will depart."

"My brother speaks wisely," Cinaed put in. "We have seen their settlements on our coast and they have made a kingdom in Ireland."

"And in the Northern Isles," another chief added.

"If we want more lands we will have to fight the Norsemen at some stage. If we fight now we have allies in the Picts," Domnall finished. "I do not wish to oppose my brother and chief, but my opinion is that the clans should fight now."

The hall descended into uproar once more, as the chiefs discussed this new information with each other.

"I am surprised, Brother," Cinaed said. "I thought you wanted a Norse alliance."

Domnall shrugged. "I am for Clan Mac Alpin and Dal Riata. In a Norse alliance, we would always be at their mercy. We can subdue the Picts easily enough."

Cinaed nodded but said nothing.

"Are you angry at me for opposing you on the matter of the clan involvement?"

"I'm not," Baena put in. "I know the support of Dal Riata is the only hope my father has."

"Good! Then you can defend me from Cinaed's wrath," Domnall snorted.

Cinaed smothered a grin as the King got up to speak.

"So if I have rightly understood the Lord Domnall, if the Norse Men conquer the Picts they will likely surround us on three sides. And of course, the Britons and Angles still press us from the South."

A murmur of assent went around the room.

"Then I think I have no choice but to commit the clans to the defence of the Picts."

Heads began to nod with considerable reluctance.

Coulym spoke once more. "And when this battle is done and our own forces are weakened, no doubt the Picts will encroach on our lands once more. What sort of deal will they understand that will stop this?"

"What sort of deal do you suggest?" asked the King.

Coulym strode round the table to look down on Baena. She shivered at the expression in the man's eyes and Cinaed's hand clenched so hard the white of his knuckles showed.

"It would seem to me, my lords that we have a hostage and a pretty one at that. A female Pict of royal blood is valuable to them. I propose that if they wish to guarantee her safety they will honour our borders. Harass us again and... Well, perhaps they'll see a bit more of her royal blood than they wish!"

The burst of laughter that greeted this was silenced by a splintering crash as Cinaed kicked back his seat.

"Your logic is off, my lord. The Picts have already proved they care nothing for the Lady Baena's safety."

He paused and his narrowed eyes bored into Coulym so hard that the man stumbled back.

"And secondly," Cinaed continued in a menacing tone "the Lady Baena is a member of Clan Mac Alpin and my beloved wife. I would fight to the death to defend any member of my clan and I do not think even death would stop me pursuing to the ends of the Earth the man who threatens my wife."

Cinaed thrust his dagger into the table with brutal strength. Within seconds two more daggers quivered next to it as Domnall and Graunt rose to their feet and stood next to Cinaed, their arms folded. As the three men of the clan glared at Coulym, King Aed broke the tension by laughing out loud.

"Don't be a fool, Lord Coulym. There is nothing to be gained by fighting among ourselves and threatening a woman is not how we conduct matters in Dal Riata. So, apologise to the Lord Cinaed and his lady. Clan Mac Alpin, I think you owe me a new table!"

Coulym mumbled a few words as he backed away. Baena smiled tremulously, as Cinaed and the others sat down. Still scowling, Cinaed put his arm protectively around Baena's shoulders.

"Ignore him, my love. He has never forgiven me for opposing his claim to the crown."

But Baena was shaken. After the happy years with the clan on Iona, it was scary to be treated as a foreigner again. And now that Cinaed was headed to one of the most difficult battles imaginable, it was almost impossible to fix a smile on her face as she listened to the King's plans.

Chapter six

Baena waved Cinaed and the clan away with a fear that seemed to crush her so cruelly that she was surprised her heart could still find room to beat. The men were all in good spirits, singing battle songs as they rode or marched away. But her eyes ached with unshed tears as she wondered how many of these young men would never return.

"Where Father gone?" little Causantin demanded.

The confusion on the boy's face was nearly Baena's undoing as she wondered how she would find the words if she had to tell him that Father or Uncle Domnall would never come back.

"He... He's gone to help your Grandfather," she told him.

Causantin frowned, looking so ridiculously like Cinaed when he was angry that Baena would have laughed at any other time. "Want Father. Want Domnall."

Baena hugged him so he would not see her tears.

"I know, my sweet. Come, let's go practise on your horse. When they come back they will see what a great horseman you have become."

The days passed slowly. Dunadd felt very empty, with so many gone. Everyone tried their utmost to keep cheerful, but it became harder as each day passed and they began to wonder if the battle had yet been joined.

The golden summer came to an abrupt end as days of torrential rain followed one after another. Lying snuggled with her children at night, listening to the rain, she worried about Cinaed resting in a flimsy shelter or trying to manoeuvre his horse through the mud.

As the weeks went by the women had less and less to say to each other and went silently about their tasks. None knew if they were already widowed or if their father or son could be at that moment dying.

One dull evening when the drizzle had finally stopped Baena was outside on the lowest terrace with little Aed in her arms. The child was fretful and so she walked him around hoping that he would soon sleep.

The sound of galloping horses carries a long way in the evening stillness and Baena stopped in her walk to listen to it, her heart thumping with both fear and hope. She placed the now sleeping Aed into the arms of one of her women and ran to the watch tower calling to the man on guard.

"I hear it too, my lady, but there's nothing to be seen in this light."

Baena stood on, as the light faded still further. The unmistakable sound of hoofs continued, but with no sound of any riders and nothing to be seen in the grey light Baena began to wonder if it was a ghost army approaching. Slowly news spread and other women drifted out to stand with her. All looked fearful.

"Why does no one come?" Kieta whispered reaching for Baena's hand.

But Baena could only squeeze Kieta's hand back. She had no answer. Flaming torches were lit, making it even harder for the watchman to see beyond the walls.

They could hear the snorts and whinnies of the horses now, but still no voices. There seemed to be no sign that any human was even with them. Some of the women crossed themselves.

It seemed a long time later that the sounds of horses stopped outside the gates. The women looked at each other, wondering what horrible spectre would be let in if the gates were opened.

The bang on the gates made them all jump, but a weary voice from the other side called out "Open for the return of the clans!"

The women relaxed and chattered excitedly, as the watchmen headed towards the gate. But Baena was still. A victorious army returning is full of songs and laughter, however weary they may be. Other than that one shout, this army was silent.

Boys who were too young to fight streamed down to take the horses, leaving the battle-weary men to make their way to the dwellings.

Baena gave a cry of joy as she realised that it was Cinaed who was leading the men towards them. She ran forward but stopped short at the sight of his face. One side of his face was bruised yellow and purple with the eye almost swollen shut. Baena wondered how he'd been able to ride.

She folded him in her arms and felt him cling to her. Looking up she tried to smile. "Oh Cinaed, you have made a mess of your face!"

But there was no answering smile. "It could not have gone worse," he whispered.

Baena looked around. Domnall stood behind him. She almost didn't recognise him. A scabbed gash ran across his forehead, but it was not so much that as the air of total dejection that hung around him. Baena looked to Cinaed's left side, but there was no sign of Cinaed's most devoted friend.

"Graunt!" she whispered and behind her she heard Kieta let out a terrified gasp.

"He's injured," Cinaed told her. "Quite badly, but he is on his way back."

Kieta closed her eyes and murmured a prayer of both plea and thanks.

"Tell me what has happened," Baena said anxiously.

She had looked round. Even for just an advance party, the returning group was tiny.

Cinaed shook his head. "It was the bloodiest day in the history of Dal Riata. So many of our best warriors are gone. Half, maybe more of our nobility wiped out. I have seen defeat before, but never anything like this."

"King Aed is dead," Domnall told her solemnly and Baena took his hand on hearing the sorrow in his voice. "He and his guard were cut down almost immediately. Cinaed and I and some of the other chiefs tried to rally the troops, but the heart had already gone from so many. And as other chiefs fell, the task became harder."

"I have fought against the Norsemen in skirmishes and defended settlements from raids, but I have never fought against them in full-scale battle before. They fight with a ferocity I have never seen. They were as a demon hoard." Cinaed fell silent.

Baena felt tears come to her eyes at the thought of so much slaughter. She wondered sorrowfully which of their clan would not be returning. And King Aed was gone. Not long ago he had been laughing with them over a feast and now he would never laugh or feast with them again.

"And what of the Picts?" she asked. "Were their losses as grievous?"

Cinaed reached out and took her hands in his. Baena felt suddenly frightened by the sorrow she could see in his eye. "Their losses were at least as terrible as our own. Perhaps even more so. Their king too was slain." Cinaed hesitated miserably. "Oh Baena, I am so sorry to bring you this news."

"My father?" she whispered, already knowing that she did not want to hear his answer.

Cinaed shook his head. "He fought bravely, my love. I was aside him when he was struck down. I carried him from the field in my own arms in the hope he could be saved, but he was dead before I reached the Pict back line."

Baena buried her face in her hands unable to believe that she would never see her father again. Cinaed put his arms around her, although he knew they would bring little comfort.

"I spoke with him the night before the battle was joined," Baena could hear Cinaed's voice as if through a fog. "He was happy to get news of you and most interested to hear of our sons, particularly his namesake."

Baena nodded and tried desperately to compose herself. She knew that there would be many in need of comfort that night.

"And my brothers?"

Cinaed shook his head sadly. Baena could hardly comprehend what he meant. "All of them?" she choked. The whole of the Third Royal House wiped out at once?

"Hago stilled lived when we departed," Domnall told her. "But his wounds were severe. I do not think he can be saved."

Baena fell to her knees, the tears flowing fast now. The union of Picts and Gaels was what her marriage had been about, but this was the result. Her father, brothers and more than half of the brightest, bravest young men of the land obliterated in one brutal day.

Chapter seven

At the usually bustling settlements throughout Dal Riata, a heavy atmosphere reigned. Grief and fear took a stranglehold of the people as the autumn drew in. At Dunadd, the priests found there were not enough hours in the day to say the required prayers for all who had been lost. Across the land clans met to choose their new chiefs, sometimes having to pick untried, bewildered looking lads of just fifteen years or less, whose fathers, uncles and older brothers had perished in the Norse onslaught.

Clan Mac Alpin was luckier in this respect. Although they too had lost many of their finest warriors, at least both Cinaed and Domnall still stood. Neither man spoke of the battle, but Baena heard from many others how brave they had both been and how given they had both spent the entire battle in the thick of the fighting, it seemed miraculous that they had survived. It was Graunt, on his return to Dunadd, who told her how Cinaed had risked his own life to save him and how they both owed their lives to the great dog Augus, who had stood guard over them as Cinaed had struggled to help his friend from the field. The faithful hound was one more casualty of the Norsemen. He had been struck down as he sank his teeth into the leg of a Norseman who was within a hairs breadth of running his sword through Cinaed.

The news on Graunt's recovery was not so good. He did survive his injuries, but they left a permanent mark as from that day on he walked with a dragging of one leg that rendered him, in his own opinion, useless.

Cinaed disagreed, assuring Graunt that he would always value his counsel even if he was no longer able to accompany him into battle. Kieta privately told Baena that she was almost glad of the injury since it meant that he would never have to risk his life on the battlefield again.

The news from the Picts was similarly glum. Following the battle the Norsemen had sacked many of the Pict settlements and plundered their costliest treasures. All seven of the Royal Houses were all but wiped out and in many cases forced to accept the most minor members as their heads. Baena wept uncontrollably when she heard of the distant kinsman who now headed up the Third Royal House. She knew that this must mean that Hago too had succumbed to his injuries. She wondered what had happened to her mother, now that her husband

and sons were all gone, but the messenger had no news on that. Drust took leadership of the First House and, as the most highborn Pict remaining, was crowned Rex Pictorum. Cinaed shrugged and took that news with a curl of his lip.

"We'll need to give some thought to our own kingship soon," he commented.

"That will be an interesting debate," Graunt said. "With the bunch of children we now have leading the clans. You might as well put young Causantin forward!"

"There doesn't need to be any debate!" Domnall said. "Cinaed, surely you will stand forward this time?"

"The matter still needs to be debated," said Cinaed. "I will have no man say that I took the crown unfairly."

"A short debate," Domnall amended. "But seriously Cinaed, even before the last terrible days you would have been chosen. You have become one of the most respected Chiefs of Dal Riata."

Cinaed waved away the tributes. "You are very quiet, my love. What do you think? You would be Queen of Dal Riata!"

Baena tried to smile. She had been feeling unwell and suspected she was with child again. It was too early to tell Cinaed, but she hoped she was. It would be good to look to the future.

"I should be very proud to see you as King of Dal Riata. But..."

"But what?" Cinaed asked.

"Eochaidh dead in battle. Oengus dead in battle. Alpin... I know he was not King, but he would have been, dead in battle. Aed, dead in battle." Baena bowed her head, tears flowing from her eyes as she thought again of her father.

"Many have died in battle, my love, not just kings." Cinaed put his arm around her.

"Our grandfather Eochaidh was an old man," Graunt said. "Every man must die of something. I would be happy to reach his age."

"I know. I am being foolish. I should be proud to be your Queen, Cinaed."

"Well, we must summon the suckling babes I mean the chiefs," Domnall said. "It will help us all if the matter is settled."

The chiefs were not quite the suckling babes that Domnall had described, but looking out at the welcome feast Baena could see that many of them were very young.

The debate started the next day, but unlike the days and nights spent choosing Aed, this one was over before noon. Cinaed staked his own claim as soon as the discussion started.

"My Lords, I am the son of the great Lord Alpin and the grandson of King Eochaidh. I put forward my name to rule you. Since the death of my father, I have led many a victorious attack on our foes. My claim is a true one. Who stands with me?"

The new young chiefs were in awe of Cinaed and were more than willing to follow him wherever he led. The older, wiser ones recognised Cinaed's abilities. Only Coulym raised a voice of dissent.

"We do not want Clan Mac Alpin in charge of Dal Riata!" he cried. "The clan is in alliance with the Picts."

The older Chiefs shook their heads. Lord Fie, who had once challenged Aed for the crown and was one of Cinaed's few rivals, rose to his feet.

"I have had the privilege to serve alongside the Lord Cinaed and his father, the Great Alpin before him. I can assure you that no one has fought more for Dal Riata than them. I would choose a king who is proven brave and wise in battle, who can triumph by strength or guile over Pict and Norse alike. There is no better choice than Cinaed Mac Alpin!"

The Chiefs roared their approval. Domnall stood up. "All hail King Cinaed!" he cried

"Hail to King Cinaed!" the Chiefs echoed.

Flushed with triumph Cinaed spoke. "I thank you, my lords, for your confidence in me. I shall serve this land well for as long as I have life." Getting up he pulled Baena gently forward. They were now certain she was with child.

"My lords, I present your queen!"

Coulym muttered something about Picts, but he was quickly drowned out as the Gael Chiefs enthusiastically accepted their beautiful queen.

The day Cinaed chose for his crowning dawned as a golden autumn day with just the faintest chill in the air.

"A good omen!" Cinaed commented when he rose at first light.

Sleepily Baena watched him pull on a white tunic of fine wool in a simple design. His ornate sword belt was the only decoration. He was to go to the church alone to pray for guidance in his new role.

They had moved into the royal chambers at Dunadd, which offered a luxury she had never before experienced and there were days when she felt like she never wanted to rise from that sumptuous bed with the fur covers.

Cinaed pulled a comb through his hair, which was still streaked with blond from the golden summer. He had seen twenty-nine years and to Baena was more handsome than ever. The years since their marriage had seen more scars on his body and a few lines on his face, but his grey eyes were as calm as ever and his body even more muscular. Catching her watching him, he grinned and sat back down on the bed.

"It will be a long day. Rest as long as you can."

"I am quite well now. Do not worry about me. This is your day."

Cinaed nodded and it was clear that he had every intention of making the most of the day. The sparkle in his eyes told her that this was a day he had been working towards his whole life. Kissing her lightly he headed for the church.

Baena lay back, but the excitement of the day prevented her from sleeping. She dressed quickly in a simple robe, leaving her finery for later and went to check on the preparations.

Outside fires were ready for lighting. As the weather was so fine it was likely that the feasting would take place outside, but just in case, the hall had been prepared. Fresh rushes were strewn on the floor and the animals that might soil them had been kept well away. Cinaed's banners, many of which she'd sewn herself over the years, were hanging from the ceiling and the King's chair at the head of the table had been freshly lined with fur.

Smells of roasting food drifted from the hearths and laughter rang out from the chambers. Baena felt her own mood lifting. It would take time for the grief of the last months to lift from Dal Riata, but there was to be no sign of it today. Her heart swelled with pride as she realised that it was Cinaed and Cinaed alone who was responsible for this good cheer. A lesser man being crowned today would have been crowned on a sea of tears, but Cinaed brought fresh hope to these beleaguered people as they fervently believed that he was the man who would lead them out of these dark times.

Baena returned to her chamber, calling for a woman to bring water. After washing her face and allowing her women to plait her hair they brought her tunic. It was of a fine green-blue wool, edged with ivory thread. Around her wrist, they fastened her bangles including the gold and amber one that Cinaed had given her at their handfasting. Baena smiled, remembering the reluctance with which she'd fastened that bangle the first time.

As they tied a silver girdle, Baena looked down with some irritation at her thickening waist. Kieta caught her eye and laughed. "My lady, if the new queen is with child, it is said to be a sign of prosperity for the land."

"I know," she sighed. "But I would look my best today."

"You know that Lord Cinaed… I mean the Lord King always considers you beautiful and perhaps never more so than when you are carrying his child."

Baena blushed at this, but there were no more comments as in silence Kieta placed a circlet of gold around her head. The Queen's jewels included a large silver mirror that the women held up for her now. Baena nodded her approval. Perhaps it was vain of her, but she felt happy with how she looked that day.

The church bell began to toll summoning them to join the prayers for the new King. The women quickly draped a soft woollen cloak edged with fur around her shoulders and fastened it with the brooch of the clan. She had many finer ones, but Baena was determined to proudly display her status as a member of Clan Mac Alpin.

"Mother!" Causantin rushed into her chamber with Aed toddling behind as fast as his fat little legs could. Both were dressed in white tunics and their scrubbed faces beamed at her. As ever she felt a huge rush of love and pride at the sight of these two lively little lads and her heart lifted still further. There was fresh hope. As a new generation grew up there would be a return to the great times for Dal Riata.

Baena took a hand of each of her sons. "Come, children, we must hurry to the church."

Chapter eight

People from the household and settlement of Dunadd lined her way as Baena made her way to the lowest terrace. Inside the church, the chiefs and other highborn Gaels were gathering with a solemnity appropriate for the occasion, but outside the mood was joyous. Many of the people waved or even burst into cheers as Baena, the children and her ladies passed through the throng.

Inside it took a few moments for her eyes to adjust to the dim light of the church. Around her, the nobility were all dressed in their finest apparel and there were many smiles directed at the little boys as they followed Baena to the front.

"Father!" Aed's tiny voice echoed in the stone church as he pointed excitedly at the kneeling figure in the white tunic. His head was bowed, almost brushing against the white stone at the base of the altar.

"Shh!" Baena whispered to the boy, but from the twitch of Cinaed's shoulders, she knew he'd heard them.

The bell of the church stopped tolling and the priest entered, blessing them all as he made his own way to the front.

Reaching the altar he raised the cross over them. As one, the nobility of Dal Riata fell to their knees as the priest began the familiar chant. Giving an added prayer that her sons would stay quiet, Baena bowed her head.

As the sacred words finished the people rose. Only Cinaed remained kneeling and the priest rested his hand on his head.

"We pray to the Lord God and to the holy Saint Columba who once stood on this very ground to guide this man on his appointed path as our Lord King. May he be ever strong and victorious in battle, may he be gentle and wise at home. Lord Cinaed Mac Alpin, I command you in the name of Saint Columba to rise."

If Cinaed's legs were stiff from kneeling for so long he gave no sign of it. At a sign from the priest, one of the young chiefs brought a basin of water. Cinaed dipped his hands in it and splashed some over his face.

"The Lord Cinaed has this day confessed all sins to me and by this blessed water he stands before you as if reborn." The priest passed the cross to Cinaed.

"Recite the oath, my son, so that you are reborn this day as King of Dal Riata!"

Silence reigned in the church as Cinaed turned to face them. In spite of his plain tunic, there was no doubting his authority.

"Good men of Dal Riata, I swear this day a sacred oath in the name of God our Father and the blessed Saint Columba to rule you fairly with wisdom and mercy. I vow to see us victorious in battle and to crush our enemies. I will bring prosperity to our fair land and endeavour to make it ever greater for as long as the Lord God grants me breath in my body. From this day, I command your obedience. I am your King!"

Everyone in the church rose. "All hail King Cinaed, Lord of all Dal Riata!"

Domnall and Graunt proceeded forward, as the two most senior members of their clan. There was a slight murmur of surprise among the nobles at the sight of Graunt and Baena's heart went out to him, as he limped painfully towards Cinaed. He had suggested to Cinaed that he not take part.

"The ceremony must be perfect," he had said. "You should show no signs of weakness by having a cripple take such a prominent part. I shall be proud just to be present."

But Cinaed would not hear of it. "There will be many to curry favour with me now," he had told Graunt. "But my true trust will remain with those that have always stood with me. Any who consider that a sign of weakness is a fool. You are my most long-standing companion. I'll not be crowned without you."

Baena had often seen old friends cast aside when men came to power and she felt proud that Cinaed would not act like that.

Over one arm Graunt carried a cloak of thick wool dyed the most wondrous shade of purple and edged with white seal fur. He knelt somewhat awkwardly before Cinaed and received his hand on his head in blessing.

Rising he looked directly at Cinaed and Baena caught the smile that went between the two, as Graunt draped the cloak over his shoulders and fastened it with a jewelled pin.

Graunt stood to one side as Domnall approached bearing a gold circlet. He too knelt to receive Cinaed's blessing. The nobles of Dal Riata held their breath as Domnall lifted the circlet onto his brother's head. Cinaed reached out and clasped the hands of both Domnall and Graunt. There was a faint shuffle in the church, as such an action was not normally part of the ceremony, but Cinaed's motives were clear. Clan Mac Alpin were in charge! And they would always stick together.

"All hail the King!" Domnall and Graunt proclaimed.

"Hail King Cinaed!" the people echoed.

For a time Cinaed stood still, looking over his people and Baena gazed at him. The simple white tunic was transformed by the cloak and the gold in his hair glinted in the candlelight. Causantin and Aed gazed too in wonder and adoration.

Cinaed stepped away from the altar to make his way from the church. As he reached her, Baena knelt before her King. She felt him lay his hand on her head in the traditional blessing he had given to the others, although she suspected he had not caressed their hair as he was stroking hers.

"Rise, Lady Baena," he said solemnly.

She did as she was bidden and he took her hand to place it over his heart. They smiled at each other, a touch of mischief appearing in Cinaed's eyes. When the priest declared Cinaed reborn as King of Dal Riata he granted him the right to leave all ties from his old life behind. It was not unheard of for the new king to sweep past an old or barren wife as a sign that she was no longer to be considered married to him. No one had expected Cinaed to do such a thing as his devotion to Baena was no secret. But even so he kept her hand firmly over his beating heart for longer than was necessary to display to anyone who wondered at their Pict born Queen that her place was not to be disputed.

Keeping her hand in his Cinaed headed slowly towards the daylight. The nobles all sank to their knees as he passed and Cinaed paused before each one to give them his blessing.

Neither Baena nor Cinaed were prepared for the rapturous welcome that greeted them as they left the church. They made a striking pair as they emerged out into the sunlight. Cinaed, so tall and powerful looking stood for a moment smiling at the people, his arm protectively around his beautiful, red-headed queen. As the sun glinted on their gold circlets it seemed to many as if God himself was welcoming them into their realm.

Many in the crowd cast white heather petals into their path as they retired to the middle terrace to break their fast. The weather had remained fine, so the great king's chair had been moved outside and Cinaed sank down into the fur with relief.

Baena took the chair next to him and they looked at each other, trying to take in everything that had happened.

"My father once told me I might be Queen of Dal Riata one day. I don't think I believed him."

"Back then you wanted to believe I was the worst match imaginable!"

Baena reached over and kissed him. "Now, you don't still hold that against me do you, my Lord King?"

Cinaed grinned and squeezed her hand. "Has anyone told you how beautiful you look today? More beautiful even than our wedding day."

Baena laughed. "I don't think you found me very beautiful then."

"Now you don't still hold that against me do you, my Lady Queen?" he teased as others joined them.

After they had broken their fast in a lavish meal of roasted pig served with thick slices of apples and many another dish of fine fruits and leaves, the second part of the coronation took place. Many of the priests started to look disapproving. Known as the Union with the Land, this ceremony was very ancient, from before the day the blessed Saint Columba had arrived on their shores. When planning the crowning some abbots had even suggested to Cinaed that this part of the ceremony should be left out, but Cinaed refused, saying that the people considered this ancient rite to be at least as important as the church blessing.

Later he had told Baena that he considered the Union with the Land to be even more important than the church.

"I know they say that it is God who appoints me and indeed I am glad to have God's blessing, but I believe that it was the land that chose me."

Shaking her head Baena had protested this. "That's heathen talk."

"Why? This is God's land blessed by the sacred feet of Saint Columba. That is the union I seek."

Only the most important people of Dal Riata would attend the Union with the Land, so Baena had not witnessed the ceremony before. Very few women ever did witness it. Certainly none had at Aed's Union, but Cinaed said he remembered his grandmother at Eochaidhs.

"It is time," Cinaed said rising to his feet. The morning was now advanced and it was important that they should be at the sacred rocks by midday.

Baena was still feeling a little uncertain, but she knew that it was important to Cinaed that she accompany him.

A priest frowned as she placed her hand in his. "My Lord King, I must protest you taking your Lady Queen to this. She is breeding and at such time, women are particularly vulnerable to the influence of evil."

Cinaed gave a dismissive wave of his hand. "Forgive me Father, but I disagree. This sacred land of ours has no evil influence. A fertile queen is a blessing for this land and heralds prosperity for us all."

"Father!" Causantin waved at them as they passed the group of children playing among the rocks.

Cinaed paused to give them the traditional King's blessing and watching them he squeezed Baena's hand. "A fertile queen is indeed a blessing. Look at those boys of ours! Did you ever see such sturdy lads?"

Baena shook her head smiling. Those freshly scrubbed, white-clad little lords she had been so proud of that morning were no longer evident, but sturdy and strong they both were. Something she nightly thanked God for.

Domnall led the procession of nobles. His blonde hair gleamed in the sun and clad in a light blue tunic, edged with shimmering duck feathers there were many who considered him to be even more handsome than Cinaed. He was still unmarried and seemed determined to remain that way, but there were several children both here at Dunadd and back on Iona with that same bright hair.

As they reached the start of the processional way to the sacred rocks the quiet conversation among the chiefs and other nobles of Dal Riata fell away as they made the traditional ascent in silence. A breeze blew around them and somewhere a bird cried, but other than that the only sound was their own footsteps on the soft ground.

The climb was steep in places and many rocks blocked their path. Baena lifted her tunic a little to stop it catching on the jagged edges and several times Cinaed put his arm around her waist to help her over some of the trickier spots.

Eventually they reached the carved boar that marked the place where the union with the Land would be celebrated. Cinaed paused and removed his shoes, leaving them in front of the boar. Although the settlement at Dunadd was just below them it seemed like a long way away as they stopped in this ancient place. The sun was almost at its highest point, which on that autumn day was not that high and shadows encroached on the grass where they gathered.

Despite the cloak she was wearing, Baena shivered. She felt even colder when Cinaed moved away from her and wearied from the climb. She would have liked to have sat down, but that was not possible. However, it made her glad of Domnall who took his place next to her. When she looked at him Baena was still struck by his Norse features, but since the terrible battle that summer a new closeness had grown between him and Cinaed. These days Baena could find little reason not to trust him. Although Domnall still professed to admire her beauty, there was none of the lechery in his behaviour that had marked his attitude in the early days of her marriage. Baena suspected that a pregnant woman who had borne two children had little attraction to him, so accepted gratefully the brotherly arm of support he put around her.

Once everyone had assembled Cinaed removed his cloak and was clad once more in just a simple tunic. Only the gold curve on his brow marked him as king. Carved from the rock in front of them was a bowl full of water. Kneeling by it Cinaed scooped the water in his hands. Cupping it he poured it over his hair, so it ran over his face. Then he stood and his great voice cried, "I am cleansed by the waters of Dal Riata!"

There was silence once more as Cinaed stood still until the water no longer dripped down him.

"I am borne by the winds of Dal Riata!"

The timing was perfect. The sun had reached its zenith. Cinaed stretched out his arms to it. "The fires of the sun will feed my reign over Dal Riata!"

Baena felt the hairs on her arm stand up. The magic of the occasion overwhelmed even her Christian soul. Cinaed was transforming before her eyes into the King he was perhaps always meant to be.

Cinaed lowered his arms. He walked barefoot over the grass to a rock overlooking the plain beneath them. Easily he pulled himself up onto it. Deep in the living rock was a footprint said to have been left by Fergus the first King of Dal Riata on these shores. Cinaed placed his right foot into the footprint. The lords of the land looked on with triumphant smiles as Cinaed raised his arms once more.

"I am one with the land of Dal Riata!" His voice echoed across the outcrop. "I Am Dal Riata!"

Everyone present fell to their knees. Their King was crowned.

Cinaed remained on the rock as one by one the nobles returned to the settlement and the celebrations that would spill over the terraces onto the plain beneath.

Soon only Domnall and Baena were left. Looking elated Cinaed sprang down from the rock and retrieved his shoes as Baena wrapped the cloak around him.

"Thanks," he smiled at her. "The winds of Dal Riata are cold at this time of year."

"Well, I'm for the celebrations below," Domnall announced giving Cinaed a sly grin. "I suppose you two are going to stay here awhile!"

Cinaed put an arm around Baena, his eyes running over her figure. "I am tempted indeed, but perhaps it would not be right for a Christian king such as myself."

Baena frowned. "What are you two talking about?"

"It is said that in the days before Saint Columba walked this land the King and Queen of Dal Riata would remain alone up here to bless the land with their fertility," Cinaed said, amused at Baena's obvious shock.

"It was said to be even more fortunate if the Queen was brought to childbed within the year," Domnall added cheerfully.

Baena crossed herself, her face scarlet. "Well, I hope I will manage that!"

"True, but go Domnall. It is fitting that Baena and I descend alone."

After Domnall had left them Cinaed led Baena to the stone basin. Dipping his fingers in the few drops remaining he traced it over her face.

"My Queen," he said looking proudly down at her. "Lady of Dal Riata."

Part five: Year of our Lord 841 - 842

Chapter one

The first year of Cinaed's reign passed smoothly. Cinaed concentrated his efforts on defending their remaining territories against further Norse attacks rather than waste men in trying to reclaim their lost lands. The strategy worked and casualties of war were minimal. Slowly the people of Dal Riata recovered and their loyalty to their king grew. In his first summer as king Cinaed made a tour of a part of his kingdom and had reported that the welcome of the people and the tributes they provided had been even greater than he had expected.

There was much rejoicing when Baena was indeed brought to childbed five moons after the coronation and safely delivered of a healthy girl. They named the latest addition to their family Coira. If Cinaed felt any disappointment at the sex of the child he showed no sign of it but appeared to take great pride in the pretty daughter who looked more like her mother as each day passed.

Towards the end of the year Baena had hopes of another child, but this time, she was not so lucky. She carried the child just five moons before it fell from her in a crimson flood shortly before Yule.

Baena wept bitterly and blamed herself for the loss, but Cinaed refused to show any reproach.

"You have done well with our three sturdy babes," he had told her, taking her in his arms. "It is not to be expected that we should be so lucky every time and there are many who are not as fortunate as us. Once you are well we shall renew our efforts."

Baena had dried her eyes and had determined to enjoy the Yule celebrations, which at Dunadd were on a lavish scale. Causantin and Aed were open mouthed as men with painted faces juggled with swords and even flaming torches. Although still weak Baena cradled her daughter on her lap and laughed as Cinaed and Domnall played with her sons in a way that made it hard to tell which were the two great lords of Dal Riata and which were just babes. As the great procession of fire wound its way to the rocks at the top of Dunadd, Cinaed took his place next to Baena with his now sleepy sons on his lap. Despite her recent loss, Baena felt her heart fill with happiness. Cinaed was right. They were fortunate.

The Year of our Lord 841 started annoyingly. Baena, still recovering from the loss of the pregnancy, became ill. For several weeks she felt weak and useless, with limbs that ached at the slightest exertion. The damp weather that hung around Dunadd did nothing to help either her strength or her spirits.

There was bad news from the border with the Picts, as they yet again began to harass them. Reports reached Dunadd of sheep and cattle being stolen and settlements burnt to the ground. The demand Cinaed sent to Drust to honour the border agreement was sent back with derision and there could be little doubt that the attacks had Drust's personal support.

"What else can you expect from the Picts? Everyone knows they are incapable of honouring an agreement," Coulym raged once Cinaed had summoned the Chiefs.

"They are fools!" cried Domnall. "They are still struggling against the Norsemen. Why harry us?"

At the head of the table, Cinaed frowned. "No doubt it is good for their spirits to make some gains on us. But our message must be clear. Dal Riata will not stand for this. What men can be spared from our western front?"

"Few from our own lands," Graunt said. "The Norse kingdom in Ireland is a grave threat."

"This is ridiculous, Lord King," Coulym burst out. "Are you proposing our men simply stand in a ring around all Dal Riata?"

Cinaed raised his eyebrows. His kingship was too new to be able to afford any weakness. "I am not proposing a defence at all," he announced. "The Picts will understand one thing - an attack."

A current of excitement rippled around the room. Cinaed sat back, a slight smile of satisfaction on his face as the matter took hold. He allowed them to discuss the matter freely before calling the council back to order.

"So, we are agreed. We fight."

This was no question. Cinaed knew that every man was with him.

"My lords, there is much to plan. Return to your clans and muster as many men as you can. Do not leave the Western front undefended. I do not want another Norse battle just yet."

The men nodded their agreement and Cinaed could see the calculations in their eyes.

"Where we attack is important," Domnall said. "I suggest sending scouts to spy on their defences."

"Agreed. I know I can rely on you, Brother, to see to that. Watch the Norsemen too. I would know when they are attacking the Picts."

Domnall laughed. "Good thinking, Cinaed. It would be unfortunate for the Picts if our attack followed hard on a Norse one."

As the scouts returned Domnall ordered them to report only to Cinaed. It was vital for both Dal Riata and Cinaed himself that the attack should be a success. So Cinaed carefully considered each bit of information and planned accordingly.

When Cinaed was ready to share his plan he did so only with Domnall and Graunt. Of all the nobles of Dal Riata, these were the only ones he completely trusted to give an honest opinion. The others were either too in awe of Cinaed or were likely to be looking to their own interests. The fortunes of Domnall and Graunt were so bound up in Cinaed's own that he had no concerns on that front.

He asked Baena to be present at this meeting to lend a family air to the proceedings and prevent the suspicions of the chiefs.

Baena was not completely recovered, but she did not mind. The King's chamber at Dunadd was warm and it felt pleasant to sit with these old friends while stitching a robe for her daughter, even if it did mean listening to plans to attack her own people.

"I assume the pattern of the Norse attacks is to raid to the North?" Cinaed asked.

"Yes," Domnall replied. "They seem to come in waves and Pict men muster there to mount a defence."

"So an attack from the South would stand a good chance of success," Cinaed mused.

"It would, but the Pict territories there are insignificant," Graunt said. "And we risk conflict with the Britons or the Angles if we head down there."

"The last thing I want is another enemy. And if we hit the Picts we must hit them hard. Not their main settlement, not yet. But not too far either."

"There is a stronghold at Forteviot. It is not well defended at the moment," Domnall suggested. "A march on that would have a good chance of success."

"Our own stronghold in Pict territory!" Graunt exclaimed. "I like the sound of that!"

"As do I," Cinaed said grimly. "An excellent suggestion, Domnall."

"I fear I am useless to you in this, Cinaed," Graunt said, looking sadly at his leg.

"You have never been less useless!" Cinaed smiled warmly at his friend. "You remain in charge here. I am happy to be able to leave someone I can trust so well." Cinaed suddenly looked soberly at Graunt. "If I and Domnall do not return, I commend Baena and my children to your care."

Baena shivered. Yet again Cinaed would be headed for battle. Yet again she would wait here wondering and worrying. While he was away she would spend her days in prayer for his victory. But all that victory would mean was a Pict retaliation later on. More and more men on both sides would be lost while the Norsemen waited to swoop down on them. One day it would be little Causantin's turn to ride off, returning with his handsome face scarred if he returned at all. Baena wondered if there was another way. A thought occurred to her and refused to go away.

"Sister! Sister!" Baena became aware that Domnall was standing before her holding a flagon of wine.

"We have tired you out, my love, with all this battle talk," Cinaed commented. "You need not stay. Rest if you will."

Baena smiled and shook her head. "No, I am well enough. Cinaed, may I say something?"

"Of course, my love, though this is men's talk."

Baena nodded and swallowed. She remembered how years ago, in this very castle, Cinaed's dying mother had told her that one day she would be the one to remind Cinaed of his heritage. Baena suddenly felt sure that day had come. He probably wouldn't be happy, but Baena knew if she didn't speak today it was likely she never would.

The three men were waiting for her to speak. She stood up and took a deep breath. "You know Drust will retaliate if you invade."

Cinaed's face froze at the mention of Drust's name on her lips, but he replied courteously enough, "Probably, but there is no choice. The Picts must be subdued. I must defend my people."

"But they too are your people, Cinaed. You are a Pict!"

It was as if the temperature in the room suddenly dropped. Domnall and Graunt both sucked in their breath sharply. Cinaed's face did not change, but the expression in his eyes nearly ripped Baena in two. She could feel him withdrawing from her.

Cinaed's hand flew to the dagger that hung around his waist. "If a man said such a thing to me I would kill him where he stood." His voice was quiet, but the threat sliced through.

From the corner of her eye, she saw the look of consternation that Graunt shot Domnall and both men took a step towards Cinaed. Graunt pulled at the hand that clutched the dagger.

Cinaed's hand fell away from his knife. "This council is over." He looked down at Baena with empty eyes. "Go. Leave me."

Baena shivered. She would have preferred to see him angry. This terrible stillness frightened her, but she had to finish what she started.

"No!"

Domnall stepped forward and gently tugged at her arm, but Baena shook him away. She kept her gaze focused on Cinaed.

"My lord, I have done everything you have ever asked of me. I have lain in your arms and bore you children. I have gone wherever you commanded. I have even renounced my own people for you. I have never asked you for anything, but I am now. All I ask is that you let me speak. After I will do what you command. I will leave this place with just the clothes on my back if that is your will."

Cinaed inclined his head, motioning Domnall away. He said nothing.

"The Pict people, your people are good. They are simply obeying their king. You have the royal blood of the Sixth House in your veins. You could be King of the Picts."

Cinaed's face did not change, but Graunt's jaw dropped still further.

"Your claim is as strong as Drust's. Perhaps even stronger as I bring you the blood of the Third and Fourth Houses. As king, you could stop the attacks on Dal Riata and combine the people against the Norsemen."

Cinaed inclined his head once more. "I thank you for the suggestion. I shall consider it." Cinaed's voice held the same tone that he used when talking to any petitioner. He turned to Domnall and Graunt. "The council is over."

Cinaed strode towards the door. No matter how busy the room Cinaed always acknowledged Baena when he left. Sometimes with just a nod or a smile, but he never just strode from the chamber as he was doing now without so much as a glance.

Chapter two

Domnall and Graunt stared at her in silence as Cinaed left. Baena anxiously wondered where he was headed. The church perhaps or Alpin's grave in the plain below.

"What possessed you to say that?" Graunt demanded, his face displaying both shock and anger. "I never took you for a fool before."

Baena shook her head but said nothing.

"You couldn't have said a worse thing," Graunt continued. "As a young lad on Iona, the boys would often taunt him and call him Pict. Once he was big enough he fought back. He was not much older than Causantin when he broke the noses and blackened the eyes of any who called him Pict."

Graunt stopped short and studied Baena's beautiful face, clearly uneasy at the thought of Cinaed doing the same to her.

"I'm surprised he agreed to marry me," Baena said dully.

"It was our father's idea," Domnall said. "Cinaed was not happy, but after the battle against the Angles, there was no objection he could make."

Baena was surprised as she well remembered the charm he had displayed to her family at their handfasting. But that was what Cinaed did best. He had displayed a similar charm to the Norse chiefs on Iona.

Domnall looked thoughtfully at Baena. He alone seemed to be considering the implications of her suggestion. "Would the Picts really accept Cinaed as their king?"

"Not now, but if he held a stronghold deep in Pictavia they might. So little of the Pict nobility remains. Cinaed is of better birth than the current head of the Sixth House. They would never accept conquest by Dal Riata, but if Cinaed claimed the crown in his mother's name and mine..."

"He'll never do it," Graunt said. "He has spent his entire life denying it."

"What will become of me?" Baena asked pleadingly. "Will he force me from Dunadd?"

Graunt looked out of the little window to the grey world beyond. It was no day for a frail woman to be out in.

"Take my advice, my lady. When Cinaed returns take back your words. Beg his forgiveness. Throw yourself on his mercy. I don't know if he'll ever feel the same about you, but he's not a cruel man. He'd not throw you out."

"I can't do that," Baena whispered. She wondered if staying with an indifferent Cinaed was even preferable to being cast aside. A future where Cinaed visited her chambers occasionally out of duty to coldly beget children on her made her shudder.

"Then you are a fool," Graunt said bluntly. "I don't know what he'll do."

Domnall shrugged. He clearly had no comfort to offer her. "I only hope he does nothing to harm you. There are places on our lands he might send you. It's what I thought he'd do when I first saw you at your handfasting. No one ever thought he would keep you with him always as he has." Domnall tried to smile. "But perhaps it won't come to that."

Baena bit back the tears. She had the rest of her life to weep.

"I'll not take back my words, but I will go where he commands. Domnall, promise me that if he ever has need of me you will bring me to him. I will always be there for him as long as I live."

Domnall nodded and squeezed her hand.

The three were still sitting there in silence when Cinaed returned. His knees were caked in mud, so Baena guessed it was the grave he had visited. She knew he was often there when he needed to think. His face was as expressionless as when he left, but Baena thought that he looked older and broken.

"Leave us," he said to Graunt and Domnall.

Graunt shot Baena a swift warning look, as he limped to the door. But Domnall remained where he was.

"Brother," Cinaed indicated the doorway.

Domnall slowly rose to his feet and took a stand beside Baena's chair. She looked at him, surprise and gratitude mingling on her face. Domnall fixed his eyes on his brother. "Cinaed, you are my king and my chief and I would obey you always. Nor would I ever interfere in your rights as a husband, but even so I will not let you hurt her. If you mark her today you will always regret it."

A flicker of irritation passed over Cinaed's face, the first sign of emotion he had shown. "Mark her? By God, Brother, what do you take me for? When have I ever struck a woman?"

Domnall looked firmly at Cinaed, his blue eyes clashing with the stormy grey ones. He only broke off his gaze to glance down at Baena and she nodded fearfully at him. Domnall gave a slight bow to them both and then strode from the room. Baena repressed the urge to call him back and looked up at Cinaed. She considered going to him, but her limbs were shaking so much she was not certain she could stand. He was staring beyond her and the silence was broken only by the crackling of the fire. Usually this was a cheerful sound, but today it brought neither of them comfort.

"Baena, when you spoke those words did you know how they would insult me?" Cinaed said, at last, his eyes fixed on her.

Baena could hear the faint plea in his voice and she was tempted. She could take Graunt's advice and beg his forgiveness. He was kind and he would forgive her.

But she had come too far. Unable to meet his eyes she bowed her head and answered honestly. "Yes."

"Do you know I can never forgive any man for those words?"

"Yes."

"Does my love mean so little to you?" Cinaed sounded bewildered and Baena hated herself for it.

She raised her head and looked at him, her heart breaking at the pain in his eyes. "No! No, Cinaed. Your love means everything to me. I am nothing without your love."

"Then why?"

Baena sought for the words. "Because once you spoke of the waste of good men lost to the endless border fights and the wish that the two people could stand together against our common enemies."

Baena looked pleadingly at him, but he did not react.

"Because the Picts need you. Like the Gaels, they have had the heart ripped out of them by the Norsemen. I have watched this last year how you have brought hope back to Dal Riata and I have never admired you so much. You could do that for the Picts. But not if you go in as a conqueror. You must go in as a Son of the Sixth House. You must go in as a Pict."

"Why should I care about them? They murdered my father. They steal my lands," Cinaed said dismissively.

"Peace will benefit the Gaels as well. With so many of the noble families of Pictavia destroyed there would be land a plenty to reward your followers. How many good men have been lost to the fights and skirmishes between the two people? You could bring all that bloodshed to an end." Baena felt faint with exhaustion. She had done everything she could. "That is why I have risked losing your love, even though it will destroy me. I am nothing compared to all this."

"I see." Cinaed sounded stunned.

"If you want me gone from Dunadd I will be gone within the hour."

For the first time, Cinaed looked angry. "First Domnall, now you. What have I done that you believe me capable of such cruelty?"

Baena flew from her chair and clasped his hand. It was icy cold. "Nothing! You have ever been the kindest of husbands, far better than I deserve. Oh, you are cold. Sit by the fire."

Cinaed allowed himself to be led to the chair that Baena had just vacated and she sank to her knees next to him.

"Have you been at your father's grave?" she ventured.

Cinaed shook his head. "No. My mother's."

Baena was surprised. She was not aware that he ever went there.

"She saw something unusual in you," Cinaed continued. "Back in the days when I saw you merely as a pretty diversion, she saw something more."

Cinaed sighed and ran his hands through his hair.

"I never thought to be King of the Picts. Dal Riata is my land. Can I be of both?"

"I think you can. The Gaels trace their lineage through the fathers, so to them you are Gael. The Picts can trace it through their mothers, so to them you are..." Baena's heart failed her at that final word. She'd said it already. There was no need to say it again.

Cinaed was silent for a long time, but Baena felt his face looked a little more alert. She remained on her knees before him determined to keep the tears back and longing for some sign that he still felt some affection for her.

"This changes everything," Cinaed muttered, more to himself.

Baena looked at him in confusion, but he did not explain.

"But what of me?" she asked, at last, unable to bear it any longer. Her knees were hurting from kneeling so long on the stone floor. She was terrified of what he would say next, but she had to know.

"You?"

"You said you could never forgive a man for those words."

Cinaed looked at her for what seemed like an age, but Baena thought she saw a hint of a sparkle come into his eyes. "Are you a man?" he asked. "And are you asking for my forgiveness?"

Hardly daring to believe the ray of hope that darted through her Baena slowly shook her head.

"Then why are you kneeling on the floor? Get up! You do think I'm a brute don't you?"

As she got up rather stiffly Cinaed pulled her onto his lap and she almost wept with the relief at feeling his arms around her again. Burying her head in the folds of his tunic against his chest she could hear the beating of his heart. He held her tightly against him and felt how she was trembling. "I am a brute. You're still not well."

Baena clung to him. "Do not worry about me. I will soon be better."

She looked anxiously into his face. The hurt was gone and his eyes were kind as he looked at her. She wound her arms around his neck, longing for more than just kindness. Her hands stroking his hair, she pressed her lips gently against his, praying he would respond. When no reaction came she sat back, scared that everything had truly changed. But slowly a smile spread over Cinaed's face and he pulled her back to him. To her delight, his lips found hers, tentatively at first before melting into a long and passionate kiss.

"You must rest and regain your health," he said at last as she still clung to him, unwilling to let him go. A teasing glint came into his eye, as he ran his hand down her body. "I'd like to have a go at getting you with child again before I leave for war."

Laughing, Baena flung her arms around him. "I will do my best, my love," she whispered.

Cinaed grinned. "But now I must speak with Domnall and Graunt. If I am to claim the Pict crown we will have much to discuss."

"You are really going to do it?"

Cinaed nodded. "You once rejected your Pict lineage for me. I shall embrace mine for you."

Baena let out a trembling breath, realising there could be no greater sign of his love than those words he had just uttered. "As a Daughter of the Third Royal House, I pledge my loyalty to you, Rex Pictorum."

Cinaed smiled "I thank you, my love. Now rest yourself." He eased her to her feet and hand in hand they left the King's chamber together.

Chapter three

His decision made, Cinaed moved quickly. The chiefs mustered an impressive number of men and the Norsemen unwittingly obliged them by launching their own attack on the Picts in the North. It seemed no time at all before the familiar scene came back to the plain beneath Dunadd, as the Gaels prepared to make their move.

"As soon as I have secured Forteviot I want you to come to me," Cinaed told Baena, as he surveyed his troops. "When I claim the Pict crown you should be at my side."

Baena nodded and wrapped an arm around him. She was fully returned to health now, apart from the anxiety that always consumed her at such time.

Cinaed guessed her feelings and kissed the top of her head. "You must not worry about me, my love. Look at these men!" He gestured buoyantly at the warriors. "We cannot fail!"

"No, we cannot!" Domnall greeted Baena with an exuberant embrace. Any last doubts she had about her brother-in-law had vanished that day when he had stood to her defence against his own brother.

"You look after Cinaed," she told him with mock severity.

Domnall grinned. "Absolutely, my lady!"

Baena hugged him. "Look after yourself too."

"I shall send word of our progress," Cinaed told Graunt and Baena. "Guard my Queen well, my friend."

Nodding Graunt backed away to allow Cinaed to say his final farewells. Knowing how hard Baena found this moment, he kept them short and formal. Pausing briefly before mounting his horse to whisper in Baena's ear, "Until we meet again, Queen of the Picts!"

And so for once Baena was genuinely beaming as again Cinaed set off for battle. Then she turned back to Graunt. He was looking awkward. During the frantic weeks of preparation, she had seen little of him and never informally so he was keenly aware that the last time he had called her a fool.

Smiling to show she bore him no grudge, she took his arm. She felt sorry for him, guessing how hard it must be for him to be left behind.

"I don't suppose Cinaed ever thought in his wildest ambitions that he could be King of the Picts," she said.

"No, but Alpin did," Graunt replied.

Baena was surprised as Graunt went on. "I suspect it was already in his mind when he married the Lady Unuis. It was certainly one of his plans when Cinaed married you."

Baena thought back to her few memories of Alpin. Clearly the bluff exterior had hidden a mind that was as shrewd as his sons. "I wish I had known Alpin better," she said. "Did Cinaed know this was his plan?"

Graunt laughed. "My lady, only one person has ever reminded Cinaed of his Pict heritage without having their nose broken! And forgive me, my lady, but I still cannot decide whether it was brave or foolish!"

"A little of both, perhaps."

"Alpin presented the marriage to him as a peace treaty, a useful ally. Nothing more. Cinaed was not best pleased, but he accepted his father's wish."

Baena stopped as a thought struck her. "Back at our wedding, I behaved... well, you know how I behaved."

"Yes, my lady," Graunt replied gently, no hint of censure in his voice.

"I gave Cinaed the excuse he needed to get out of the wedding. Why did he not take it?"

"I don't know," Graunt replied. "I wondered it myself. I think you know that it was I who reported you to Cinaed."

Baena nodded, smiling at the irony that she was now on such friendly terms with this man.

"I thought I was giving him the escape he wanted. But he didn't take it. I know the Lady Unuis liked you from the moment she first met you, but I do not think that would have swayed Cinaed."

"Then what? I held no attraction to him then."

"And yet I think it was you who stopped him. If he had reported your actions to your father and backed out of the marriage your name and reputation would be destroyed. What would your punishment have been?"

Baena grimaced, remembering the temper of her mother. "I'd have been beaten for sure. Probably many times."

Graunt nodded. "On Iona during our boyhood, there were many women who bore the scars from the Norse raids. Cinaed's wet nurse had lost the sight in one eye and was scarred down her face. I do not think he ever forgets that. Cinaed is one of the bravest men I know on the battlefield. There is no man I'd rather fight alongside and no man I'd like to fight against less! But however much he insists on his own way, I have never known him strike a woman."

Baena was amazed. "You think he continued with the marriage to protect me?"

Graunt nodded. "I remember you on that day. So defiant, yet completely powerless. You have no idea how much you angered him, but he could not bring himself to see you punished. Even when the treaty broke down and the alliance was useless to him, he refused to allow you to be disgraced."

"I remember you three on that day as well. I do not know which one of you I hated the most! Now look at us. You and Domnall are my good friends and Cinaed... Cinaed is everything to me."

"So enmity can become friendship! There is hope for us all."

At the fort Causantin and Aed were excitedly watching the troops streaming across the plain beneath them. Baena put her arms around them, looking at the figure at the head of the troops with a smile on her face. Cinaed's optimism had affected even her.

Cinaed's messengers returned regularly, so they knew when Cinaed reached the Pict borderlands. As he fought his way across Pictavia reports continued to be favourable and at Dunadd the mood was high.

"Cinaed our king so strong and brave, beat the Picts seven times in a day," the musicians sang.

Then the messages stopped. Baena knew he was close to Forteviot and had hoped that the end was in sight.

As the days went by the mood dampened. Graunt limped around the fort clearly wishing he was at Cinaed's side. Baena busied herself with her children and tried not to think the worst. She was playing with her daughter one day when one of the serving lads came upon her.

"My Lady Queen," the boy bowed low before her. "The Lord Graunt begs for your presence. Lord Domnall has returned."

Baena's heart stopped. Domnall? The man who never left Cinaed's side?

"Is Lord Domnall alone?" she asked faintly.

"Yes, my lady."

Baena left her daughter with her nurse and picking up the hem of her tunic she dashed down the passages to the hall. She could hear Domnall and Graunt talking, but was unable to make out the words.

She burst into the room crying breathlessly, "Domnall, what news?"

Domnall's grin told her everything she wanted to know. He showed no weariness from his ride as he crossed the hall in a few strides and swung her off her feet.

"The best news! The Picts tried their utmost, but they were no match for us. Cinaed has made himself quite at home in Forteviot."

Baena muttered a quiet prayer of thanks.

"I'm surprised you left him there," Graunt commented.

Domnall cast a sly glance at Baena. "I once promised my sister that if ever Cinaed had need of her I would bring her to him. Well, here I am!"

Baena shook her head, laughing.

"Seriously, we have made the passage to Forteviot as safe as we can, but there are still dangers. Cinaed trusts me to keep Baena safe."

"He wants me to join him now?"

"As soon as you can be ready," Domnall nodded. "The children are to stay here."

Baena nodded a little hesitantly. Domnall noticed her mood.

"It is the safest place for them. You'd not want to subject them to the dangers of the journey, especially when the Picts could attack Forteviot any day. Even if a foe was to come here, Dunadd is well defended and no man is better than Graunt at withstanding a siege."

"I would guard those children with my life, my lady."

Baena nodded, still smiling. "I know you would. There are few I would trust as well as you." she looked at Domnall. "I can be ready to ride in the morn. How many ride with us?"

"Not many. A small group attracts little attention. Who is to know if we are Pict or Gael?"

"Not even us, perhaps."

Chapter four

Baena bade a sad farewell to her children and entrusted them to Kieta's care. It was hard to leave them. If they were besieged at Forteviot who knew when she would see them again, but as they sped away from Dunadd the wind quickly dried her tears.

"How are you bearing up, Sister?" Domnall asked her when they stopped to rest the horses and refresh themselves. He studied her with a touch of anxiety.

Baena, her eyes bright and her cheeks pink, laughed. "As well as you."

"Cinaed reminded me before I left that you have not been well."

"That was months ago." Baena tossed her tousled hair. "I am quite well now."

"I think Cinaed thought that you might… that is you could be…"

"Oh," she replied a little flatly. "I am not."

Domnall noticed her dampened mood. "Forgive me, Sister. I meant no offence. With those two fine boys, no one could find any fault with you." He passed a flagon of ale to her. "But I had to check. I'd not risk Cinaed's wrath by delivering you in a frail state."

Baena drank deeply. The loss of her hopes the previous year still weighed heavily on her and so far it seemed that she would not be blessed this year.

"It's probably as well," Domnall tried to cheer her. "We are heading into dangerous territory."

But to Baena, it did not seem dangerous at all. She felt she was coming home. They took a roundabout way to Forteviot, to avoid the settlements and Baena was impressed by how little destruction she saw along the way.

"We fought only if there was resistance," Domnall told her. "Cinaed did not wish to waste our energies attacking farmers and shepherds."

At night the men took it in turns to sleep, so that one always guarded her shelter to protect her from dangers both human and animal. Dangerous territory? Baena had rarely felt so well cared for.

Late one morning, several days after leaving Dunadd, Domnall announced that they were but an hour from Forteviot. The last days had seen them pass through more populated areas and for the first time Baena saw the signs of past skirmishes. The settlements seemed subdued and no one questioned them.

"We'll wait a while here," Domnall announced. "Kynon!" he gestured to one of the lads that had ridden with them. "Ride on to Forteviot and see if it is still secure. We cannot bring the Lady Queen into a siege."

"If all is well we will be in Forteviot by nightfall," Domnall told her.

"And if it is not?"

Domnall shrugged. "I promised Cinaed I would keep you safe and so I must not return to his aid until I have got you to sanctuary."

Baena, whose heart had lifted at the thought of seeing Cinaed that night, shivered. Trying to lighten the mood she said, "And yet you promised me you would look after him!"

Domnall laughed. "So I must break one of my promises. I shall have to think awhile on whose wrath I fear most."

Their eyes fixed on the path to Forteviot, they did not notice the group of dark-clothed men who crept closer to them, until with a roar they had charged. Domnall and the other men swiftly leapt to their feet, drawing their swords.

"Get to your horse, Sister," Domnall yelled, as he engaged the first man.

Baena's first terrified glimpse showed her that they were outnumbered, almost two to one. Turning away, she darted towards her horse, hearing the clash of metal behind her, as well as the sound of pursuit. Just as she reached the horse a heavy hand grabbed her shoulder, pulling her around. She looked into the thin face of an unkempt looking man. He held his sword at her throat and she froze, staring at him out of wide eyes.

"Hand over anything of value," the man snarled. "And I may let you go unharmed."

With shaking hands Baena pulled a chain from her neck and handed over the pouch at her waist. The man lowered his knife, as he sorted through the contents. His dirt-begrimed fingers went to the buckle of her belt and she screamed in terror. He shot her a look of contempt as he threw the belt into his sack.

She could see that Domnall was trying to fight his way towards her, but several men still blocked his way.

"And that," the man pointed at her shoulder.

Baena glanced down to see the brooch that Cinaed had sent to her long ago on Iona. Of all her jewels it was the one she would least wish to part from, but she knew she had no choice. She handed it over and shivered as her cloak fell to the ground.

The man studied the brooch, a pleased smile on his face. "Open those packs," he demanded.

Baena turned back to her horse, looking longingly the saddle. "Let the men go," she pleaded, noticing that several of the men had been disarmed. Only Domnall and one other were still fighting. "Take what you will, but leave us unharmed."

The man laughed. "Open those packs, my pretty. We'll decide what to do with you later."

Almost beyond fear Baena hunched over the packs, her shaking fingers struggling with the fastenings. Suddenly she heard a new shout.

"For Clan mac Alpin and Saint Columba!" the voice bellowed.

The newcomers were many and well-armed. Baena felt her heart beat louder than ever, but this time with hope. The man charging towards her was Cinaed, his face twisted with rage as he clashed his sword against one of the robbers. It did not take long before the man took to his heels.

Cinaed stopped short as the man with Baena put his knife back to her throat. She looked pleadingly at Cinaed, as the other Gaels gathered around.

"Lower your weapons and this lady goes unharmed," the man cried.

Cinaed motioned to the Gaels to obey, his grey eyes fixed in fury at the man.

The man picked up the sack and pulled Baena with him as he backed away. Baena wanted to scream at Cinaed to do something. It was mere seconds, but it felt like hours before in a swift movement Cinaed shot out his lowered sword to strike the man hard on the leg with the flat of the blade. The man stumbled, loosening his grip on Baena. Cinaed darted forward and pulled her into his arms. With a sob of relief, she clung to him.

The robber grabbed his sack and sprinted away, the young Gael who had been fighting alongside Domnall hard on his heels, but Cinaed called him back.

"Your mission is to guard the Queen. Do not lose your focus on that," he said sternly, before smiling at the crestfallen boy. "But I have noted how bravely you fought, my lad. You greatly impressed me."

"And me," Domnall added. "I sympathise with your wish to chase. If the Queen were not present I would have joined you in your pursuit." He arched an eyebrow at Cinaed. "And I suspect the King would as well."

Cinaed grinned and did not deny it. He looked down at Baena, who was still clinging to him, her face buried in his cloak. "Are you hurt, my love?"

Baena shook her head, looking up into his concerned eyes. Cinaed pulled her even closer. "This was not the welcome I had planned for you. Did you lose much?"

"My pouch. It did not contain much," Baena whispered. "And a chain and brooch."

"Not your brooch," Cinaed said, picking something from the ground. "He dropped it as I approached."

Gently Cinaed draped the cloak around her shoulders and fastened the brooch back into place. She smiled bravely. "Thank you. I am so glad you came."

Cinaed kept his arms tightly around her and looked at the men. Domnall was passing out flagons of ale to them all. Cinaed took one and held it to Baena's lips. She drank, feeling her nerves gradually calming. He took Baena to his own horse and lifted her onto the saddle, before mounting behind her. She leant gratefully against his chest, glad she would not have to guide her own horse.

"Come, my friends, let us bring the Queen safely to Forteviot."

Baena got her first view of Forteviot as they passed an ornate stone cross. The castle was built in the Pict style with a stockade of stout logs surrounding many dwellings of turf and stone, as well as the circular hall and church. As they approached people stopped their work in farms and houses nearby to stare at them with a mixture of fear and resentment. Cinaed's stronghold was secure but it was obvious that the conquered people would turn on them at any chance.

By the next day, both Cinaed and Domnall seemed to have forgotten the attack. Baena looked on in surprise when she came down from her chamber to find them joking with each other in the hall and she tried resolutely to put the attack from her own mind. Cinaed had summoned a group of Pict men to the hall. These men were the highest ranking Picts that had been found at the settlement when the Gaels had stormed the citadel. Cinaed had been keeping them prisoner since he captured the castle, although he had ordered them to be well treated. Now they were before him in the hall he acted as if they were honoured guests.

The three men stood awkwardly, confused as to how to behave in the presence of their captors.

"It is customary to bow before a king," Domnall pointed out helpfully.

With consternation on their faces, the men fell to their knees, but Cinaed waved them up.

"No! No! Such formality is unnecessary. Be at ease, my friends. Refresh yourselves." Cinaed gestured at the ale jug.

But not one man dared do such a thing.

"Remind me of who you are, my friends."

"My name is Kai, my lord," one man said and gestured at the other two. "Broide and Nektan"

"We are of the Fourth Royal House, my lord," Broide added.

Baena studied them. Her mother was of the Fourth House, but Baena could recall no one of these names. Clearly they were very minor members.

"Excellent." Cinaed gestured to Baena, who was seated next to him. "I present to you the Lady Baena, Queen of Dal Riata."

The men bowed low before her and Baena smiled graciously upon them.

"Do you know who I am?" Cinaed asked the men.

The men obviously suspected trickery and looked worriedly at each other. Cinaed leant back and smiled encouragingly at them.

"The… the King of Dal Riata?" Nektan stammered at last.

"Very good," Cinaed replied. "But you are only partially correct. I am Cinaed Mac Alpin, the son of the Lady Unuis of the Sixth Royal House. I am also the King of Dal Riata," he added, as the men looked completely confused.

Cinaed rose to his feet, drawing himself up to his full height. The men fell back, more frightened than ever.

"Do not be afeared, my friends. I mean no harm to you. I am here to announce to you that I Cinaed Mac Alpin, King of Dal Riata claim the crown of the Picts in the name of my mother the Lady Unuis of the Sixth Royal House and my wife the Lady Baena of the Third Royal House."

The men's shock was complete. They stared open mouthed at Cinaed.

"Kneel before your King and Queen!" Domnall thundered suddenly, making the men start.

Nektan and Broide fell to their knees, but Kai, clearly the bravest of the group, remained on his feet.

"What of King Drust?" he ventured.

"I dispute the claim of Lord Drust," Cinaed said. "You are released from any loyalty to him. From this day you serve me."

The three men stammered and looked around the hall as if hoping for someone to come to their aid. All around them were warriors of Dal Riata. One stepped forward and firmly, but not cruelly pushed Kai to his knees.

"I am pleased to see your obedience," Cinaed smiled. "You are free to go. You will see that the settlement here is running as well as ever and I will wreak no harm on my loyal subjects. You may spread the good news of my coming to all."

As the men kept kneeling, Cinaed waved a hand impatiently at them. "Go!"

Domnall stood with his arms folded and watched impassively as the men stumbled out. Only when they were gone did his face collapse.

"Good God, Cinaed, could you not have found anyone better to proclaim yourself to than them?" he choked.

Cinaed too gave way to laughter. "The very finest this settlement has to offer!"

Wiping his eyes, Domnall shook his head. "Ah well, they will serve their purpose I suppose. The word is out."

"Exactly. It is of no matter if the news takes a little while to filter through to Drust. In fact, it gives us time to strengthen our position here further."

As the spring merged into summer Cinaed did exactly that. More and more of the land around them came under control from Forteviot. Accompanied by a strong guard, Baena rode out to each settlement to meet with the leaders to persuade them to accept Cinaed's rule and the professions of loyalty gradually increased. It was not to be expected that Drust would accept Cinaed's claim and soon the retaliation began. The skirmishes were easy enough to deal with, but Cinaed began to suspect that a full-scale battle with all the related losses would be hard to avoid.

He sent messages to the heads of the Third, Fourth and Sixth Royal Houses, demanding their support by the right of the blood of Unuis and Baena. Only the Sixth responded, sending men to swell Cinaed's forces. The Third and Fourth ignored them completely, although Domnall's scouts reported that they did not appear to be supporting Drust either.

As the summer drew to a close Cinaed had made some gains, but they were not sufficient for him to push home his claim.

"At least while they are here they are leaving the Dal Riata border alone," Domnall commented, as they sat one day outside the hall of Forteviot.

"True. I have word from Graunt that all prospers there. And the children are all well," he added to Baena.

Baena smiled, but a pain seemed to be permanently in her heart. It had been so long since she has seen them. Sometimes she considered asking Cinaed if she could return to Dunadd, but the thought of being away from him again was unbearable. In any case, she doubted if he would agree to it. Away from the safety of Forteviot, she would be an easy target for Drust's forces to capture. She remembered the robber band who had attacked them on her previous journey. Such an attack would be nothing compared to what Drust's forces were capable of.

"I'll not withdraw from here," Cinaed was saying to Domnall. "But I do not want to be cut off from Dunadd."

"Could that happen?" Baena asked in alarm, as she imagined being cut off from her children for years.

"It's what I'd do if I were Drust," Domnall said bluntly.

"But he has not done it yet," Cinaed pointed out. "He seems more concerned with harassing us here."

"Perhaps he is deliberately leaving the way open for you to leave," Baena suggested.

Cinaed looked doubtful, but Domnall nodded. "You could be right. Perhaps Drust has as little heart for a full battle as we do."

"I'll not take the way out. The Pict crown is to be mine," said Cinaed. "So where does that leave us?"

"At the same place we were at the start of the summer," said Domnall. "I suppose if you needed to return to Dunadd I could hold Forteviot for you."

Baena kept her face still. She knew she mustn't let her longing for the children influence Cinaed, but she liked the sound of Domnall's suggestion.

However, she was unsurprised when Cinaed rejected the idea. "That would mean splitting the army. We'd be vulnerable on both fronts."

"We have three choices. We carry on as we are; we all return to Dunadd; or we force a full-scale battle and hope we are victorious."

"There must be another way. I am not giving up," Cinaed said, his brow creasing thoughtfully.

Domnall and Baena both withdrew to let Cinaed think. At length he re-joined them, his face set into lines of grim determination.

"My love, I must talk with Domnall. Leave us a while."

"Why? What are you planning?"

"Just leave us."

Baena felt a little hurt and Domnall raised his eyebrows. It was most unusual for Cinaed to take that tone with Baena.

Cinaed caught Baena's hand as she left. "Baena, I will tell you, I promise. But I must talk to Domnall first."

Baena watched from the open doorway of the hall as the brothers headed into the courtyard. The conversation did not seem to be going well. Domnall looked horrified. He gestured wildly and shook his head. Cinaed put his hand on Domnall's shoulder and talked some more. Baena bit her lip as she tried to imagine what Cinaed could be saying, especially when Domnall strode away before whirling around to confront Cinaed once more.

This sort of confrontation between the brothers was unheard of in recent years. The two often had differences of opinions, but they always listened courteously to each other. Baena turned away from them, her mind racing as she wondered how dangerous Cinaed's plan could be that Domnall, one of the bravest of men, was acting like this.

When she looked back towards them the scene was more normal. Cinaed had one hand on Domnall's back and was talking intently to him. Domnall was nodding. At last the men embraced, Domnall's blonde hair mingling with Cinaed's darker locks. Baena breathed a sigh of relief. At least they were in agreement.

When they returned to her Domnall gave a grim smile.

"Good luck explaining all this to her," he said to Cinaed, as he left them together.

"Baena, I am a brute to be asking for your support in this and more than your support - your help," Cinaed said, taking her hand.

"I would always support you. You know I will be happy to help."

Cinaed shook his head. "Not this time. And my love, please note I am asking for your help not commanding it. This plays no part in your wifely duties. If you want no part in this I shall understand. You can be kept away, I might even be able to return you to Dunadd."

Baena nodded, but Cinaed noted how her eyes brightened. "Yes, I know you long to be there," he commented dryly.

"I do. But if I was there I would be wishing I was with you," Baena replied. "Tell me what you want."

"You won't like it," Cinaed warned.

And so he told her his plan and he was right. She didn't like it. She was shocked that he was even thinking it. But there was never any doubt about her help. Baena would support Cinaed. She always did.

Chapter five

Cinaed's plan started simply. He summoned seven men to take a message to each of the Heads of the Royal Houses.

"Tell them this. It is time to bring this intolerable situation to a close. The matter of the Pict crown and the borders with Dal Riata must be settled. I, therefore, request your presence at the Place of Scone to arrange terms that we can all agree. As a token of my good will, I and my lady would like to invite you and your closest kin to dine at that place on the evening of the new moon, twenty-four days past the equinox. This message was issued on this day by Cinaed Mac Alpin, son of Unuis of the Sixth Royal House, King of Dal Riata."

Only the messenger to the Sixth House was given an amendment, as remembering how they had sent men to aid him, Cinaed told them that if they were happy for him to represent them there was no need for them to attend.

He looked at Baena. "This message is going to the Third House. Do you understand?"

Baena swallowed over the lump in her throat and nodded. "I know he is my kin, but I have no recollection of this man."

"Then ride my men!"

The Place of Scone was on the edge of the territory that Cinaed had conquered and was an ancient meeting place. The stronghold there had fallen into disrepair in recent years and the only residents nearby were a reclusive order of monks. It was not easy to defend, but that was of no concern as Cinaed did not want a fight. More important to Cinaed was that it would be hard for the Picts to launch a surprise attack on him there. If there was the slightest hint of arms they would simply retreat to Forteviot and defend themselves from there.

"Do you think they'll come?" Baena asked in a low voice, a few days after the messengers had ridden out.

"They'll come," said Domnall. "What choice have they? If they don't they must spend a cold winter camped around Forteviot, as if they leave they know we will increase our territories here."

"I have dangled the bait of the borders with Dal Riata," Cinaed added. "If they think there is any chance they can persuade me to be content with a secure border and forget my claim to the Pict crown they will have to take it."

"It's going to be dangerous," Domnall warned. "Are you sure you want Baena there?"

Cinaed gave a mirthless laugh. "No, I do not want Baena there. But her presence will fool them. It would be a strange merriment without my lady there. Besides, the whole plan will be useless if Drust does not come. If the Pict crown is not bait enough, I am certain that her presence will entice him there."

Domnall looked at Cinaed in shock.

"She will be away before the danger starts," Cinaed said defensively, avoiding his brother's eye.

"I still think it is a bad idea. You could pay a high price for your triumph."

"I am there by my free choice, Domnall. Cinaed does not order me there. If a sacrifice must be made for the sake of a union then I think any one of us three are prepared to make it."

Domnall shook his head. "My poor sister. You do nothing but sacrifice yourself for the sake of a union. Which is worse do you think? A Pict sword or marriage to this brute?"

"I think at the time she would have infinitely preferred the Pict sword," Cinaed said, with grim irony. "But back to the matter in hand, I am determined that no sacrifice will be necessary on our part. The serving men there will be my best warriors in disguise. They will be under strict orders to protect Baena before all else."

"Protecting you should be the priority, Cinaed," Baena protested. "I am unimportant. You are of the greatest necessity to both lands."

Cinaed kissed her hand. "But you are of the greatest necessity to me."

A few weeks passed. Messengers returned with an agreement to come from the heads of the Royal Houses. The words differed, but the messages were the same. They trusted they could come to an agreement where Cinaed would forget his pretensions and get back to Dal Riata.

Cinaed accepted these messages with amusement, but Baena felt her terror increasing with every day. If Cinaed could pull this plan off he would become the greatest King this land had known, but failure would almost definitely spark another bloody conflict. Baena closed her heart to any softer feelings and prayed for success.

Cinaed's preparations went well. He had ordered repairs to be made to an assembly hall that stood outside the little stronghold. Inside he placed a huge table and wooden benches.

"Don't sit on those," commented Cinaed with a touch of humour when he and Baena rode over one cloudy day to check on the preparations.

Baena shuddered and turned away.

"Baena, get used to this place. I'll not see that face when the night comes."

Baena tried to compose herself as Cinaed strolled around. He seemed pleased as he looked behind the hanging cloths to the hidden spaces. Clearly excited by the progression of his plans he caught Baena up in his arms and went to kiss her. But she pushed him away.

"Not here, Cinaed."

"What's wrong?"

"This place... I cannot like it."

Cinaed released her, looking angry. "You must not ruin this for me. Everything rests on this night."

"I know," Baena said in a low voice.

"Then start smiling your pretty smile. Be the gracious queen everyone knows you to be."

Baena tried, but she knew her efforts were not pleasing Cinaed.

"I'll not disappoint you, I promise," she said. "But I shall be so glad when that night is passed."

Cinaed still looked unimpressed. "I suppose none of them know you. Perhaps they won't be surprised to meet a miserable shrew."

Baena's eyes flashed. "I am not a miserable shrew!"

Cinaed grinned. "That's more like it!"

"Anyway, I think you're forgetting that one of them knows me very well."

Cinaed's smile faded. "I suppose I deserve that you remind me of that. But do not let your old friendship interfere with my plans."

Despite her misgivings, Baena almost laughed at him. "If you scowl like that every time Drust's name is mentioned I think it will be you who lets my old friendship interfere with your plans." She looked up at him. "Now smile your pretty smile and be the gracious king everyone knows you to be!"

With that Baena swept from the room, relieved to be out of there, even as the first drops of rain started to fall. Cinaed caught her up easily.

"Why have I ended up with the most disobedient wife possible?" he demanded, pulling up the hood of his cloak, but even he looked back at the hall with a concealed shudder. As the rain fell harder he did not suggest returning.

Chapter six

A few days before the arranged night Cinaed, Baena and Domnall moved to the little castle at Scone and Cinaed's trusted warriors took up their roles as serving men. The rest of the army were stationed nearby without any attempt at concealment. It was expected that the Royal Houses would arrive with their own armies, so it was reasonable for Cinaed to do the same.

After the weeks of planning, it was almost a relief when the day finally arrived. Cinaed's excitement was bubbling over when he rose that morning.

"Be of good cheer, my love," he cried. "By the time we return to this bed tonight it will all be over. The Pict crown will be mine."

"How can you smile, Cinaed?" Baena asked, longing to go back to sleep and not awake until Yule. "Is this not the hardest thing you have ever done?"

"No. The hardest thing was making a deal with the Norsemen. That still weighs on me. I often wonder if it was I that caused the battle with the Norsemen." Cinaed replied, his own mood flattening.

"You cannot blame yourself for that," Baena exclaimed. "The Norsemen would have attacked in any case. Perhaps the attack would have been in Dal Riata, rather than Pictavia. But they would have still triumphed."

Cinaed shrugged. "Your father might be still alive," he pointed out.

Baena flinched. "And you might be dead," she hit back. "Cinaed, I keep telling you that if I have to choose between you and my family, I choose you. Why do you never believe me?"

"I do believe you, my love," Cinaed said, folding her into his arms. "I am just not sure I deserve it."

When she left her chamber she found Domnall watching the rising sun. "The sky is already stained with blood," he said.

Baena looked and the sky did seem unusually crimson. She shivered.

Cinaed shook his head in exasperation. "It is not too late. We can make this the festivity the Picts are expecting. I'll not go ahead without you two behind me."

"What happens then?" Baena asked.

But it was Domnall who replied. "We either retreat to Dunadd with our tails between our legs or we fight a bloody battle. I'm with you Cinaed. You know that."

"Then look cheerful. Both of you."

Domnall and Baena exchanged glances.

"The King has spoken," Domnall commented with a grim smile.

Baena smiled weakly back and wished with all her heart that the day was already over.

That day the heads of the Royal Houses arrived and set up camp in the meadows around Scone.

As the afternoon wore on and with news of the arrival of the last Royal House Cinaed commanded Baena, "Make your special brew."

Baena did as she was bidden, remembering the last time she'd made that drink. How innocent that day was when Cinaed had tricked the men of the clan into believing an angel was among them. She stirred the ale and herbs together before picking up the costly jar of Water of Life. Suddenly the tears started to flow dropping into the brew as she reflected on the stupidity of that name on this night. This was no water of life.

But as she hesitated a picture of Cinaed's head on a spike like Alpin's had been floated into her mind. She could almost see his sun-streaked locks matted with blood and his grey eyes no longer filled with love but instead with an unspeakable terror. And so, resolutely, she picked up the jar again and poured copious quantities into the brew. She took a sip and nodded harshly. The Water of Death was ready.

Baena's face was pale as she, Cinaed and Domnall, dressed in fine raiment, awaited their guests. Cinaed and Domnall were both unarmed, apart from the usual daggers at their belts.

The hall which had been festooned with banners and lit by bright torches had a festive appearance. But this only contrasted greatly with the silence of the hosts. She felt they had been waiting an age before they heard the sound of the first horsemen arriving. Baena started and Cinaed squeezed her shoulder reassuringly.

"God be with us all," Domnall muttered in a low voice.

Cinaed stepped forward to meet the first of their guests, a winning smile lighting up his face, welcoming the head of the Seventh House with apparent pleasure. As Baena joined in the greetings she could feel how false her smile felt. The only surprise was that none of the Picts seemed to notice.

"My dear kinswoman!" the Head of the Third Royal House greeted her. "How like your noble mother you look."

Baena froze. To her knowledge, she had never met this man before, but his greeting cut her to her heart.

Cinaed shot her a sharp look as he gripped her hand almost painfully. "My dear lady wife is quite overcome at seeing a kinsman after such a long time," he explained cheerfully to the man.

Baena tried to smile. She longed to ask him about her mother but making such familiar talk seemed wrong when she knew only too well what the night had in store for him. Cinaed kept his eyes fixed on her, but before he could say anything, Domnall muttered, "You should not have brought her here."

Cinaed shrugged and put his arm around Baena. She blinked back the tears and looked at the Pict lords starting on the refreshments. If only they had left the border alone Cinaed might have remained contentedly the King of Dal Riata and right now they would be happily presiding over the great table at Dunadd.

The last glimpse of the sun had almost completely gone when Drust finally arrived. Glancing at Cinaed, Baena saw his jaw tighten, as his father's murderer strode towards them.

"My Lord Drust, I thank you for coming. It is an honour to receive you," Cinaed said in what sounded to Baena as a very false tone.

"Is it Lord Cinaed? I am here for one purpose - to make you understand the Pict crown shall never be yours."

Cinaed waved his hand airily. "Not tonight, my lord. Tonight we are merry. We must not discuss such weighty matters with a lady present. Allow me to present my lady wife, the Queen of Dal Riata."

Drust sneered. "Surely you have not forgotten how well I know her."

But Cinaed refused to be ruffled. "Of course. Well, it is always good to meet old friends, is it not, my lady?"

Baena took a deep breath and smiled a dazzling smile that would make Cinaed proud. "Indeed it is, my lord. Most pleasant. I trust all is well with you, my Lord Drust?"

"I am sure you know it is not," said Drust bringing Baena's hand to his mouth. He kept his lips there longer than necessary with one eye on Cinaed to see his reaction.

Baena pulled her hand free with some difficulty and studied her old friend. His eyes were as blue as ever, contrasting dramatically with his dark hair, but he was not as handsome as Baena had expected. Like many men, he bore the scars of multiple battles, but it was not these that marred his appearance so much as the sneer that seemed fixed to his mouth. His eyes too seemed changed. They still sparkled but with a cold glitter that seemed to cut cruelly through the air.

"My dearest Baena, it has been too long since we last met."

Baena did not look at Cinaed, but she could guess his expression on hearing Drust speak to her so familiarly.

"Many years. Why I have had three babes since I last saw you! There will be much news to exchange." Throwing herself into the part she stepped forward and took his arm. "Now refresh yourself, my lord. And hurry. I have prepared this drink myself, but there will be little left now my Lord Domnall has started helping himself!"

Baena kept her smile bright, but she didn't miss the expression in both Cinaed and Domnall's eyes. She'd pleased neither man with this speech although both felt a reluctant admiration for her. Suddenly she seemed to be far better at this ruse than they were.

"Ah, sweet Baena, how good it is to be with you again," Drust proclaimed loudly, sneering once more at Cinaed.

Baena's drink went down well and the men grew merry. Drust continued to fawn over Baena at every opportunity and whenever she felt her heart fail her at the plan ahead she reminded herself that it was obvious Drust, at least, had not come with peaceful intentions.

Just how unpeaceful Drust's intentions were Baena found out the hard way. As the ale was running low she left the hall to fetch fresh supplies. Away from the torches the night was black and cold, but she paused a moment, relieved to let the mask slip.

Suddenly she felt a hand on her shoulder. Wheeling around she found herself face to face with Drust.

"Drust, what are you doing here?" she tried to keep her voice light.

Drust smiled his sneery smile. "Why, I have come to see you of course. Are you not pleased to see me?"

"Of course, but I must not be alone with you. Cinaed would be so angry. You would not want to cause trouble for me." Baena tried to back away from him. A sound of raucous singing and laughter drifted from the shelter and she knew it would be useless to call for help.

Drust pushed his face close to hers. "Cinaed does not need to know."

Baena felt her heart thumping as she backed into the castle wall. There was nowhere else to go. Desperately she tried to make light of the situation. "Don't be foolish, Drust. Return to the feast. I will be there presently."

"You should have been mine, Baena. Tonight you will be mine," Drust whispered, pushing his lips against hers.

Truly frightened now Baena pushed her hands against his chest but to no avail. His strong body pressed her even harder into the castle wall and she felt the rough stones digging into her back. His lips seemed to scorch her, as she tried desperately to extricate herself.

She dug her fingernails into his neck and, for a moment, he stopped kissing her and caught her hands together. She gasped for breath, trying without success to wipe away the wetness from her mouth.

"Fiery little thing, aren't you?" Drust sneered. "Do you kiss Cinaed like that?"

"Cinaed will kill you," she hissed, totally forgetting the plan for the night.

"I don't think so." Drust gave a low laugh. "Because you won't tell him, will you? He would likely kill you for your faithlessness."

She cried out in horror as his lips went to her neck. She continued to struggle, oblivious to the bruises the stones were inflicting on her shoulders. All she could feel was his grip like an iron cuff around her wrists and the force of his strong body pressed up against hers.

He pinned her hands to her sides with one arm and she felt sick as she felt him run his other hand hard over her stomach. She struggled some more but he kept her firmly against the wall.

"Doesn't feel like you're with child, but perhaps you will be soon," he chuckled in her face. "Now that Cinaed values Pict blood so highly, wouldn't it be amusing if his next child had even more Pict blood than he expects."

As if through a thick fog Baena heard more laughter coming from the gathering. It was impossible to fight harder.

"Please, Drust. Stop. Please stop," she begged now.

As he pulled at her tunic she closed her eyes, trying to blot out the horror that was coming. She tried to picture Cinaed's face, his eyes looking at her with love, but in this vision even he looked at her with disgust and condemnation.

Beyond all thought, she suddenly felt sharp fingernails raking across her wrist as the grip was released and her tunic fell back to her ankles. It took a few seconds for her to realise she was free. Opening her eyes she saw Drust sprawled on his back on the floor. Domnall, his face almost unrecognisable with rage, was standing over him.

"Do not dare to touch the Queen," he spat.

Baena stumbled forward, breathless and sobbing with a mixture of pain and relief. She clung onto his arm. Domnall looked angrier than ever at the sight of her.

"My brother will kill you for this." Domnall kicked at Drust.

Drust shrank back. "And what of her?" he leered "How will the great Cinaed feel to have a faithless wife?"

It was surely impossible for Domnall to look any angrier. Baena shook her head as the plan for the night came flooding back. She realised if Domnall fetched Cinaed he would most certainly kill Drust, but the evening would be over and the other lords would be free to continue the conflict.

"Please don't tell Cinaed," she begged. "He will be so angry with me."

Domnall looked at her incredulously.

"I fear he would beat me for my faithlessness," she stumbled on, making her statements even more outrageous in the hope that Domnall would catch on. "I have not yet recovered from the last beating he gave me. Please, Brother."

It was plain that Domnall had understood. "I shall think on the matter. My brother is ever just. You have received no punishment that you have not deserved." He kicked at Drust again. "Go back, Pict scum."

Once Drust had slunk away Domnall helped Baena into the castle. By the light of the torches inside he studied her, shaking his head. Her hair was unbound and the back of her tunic was torn. Livid finger-marks were appearing on her skin.

"Cinaed will have to know," he said in the gentlest voice that Baena had ever heard from him.

"How angry will he be with me?" Baena sank her face into her hands, unsure how much more she could take that night.

Domnall shook his head. "Surely you know him better than that."

"I was so nearly false. My body would have betrayed him." Shame stung her as she realised how close she had come to allowing another man to take her and to perhaps even bearing his child.

"A little thing like you has no chance against a man." Domnall looked helpless as he tried to console her. "I told Cinaed it was a bad idea to bring you here."

"Let us bring the night to an end," she said wearily, but resolutely wiping her eyes. "Then we can all be safe."

"You're not going back?" Domnall sounded horrified. "Go to your chamber. I'll tell them you have been taken ill."

"I must. Cinaed trusts me to play my part. I'll not let him down again. I shall straighten my hair and change my attire." With an effort, she smiled a festive smile at Domnall. "I must do this for Cinaed."

Domnall stared at her, but finally, he found the right words to say. "My lady, when men look on your sons they often hope they will have the courage of their father. I hope they will have the courage of their mother."

Chapter seven

Baena ignored the pain in her arms and back as, accompanied by a couple of men Domnall had appointed to guard her, she returned to the feast with a great jug of ale in her arms. The scene was as merry as ever and as she met Domnall's concerned eyes she smiled slightly to show him all was well. In a quick glance around the hall, she spotted Drust sitting in a group with his back to her. Determined never to meet his eyes again she carried the jug to the table.

"There you are, my love," Cinaed called. "Our guests are quite parched with thirst!"

Baena wished for nothing more than to throw herself into Cinaed's arms and sob. It was a real effort to casually pour the drinks and say "Forgive me, my lord. I spilt some ale on my tunic and took the time to change."

"And you look as charming as ever, does she not, my lords?"

Baena bowed her head to hide her expression as the drunk men all enthusiastically agreed. More male attention was the last thing she wanted.

She did not have to wait too much longer before Cinaed took a moment when she was alone to say in a low voice, "It is nearly time. Go to our chamber and bolt the door. Do not open it unless I or Domnall command it."

Baena gave him a strained smile and slipped from the feast. While she longed to run to the safety of her chambers the thought of waiting alone for news was unbearable. She hesitated, looking fearfully around before concealing herself behind some shrubs near the entrance to the hall.

The first sounds quickly came. There was a loud crash followed by a curse. Baena crept to the doorway and peeped round the hangings to see that Domnall had, apparently accidentally, knocked a platter to the floor.

Cinaed cursed his brother for his clumsiness while a couple of serving men scrabbled on the floor to clear the debris or so it seemed. So subtly, that even Baena did not see them do it, the men were loosening the bolts that held the bench together.

"Do not curse me for a fool, Brother," Domnall roared at Cinaed.

"I call you a fool because you are one. And a drunkard to boot," Cinaed yelled back, sounding strongly affected by the drink himself.

"No man shall call me that!" Domnall threw the remains of his drink at Cinaed.

The pain and terror faded momentarily from Baena's mind, as she watched the brothers appear to glare angrily at each other.

"You forget yourself, Brother," Cinaed said icily. "And you forget the honour due to my rank."

"Oh yes, the mighty King Cinaed! We should all grovel and beg your pardon."

"Retire to your chamber you drunk fool!" Cinaed thundered.

Domnall laughed. "Come, my friends, shall we all sing the praises of the Great Cinaed?"

The noble heads of the Pict Royal Houses roared with laughter and needed no encouragement to join in the jeering at Cinaed.

Cinaed kicked his chair backwards in an apparent rage and in doing so knocked against the bench. With the bolts loose the bench collapsed sending men flying to the floor. The burst of laughter that followed was abruptly cut short as the sprawling Picts realised that Cinaed, Domnall and every serving man present held a gleaming sword in his hand.

Baena froze, wishing now she had gone to her chamber. She put her hands over her ears, but this did nothing to stifle the screams of terror and anger that tore apart the air. Cinaed was unrecognisable to her as he ordered his men to attack. She winced as he brought his own sword slicing down onto the shoulder of the Head of the Third Royal House. Blood spurting from the wound, the man stumbled backwards, but that didn't stop Cinaed. He thrust his sword on, not even stopping when the man lay groaning on the ground. In a valiant attempt at defence, the Pict men pulled out their ceremonial daggers, although these were near useless against the huge swords of the Gaels. Through the muffling of her fingers, Baena thought she heard Drust cry out in rage, but it was hard to be sure of anything in that maelstrom of clashing metal.

Some of the men tried to make a break for the doorway, but warriors moved quickly to obstruct their path. There was nowhere for the terrified Picts to go, as the Gaels encircled them. With her view blocked Baena felt able to turn away at last, her heart thundering with terror. Falling to her knees she thought she would be sick, but as she shivered and retched all she could hear was the gasps and gurgles of men struggling to take their final breaths.

When silence fell Baena plucked up the courage to peer again into the hall. An acrid smell of blood hit her first before her eyes could make sense of the sight. It was to be one she would never forget although for the rest of her life she tried very hard to. The ground appeared to be covered with a crimson carpet that oozed ever larger. The bodies of men who just a short while ago had been drinking and laughing now lay everywhere.

She tried not to think of the jovial greeting of the Head of the Third House, as she looked at him slumped on the ground, his grey tunic splattered in red drops. Across his chest, the cloth was torn and she could see a scarlet slash where Cinaed's sword had marked him from neck to belly. Before her lay an arm, no telling who it belonged to among that heap of bodies, its fist clenched uselessly.

Quietly, Cinaed's warriors moved around the bodies, stripping them of their jewelled pins, sword belts and chains. It seemed foolish to care about this last indignity, yet it was this that caused Baena to open her mouth in a silent scream at this gruesome tableau of slaughter.

Cinaed stood in the middle of the hall with his back to her, his sword at the throat of a man on his back. It was Drust and it seemed he still lived.

"Come, Brother, it is fitting that we dispatch this man together," Cinaed called.

Domnall crossed the room to face Cinaed.

"And so our father is avenged at last," Cinaed said.

"You will never get away with this!" Drust cried. "Murdering men who have come to you in peace."

"Peace?" Cinaed exclaimed. "Every treaty, every alliance broken by you and your kin." Cinaed gestured at the bodies around him. "Even after we went to your aid against the Norsemen. For once the peace is broken on my terms. Are you ready, Brother?"

Domnall raised his sword but then lowered it.

"Wait. Cinaed, there is something you should know. Earlier this night Drust most grievously attacked your lady."

Baena shrank away, horrified that Domnall had so quickly reported the events to Cinaed. Even from behind Baena could see the rage that consumed him. He kicked Drust hard in the ribs several times ending in a splintering crack of bone. Drust howled in pain. Baena bit back a sob wondering if Cinaed would want to inflict a similar punishment on her.

"She wanted me!" Drust screamed. "She has always wanted me."

Baena longed to scream a denial, but no voice would come out. She could only stare in horror as she waited for Cinaed's reaction.

Cinaed slowly looked up and she got a glimpse of the fury on his face. At that instant, she longed for death to take her, so she would never have to see Cinaed look at her in that way. "Did… he… force himself on her?" Cinaed seemed almost unable to get the words out.

Domnall shook his head. "No, I came upon them in time. She had fought most valiantly against him, but her strength was at an end."

Cinaed aimed one last kick and spat at Drust. "I would I could kill him twice. Come Brother, let us end this now."

As the two sons of Alpin raised their swords Baena stumbled away and collapsed weeping by the wall. She wept for all the men who had perished both this night and in all the years of conflict. She wept for Cinaed. Her love for him would never change, but she had seen a new side to him that night. She had always known of his reputation as a warrior, but knowing only the loving husband and father it had been easy to forget. She wept for herself, for the deeds she had done that night and her fears that Cinaed would now view her with distaste.

She even wept for Drust. Not the man who had attacked her that night, but for the merry, dark haired lad she had played with so many years ago.

Chapter eight

Baena was slumped against the wall when Cinaed and Domnall strode from the shelter, their swords still in their hands.

"Baena! What are you doing out here?" Cinaed exclaimed.

Baena did not stop to think before she uncurled herself and flung herself towards him. Cinaed dropped his sword with a crash and caught her. He held her at arm's length.

"I am covered with blood," Cinaed told her as she looked at him questioningly with anguished eyes.

"I don't care. Their blood is on me in any case," Baena begged, frightened that the blood was but an excuse to avoid enclosing her in his arms.

But she needn't have worried. Cinaed gave a slight smile and pulled her against his chest. His strong arms folded around her and for the first time that evening she felt safe.

"I'm sorry. So sorry," she sobbed. "I betrayed you this night."

"No, no, my love. Don't say that."

"My body failed you. I would not have stopped him. I am sorry," she cried, still waiting to be punished. Still certain that she deserved to be punished.

But Cinaed pulled her closer still. The weight of his arms hurt her bruised back, but she did not complain. "Baena, when you cared for the women after the Norse attacks did you blame them?"

Baena shook her head.

"Then why would any man blame you? Your strength may have failed you, but I know your heart did not."

Baena lifted her head so she could look into his face. "Then you forgive me?"

Cinaed smiled a tortured smile that was surprisingly sweet. "My love, if you need my forgiveness then, of course, you have it. But I do not feel you have done anything to forgive." His face crumpled. "The truth is that it is I who have betrayed you. I swore I would protect you above all else this night and I failed. I hope you can forgive me. I do not think I will ever forgive myself."

Baena clung tighter to him, her sobs gradually calming. Cinaed looked over the top of her head at Domnall. "Brother, we can never speak of what has happened this night."

Domnall looked insulted. "I know that. You cannot think I would ever besmirch Baena's name."

But Cinaed took one arm away from Baena to embrace Domnall. "You misunderstand me. You saved Baena this night. We will never speak of it again, but I will not forget it. I am forever in your debt."

Domnall waved it away. "Far too many shameful deeds this night. Glad to have stopped one of them. Well, I'm to my rest. There will be much to do in the morn. A good night to you both."

With no words left to say Cinaed and Baena clung to each other for a long time in the darkness of the night. A deep weariness came over her, but every time she closed her eyes images of dying men flashed before her, men killed by the man now standing in her arms. Feeling his hands gently stroking her hair it seemed impossible to believe that he had been capable of such deeds. She looked up at him.

"Domnall is right. This is no way to conduct a war," Cinaed sighed as he met her eyes.

"What was the alternative? A huge battle? Endless border skirmishes?" Baena cried, a touch of hysteria in her voice. It was far too late for Cinaed to be regretting his plan.

"I do not know, but I never thought to kill helpless men."

Baena put her arms around his neck, feeling strangely comforted by his change in mood. "They might have perished in battles in any case along with many others. Look out there, Cinaed," she gestured to the world beyond. "All around you men are sleeping. Good men, both Gael and Pict who thanks to you may now not die in senseless border disputes. As a mother of sons, I thank you for what you have done this night."

"I hope you are right, my love. If we bring peace to this land it will be worth it, but I shall never forget what I have done this night."

Baena clasped his hands and cried a little wildly "Then come to bed. Let me help you forget this night!"

"Tonight?" Cinaed sounded shocked. "No, I cannot expect that of you tonight."

Baena stepped back. Her face was smeared with blood from where she had rested it against Cinaed's chest and further streaks marked her tunic. She didn't care. She would never want to wear anything from that night again.

"Have I given you so great a disgust of me?" she asked forlornly.

Cinaed cursed himself for his reaction and put his arms back around her. "No, my love," he said softly. "You could never disgust me. I desire you as much as ever. But what of you? Do you truly want me this night?"

Standing on tiptoes Baena kissed him, ignoring the stench of blood that still clung to him "Yes my love. I too need to forget this night."

It was not for some weeks that Baena realised that it was on this night of blood that her next child must have been conceived.

Chapter nine

When the first light of the new day filtered through the smoke hole of their chamber Baena and Cinaed were both already awake.

Cinaed quickly dressed himself, his ears straining for the slightest sound that his deeds had been discovered. He was taking no chances with this day and he knew that his army would have already crept closer to Scone under the cover of darkness. In a bout of apparent generosity, he had given vast quantities of ale to the Pict armies the previous evening. Of course, he couldn't be sure, but if those Pict men were anything like his own they would have taken full advantage of his hospitality and be in no state to fight today, especially without their leaders to urge them on.

Baena too slipped from the bed and in the grey light, Cinaed noticed the bruises and torn skin across her shoulder blades. He was horrified.

"My God, I had no idea you were hurt so badly!" he exclaimed.

Pulling on a loose tunic Baena tried to smile. "It is not so bad."

Cinaed frowned, remembering how he had clung to her in the night. "Did I hurt you?"

Forcing herself to maintain her smile, Baena shook her head, although this was not true. Her shoulders stung with every movement and the slightest pressure on the bruises brought fresh pain. But Baena knew it was useless to explain to Cinaed that the pain was of little consequence compared to her need to feel safe in his arms or that she'd rather feel that sharp pain in her back than the milder one on her arms where Drust had grabbed her. The thought of those dead man's fingerprints still marking her even now the blood had been washed away made her shudder and it was with relief that she covered them in the sleeves of her tunic before Cinaed could notice them.

Cinaed still looked tormented and he put his arms very gently around her. "That man died too easily."

A noise from outside made them both start.

"I must go. Bolt the door when I am gone."

"No. I am coming with you."

"It could be dangerous and I've put you in enough danger already. Stay."

"I'm not waiting here to be slaughtered. If there is danger, I would rather die at your side," Baena cried in panic.

Cinaed sighed. "Very well. I suppose it is useless to dissuade you. But remember, a clansman at war must always obey his chief. If you come down you must obey me without question." He gave a slight laugh. "And yes, I know that is hard for you."

Baena smiled a small, but genuine smile at this as she slipped her hand into her husbands.

Domnall was already outside, his sword in his hand.

"Our troops are here," he reported to Cinaed in a low voice. "But I've seen Pict men at the chapel." He raised an eyebrow upon seeing Baena at Cinaed's side.

"She insists on joining us," Cinaed answered the question that was so obviously in Domnall's mind.

"My dear brother, why is it that you can so effortlessly command a thousand men, but struggle to control one woman?"

"That is one of life's great mysteries."

The light-hearted mood between the brothers was short lived. A group of Pict soldiers had just come out of the chapel where Cinaed had ordered the bodies to be placed. Their anger was obvious. Cinaed drew his own sword and put a protective arm around Baena.

"If I give the word you must stand back," he whispered.

Around them armed Gael warriors were gathering. As the Picts got closer the Gaels drew their weapons. Cinaed raised a hand, as he waited to see what the Picts would do.

"What is the meaning of this, Lord Cinaed?" one man asked.

Indicating for everyone else to keep back Cinaed stepped forward. Baena held her breath as she watched him. There was no sign of the stresses of the previous night. He seemed completely in charge of the situation and his voice was almost insolent as he answered the Picts.

"The meaning of this is that the matter of the Pict crown is settled. I am your king. If you fight me you will be dealt with as traitors."

The Picts muttered among themselves before the Pict man spoke again. "We do not recognise your authority."

The Gaels raised their weapons and awaited their King's orders. Cinaed held up a hand to stall them a moment. He glanced back at Baena and his look was stern. Baena shivered as she was reminded of the look on Cinaed's face the night before. This was no look from a man to his beloved wife, but from a Chief to one of his subordinates.

"Stand back," he ordered.

Domnall shook his head as she quickly returned towards the castle. Baena was already regretting coming with Cinaed. It seemed that she was now to witness another slaughter and this one in broad daylight. Seeing the grief-stricken anger on the Pict faces she realised that it was even possible that Cinaed might be the one she saw slaughtered before her very eyes. No one took any notice of her. The eyes of every Gael were focused on Cinaed, as the Pict archers lifted their crossbows.

But before Cinaed could give the order to advance one of the Picts cried aloud and pointed to the sky. As the other Picts followed his gaze their faces went white and their weapons dropped.

"The sun! Jesu, the sun!" cried the man.

"It is a judgement upon us!" cried another.

The Gaels shifted, uncomfortable with the change of mood. Cinaed suspected trickery and kept his gaze fixed on the Picts as their terror seemed to increase. But it was the gasps from his own men that convinced Cinaed that the Pict reaction was genuine.

"My Lord King," one of them called in a trembling voice. "Look at the sun!"

Baena turned to where the sun was rising between the hills and the colour drained from her face. On this fateful day, only half the sun was rising. The men of Dal Riata looked at each other with consternation on their faces and the tight formation behind Cinaed relaxed.

"What does it mean?" men asked each other.

"What does it mean?" a Pict called back. "It is obvious. The sun is leaving the Land of the Picts. It will shine no more now that our king is dead."

Baena knew that Cinaed had to be shaken, but there was no sign of it in his voice. "That is nonsense. You have lost kings before, but the sun has continued to shine."

"It is a sign that God does not accept your claim, Lord Cinaed. And it is our punishment for our failure to protect the good King Drust."

Cinaed's lip curled, but the warriors of Dal Riata shuffled their feet and looked uncomfortable. Baena ran forward again and stood behind Cinaed. Domnall looked worried, his eyes darting around. If the men failed them now the danger to Cinaed would be immense.

"Sister, you should flee while you still can," he whispered in Baena's ear. "I do not know if even Cinaed can hold the army together through this."

"Only if Cinaed commands it," she said in a low voice. "Otherwise, I'll stand with him even if no other does."

Domnall raised his eyebrows and Baena gave a shaky laugh, her eyes still looking up through her lashes on that terrible half sun, sure that a terrifying judgement was to be visited upon them. "I'm sorry, Brother. I know you will always be true."

"So you know that Cinaed will not stand alone." He tugged on Cinaed's arm. "Brother, I beg you to order your wife to safety."

Cinaed ignored the suggestion. Turning, he put an arm around each of them. "I think the sun is growing again. What do you think?"

The three of them clung together watching, as did every Pict and Gael present and probably across the land. The sun climbed higher and Baena began to think that Cinaed was right. It did seem as if the sun was increasing.

As the minutes passed they were sure of it. Both Gaels and Picts began to smile nervously as it seemed that God's wrath would not, after all, be delivered upon them. Many of them began to pray.

After an hour the sun shone on them with as much splendour as could be expected on an autumn day and Cinaed allowed himself one sigh of relief.

Striding away from the Gaels he stood between the two groups. "My People," he started and with a shock, Baena realised he was addressing them as one. "We have indeed had a sign today and one I thank God for. Never have I been more confident of his blessing."

Cinaed smiled almost affectionately on the groups of bewildered men. "These past years Gaels and Picts alike have seen too many of their great men fall. This morn we could rightly feel that only half of the sun shone upon us. But we have had a sign from God himself that this is no more! Allow the half that remains to lead and guide you and as we have seen, the sun will shine once more on the combined territories of Dal Riata and Pictavia."

The Picts whispered among themselves, unsure of what to make of this speech.

"I am the son of Lord Alpin, the greatest chief Dal Riata has ever known and of Lady Unuis, of the Sixth Royal House. In their names, I command you all."

The Gaels all knelt on the ground, but the Picts still looked uncertain and looked at each other as if waiting for some other man to make the first move. When the Gaels knelt Domnall knelt with them, but Baena remained standing. Now she walked forward to stand before the Picts and her own clear voice rang out.

"I am Baena, daughter of the great Causantin, former Head of the Third Royal House and Sabina the Beautiful of the Fourth Royal House. In their names, I, Baena, Queen of Dal Riata command you to bow before your King, the mighty Cinaed!" She half expected the Picts to hurl spears at her, but at that moment, she didn't much care. She would die trying to win the Picts for Cinaed.

Baena could see the shock in Cinaed's eyes and Domnall too raised his head to stare at her from the Gael lines. Cinaed took a step towards her, and grabbed her hand as if to pull her back, but then he stopped. None of the Picts had so much as moved.

"Daughter of the Third and Fourth Royal Houses I thank you for your loyalty," he said as he brought her hand to his lips. "Men of these Houses do you still revere the names of Unuis, Causantin and Sabina?"

"Yes, my Lord King we do," Baena replied, and to Cinaed's total astonishment she dropped to her knees before him. It did not take long after that. One by one the Pict men knelt until only Cinaed was left standing. For a minute, he looked at the bowed people.

"Lord Domnall Mac Alpin of Dal Riata rise and stand before me."

Domnall did as he was told, bowing his fair head as he stood before his brother.

"Lady Baena, Daughter of the Third Royal House rise and stand before me."

For an instant Baena forgot the horrors of the last day and her face lit up in a burst of joy. For so long her Pict heritage had been ignored. Now, at last, Cinaed of all people was publicly acknowledging it and acknowledging it with pride.

"My people, these two are most beloved to me. And in that love you can place your hopes. Just as my love and trust for these two will never waver, so you can rest easy that my love for my people, both Gael and Pict will remain as true. Go in peace my friends. Mourn the dead if you must, but look to the future as the sun shines on us all once more."

There was a rustling as everyone present rose from their knees. Many felt a sense of awe as they looked at the tall man standing in the sunlight, his Pict queen and his Gael brother at his side. Cinaed's powers of persuasion had worked their usual spell and no one present had any heart for a fight. Later that day the bodies of the murdered Pict lords were given a quiet, yet respectful burial, but by then Baena, Cinaed and Domnall had returned to Forteviot as Cinaed started to plan how to best secure his new kingdom.

Chapter ten

Can the circumstances around conception affect the growing child? That was a question Baena was to ask herself many times over the next wretched months. Cinaed was delighted when some weeks after that terrible night she told him that she thought she was with child.

"A most auspicious omen," he commented. "I had thought you were looking pale. Are you feeling very unwell?"

"A little sick," Baena admitted, not wanting to tell Cinaed the true extent. Even the smell of food was making her sick and for several days now it was only in the evening that she felt able to nibble on a small portion of her meal.

"You must take things easier. We shall all pray for your health and that the babe is born well this time," Cinaed smiled.

Baena felt her smile slip slightly. She knew that Cinaed had never blamed her for the loss of her child the previous year, but the memory still pained her.

"We must hope for another fine son, now that I have such a big kingdom to control," Cinaed said, not noticing her that her expression.

"Cinaed, might I return to Dunadd?" she asked, as she felt the familiar urge to cuddle her children. She was certain that looking at their sweet faces would drive away the hideous memories of those blood-stained Pict faces lying among the remains of the feast.

"Dunadd?" Cinaed looked surprised. "The journey is dangerous, my love. Our enemies are not all vanquished. I would need to send many men to protect you this time. And the weather is so uncertain. I do not think such a journey would be good for you or the babe within."

"Please, Cinaed. It has been so long since I have seen the children. And it is nearly Yule Tide…" Baena struggled to compose herself, but the thought of the Yule festivities without her children was too much and she was unable to stop the tears spilling out.

With a mixture of exasperation and concern Cinaed tried to comfort her. "Don't cry Baena, please don't cry." Smoothing her hair back from her forehead he looked down at her pale face, now blotched with tears. He was painfully aware of how much she had done for him this past year. It would be too cruel to refuse her this one thing she had asked for. "My love, I can make no promises, but if it is in my power I will get you to Dunadd for Yule."

"Oh Cinaed, thank you!" Baena breathed.

"Do not thank me yet, my love. It may not be in my power. I shall send men to check the path and locate places where you can rest on the way. But the weather too could turn against us at any time."

"Can you spare the men to escort me?" she asked.

Cinaed nodded. "I shall escort you. Domnall can hold things here over the winter," he grinned sheepishly. "I'd like to see those little rascals myself!"

Overjoyed Baena flung her arms around him, certain she would soon be with her children. After all, it was rare indeed that Cinaed did not succeed in anything he set out to do.

Cinaed wiped away the last remains of her tears. "You must rest and try to eat a little more than you have the last few nights. You need your strength."

Baena tried desperately to follow his instructions, but it was so hard. Never before had she experienced sickness like this. During the day the Pict women, Cinaed had appointed to care for her, brought honeyed water, which she drank in small sips. Any more than that and she gagged and retched once more.

In the evening she made the effort to eat in the hall with the others, but she could feel Cinaed's eyes on her as she could only nibble on morsels of pork or venison. She always left the table as soon as she could to lie down and feel the nausea fade at last.

Three nights later she rose from the table as she always did and felt everything blur around her. Cinaed, who had risen also to bid her goodnight, caught her in his arms and carried her to her bed, shouting loudly for her women to attend her.

"I do not think anything is wrong with the child, my Lord King," one woman reported afterwards to Cinaed. "Fainting is not uncommon in breeding women. It would be better if she could eat. Perhaps once she quickens all will be well."

Cinaed went to Baena's bedside filled with guilt.

"I know what you have come to say," she whispered, feeling her heart break at the look on his face.

Cinaed kissed her hand, wishing he could deny it. "I am sorry. I am afraid you would not survive the journey."

"I know," she shut her eyes and let the tears flow from beneath her lids.

Knowing that there was nothing he could do to help, Cinaed lay next to her on the bed and took her in his arms. He held her until her tears stopped and she slept.

Baena spent a miserable Yule alone. The unusually mild weather mocked her and made it possible for some of the Picts to launch a rebellion to the North of the territory that Cinaed commanded. With considerable regret, Cinaed knew that both he and Domnall were needed elsewhere and he rode away bitterly wishing that he had never brought Baena to Forteviot.

The Pict women who were left with her cared for Baena as well as they could, but they were strangers to her and all too frightened of their new ruler to relax into the laughter that had so characterised Baena's chambers at Dunadd.

"Are you sure you are with child?" a shocked Cinaed demanded when he returned two moons later.

Baena had risen shakily from her chair to greet him, but Cinaed had been horrified by the white face she offered up for a kiss and the thin hand and wrist he clasped.

With a forced smile, Baena smoothed her robes over her stomach so he could see her swelling belly.

"He moves," she told him. "If not a child then I know not what else it could be."

"But if you've quickened you should be feeling better," Cinaed exclaimed looking with censure at the other women as if they were to blame.

"My lady would be well enough if she could but eat," one woman spoke up quickly. "We try to tempt her appetite as best we can, my Lord King."

"Baena, you must eat," Cinaed ordered almost angrily.

Baena gestured to the women to leave the room, longing for the happy reunion that was their custom.

"I cannot," she said helplessly.

"What is wrong? You've had no trouble carrying the other babes."

"Perhaps it is a judgement upon us," Baena whispered.

"No," Cinaed said firmly.

"We killed helpless men."

"I killed, Baena. I and my men. Not you, so why would judgement be visited on you?"

"I know not, but I think this sickness is God's will and I must bear it." She sank back down onto her chair and shut her eyes. "Do not be angry with me, Cinaed. I will do everything in my power to present you with another son."

"But that son needs to be strong. How can he be if you don't eat?"

"I do not know," Baena replied, trying to hold back the tears.

Cinaed knelt down by her chair, laying his hand gently on her stomach. "My love, it is not just the child that concerns me. I am not angry with you, but I am… scared."

Baena managed a smile at that and stroked his face. "The Great Cinaed scared? What would the men say?"

Cinaed smiled too. "I am depending on you never to reveal it to a soul. Now, no more talk of judgements."

But Baena's belief that they were being punished was only strengthened when shattering news arrived a few days later.

To try to make up for leaving her alone over Yule, Cinaed was spending as much time as possible with Baena to raise her spirits. And so she was with him one morning when a muddy man burst in.

"My Lord King!" the man cried, as both Baena and Cinaed looked at him in surprise. "I have an urgent message from Lord Graunt. The Norsemen have attacked Dunadd!"

Chapter eleven

To Baena, it seemed as if time itself stood still. Cinaed had risen to his feet, horror bleaching his face.

"My children!" she shrieked. "What of my children?"

At the same moment, Cinaed strode across the room to grasp the man by the shoulders.

"Speak man! How bad was it when you left?"

"Some farms burnt. Cattle stolen," the man stammered.

"Never mind the cows!" Cinaed cried. "What of the fort?"

"The fort was not yet breached, my lord. Lord Graunt said your children were well."

Cinaed wiped his brow, some of the horror draining away. "Refresh yourself, man," he waved the messenger away. Turning back to Baena they looked at each other speechlessly. "Dunadd is the best fort in all Dal Riata. Graunt will keep them safe until I get there."

Without another word to her, he strode from the room shouting orders. As soon as they grasped the news the men moved quickly and by the afternoon a sizable force of both Picts and Gaels had gathered at Forteviot. Even Picts who had not welcomed their new king were outraged at the Norsemen encroaching on a settlement as well defended as Dunadd and the thought of the King's innocent children there seemed to touch everyone.

Baena wrapped herself in her warmest cloak and hurried out, all weakness forgotten. She hesitated in the doorway, looking at the troops. The numbers reassured her if only they would get to Dunadd in time. But her mind drifted back to the terrible battle that had killed her father and her heart failed her at the thought of these Norse fiends getting so close to her children. She quickly located Cinaed talking to Domnall. Cinaed's face was pale, but he wore the same look of brutal determination that Baena had witnessed on the night he had slain Drust. This time she could only be glad. Such brutality might yet save her babes.

"We'll not get far before nightfall, but we can make a start," Domnall was telling Cinaed as she came out. "Are we ready to fight for King Cinaed?" he shouted to the men.

The answering roar was deafening. Domnall clapped Cinaed reassuringly on the shoulder before they both noticed Baena coming towards them.

"Baena, it is cold. You should not be out," Cinaed said, kissing her. "Try not to worry."

"I'm coming with you!" Baena cried.

"Don't be so foolish. Return to your chambers."

Baena shook her head wildly. "No! My babies need me. I should never have left them." Baena pushed past them and ran toward the waiting horses. Domnall's mouth dropped open and he stared at Cinaed as if he half expected Cinaed to agree to Baena's plans.

But Cinaed strode past her and blocked her way. "Do as you are ordered!" he thundered.

A silence suddenly reigned over the army as everyone froze. No one had ever heard the king address the queen that way. Cinaed folded his arms and looked sternly at her. "If any clansman, any subject, whether Gael or Pict disobeys my order I have them beaten." He did not quieten his voice. "Do not presume on either your womanhood or your condition to prevent me doing the same to you."

Baena backed away in some terror, her arms protectively over her stomach. At the doorway she stopped, gaping at Cinaed. There was no love in his face. Almost she could believe he hated her. All eyes were on him and no man moved. Even Domnall was expressionless.

"Your orders, my lady, are very simple. Return to your chambers and look after the babe in your belly. It may be the only one we have left," Cinaed turned away and did not see how Baena had slumped against the doorway, trembling with the shock of hearing her worst fears out loud. "Mount your horses, men. Foot soldiers prepare to march. To Dunadd!"

"To Dunadd!" came the answering roar.

Cinaed and Domnall strode towards their horses at the head of the men. Baena slid to the ground, too devastated at the way they had both deserted her to care how the cold seeped through her tunic.

"Mount your horse, Brother," Cinaed said sternly to Domnall, who was frowning at him over the horses back.

"Yes, my lord." Domnall did as he was ordered, but he dared to glance back at Baena. "Are you sure you want to do the same?" he asked.

Cinaed was already on his horse and nodded curtly. He lifted the reins before he too glanced back.

"Domnall?"

"Yes, my lord?"

"Lead on. I will join you presently."

Beneath his helmet, Domnall gave a slight smile. "Yes, my lord." He urged his horse forward as Cinaed slid down.

As the horses trotted out Cinaed returned to where Baena was huddled on the ground.

"Baena," he said hesitantly, afraid she had collapsed.

She looked dully up at him and Cinaed knelt on the floor next to her. "Baena, you cannot come with me. You are not well enough. What am I to do if you become even more unwell? Abandon you alone in the hills? Or leave men from the army I cannot spare to guard you? If I know you are safe here I can put all my efforts into saving our children."

Baena looked at him pleadingly. "Do you have any idea how horrible it will be for me being here, not knowing what is happening?"

"Yes, I do. You will go on feeling how I am feeling right now. But you must bear it for the sake of the babe you have within you and for our babes back at Dunadd."

Broken hearted, Baena nodded and allowed Cinaed to pull her to her feet.

"Would you really beat me if I refuse to obey?" she looked miserably at Cinaed, expecting a swift denial, but none came.

Instead, for a long time, he looked at her from stern, grey eyes. Her husband was gone again and the warrior had returned. "I have never beaten a woman and I never want to, but every man in my army must obey me without question. If one does not the whole army could fall. I can have no favourites that have not truly earned my regard. If I do, I might as well hand over control of my kingdom to them. There must be one rule for all. That is why I must be prepared to give my life for these men because if I do not I cannot expect them to give their lives for me."

Baena nodded fearfully and Cinaed took her in his arms at last. "That is just one more reason why I do not want you with my army anymore. Please, Baena, be my wife. Welcome me into your arms when I return, bear my children and give me your blessing when I must leave again."

Baena made herself stand up straight and meet his eyes. They were gentle again. "My Lord King, it has been an honour to serve you."

Cinaed laid a hand on her shoulder "Daughter of the Third House, I have never served with anyone more valiant."

"But from now I will be content to be just a wife."

Cinaed smiled very tenderly. "Oh Baena, you will never ever be just a wife." He glanced around at the foot soldiers filing away. "I must go, my love, but remember this: I have an army full of men, but just the one wife."

Making the effort to smile back Baena pulled his head down to kiss him. "Go save our babes, Cinaed. May god speed your journey and send you victorious."

Chapter twelve

Baena walked up the steep path at Dunadd to the sacred rocks, as the sky grew ever darker. In the distance, she heard a rumble of thunder and saw lightning split the sky. At the top Cinaed stood on the rock, one foot embedded in the ancient footprint. His bloodstained sword was in his hand and red drops dripped into the basin mingling with the water of Dal Riata. Kneeling there, Baena scooped the crimson liquid over her face. It dripped down forming livid fingerprints on her bare arms.

Cinaed turned to face her, his eyes like stone. Silently he extended his hand. She was pulled onto the rocks and they stood there together while the thunder rumbled around them. Slowly Cinaed pointed with his sword to the ground below. Wearing his white tunic Causantin lay sprawled on the rocks, his neck at an unnatural angle. As Baena watched an eagle swooped down. It pecked viciously at his face, spattering the white tunic with bloody streaks. Baena screamed a silent scream and the eagle turned its head to glare at her out of Drust's glittering blue eyes…

Baena sat bolt upright in her bed, screaming aloud.

"Are you in pain, my lady?" came a voice.

Baena's heart was beating loudly as she looked wildly around. She was in her chamber at Forteviot.

"No, no. Just a dream." Baena dismissed the woman, then thought better of it. "No, wait, leave me a light."

The flickering oil lamp cast eerie shadows around the room, but Baena couldn't bear the idea of lying alone in the dark. Cinaed had been gone for weeks now and she had heard nothing since he left. Thinking of the ferocious Norsemen he would have had to face, she realised that it was more than possible that they were all dead. The child moved inside her, but she could find no comfort in it. The fleeting thought occurred to her that if it wasn't for this child she would be with the others at Dunadd and if they were dead, she would be dead with them.

Ignoring the nausea that built up as she moved Baena reached for a cross and prayed for forgiveness for that thought. The child was a blessing sent by God and she was the most terrible of sinners to wish it gone even for a moment. She knew the sickness and loneliness were just things she would have to accept to bring it safely into the world.

Lying back down again she watched the little window in the chamber until light started to creep in.

That long, lonely night was far from rare, leaving Baena even more exhausted each day. She mostly kept to her chambers and often returned to her bed in the afternoon to doze uneasily. One afternoon a noise disturbed her and she awoke to see Cinaed standing with his back to her in the doorway. She stared at him, thinking she was dreaming and tried desperately to get back to sleep so she could stay in such a pleasant dream.

"Cinaed?" she called half questioningly, still not completely sure he was really there.

But he turned and looked down on her. "I did not mean to wake you, my love," he said, not moving from the doorway.

"I am awake now," Baena sat up gingerly and looked pleadingly at him. "What of our babes? Are they safe now at Dunadd?"

Slowly Cinaed shook his head.

Baena felt an icy dash of fear clutch her heart. "What do you mean?" she whispered.

A smile twitched at Cinaed's lips as he simply stood to one side and two little figures darted past him.

"Mother, Mother!" Causantin flung himself at her. "I rode all the way all by myself."

"I rode on Uncle Domnall's horse!" Aed launched himself after his brother.

Certain now that she must be still dreaming Baena clasped the boys to her, covering the tops of their heads in kisses. They beamed up at her, chattering excitedly about their long ride.

Still unable to speak she looked at Cinaed, who stood smiling at her. "As you are not well enough to travel to Dunadd I thought I would bring your babes to you." In his arms was a little red headed girl. Baena reached up to her.

"She has changed so much," Baena breathed. "I wouldn't have known her."

The girl looked at her, then turned to bury her head in her father's shoulder.

"She doesn't know me either."

Joining his sons on the bed Cinaed put one arm around Baena and kissed her. "She'll get to know you again. She didn't recognise me a few weeks ago, now look at her!" he said as Coira wound his hair around her fingers.

Baena laughed for the first time in ages. "We are together again, that is all that matters."

"We are truly all together again. Graunt rode with us. I thought you could use Kieta with you."

"Oh Cinaed, thank you," she breathed, smiling in gratitude at her husband who among all his other cares had realised how to ease her loneliness.

But Cinaed shook his head ruefully. "Don't thank me, my love. I've done little enough for you this last year to deserve any gratitude. Bringing Kieta is a small thing to manage, especially as I shall be glad to have Graunt's counsel once again."

"But what of Dunadd? Was there much damage?" she pulled her children even closer. "Were they in danger?"

Cinaed looked solemn. "When we came down from the hills I thought all was lost. So much of the settlement was up in smoke I could scarce see the fort. Graunt did well to keep them at bay. Messengers had brought news of the Norsemen's approach to him, so most of the people were already in the fort and much livestock had also been brought in. The Norsemen burnt the farms and the metal works, but there was little they could do against the solid rocks of Dunadd. They tried to burn the gate, but Graunt had the men pile rocks behind it and stationed archers to fire on any Norseman who approached. He kept the children safe as I knew he would."

Baena shook her head sadly at the thought of the wreck of the bustling settlement. "We owe him a greater debt of gratitude than we can ever repay," she said quietly.

"I saw the fires!" Causantin announced proudly.

Cinaed gave Baena a look of half pride, half vexation. "This young lad kept climbing the rocks to watch the Norsemen." He ruffled his son's head. "Led Graunt a merry dance, did you not?" he said sternly.

"I'm hungry!" Aed complained.

"Go to the hall, my sons. There's plenty there," Cinaed told them.

"But come back here afterwards!" Baena called, unwilling to see them go for even a few minutes.

"Did Causantin really ride the whole way on his own?" she asked in amazement.

Cinaed laughed. "If he had we might have just arrived in time for next Yule! But he did well, my love. He'll be a great horseman one day. But what of you?" Cinaed lay the now sleeping Coira on the bed and put his arms around Baena. "You are still so thin."

"The sickness will not leave me. The babe grows ever bigger and stronger though so be not concerned."

"How much longer do you have?" he asked.

"The women think he will be here soon after midsummer."

"That is still some moons off." Cinaed looked worried. "Baena, surely you know that it is not the babe that concerns me. It is you that I would see stronger."

Chapter thirteen

With the arrival of the children, happiness and laughter came to Forteviot, but although Baena's spirits rose the sickness barely eased and she remained very weak. Kieta did all she could to nurse her and both Graunt and Domnall were often in attendance. They appeared ever merry in her presence, but always Baena could see the look of worry in their eyes as they left. As the weather improved Cinaed carried her outside so she could watch the children at play, hoping that the fresh air would do something to restore her appetite, but it was to no avail.

When Cinaed helped her back to her chamber after the midsummer festivities she asked him to stay with her awhile.

"I must talk with you if you have the time."

"Of course, my love." Cinaed sat down and tried to smile. She was unrecognisable from the vibrant young woman who had arrived in Forteviot last year. The child hung on her like a sack on a skeleton, her hair was thin and dull and her face white. Only her eyes remained the same, as full of love and courage as ever.

"It will not be long now I think. There are signs that the babe will come soon."

"I will be glad when he is safely here and then you can get strong again."

"Oh Cinaed," Baena shook her head. "My love, look at me. I do not know how I can survive this. Childbirth can take away even a strong woman and I am no longer that."

Cinaed rubbed a hand over his eyes. "Do not talk this way. I know it has been hard, but you have always come through before."

"I was strong then. Oh, I know as the birth grew near I was tired and irritable, but this time has been so different. I know you do not want to hear this, but I do feel it is a judgement upon me."

"No, Baena. How can that be? Any judgement would be on me."

"You are needed, Cinaed. I am not. That is why the judgement must be on me."

Cinaed held her very gently in his arms, afraid that too tight an embrace would snap her fragile bones. "You are needed. I need you," he said quietly. "Perhaps you are right and it is a judgement upon me. God knows that I do not value my own life as I value yours."

"I did not want to marry you nor you marry me, but we have been so happy have we not?"

"Happier than I ever believed was possible," Cinaed replied, kneeling at her side. "Do not speak this way, my love. You must come through."

"It is in God's hands, but promise me you will love this child if it lives and I do not. Love it like you do the others."

"I promise, my love. If this babe is to be your last gift to me I shall cherish it all the more." Cinaed kissed her, aware of the tears that were flooding to his eyes, before his old spirit came rushing back. "If this is a judgement I will atone. I will found an abbey, no matter the cost. I pledge this to God, if he will but spare you."

Baena smiled sadly at Cinaed's determination never to give up, although she felt certain that this was one battle he would not win. She wondered if Cinaed would marry again when she was gone. Perhaps by this time next year, there would be a new queen at Forteviot. Worry lined his face, but he was still such a handsome man with grey eyes that could sparkle with humour, as well as cut like a knife. She knew that it would be unlikely for so vital a king to remain long unwed. Nor could she wish for Cinaed to be alone.

Baena's pains started a few days after that conversation, late one night. Fearfully Cinaed kissed her, praying it would not be the last time and called for her women. For Baena there was a sense of relief that the day had finally come. She was so glad to have Kieta with her. She had been with Baena at every birth and it meant that she was not left alone with the formidable old Pict woman who had been summoned to the castle these past weeks. She had a reputation among the women for helping mothers through the most difficult of births, but Baena had found her highly intimidating.

When dawn came to Forteviot there was still no sign of the baby and throughout that long day, men tiptoed around waiting for the moment to be announced. Cinaed sat in the hall at the foot of the steps to the birthing chamber. He waved away all offers of food and drink with increasing temper as the day wore on with no news.

In the birthing chamber the mood was similarly glum. Baena lay on the straw without even the strength to cry out as her body was wracked with pain. Kieta sat next to her helplessly, sometimes trying to give her sips of a honeyed concoction that the old Pict woman insisted would help. Night came again and still there was no sign that the end was in sight.

"Is there nothing we can do?" Kieta begged the old woman.

"Not yet," came the grim reply.

Kieta smoothed Baena's hair. She was carrying a child herself and was feeling exhausted, but there was no question of her abandoning her friend.

At last, as dawn came Baena's body began to push out the child. But if the women hoped that the ordeal would soon be over they were to be disappointed. Hours went by and they could still barely glimpse the head.

"The babe is stuck," the old woman said, after a lengthy and painful attempt to reach the child. "I feared that would happen with her so small and thin and the King so big and strong."

"What can we do?" Kieta sounded frightened.

"I might save one."

Baena's eyes flicked open. "The babe. Save the babe," she whispered. She had heard stories of what would have to be done to release the child, but she was beyond caring. Whatever was done to her this day it could be no worse than the fate she had helped to condemn the Pict lords. All she could hope for was that God would be merciful to her soul.

"I take my orders from the King," said the woman as she stalked out.

In the hall, Cinaed looked up eagerly. "What news?"

"Nothing yet, my Lord King. I would know which of them I should try to save."

Cinaed froze in terror and was unable to answer.

"The Queen or the child?" the woman asked impatiently. "The Queen has requested I try to save the child."

"What will you have to do?" Cinaed whispered.

"That is not your concern, my Lord King. I must know which one."

Exhausted and out of his mind with worry Cinaed was still the King. He stood up very tall. "What will you do?" he repeated.

The woman shook her head, not even attempting to hide her annoyance. "To save the Queen I must reach into her and crush the child's head." She withdrew a thin knife from her robes. "Sometimes it is necessary to remove an arm as well. The birth should follow easier and God willing, the Queen can regain her strength. If all is well she can get with child again in a few moons."

Cinaed's hands twitched as he itched to strike the old woman who spoke so calmly, but she was not finished.

"To save your child I must cut into the Queen's belly and remove the babe."

Cinaed stared in horror at the knife. "I must speak with Baena."

"The birthing chamber is no place for a man," the woman protested.

But Cinaed pushed past her and ran up the steps. He'd witnessed horrors a plenty on a hundred battlefields but none was to be as terrible for him as the sight of his beloved wife huddled against Kieta on the straw. Meeting Kieta's eyes he saw the bleakness in them.

"Baena," he called gently.

Baena looked up. "Save the child, my love. I beg you."

Cinaed looked at her, unable to bear the courage in her eyes. Moving his gaze reluctantly to the knife still in the old woman's hand, he nodded slightly, unable to speak.

"Very good my Lord King. Leave now and, God willing, I will present you with your babe soon."

Cinaed knelt down next to Baena and lifted her gently from Kieta. He looked down sorrowfully at her face.

"I will stay with her until the end, my lord," Kieta said in a low voice.

Cinaed flinched as a spasm racked Baena's body. When it passed she opened her eyes again.

"Do not grieve, my love," she gasped. "It is my duty to die for my child to live."

Cinaed knew what he had to do. There was no point prolonging her agony. He should kiss her farewell and run from the room to be as far away as possible when they cut her open. He'd slashed many a man across the belly in battle and knew only too well the screams of agony that would follow. That this was now to be done to his precious wife was more than he could bear. He brushed his lips gently across hers. Tears ran from his eyes as he realised it would be the last time he would ever do this, then he rested her back on the straw. Cursing himself for his cowardice, he realised that he was glad her eyes were shut. He would never look into them again, but the courage in them would surely destroy him if he could witness it now.

For a while he gazed at her, as so many memories flooded back. Baena running to meet him on Iona with baby Causantin in her arms, the proud smile on her face when she showed him the ridiculous fish skin tunic, and her eyes looking up at him in wonder on that first sweet night they had spent together back at Dunadd.

Then came the less pleasant memories of the last year when he had forced her into a man's world. With guilt crushing his heart, he wondered how much that had to do with transforming that bright, laughing girl to the broken woman he saw before him.

Slowly he backed away. The two women were barely aware of him. Kieta, tears running down her own face, pulled up Baena's robe, exposing her stomach and gently cradled her head on her lap. The old woman, her face grimly resolute, knelt down beside her the thin blade in one hand and her other probing Baena's stomach, working out where to cut.

"Stop!" The words were out of his mouth before he even realised it and the old woman looked up at him in irritation. His grey eyes cut into her. "What happens if you do nothing?"

"Nothing? My lord, you will likely lose them both."

"It will be in God's hands." Cinaed knelt down and stroked Baena's hair as another spasm coursed through her body. "If it is Gods will that you be taken, he will take you," he whispered. "But I can't order it." He took the knife from the woman's hand and flung it across the room.

"Very well, my Lord King," the woman said in a contemptuous tone. "As you wish."

Cinaed didn't move and Kieta gently touched his arm. "My lord. Cinaed, this is a woman's place. You should not be here."

Ignoring the outraged gasp of the old woman and with a defiant look at Kieta, Cinaed took Baena back in his arms.

"If the Queen can enter a man's world," he muttered.

Kieta looked mystified, but through the pain, Baena heard him and sank her head gratefully onto his chest. She knew she was still likely to die, but somehow in his arms the agony seemed easier to bear. If she had to die there was no place she would rather be.

It was impossible to say how long Cinaed knelt on the floor as spasm after spasm shook Baena. Suddenly Kieta looked excited. Both she and the old woman were very busy. Cinaed buried his head in Baena's hair, not wanting to see what they were doing to her.

"My Lord King, the babe is nearly here."

It did not take much longer before at last a motionless baby slithered out onto the straw.

"It's a girl," the old woman said in a flat tone as Kieta frantically rubbed the baby.

Cinaed held Baena very close, his eyes fixed on the baby. The infant did not move and the old woman shook her head. The prayers on Cinaed's lips were unable to come. All he could feel was an overwhelming rage that everything Baena had endured would be for nothing. Kieta struck the baby hard on the back, again and again. There was a faint choking sound. Again Kieta struck the baby. Suddenly came the most beautiful sound Cinaed had ever heard. The baby let out her first cry. Tears fell down Kieta's cheeks as she cradled the baby and she smiled in relief at Cinaed. His face lit up. "She lives! My love, you have done it! The babe is here."

But Baena remained slumped against his shoulder. Very gently Cinaed turned her over. Her head lolled back and her eyes were shut.

"Baena," he whispered, his eyes widening in horror at her shallow breathing. Carefully he laid her down on the straw and looked on helplessly as the blood flowed from her.

Chapter fourteen

Baena remembered nothing of the next days. Afterwards she was told how she had drifted in and out of consciousness. How during those moments that she stirred they had fed her of sips of honeyed drinks and milky porridge. And how Cinaed handed over nearly all of his kingly duties to Domnall and Graunt, to divide his time between sitting by her side and praying in the church.

But eventually came the day when, still very weak, she opened her eyes and knew where she was. They had not dared move her from the birthing chamber but had tucked plump feather pillows under her to make her more comfortable.

"My lady!" Kieta was sat nearby. She reached for a pot of porridge that was being kept warm and began to spoon it into Baena's mouth.

Kieta looked up as the old woman entered. "My lady is eating. She has had eight full spoons!"

Kieta sounded delighted, as well she might. It had been a long time since Baena had eaten so much.

She managed another two, before turning her head away. "The baby?" she questioned, half afraid of the answer. She remembered so little of the end of the birth that she wondered whether Cinaed had eventually given the order to destroy the child to save her life.

"You had a girl, my lady. She seems a strong little lass."

"Where?"

"Let us refresh you a little, my lady, then I will bring her. And summon the Lord King. He will be most happy to see you."

When the baby girl was brought to her, Baena managed a weak smile. Normally she would have laughed at seeing Cinaed's features so clearly on a tiny baby and a girl baby at that.

She ran a finger down the baby's soft cheek. "Perhaps Cinaed's next child will be a boy," she said.

The old woman and Kieta looked at each other. "My Lady Queen," the old woman started. "I have attended many births and seen many as hard as yours. Of course, I cannot be certain-"

Kieta interrupted her, "Stop."

"She must know," said the old woman.

Baena looked at them and Kieta sighed. "Let me tell her." Kieta smoothed Baena's hair back from her face and took her hand. "My lady, whenever the woman has seen births like yours, she has never known them to bear another living child. Baena, forgive me for this news, but it is likely there will be no more."

Baena stared at Kieta almost unable to take in her words. Not only was the baby a girl, but she would bear no more. Knowing she had truly failed she closed her eyes and let a tear trickle down her cheek. A barren queen was a useless one.

At that moment, Cinaed entered the room. He took the baby in his arms and motioned for them to be left alone. Sitting down by Baena's side he lifted her limp hand. He looked at her, searching anxiously for the signs of life that had been reported to him.

"Baena," he whispered.

He smiled slightly as Baena's eyes fluttered open. "They tell me there will likely be no more babes."

Cinaed looked vexed. "I ordered them not to tell you that yet."

"I am sorry," she whispered as tears spilt over again. "I know you must think that two sons are a poor brood."

"I do," Cinaed agreed. Baena's eyes flew to his face. It was true, but she had expected him to say something soothing. He smiled gently at her. "But two sons and two daughters I consider a very fine brood indeed."

"Oh Cinaed," somehow Baena managed a smile. "I know that is not true, but thank you."

"It is true," Cinaed insisted. "Of course I value our daughters as I do you. I need my strong sons to help with this new kingdom. But this new kingdom was not just created by strong men. You and my mother before played a part. A vital part. Who knows what our daughters will achieve for us when it is their turn to marry?" The baby began to squall and Cinaed smiled as he kissed her. "And you will lead your husband a merry dance, won't you? Just like your mother!"

He looked again at Baena. "I'd like to call her Mael Muire. I have spent so much time this week in prayer to the blessed virgin it seems appropriate."

"A goodly name," Baena whispered, her mind still on the lack of sons. "Cinaed, a long time ago there was a woman. Annis. She bore you a son. Do you want to bring him to Forteviot to be raised with our sons?"

Cinaed flushed. "I didn't realise you knew about her," he said rather uncomfortably. "But no, he shall not come here. I would not supplant Causantin as my eldest son."

"Can I speak freely to you?" Baena's voice sounded stronger and her eyes were firm.

Cinaed nodded, feeling surprised. "You don't usually ask permission for that!"

Baena gazed up at him. "I think I would prefer you to bring that boy here, than someone younger. But you must do what is necessary. If you need to find a way to beget more sons I would support you as ever." It was an effort to keep the pain out of her voice. She knew that if Cinaed took a mistress she would be heartbroken, but needs must. Her own body was useless to him now.

For a long time Cinaed just looked at her, before laying the baby in her crib and taking Baena gently into his arms.

"Annis was a moment of weakness when you were but a child." Cinaed hesitated a second and Baena thought she saw a hint of mischief come into his eyes. "Did you know there was another woman after Annis? A little red headed Pict brat. The cheekiest woman imaginable. But somehow she found her way into my heart." To Baena's astonishment, Cinaed's voice broke. "And these past days when I thought she would depart this world it felt like my heart was being ripped from my body." He raised her hand to his face where she could feel the wetness from his eyes. "Baena, I could never share either my heart or my body with another woman."

Baena found that no words would come. She could only look at him, feeling as if her own heart would burst. Cinaed kissed her gently as he laid her back down on the pillows and they gazed at each other.

"Get strong, my love. It grieves me greatly that we will likely have no more children, but I shall learn to be content with the four bonny babes that we have if only you recover to stay at my side and lie again in my arms."

Chapter fifteen

It was a long climb back to health for Baena and, because trouble can never come singly, that summer the Picts rebelled against their new king, forcing Cinaed to be away from Forteviot. He returned briefly in the autumn to find Baena seriously ill again. When he had to head back to his troops he went crushed by sorrow. He expected at any day to receive a messenger telling him that his beloved Queen had succumbed to one of the illnesses that were so rife in winter.

It was a relief to him when the cold weather and dark nights finally forced the surrender of the most determined of rebels and Cinaed was able to return. He was so eager to be back that when the men stopped one night not far from Forteviot, he and Domnall took advantage of the full moon to ride on, arriving quite unexpectedly.

A busy scene awaited them in the torch-lit hall. Graunt, perhaps remembering his own boyhood ambitions, was helping Causantin and Aed to make a ball of fat and sticks to be lit at Yule.

"Father! Uncle Domnall!" Causantin cried suddenly, as the two men strode into the hall.

Causantin and Aed charged excitedly into their father's open arms.

Baena had been sitting by the fire watching the peat crumble and glow. She rose in delighted surprise when she heard the children shout.

Laughing, Cinaed embraced the lads before letting them jump on Domnall. He cast his eyes quickly round the smoky hall and then stopped, staring in amazement at Baena.

"Welcome home, Cinaed! We were not expecting you this night," she called, her hair sparkling in the firelight and her cheeks pink from its warmth.

Cinaed swallowed the lump that had come to his throat. "Look at you!" was all he could stammer.

Baena glanced down at her old grease stained tunic and wished she'd combed her hair after the stick gathering mission she and the children had been on earlier. "I wasn't expecting you, Cinaed. I'd have put on something finer if I'd known you were arriving this night."

"Don't be foolish!" Cinaed strode across the hall hardly able to believe his eyes. "You have never looked more beautiful."

He put his arms gently around her but finding to his joy that he no longer felt he would break her in two, whirled her off her feet in exuberant fashion. "You look so well!"

Baena smiled. "And you feel cold! We have nothing prepared for you, but come sit by the fire and they can bring you something. I'm afraid it is a poor homecoming."

But Cinaed, sitting down, pulled Baena onto his lap and kissed her heartily. "It is the best homecoming!" he told her.

"Father, Father!" Causantin cried. "Graunt said I could help carry the fireball with your permission. Can I? Please?"

"I am sure you can," Cinaed smiled at the boy. "If you promise to be careful."

Domnall too gave Baena a heartfelt embrace with Aed still clinging to his back. He ruffled Causantin's head. "Just don't set your hair on fire like a foolish boy I once knew!"

Graunt snorted and Cinaed grinned at him. "And what news of you, my friend?"

Graunt's usually stern face lit up. "The best news. Kieta was brought to bed not ten days ago and delivered of a fair son."

Cinaed clapped his friend on the back in delight, firing questions about his newest kinsman. But as refreshments were brought and Coira had climbed onto his lap Cinaed looked soberly around at them all.

"What ails you?" Baena asked slipping her hand into his. She wondered whether Graunt's happy news had only served as a painful reminder to him that he would probably have no more sons.

Cinaed's eyes were glistening and Baena was sure it was not just from the smoke. "I've just realised that in this last year I truly feared I would lose every single one of you here." He took a long drink of his ale and then perhaps feeling ashamed of his emotion he cuffed Domnall. "Except you of course. I know I'll never rid myself of you!"

Baena looked down to the crib where little Muire was sleeping peacefully through the noise. "We have been lucky," she whispered.

Cinaed squeezed her hand. "This next year will be better. Starting with Yule." He smiled at Baena as they both remembered the previous miserable Yule Tide. "It will be the happiest one we have ever spent."

"And next year Cinaed will be crowned," Domnall announced.

"Another crowning?" Baena exclaimed.

"Yes, I will not be truly accepted here until I have been officially crowned Rex Pictorum."

"We shall make it the greatest of celebrations," said Graunt. "By the end there will be none to doubt that you are the King."

Part 6: Year of our Lord 843

Chapter one

The preparations that summer for the crowning of King Cinaed as Rex Pictorum were extravagant, even more lavish than the ones at Dunadd had been. Now that Dunadd had proved vulnerable to Norse raids Cinaed had decided to make Forteviot his main residence and that summer it was filled with merriment. Cinaed had sent summons all over Pictavia and Dal Riata calling on his people to show their loyalty. The response from the Picts was mixed. There were still rebels, remnants of the old Royal Houses who clustered together to the North to plot among themselves, but for the most part, the Pict people had begun to accept their new king.

"I think they're a little afraid of you still," Domnall commented, as they surveyed the preparations from the gateway of the enclosure.

"That's no bad thing," Cinaed replied. "Getting a new kingdom is like getting a new wife. It's easier to subdue them if they're a little afraid." Baena glared daggers at him for this and even more so as he continued. "The trick is to keep her a little afraid, otherwise she gets cheeky and never shows you any respect."

Domnall grinned and shook his head. "Why," he demanded "have I heard them call you Cinaed the Hardy? Cinaed the Foolhardy would be a much better name! I've stood beside you against a hundred enemies, but if you upset her" he gestured at his sister-in-law "you're on your own. Some foes are too terrible even for me!"

Baena frowned at them both, pretending to maintain her annoyance. Sometimes Cinaed and Domnall seemed more like Causantin and Aed than the two most powerful men in the land. Cinaed laughed before his mood turned serious.

"You have stood beside me well, Brother and your reward is long overdue. The lands we took last autumn are fair ones and they shall be yours."

Baena could see that Domnall was pleased, but he waved the compliments aside in his usual fashion. "I shall always stand with you, Cinaed. Clan Mac Alpin sticks together!"

Cinaed put his hand on his brother's shoulder. "Yes we do and I think our father would be proud." He glanced down at Baena for a moment. "The reward I am offering is a poor one compared to how well you have served me."

Domnall glanced at Baena too. "Like I said, Brother. Clan Mac Alpin looks out for its own."

"Father! Father!" an excited voice called and they turned to see Causantin headed towards them.

The boy's dark blonde hair gleamed in the sunlight as he half ran, tugging on the hand of a man in religious dress. Priests and monks had come from all over the land to lend their blessings to Cinaed's crowning, but it was surprising to see Causantin on such familiar terms with any. But as he came closer they realised who it was. His hair and beard were whiter and his face more lined, but his smile was as gentle as ever.

Cinaed ran towards him, his hands outstretched. "Welcome, Father," he said, bowing. "I had hoped that Iona would send a representative, but I never dared think it would be you."

The Abbot smiled as he greeted Domnall and Baena. "It is perhaps a little indulgent of me, but I could not resist coming myself. My sons, I remember you both as little lads, no older than this one." And he patted Causantin's head. "I could never have dreamed that you would rise to such greatness."

"What news of Iona, Father?" Domnall asked. "Have there been many raids in the area?"

"Mull was raided last year," the Abbot admitted. "I think you were wise to remove your family, my Lord King. But the Abbey still stands."

"And the sacred bones of Saint Columba rest with you still?" Cinaed asked

"They do."

Cinaed frowned. "Father, if the threat grows too great those sacred bones must be moved. They could be brought here. I have founded an abbey not far away where they would be safe."

The Abbot looked startled. "I cannot imagine the sacred bones of Saint Columba being moved from Iona, my lord."

"But they must not fall into the hands of the Norsemen," Cinaed insisted. "They would steal them for the few scraps of gold on the casket and care nothing for the sacred treasure that lies within. Think on it, Father and if the threat grows too great, send word. I would send only my most trusted and god fearing men to bring our most sacred relics to safety."

"You may be right, my son. I shall think on it. I must not allow my vanity in Iona as the guardian of Saint Columba to come before the protection of the holy treasure."

Cinaed laughed. "I shall make a poor exchange," he said. "But if you entrust the bones of the blessed Saint Columba to me, one day I will trust Iona with my own bones."

"But not for a long time, I hope," Baena put in.

Cinaed shrugged. "These matters lie in God's hands. But as both man and boy, I spent many happy times on that isle. I can think of no better place to spend my eternal rest."

"Iona would be honoured," the Abbot replied gravely. "But I must agree with my Lady Queen and say that I pray that day is long off. I think this land will have need of you for a while yet."

The Abbot of Iona was not the only familiar, yet unexpected guest at Forteviot that summer. A couple of days later Baena had taken Coira into the settlement to listen to the storytellers and musicians who had gathered there.

She had always loved it when the settlements were in a festive mood and had lingered a little longer than she should. She almost wished she could join the people dancing by the fires rather than attend the feast for the nobles. Hurrying back to the fort she noticed a couple loitering near the gateway to the wooden stockade. One was a tall woman with abundant white-streaked hair. The other was concealed in a cloak. As Baena approached the woman turned and Baena saw her eyes.

"Mother!" Baena gasped.

The woman looked at her steadily as Baena ran forward.

"Mother, it is you!"

Sabina's face was lined, but she was still tall. Even now she stood almost a head taller than her daughter. She was dressed in a grey tunic which shocked Baena with its plainness. A silver chain around her neck was her only jewellery.

"Baena! Oh, my dear child!" Sabina stared at her in shock before her sharp eyes shifted to Coira.

Deciding that introducing her children could wait until after her own reunion, Baena sent Coira ahead. For a moment she and her mother just looked at each other and then Baena flung her arms around her. "I thought I would never see you again," she whispered, close to tears.

Sabina's companion had turned as well and the hood fell back from his face. It was a young man with eyes much like Baena's own.

"Hago! Brother!" Baena cried, releasing her mother. "We thought you had perished."

"Would I had," the man said bitterly. And as the cloak slipped away from his arm, Baena realised his hand was missing.

"Oh Hago, Domnall told me you had been grievously injured. But I had no idea." The tears were now spilling from her eyes.

If anything the bitterness in Hago's face increased. "Domnall," he spat. "Him and Cinaed strutting around the place."

Baena looked at him in surprise. "What do you mean?"

"Have you not heard, Sister? The Great Cinaed has taken our lands and given them to Domnall."

Baena was silent for a moment. "I did not know," she said.

"No, I suppose they didn't bother to tell you they were tramping all over our lands last year."

Baena decided not to mention her ill health of that time and simply replied, "I know they were putting down a rebellion."

"Rebellion?" Hago raised his voice. "It was a fight to drive out a foreign invader, not a rebellion."

"Hush, Son," Sabina whispered. "You must not speak so."

"Why not? Who is listening? Surely you are not going to betray our part to your husband, are you, Sister?"

Baena looked from her mother to her brother in bewilderment. "Were you part of the rebellion?" she whispered. "Cinaed would not have known they were your lands, Hago. We thought you had died after the battle."

"So will he take them from Domnall and return them to me? Will you ask him to do this?"

Baena's face fell. "I can't," she said as she reflected that Domnall was the last man she could ever take anything from.

"I didn't think so. Drust told me you had become Cinaed's creature," Hago scowled. "Then I am forced to try other methods. Oh, Baena, our father made a poor deal when he married you to such a monster."

Baena had frozen at the mention of Drust, but she almost laughed at the last part of Hago's speech. "No, no. He made the very best deal!"

"Do you know how Drust died?" Hago whispered.

Baena paled. "Do not ask me such a thing. Terrible things happen in war."

"I heard that he was thrown into a pit full of spikes. He screamed in agony for hours before he died."

"No!" Baena protested. "That is not what happened!"

"How do you know?" Sabina demanded.

A bit late Baena remembered that she was the Queen and should take charge of the situation. "Because the Lord Cinaed is a most merciful and noble king," she smiled.

"Mother!" Causantin called, running to the gateway. "Father sent for you. The feasting starts soon."

"Go, my daughter," Sabina whispered.

"Presently," Baena smiled. "Causantin, come here my son. This is your grandmother and uncle. Mother, Hago meet my firstborn, Causantin!"

Causantin bowed politely, but Sabina barely glanced at him. She seemed agitated. "Baena my child, why must you always try to flout him? Have you learnt nothing over the years? Go if he has summoned you. Do not risk his wrath."

"Oh Mother," Baena shook her head. "Come with me. You must both join the feasting."

"How can we?" Hago asked. "We were not invited. We would not presume to be there and risk the king's wrath. Besides, I hear terrible things happen to Pict men who are guests of the Great Cinaed."

"That is nonsense," said Baena with a sharp glance at Causantin. "Cinaed is most happy to welcome all loyal subjects to Forteviot. We did not know you were alive. If we had known of course you would have been invited. You are still ever welcome. Come!" Baena took her mother's arm and pulled her along, hoping she was doing the right thing in welcoming potential rebels into her home.

The hall was bright with banners and torches were already lit, although the light had not yet faded. Cinaed was talking to Graunt and he smiled when he saw Baena.

"I thought I had lost you to the festivities outside." he called.

Baena pulled her mother and brother over. "Look who I have found!"

Cinaed looked puzzled before recognition lit up his face. "Why Lord Hago! It is indeed good to see you. When I saw you carried from the battlefield that terrible day I did not think you would survive."

"I would I had not. I am unable to fight. I am useless now."

Cinaed took Hago's remaining hand between his. "You have been dealt a most grievous injury, but there is more to a man than fighting skill. May I present my kinsman, Lord Graunt? You may remember him perhaps?"

Hago stammered a few words, clearly surprised by so affable a king.

"I remember you well, Lord Hago," Graunt bowed. "I too was badly injured on that day and have been unable to fight since."

"And yet never has he served me better!" Cinaed clapped his friend on the back. "I owe the lives of my three elder children to his wisdom and courage."

Baena smiled, hoping that Cinaed would charm Hago from his black mood.

Cinaed's eyes wandered to Sabina. "My lady, forgive me for not greeting you! This is a happy reunion."

"Forgive us, my lord, for the intrusion. My daughter was most insistent that we come here. I fear we should not."

"But of course you are most heartily welcome," Cinaed cried. "You are my kin."

"Thank you, my Lord King. And what of my daughter? I trust she has been a most amenable and obedient wife."

Cinaed looked at Baena with a faintly incredulous look on his face. Seeing the mischievous glint appear in his eye she shook her head warningly. The glint deepened as he smiled his most charming smile on Sabina.

"Indeed she has, my lady. You have raised a most dutiful and obedient daughter."

Baena narrowed her eyes as Cinaed turned the charming smile on her. "I do not think I have ever had cause to complain of your lack of obedience, have I, my dear lady?" From the corner of her eye, Baena could see that Graunt was struggling not to laugh. "Although I trust you are now ready to dine," Cinaed continued a touch reproachfully. "We have been waiting for you."

Baena looked at Cinaed in exasperation as he continued to smile charmingly. Firmly she turned her back on him, indicating to her mother where she should sit. Sabina made no protest but stared in consternation at the flagrant disobedience her daughter was showing to the supposed tyrant. Only once her mother and brother were seated did she look defiantly at Cinaed, merriment brimming in her eyes. The amusement in his face increased, but he said nothing more, as he escorted her to their places at the head of the table.

Before anyone could start the feasting Cinaed addressed his guests. "A warm welcome to you all. I am most happy to see you, both Picts and Gaels sitting side by side at my table. This night we feast together happily, but I know that not everyone in this land stands with me. In a few days I will be crowned Rex Pictorum. I am already the King of Dal Riata. Any who do not acknowledge this will be dealt with as traitors. So make merry my friends, but when you return to your lands beware of who shelters there. Any who betray their king will suffer the penalties of our laws." There was silence in the hall as Cinaed spoke. "But you, my loyal subjects be of good cheer. Whether you are Pict or Gael your loyalty will see me ever stand with you."

"All hail King Cinaed!" Domnall shouted.

This cry was echoed round the hall as guests began to help themselves from the platters of food. But Baena could see the Picts were nervous as they glanced warily at the serving men. She shrugged. It would take time for this to go away and Cinaed was probably right. It was no bad thing if they were all a little afraid of him for the time being.

Chapter two

The men went on feasting late into the night, long after most of the women had retired. But Baena was not yet asleep when Cinaed finally left the smoky hall to head to their chambers.

"You still awake, my lady?" Cinaed smiled, when he saw her watching him.

Baena nodded. "I have much to think about. I thought never to see my mother or brother again."

"Happy news indeed," Cinaed agreed.

"When you put down the rebellion last year did you know you were on Hago's land?" Baena asked as Cinaed lay down next to her.

"I knew that some of those lands had belonged to the Third Royal House. I did not know that Hago was alive."

"He is angry at the loss of his lands."

Cinaed propped himself up on his elbow and looked at Baena. "I have given those lands to Domnall. Are you asking me to take them away from my brother to give to yours?"

"No!" Baena replied indignantly. "I would never ask you to take anything from Domnall."

Cinaed lay back down. "Good."

Baena put her arm around him and laid her head against his bare chest. "I am scared, my love. Hago has no love for you and he is one of the highest ranking Picts remaining. In spite of his injuries, he could become a leader for rebel Picts. What would you do then?"

"Yes, I would be a pretty figure to execute my wife's brother," Cinaed sighed. "Let me think on the matter. I will find a way to win his loyalty."

Baena lay back down, but as Cinaed went to snuff out the candle he said, "I have decided on a place for my crowning."

Baena knew that he did not mean the religious blessing. That would take place in two days at the stone arched church of Forteviot. Cinaed wanted a Union with the Land, as was the tradition in Dal Riata.

"That is good news," Baena said sleepily. "Where?"

"I will show you in the morn if you can ride with me."

They rose early while most of the inhabitants of Forteviot were still sleeping off the effects of the feast. They quickly broke their fast on chunks of beef and barley bread washed down with ale and were about to go to their horses when Domnall approached them. He was looking thoughtful.

"Cinaed, I must speak with you. Lord Hago spoke to me last night. He is angry that you have taken his lands and bestowed them on me," Domnall glanced awkwardly at Baena as he spoke and she guessed that Hago had been a lot more forceful than Domnall was reporting.

"I know," Cinaed replied.

Domnall glanced at Baena again. "I see. Baena has already asked you to restore his lands, hasn't she?" he said a little flatly.

Cinaed smiled at this. "No, she has not. You should know that she would not urge me to take anything from you. But she has raised concerns that Hago would be an unfortunate enemy. I do not wish to execute him of all people."

"Would be a cruel way for him to die after everything he has survived," Domnall agreed. "Well, my lands are always at your disposal, Cinaed. If you wish to give them to Hago…"

"I don't wish to give them to Hago," Cinaed said. "A man cannot be given lands just because he has a beautiful sister."

"Ah, I fear I have just lost my entitlement to them as well!" Domnall said with a wink at Baena.

Baena smiled, relieved to see that Domnall bore her no ill will.

"I have no attachment to those lands," Domnall went on. "And I am perfectly content with a smaller reward."

Baena protested at that and Cinaed nodded. "I agree. If I take away the portion that Hago wants your reward would scarce be a reward at all. But if it is true that you have no attachment to them…"

"How can I have an attachment for them?" Domnall demanded with a grin. "I was only there once in my life and if you remember that was the time when the river swept away half of our tents. I had to share one with you. That scarcely gave me any affection for the place!"

"I have had pleasanter and far prettier battle companions myself!" Cinaed retorted, but from the looks on their faces, Baena guessed that they had spent those nights in laughter and reminiscence. "I will not take away your lands, Brother. But if you have no attachment to them perhaps you will agree an exchange?" Domnall nodded and Cinaed went on, "Hago wants the lands that make up the Eastern portion. The lands to the West of yours are still under my ownership. Later, we will discuss a fair exchange."

"And will you restore the lands to Hago?" Baena asked.

"Not immediately, my love. Hago must earn my trust as all men must. But I shall appoint him to manage them. In time if he is loyal to me I shall pass the ownership of them to him. Do you think he will be happy with that arrangement?"

"If he is not, he is a fool," Baena replied. "But what of you, Domnall? Are you sure you are happy with this?"

"Hago fought bravely on that day against the Norsemen and paid a terrible price. I could not enjoy taking his lands. I hope he will show his loyalty." Domnall frowned. "He let slip some words last night. Do you think he was part of the rebellion last year?"

Cinaed shrugged. "I know not. I have had no information on his part."

Baena lowered her eyes, struggling with her knowledge. But she knew where her own loyalties had to lie. She only hoped she could influence Cinaed to leniency. It would be hard to lose her brother again.

"Cinaed, Hago was-"

"My love, I have not asked your opinion," Cinaed interrupted. "And the prattle of women is of no interest to me!" He looked Baena firmly in the eye, a teasing smile on his face. But he was pleased at her loyalty despite his words. "I have had no information on his part and so he will have a chance to prove his loyalty."

It seemed strange that day to ride away from the festivities of Forteviot, but much as she loved them Baena was not complaining. It was not often that she had Cinaed all to herself these days. And so she was happy cantering across the land until she realised where they were going.

"Here?" She looked in shock at Cinaed, as they arrived at Scone. "This place of blood?"

"As you must know, this mound is sacred land to the Picts," Cinaed said, pointing to a slope. "It would please them to hold the ceremony here."

"And you will command me to be present?"

"No, my love. I will not command you to be present. Indeed, I will go further and say if you hate it so much the crowning will take place elsewhere. It is important to me that you are happy. This union of the peoples should be a happy one, as a wedding celebration."

In spite of her horror at the place Baena raised her eyebrows at that. "Do you even remember our wedding celebrations? We were both far from happy."

"We were young and foolish then and are fortunate that our fathers were wiser. Not everyone in the land will be happy with this union, but they must trust my wisdom."

Baena couldn't help but smile. "You are right Cinaed, but here?"

Putting an arm round her Cinaed realised she was trembling. "No, not here. Not if it frightens you this much. I know that our wedding celebrations were not happy for you. But this day, the one you have worked for as hard as I, must be joyous."

"Tell me why you thought here, this place of blood and pain could ever have been the right place for such a celebration."

"What is the best thing to come out of our union?"

"Our children," Baena said promptly.

Cinaed smiled. "And yet there was pain and blood then. My God, until last year I had no idea there was so much blood! But from the pain you endured and the blood you shed came the two finest sons and the two most beautiful daughters that any man was ever blessed with. And from the pain and blood of this place can emerge a new land, the finest, and the most beautiful of any on God's Earth. A land that we shall be blessed to call our own."

Baena looked around Scone anew, listening to the sleepy drone of the bees. This was a beautiful place with flowers growing among the grasses and the sun shining through the trees. The rich scent of gorse wafted on the breeze. There were ghosts here of course, but this place was hardly alone in that respect. Blood had been shed all over the land.

"Hold your crowning here, my love. This is the right place," Baena said simply.

"Are you certain?"

Baena nodded. "But Cinaed, when you come here to be crowned make time to pray for those that perished. Not just on that night, but over the years both in unity and enmity. Some whose names we know. Eochaidh, Aed, my father and brothers, Oengus…"

"Gregor and Mathan," Cinaed added.

"And Alpin. Perhaps especially Alpin. He too worked hard for this day, but has not lived to see it."

"And the many whose names have been forgotten," Cinaed agreed. "It shall be as you wish. We shall pray for all who have been lost."

"And there is one other prayer I would have you make that day. Pray for Drust. Pray for his soul."

Cinaed frowned, his arms falling away from her. "After the way he slaughtered my father? And, forgive me my love for mentioning this, after what he did to you? You cannot ask me to do such a thing."

"Yes. In spite of all that. Forgive him and pray for his soul. When a woman gives birth evil spirits muster to attack her and her babe. Great care must be taken to keep them safe. At the birth of a new land do you think the evil spirits are not gathering with misery and bitterness? Do not allow this new kingdom of yours to emerge with hatred in your heart."

Cinaed stared at his wife in awe, as her red hair fluttered around her in the breeze. In the bright sunlight, he could see the faint marks the stresses of the last few years had left on her face but the expression in her eyes was filled with nothing but love. "How did you become so wise?" he asked softly.

Baena smiled. "Then you will do as I ask?"

"I will. This land of ours will come forth in love, faith and celebration."

Baena looked around her once more, feeling at peace with the land. "The only thing missing from here are the sacred rocks," she said.

But Cinaed put his arm around her and smiled a mysterious smile. "Oh, there will be a sacred rock. Trust me on this."

Chapter three

Cinaed's knack for choosing a fine day for his crowning held as the day dawned to the most glorious summer day. Across the surrounding area, men rose even earlier than usual to see to livestock before making the trek to Scone. To many it seemed almost as if every Pict and Gael alive had gathered there.

Laughter rang out as Cinaed's inner circle of family and most trusted companions gathered in the new hall. The place where Drust had died had been allowed to fall into ruin and Cinaed had ordered a new one to be constructed not far from the foot of the sacred mound. Among the bright finery of the nobles, the plain robes of the religious men stood out starkly. Abbots and priests drank deeply of the refreshments on offer, but the thirteen men of the reclusive Order of Scone stood to one side in silent contemplation.

There was a rustle of greeting as Baena entered surrounded by her children. Causantin was clearly bursting with pride to be the one escorting his mother to that place. Both he and Aed were dressed in blue tunics and with a slight guilt at the extravagance Baena had dressed Coira in an embroidered robe of the same costly blue cloth. All three children were popular among Cinaed's companions and they were greeted with many a smile and pat on the head as Baena moved smiling among them. In her arms, Baena carried Mael Muire. The child whose birth had nearly killed them both had grown healthy and strong. She had her father's slate grey eyes and her mother's red hair and there were many to prophesy that she would be a great beauty one day.

Domnall and Graunt bowed before her and both men looked appreciatively at her. She had left her hair mostly loose that day with just two thin plaits at the front to stop the breeze blowing it into her face. Her own tunic was of a creamy white richly embroidered in a blue silk that matched her sparkling eyes. The circlet of the Queen of Dal Riata was on her head and gold and silver bangles jangled on her wrist. As ever on such occasions, she had used the brooch of Clan Mac Alpin to fasten her cloak and she remembered with a smile how Unuis had presented it to her all those years before when she was just the young, very new wife of a young, very new chief. She handed Muire to Kieta for a moment so as to be able to clasp the hands of her two old friends.

"My lady, you are undoubtedly the fairest queen to ever grace this land," Graunt told her.

"I am not sure it is the done thing to outshine the King on such a day, Sister," Domnall joked.

But a hush had descended on the room as Cinaed strode in and all eyes turned to him. "I do not think that is possible," Baena murmured.

Cinaed was bareheaded and like Baena he had left his blonde streaked hair to flow around his shoulders. He was dressed in a blue tunic of a deeper shade than his sons but his was edged with fine white silk thread that Baena had stitched herself. She had chosen to do a knotted design that was reminiscent of the now much-faded marks that the old Pict man had tattooed on their wrists at their handfasting back in Abernethy. His muscular body filled out the tunic and a silver sword belt only added to the impression of power. Sweeping from his shoulders was the purple cloak that had been presented to him as King of Dal Riata, fastened with a bejewelled pin. Despite the faint scars that marked his face and hands, everyone was in total agreement. He looked magnificent.

Baena and her children watched in silence as Cinaed acknowledged the greetings and bows with a smiling graciousness which melted into genuine warmth as Domnall and Graunt both bowed deeply. After greeting these two his eyes were drawn to Baena and the children who were still looking at him in adoration. The children knelt, but as Baena prepared to do the same Cinaed strode forward and caught her hand. For a moment they looked at each other and in the smile on his face and the glint in his eye Baena could see the beloved husband and father beneath the King.

Cinaed bent his head and kissed her passionately to the laughter of his friends and the slight disapproval of the religious men present. Baena's laughing face was scarlet when Cinaed finally released her and he kept her hand clasped firmly in his.

"Never," he announced "was a King more fortunate than I. The finest land and the most loyal of subjects, the very best of kin and friends. Four bonny babes and the most beautiful wife any man ever had."

More laughter and cheers greeted this and perhaps a few regrets from some of the Pict men present who had wondered whether to curry favour with their new king by bringing their own daughters under his eye.

Cinaed smiled benevolently on them all and then gestured to the doorway. "My people, it is nearly time. Make your way to the Hill of All Men and take your places.

The room swiftly emptied until only Cinaed, Baena and Domnall remained with the four children, along with the men of the Order of Scone and the old Abbot of Iona who had been charged with the sacred rites that would unite Cinaed with his new land.

The children chattered excitedly, plying their mother and Domnall with questions. Cinaed stood a little apart from them, watching them with a proud smile. At last the Abbot of Iona went towards him and laid a hand on his shoulder

"My son, it is time."

Cinaed stood up very straight and stretched out his hand to Baena. Behind them, Domnall and Causantin took their places, followed by Aed and Coira. The first of the monks who were to make up the end of the procession bore Mael Muire, although the little girl could walk now and they hoped she might make the final sacred steps by herself.

Cinaed had expected a crowd of faithful and curious onlookers, but even he was surprised by the numbers of people as they followed the Abbot and the Elder of Scone out into the sunny morning. Although Cinaed intended for this to be a peaceful day he was taking no chances with the safety of his family. Mingling with the crowd were many from his army, but so far it seemed that he would have no need to worry. The mood was jubilant as Picts and Gaels alike cheered their King.

Cinaed paused at the base of the Hill of All Men and removed his shoes allowing his bare feet to sink into the soft ground. At the back of the procession the brother carrying little Muire placed her on the ground, but to everyone's amusement, she toddled forward and clung onto Cinaed's legs. Cinaed caught Baena's eye and laughed out loud. Then in a gesture that won the heart of every woman present, he picked up the little girl and bore the child on his own arm as they began their ascent of the hill. A hush descended on the crowd as they made their way and both Cinaed and Baena forced their own features into more sober ones.

As they neared the top of the mound Baena recognised more and more faces until they reached the semi-circle of people near the summit. There stood Graunt and Kieta, Sabina and Hago, Fie, Coulym and even those three hapless Pict men Broide, Nektan and Kai who had been the first Picts to acknowledge Cinaed as King. There had been some muttering among the Gaels at the amount of Picts in the most prominent position, but Cinaed had been firm.

"Any man, Gael or Pict who swears loyalty to me shall be placed according to rank. All must earn my favour and not expect to be granted it by their blood."

He had privately told Baena and Domnall that he was happier having the Picts and Gaels well mixed. The last thing he wanted was the Picts to be grouped together in any kind of resentful band.

At the very top of the hill was an object draped with cloth and the two religious leaders took up their places on either side. Cinaed looked at it with a satisfied smile and everyone else with considerable curiosity. Cinaed handed over the obstinate little Muire to Kieta while Domnall and the rest of the children quietly took their places in the semi-circle around the summit. However, those who expected Cinaed to proceed quickly with his crowning were surprised. He kept Baena's hand in his and stepped forward into the circle. Before he could accept the crown he had a promise to keep.

"My people!" he cried. "From this day there is to be a new land. One where Gaels and Picts are no longer in enmity. Some of you here were present, as I was at the battle against the forces of the barbarian Angle king. You will remember how when all seemed lost we charged and drove the scum from our land."

There were mutters of agreement and a few cheers. Cinaed acknowledged these, but his mood remained serious.

"We did this, Picts and Gaels together. We should have learnt that day what can be achieved when this land stands together. But we did not learn it and we allowed enmity into our hearts. Men fought against their former companions and many brave men on both sides fell. If I tried to name all of these we would be here an age and I think you, my people, would not thank me for keeping you from the feasting."

A ripple of laughter greeted that, but a few tears were shed as well. Everyone present remembered someone who had been lost.

"For now, I would name one man, my father, the great Lord Alpin. He always believed that one day this land could stand together. It was with this end that he arranged for me a union with this noble Pict lady." Cinaed raised Baena's hand. "Being a foolish youngster at the time, I did not thank him."

There was more laughter and in the crowd many a man looked sternly at their own wayward sons.

"But today I remember him and thank him for his wisdom in not only working towards the union of the lands but also in securing for me a wife beyond compare." He kissed Baena's hand with a smile before his face turned serious once more.

"I would now take a moment to pray for the souls of all the brave men who have been lost, whether men of rank like Alpin and Oengus or the no less brave foot soldiers whose names I was never privileged to learn. Whether they fell at the sword of a Gael, a Pict or a Norseman kneel with me now and pray for their souls."

Cinaed drew his sword and thrust it into the ground to form a cross. Carefully keeping her tunic out of the dirt Baena sank to the ground while Cinaed went down on one knee facing her. There was a rustling as Cinaed's words filtered to the back of the crowd. As everyone knelt Cinaed looked at Baena and smiled to let her know he would keep his promise. Baena smiled too, thoughts of her father filling her mind as she bowed her head into the silence that consumed the Hill of All Men.

At length, she lifted her head as Cinaed raised his. He nodded and Baena felt herself relax. She knew it would have been no easy task for Cinaed to look into his heart and forgive his father's murderer, but it seemed as if the very air had turned lighter. Baena knew that if the evil spirits had gathered that day they had found, like many a foe before them, that Cinaed Mac Alpin was not an easy man to defeat.

Cinaed stood and reached out a hand to Baena to help her up. But before rising she kissed it.

"My love and loyalty always, my Lord King," she said in a low voice.

Cinaed raised her to her feet with a slight smile and watched her with pride as she took her place in the circle between Causantin and Domnall. A hush descended on the crowd as they waited for what would come next.

At the summit of the hill, the holy Fathers removed the cloth that still covered the mysterious object to reveal a pure white rock. Sunbeams gleamed on its shiny surface. There were gasps of wonder from the Picts as they gazed at a rock that appeared as if sent from heaven and as word spread to the back of the crowd everyone craned their necks to get a glimpse of this marvel. The Gaels too were stunned and exclaimed in recognition. It was the white rock from the altar at Dunadd. Baena and Domnall exchanged looks of admiration that Cinaed had so effortlessly appeased the Gaels who had been angered by the move to Forteviot. He had brought a piece of Dunadd and saving only the sacred rocks, the most important piece of Dunadd here to Scone.

The Abbot of Iona and the Elder of Scone knelt and kissed the rock and Cinaed's voice rang out. "This sacred stone has come a long way. Once it was the pillow on which Jacob laid his head to dream of a stairway to heaven. But from this day forth it will be the beating heart of our land. No man shall ever call himself King of this land unless he receives the crown over this Stone of Destiny."

With these words, Cinaed too went down on one knee and kissed the stone. He kept his head bowed over the Stone, holding his sword in front of him and the religious men began to pray. The Abbot of Iona took a bowl of holy water that he had brought from the sacred wells of Iona and marked a cross on Cinaed's forehead.

"The blessings of Saint Columba be on you, my son. May you be ever victorious and may Christ bless your people."

The Elder of the Order of Scone raised aloft a crown for all to see. Clever metal smiths had softened the gold circlet of Dal Riata and entwined it with the bejewelled crown of Rex Pictorum. The new crown was heavy, but Cinaed had said that it would be a reminder to him of the greater duties he now bore. His white robes flapping slightly in the breeze the Elder of Scone slowly lowered it over the Stone of Destiny onto Cinaed's head.

"By this crown Cinaed Mac Alpin is appointed to rule over this land. Good men of Pictavia and Dal Riata, be ever obedient and dutiful to him or feel the wrath of our Lord God upon you. In the name of God our heavenly Father, I command you to rise Lord Cinaed, most noble King of the Gaels of Dal Riata and Rex Pictorum, gentle and merciful ruler of this land. All hail King Cinaed!"

The cheers as Cinaed rose shook the very ground they stood on. Baena watched him in wonder. It was done. The two lands were truly becoming one. As the cheers went on, Cinaed held up a hand for silence.

"Fathers, I thank you both for your blessings. My people, from this day forth I command your duty and obedience. Serve me well for I am your King. I am the son of Alpin, the greatest Chief of Dal Riata. I am a true Gael. I am proud to be a Gael. But I am also the son of Unuis, Daughter of the Sixth Royal House of the Picts. By her blood, I am a Pict and I am proud to be a Pict!"

Chapter Four

There was a stunned silence before the loudest cheers of all erupted from the people. On and on they went and many a man reached out to embrace his former enemy. Probably the only three who were not cheering were Baena, Domnall and Graunt. Instead they stared at Cinaed with open mouths.

"I never thought I would ever hear Cinaed say that," Graunt breathed at last.

"I suppose that means now there are two people who can call Cinaed a Pict without getting a black eye," Domnall joked to Baena before he realised she was wiping her eyes. "Tears, Sister?"

Baena smiled. "A few. I was thinking how proud Unuis would be if only she'd lived to see this moment."

Graunt agreed. "Yes, she would. She always believed that Cinaed would accept his Pict heritage one day. Just as she believed that you would be the ideal wife for him. She was right about everything."

But Baena looked at Domnall. "No, not about everything."

Domnall shrugged. "Do not mind for me, Sister. She had her reasons not to like me much."

"Maybe," said Baena taking his hand in hers. "But she had no reason to ever doubt your love for Cinaed. He has the best of brothers."

Domnall flushed. "Does he? I thought I had the best of brothers!"

As Cinaed held up his hand to silence the crowd once more Baena looked down at her own two sons and prayed that they would always stand by each other as Cinaed and Domnall did.

"My people, the feasting awaits us. Go and be of good cheer! But if any would receive my personal blessing I shall receive you."

If Cinaed had hoped to be able to head straight to the feasting himself he was out of luck. But seated on the Stone of Destiny he gave no sign of any impatience as men, women and children alike queued to show their loyalty and receive his blessing.

Domnall and Baena were the first to kneel before him and they remained seated on either side of the stone as others of all ranks followed. The children abandoned all formality to embrace their father before Graunt and Kieta came forward.

"There shall be fine lands for you, my friend," Cinaed told Graunt. "But I hope you will not feel you must always be on them. I would welcome both your counsel and your companionship often at Forteviot."

Graunt nodded, smiling with pride as Cinaed blessed his two children. Then Cinaed laid his hand on Kieta's head, but instead of sending them quickly on their way he took Kieta's hands in his and kissed them.

"Since the day I first brought her to Iona, you have served my Queen well," he said. "But your devotion during her confinement last year was beyond anything I had the right to expect. I think it is you more than any other that I have to thank that she sits beside me this day. Please accept this small token of my eternal gratitude." Cinaed pressed a gold and enamel brooch into Kieta's hands.

"My… my Lord King…" Kieta, stammered, tears filling her eyes.

Baena, her own eyes misty, leant forward to embrace her friend. "I hope you too will be often at Forteviot," she whispered.

Over their heads Cinaed and Graunt exchanged amused smiles, before allowing the next subjects to approach. Some, particularly Picts, approached their King with anxiety, but Cinaed's charm was on full force that day and everyone appeared to leave his presence with pride and loyalty in their hearts.

Baena held her breath with some trepidation when Hago came forward. He had accepted Cinaed's offer to manage his lands, but Baena knew that he was still angry that they had been taken. However, he had been at Forteviot for long enough now to know that the public esteem the King showed his sister was just a small part of a far greater affection. For a moment he hesitated, his eyes taking in the way Baena leant against Cinaed before he too knelt down and swore loyalty to his king.

At last only the religious men remained and Cinaed rose up from the stone with a slight grimace. "For a pillow that is not very comfy," he said in a low voice so that only Baena and Domnall would hear. Baena did her best to hide her smile at that as they all turned to the two holy men.

"Fathers, I thank you for your service this day," Cinaed said, bowing to them both.

"My son, it has been a privilege." The old Abbot of Iona seemed moved almost to tears. "I never dreamt I would see the day. My Lord King, you have brought forward God's peace this day."

"Perhaps," Cinaed replied. "But there is still much work to do."

"Not today, Brother," Domnall put in. "Today is for celebration."

"True. I hope they have left some for us down there!"

"I can't believe you brought this stone here," Baena said, marvelling again at the creamy whiteness. "But it was revered by so many. I think it will become the land's most precious treasure."

Cinaed too looked down at the stone. "If I have learnt anything about precious treasures it is that there are always men wanting to steal them."

"But if this is truly the beating heart of our land we must make sure it is always protected," Domnall added.

Cinaed agreed. "In the wrong hands this Stone of Destiny would be dangerous indeed. We must ensure this stone is always safe. Father," he said to the Elder of Scone. "I will entrust the sacred Stone of Destiny to your Order. It will not be needed again while I live, but bring it forth for the man who succeeds me."

"Scone will be honoured," the man said simply.

"With respect, Father," Domnall protested "I am not sure this is a good plan. This stone needs strong men to protect it. Surely it would be safer at Forteviot."

Cinaed shook his head. "No. The house of Kings would be the most dangerous place of all. There are probably more there who would steal it than anywhere else."

Domnall nodded, but Baena thought he looked a little offended. "I do not think Cinaed meant you, Brother," she said.

Cinaed looked up in surprise. "My God, no. Most certainly not. If I were to entrust this stone to a man that man would be you. But you and I will not stand forever. And I cannot be certain that the Kings who are to come will be as fortunate as I. They may have brothers, uncles, cousins, perhaps even sons who would steal the crown from them. It is too precious to entrust to any man. That is why I would place the Stone of Destiny with God. He will stand forever."

Domnall understood. "But what of the Norsemen? They have never yet come so far, but we cannot be sure that this will always be the case."

"That is true," Cinaed frowned. "And terrible as it would be for the Stone to fall into the hands of a pretender from this land, it would be truly disastrous if it fell into foreign hands."

"Men must always be stationed here to defend the Stone," Domnall said.

Cinaed nodded but looked at the Elder. "Father, are you from these parts?"

"Yes, my son. I have lived here both man and boy."

"Then perhaps you would know of some secret place. A cave or hollow where the Stone could be concealed in times of danger."

The Elder thought for a moment and then his face lit up. "Why yes, my Lord King. I know of the very place! It is-"

But Cinaed held up his hand. "No. Such a secret is too important even for Kings. Share it only with your most trusted brother. And so must it always be that only two will know of this. If danger nears the two, whether it is yourself or an Elder six generations from now, must take this sacred Stone of Destiny and conceal it. It is a hard burden I place on your order, Father. The two must be prepared to defend the secret with their lives."

"I am still honoured by your trust, my lord. Scone will earn it well."

"I am sure you will, but make it a little easier. If the Stone of Destiny is to be concealed have some other stone in its place. Something like that." Cinaed prodded a sandstone block that was lying nearby with his foot. He grinned. "It would please me greatly to think of the Norsemen sailing away with that weighing down their hold!"

Baena and Domnall both laughed at the image, a sound that was echoed in the noises drifting up to them. Music and laughter mingled with the smells of roasting meat.

"Come," Cinaed stretched his hand out to Baena. "Let us join the festivities!"

The celebrations that day were spectacular. Baena was sure that never had so many jugglers, storytellers, musicians and dancers gathered in one place. Nor had anyone there ever seen feasting on that scale. It was certainly beyond anything Forteviot could have produced, but when proclaiming his crowning Cinaed had demanded that all bring a tribute from their land. Whether out of fear or loyalty the nobles of both Pictavia and Dal Riata had risen to the occasion, vying with each other to provide the finest meats, ales and other delicacies. There were even rumours of deals with foreign traders for more exotic tributes and fine wines from men particularly keen to win favour with the King

And it was not just the nobles that had contributed. Even the lowliest settlements had sent breads of barley and oats and cakes sweetened with honey and fruits.

As the afternoon wore into a golden evening the musicians started playing so that the people could dance. Cinaed took Baena by the hand.

Joyfully they danced together until both were breathless and more ale was brought to quench their thirst.

When the sun dipped behind the hills torches and fires were lit and men gathered around the fires to tell stories of the past or to sing and drink some more. Baena was delighted by how well the day had gone. She was certain that this was a festivity that men would talk of for years.

As she looked around she realised that for perhaps the first time that day Cinaed was standing alone. Slipping an arm around his waist she could see that he was smiling as he watched the men laughing by the fire.

"Look at them, Baena," he said in a low voice. "Those men were fighting each other not long ago."

"We must pray that such friendships are formed that they never will again."

As the singing got louder and more than a little bawdy Baena shook her head disapprovingly, although inside she was trying not to laugh.

Cinaed grinned. "Those lads have had many a tough day. Let them have their fun this night."

Standing on tiptoes Baena kissed Cinaed's cheek. "I will, my love. But I think such things are not fit for my ears. I'll bid you all a good night."

There were a few cheers and whistles as Baena threaded her way through the fires towards the castle, which she accepted with a smile and a wave. It had been a long day and she would be glad to reach her chamber. A few nights before she had worried about sleeping again in this place, but no more. The laughter of the day had surely driven away all evil spirits and now peace would reign. Well, a sort of peace Baena reflected as she paused for a moment in the doorway and listened once more to the shouts and laughs that drifted over the still night.

"Baena!" a voice called and turning she saw Cinaed running to catch her up.

"Are you checking up on me to make sure I go to our chamber?" she asked. "You surely can't think I'd be hanging around the fires listening to that lot."

"Not at all. I thought I would retire too," he said.

"Don't you want to stay up with the men?" Baena asked in surprise.

"No. Those sort of nights are fine for the young, unwed lads. An old married man such as myself has a much better place to be." He put his arms around her and grinned. "That won't be so bad will it?"

Baena put her head on one side, pretending to consider it. "I suppose that won't be too bad," she replied trying unsuccessfully to hide her own smile.

"I never did teach you to respect your husband, did I?" Cinaed teased and swept her up in his arms. Ignoring her laughing protests he did not let her go until they reached their chambers.

Drifting over to her coffer Baena carefully began to remove all the jewels she had worn that day. She could see that Cinaed was watching her.

"I used to think you were the most beautiful woman in Dal Riata," he commented. "But now I know that you are not only that, but the most beautiful in Pictavia as well."

"Don't be foolish," Baena shook her head. "But if I am beautiful in your eyes, then I am content."

Cinaed removed the crown from his head and in the oil light admired the workmanship. Baena looked too at how the two crowns were intertwined.

"I never thought the day would come when you would call yourself a Pict and much less be proud to be one."

"I never thought I'd ever say that I was proud to be a Pict," Cinaed said laying the crown on top of Baena's coffer and taking her in his arms. "But I'll tell you something even stranger. I truly meant it."

Postscript: Year of our Lord 849

Dressed soberly in grey Baena kept her head bowed as she followed the battered coffin into the new church at Dunkeld, her hand resting on the arm of Causantin. The lad was nearly as tall as she was now and even on this solemn occasion Baena could not help but feel proud of his good looks and noble bearing. The air was thick with incense and the sounds of the monks chanting filled the space. Around her many of the nobles of the land gathered, awe on their faces as the casket made its slow procession to the front. All fell to their knees as it passed them.

The casket was borne by two men in dusty, travel-stained clothing, who placed their precious burden at the altar. Both knelt down and kissed it, as Baena, Causantin and the others who made up the procession too knelt on the stone floor.

Earlier that year the message had come from the Abbot of Iona reporting that the Norse activity in the area had increased. The sacred relics of Saint Columba were no longer safe. Cinaed did as he promised and sent a group of his most trusted men to bring the relics from the isle. As the casket had progressed across the land people flocked to see it pass. Cinaed and Domnall had ridden to accompany the relics on the last stages of their journey and it was they who had carried the sacred casket into the church.

The Abbot of Dunkeld was new to his position, but there was no sign of that as he began the sacred rites to lay the bones of Saint Columba in their new resting place.

The solemn mood deserted the nobles as they gathered for a simple meal after the ceremony and laughter filled the refectory. In the last few years, the remaining Pict rebels had been put down and every man present was loyal to Cinaed.

"Are you returning with us to Forteviot? Domnall is biding with us a while," Cinaed asked Graunt, as he greeted his most longstanding companion.

"Not this time, my friend," Graunt smiled. "I must return to my lands. Kieta is near her time and may already have been brought to bed."

"Pass my greetings to her and tell her I think often on her," Baena said. "Send word once the babe arrives."

"I am planning a progression in your direction in the autumn," Cinaed added. "It will not be so long before we are together again."

"We shall be most happy to receive you," Graunt replied, giving them both a warm embrace. His limp was still pronounced, but Graunt never complained and in the six years since Cinaed's crowning his lands had prospered.

The afternoon was already advanced when Cinaed and Baena left the abbey. Outside they looked on smiling at Domnall and Causantin who were engaged in a sword fight.

"The lad has improved since I last saw him," Domnall called, expertly blocking Causantin's latest thrust. Throwing an arm around the boy they joined Cinaed and Baena. "You'll be as good a swordsman as your father one day."

"Or perhaps even your uncle!" Cinaed grinned, ruffling his son's hair.

Their horses were saddled and the four of them made a leisurely return to Forteviot. Baena never forgot how fortunate they were to finally be able to ride through a land that was at peace. She only wished the other conflicts could also be stopped.

"What are your plans now for the western coast?" Domnall asked.

Cinaed looked regretful. "I think we must accept that the Norsemen are there to stay now. Trade and fishing can be concentrated in the east. Our efforts in the west must be to ensure they do not encroach too far into Dal Riata, but it would be a waste of men to keep trying to defend the coast." He looked at Causantin. "I would not want to risk my son in such a fight. I cannot ask other men to risk theirs."

"Agreed. We may have a new problem in any case. Strathclyde has a new king. A man named Arthgal. He is said to harbour ambitions in our direction."

Cinaed laughed. "He can try! But I do not think he can achieve much against us. I would be sorry to be at war with him, though. Those Britons could be a useful ally against the Norsemen."

"Arthgal has a son," Domnall commented. "A lad a little older than Causantin."

"Does he?" Cinaed said thoughtfully.

Baena cast her eyes upwards. "Coira is far too young," she protested.

"She is now, but it will not be so many years before we must think of such things. I would see our daughters as queens."

Baena still looked troubled but said nothing.

"I will choose carefully, my love. I would not give our daughters to any unless I can be assured they are good men."

Baena sighed as she nodded her agreement. "And I will ensure that our daughters are better prepared for their new lives than I was. I do not want them to feel the fear and loneliness that I felt that first year."

Cinaed shot a look at Baena but did not say anything as they neared Forteviot.

"Do not waste your efforts preparing little Muire," Domnall laughed. "That girl has her mother's cheek and her father's temper. She will be fine wherever she goes! I'd have more concern for the wellbeing of her husband!"

Domnall responded only with a grin to Baena's indignant defence of her feisty younger daughter as he slid down from his horse.

"Come lad, I must greet young Aed," he said to Causantin.

After Cinaed, Domnall was the most powerful man in the land and was well respected, yet in so many ways he remained unchanged. Baena smiled affectionately. It would be good to have him back at Forteviot for a while. As she began to follow them, Cinaed caught hold of her hand.

"I did not know how afraid and lonely you were back then," he said softly. "I saw only a defiant little brat."

"Do not look so troubled, my love," Baena replied with a shake of her head. "I never think on those days now, except to reflect on how foolish I was. Those lonely times only remind me of how fortunate we now are."

"And God willing, we will have many happy times to come," Cinaed replied, pulling her close to him.

"Do you truly not mind that I have borne you no more children?" she asked, as she wondered if Kieta's latest baby had arrived. "I still pray to be blessed, but I feel that this is the price we had to pay for the actions we took to secure this land."

"If it is, then it is a price I am prepared to pay." The memories made him tighten his arms around her, kissing the top of her head. "I once feared I would pay a much higher one. Our children are growing well, you are still at my side and the land is finally at peace with itself. I could not ask for more." He gave Baena an embarrassed grin. "I know I am a coward, but the truth is I am almost relieved that I have never again had to hear you cry out in the agony of birth, knowing there is nothing I can do to aid you."

Their arms still around each other they strolled towards the castle, the bustle of the evening continuing around them, as many from the household called out greetings. Children were bringing wood to light the great fires, where chunks of beef would be roasted for their meal that night. They stopped briefly to look on them and Cinaed smiled proudly.

"These children will grow up not caring if they are Pict or Gael," he said. "And they will not die in senseless border skirmishes."

"I think this land will never forget what it owes you," Baena replied. "The generations who are to come will ever sing your praises."

Cinaed laughed and he glanced at his wife. "Will the generations who are to come remember what they owe you, the most beautiful queen to grace this land?"

Baena laughed as well, as they entered the castle hand in hand. "Me? Any beauty I have will be quickly forgotten. I expect there will be few to even remember my name. But even if I am only remembered as Cinaed's queen I am happy. It is the proudest name of any woman."

Notes on the characters.

This book is a work of fiction, but many of the characters and events are true. Records from this time are limited and the dates of many of the events are disputed. Unknown dates include Cinaed's marriage and the births of his children. These could have taken place at any point between the late 820s and the 850s. It is known that his wife was a Pict princess and so it is possible that the marriage took place in the 840s when Cinaed was pushing home his claim to the Pict throne. But Cinaed was born in 810 and to me, it seems likely that in those dangerous times a man would not leave it until after the age of thirty to marry and beget children. This is why I have placed the marriage in 833, after the Battle of Athelstaneford when the Picts and Gaels had joined forces, but before Alpin's grisly end in 834 when it seems less likely that Cinaed would have sought a Pict alliance

Cinaed (Kenneth mac Alpin, Kenneth I) ruled Dal Riata and Pictavia until his death in 858 of natural causes. During his reign he continued to fight against the Norse and Britons, but compared to the bloodshed of the previous years his reign was a comparatively peaceful one. His death appears to have been widely mourned as recorded in the Annals of Ireland 'That Kenneth with his host is no more brings weeping to every home. No king of his worth under heaven is there, to the bounds of Rome'. He was buried on Iona and passes from there into a mixture of Scottish history and Scottish legend. Historians continue to debate whether he was a Gael or a Pict, a warrior or a diplomat, a hero or a villain, the first King of Scots or one of the Last Kings of the Picts. What is perhaps undisputed is that from his reign the Picts and the Gaels remained united, forming the seed of the nation that would eventually be known as Scotland and Scottish monarchs are numbered from him. Whether he was survived by his wife is unknown.

Domnall (Donald I) succeeded Cinaed to the throne. He is unflatteringly described as the 'wanton son of a foreign wife' leading to speculation that his mother was of Norse descent. If the people had been frightened that Cinaed's death would bring an end to the peace, they need not have worried. Domnall reigned for four years and was, at least, able to maintain the borders of the kingdom Cinaed had created.

Like his brother and most unusually for Kings in those warlike times, he died of natural causes in 862.

Causantin (Constantine I) succeeded Domnall to the throne. His reign coincided with the most active period of Viking attacks in Britain and he was killed by them in 877. He left at least one son, Domnall (Donald II).

Aed succeeded Causantin to the throne but reigned for only one year before he was murdered. He left at least one son, Constantine II.

Coira is not the real name of one of Cinaed's daughters. However Cinaed did have a daughter who married Rhun, King of Strathclyde, but her name is unrecorded. She had at least one son Eochaid who jointly ruled with a man named Giric after the death of Aed. Giric is a shadowy figure of unknown origin. He is variously described as a guardian, cousin or cousin once removed to Eochaid. A cousin once removed raises the possibility that he could be Domnall's son. One source does name him as 'Mac Domnail', but this is generally considered to be a scribal error.

Mael Muire was married to two Irish kings. Her first marriage was to Aed Finliath and after his death, she married the next High King Flann Sinna. She had at least one child by both her husbands. She seems to have remained in contact with her family, as after the murder of Aed it was to her that the young sons of Causantin and Aed fled. As the wife, mother and daughter of kings, her death in 913 was recorded in the Annals of Ulster making her the only female character in this book whose real name we know.

Other children. If Cinaed did marry as a young man it seems likely that there were other children. But if these were boys they did not take the throne and if they were girls their marriages were not as glorious as their sisters, although another Mac Alpin girl is another possibility for the parentage of Giric. It is also possible in these days of high child mortality that any further children did not survive into adulthood.

Drust was the King of the Picts before Cinaed and was likely to have been murdered by him in the events I have described which are popularly known as Mac Alpin's Treason. Nothing more is known about him. His relationship with Cinaed's Queen and naming him as the murderer of Alpin is fictitious and it is impossible to say what dealings he had with Cinaed and his family before the dark events at Scone. If this makes me responsible for the worst character assassination of a Scottish king since Shakespeare wrote Macbeth I can only apologise!

The Stone of Destiny (Stone of Scone) continued to be used in all coronations of Scottish kings until it was stolen by the English King Edward I in 1296. It was then used in the coronation of the English and later the British monarchs up to the present day. It was returned to Scotland in 1996 and can be seen at Edinburgh Castle. Or can it?

The sandstone block that Edward stole seems different from the early descriptions of the Stone of Destiny, which records say was made of black basalt or white marble. Furthermore, it is geologically similar to the stone around Scone and therefore probably did not even come from Dal Riata, let alone Ireland, Spain, Egypt and Syria as the Stone of Destiny allegedly did. Could Cinaed or one of his descendants have come up with a plan to keep the true Stone of Destiny safe from foreign invaders? When it comes to these wily Scottish kings nothing would surprise me! And the thought of Cinaed laughing from beyond the grave as Edward rode away with his horses weighed down by an ordinary chunk of sandstone pleases me greatly!

I hope you have enjoyed reading 'Kenneth's Queen'. This is the book I never intended to write. My original plan was the story of a much later queen, but being a great procrastinator I started clicking on links to other Scottish monarchs. These eventually led me back to Kenneth Mac Alpin. Before long I had fallen in love with the story of this warrior king who united the two enemy nations. I also became fascinated by the unknown woman who must have been at his side throughout these events. Good reviews are critical to a book's success, so please take a moment to leave your review on the platform where you bought the book. I look forward to hearing from you!

About the author

Anna Chant was born and spent her childhood in Essex. She studied history at the University of Sheffield, before qualifying as a primary teacher. She currently lives in Devon with her husband and three sons. In her spare time she enjoys reading, sewing and camping. Kenneth's Queen is her first novel.

Printed in Great Britain
by Amazon